The Co
Supernatural and Weird
Fiction of
Florence Marryat
Volume 2

The Collected Supernatural and Weird Fiction of Florence Marryat Volume 2

One Novel 'The Blood of the Vampire,'
& Seven Short Stories
of the Strange and Unusual

Florence Marryat

LEONAUR

The Collected
Supernatural and Weird
Fiction of
Florence Marryat
Volume 2
One Novel 'The Blood of the Vampire,' & Seven Short Stories of the Strange and Unusual
by Florence Marryat

FIRST EDITION

Leonaur is an imprint of Oakpast Ltd

Copyright in this form © 2017 Oakpast Ltd

ISBN: 978-1-78282-620-0 (hardcover)
ISBN: 978-1-78282-621-7 (softcover)

http://www.leonaur.com

Publisher's Notes

The views expressed in this book are not necessarily those of the publisher.

Contents

The Blood of the Vampire

CHAPTER 1

It was the magic hour of dining. The long Digue of Heyst, was
almost deserted; so was the strip of loose, yellow sand which skirted
its base, and all the *tables d'hôtes* were filling fast. Henri, the youngest
waiter of the Hôtel Lion d'Or, was standing on the steps between
the two great gilded lions, which stood rampart on either side the
portals, vigorously ringing a loud and discordant bell to summon the
stragglers, whilst the ladies, who were waiting the commencement
of dinner in the little salon to the side, stopped their ears to dull its
clamour. Philippe and Jules were busy, laying white cloths and glasses,
etc., on the marble tables in the open balcony, outside the *salle à manger*, where strangers to the hotel might dine à *la carte*, it they chose.
Inside, the long, narrow tables, were decorated with dusty geraniums
and fuchsias, whilst each cruet-stand had a small bunch of dirty artificial flowers tied to its handle. But the visitors to the Lion d'Or, who
were mostly English, were too eager for their evening meal, to cavil at
their surroundings.

The Baroness Gobelli, with her husband on one side, and her son
on the other, was the first to seat herself at table. The Baroness always
appeared with the soup, for she had observed that the first comers
received a more generous helping than those who came in last. No
such anxiety occupied the minds of Mrs. Pullen and her friend Miss
Leyton, who sat opposite to the Baroness and her family. They did not
care sufficiently for the *potage au crouton,* which usually formed the
beginning of the *table d'hôte* dinner. The long tables were soon filled
with a motley crew of English, Germans, and Belgians, all chattering,
especially the foreigners, as fast as their tongues could travel. Amongst
them was a sprinkling of children, mostly unruly and ill-behaved, who
had to be called to order every now and then, which made Miss Ley-

ton's lip curl with disgust. Just opposite to her, and next to Mr. Bobby Bates, the Baroness's son by her first marriage, and whom she always treated as if he had been a boy of ten years old, was an unoccupied chair, turned up against the table to signify that it was engaged.

"I wonder if that is for the German princess of whom Madame Lament is so fond of talking," whispered Elinor Leyton to Mrs. Pullen, "she said this morning that she expected her this afternoon."

"O! surely not!" replied her friend, "1 do not know much about royalties, but I should think a princess would hardly dine at a public *table d'hôte.*"

"O! a German princess! what is that?" said Miss Leyton, with a curled lip again, for she was a daughter of Lord Walthamstowe, and thought very little of any aristocracy, except that of her own country.

As she spoke, however, the chair opposite was sharply pulled into place, and a young lady seated herself on it, and looked boldly (though not brazenly) up and down the tables, and at her neighbours on each side of her. She was a remarkable looking girl—more remarkable, perhaps, than beautiful, for her beauty did not strike one at first sight. Her figure was tall but slight and lissom. It looked almost boneless as she swayed easily from side to side of her chair. Her skin was colourless but clear. Her eyes, long-shaped, dark, and narrow, with heavy lids and thick black lashes which lay upon her cheeks. Her brows were arched and delicately pencilled, and her nose was straight and small. Not so her mouth however, which was large, with lips of a deep blood colour, displaying small white teeth.

To crown all, her head was covered with a mass of soft, dull, blue-black hair, which was twisted in careless masses about the nape of her neck, and looked as if it was unaccustomed to comb or hairpin. She was dressed very simply in a white cambric frock, but there was not a woman present, who had not discovered in five minutes, that the lace with which it was profusely trimmed, was costly Valenciennes, and that it was clasped at her throat with brilliants. The new-comer did not seem in the least abashed by the numbers of eyes which were turned upon her, but bore the scrutiny very calmly, smiling in a sort of furtive way at everybody, until the *entrées* were handed round, when she riveted all her attention upon the contents of her plate.

Miss Leyton thought she had never seen any young person devour her food with so much avidity and enjoyment. She could not help watching her. The Baroness Gobelli, who was a very coarse feeder, scattering her food over her plate and not infrequently over the table cloth as well, was nothing compared to the young stranger. It was not so much that she ate rapidly and with evident appetite, but that she kept her eyes fixed upon her food, as if she feared someone might deprive her of it. As soon as her plate was empty, she called sharply to the waiter in French, and ordered him to get her some more.

"That's right, my dear!" exclaimed the Baroness, nodding her huge head, and smiling broadly at the newcomer; "make 'em bring you more! It's an excellent dish, that! I'll 'ave some more myself!"

As Philippe deposited the last helping of the *entrée* on the young lady's plate, the Baroness thrust hers beneath his nose.

"'Ere!" she said, "bring three more 'elpings for the Baron and Bobby and me!"

The man shook his head to intimate that the dish was finished, but the Baroness was not to be put off with a flimsy excuse. She commenced to make a row. Few meals passed without a squabble of some sort, between the hotel servants and this terrible woman.

"Now we are in for it again!" murmured Miss Leyton into Mrs. Pullen's ear. The waiter brought a different *entrée*, but the Baroness insisted upon having a second helping of *tête de veau aux champignons*.

"*Il n'y a plus, Madame!*" asseverated Philippe, with a gesture of deprecation.

"What does 'e say?" demanded the Baroness, who was not good at French.

"There is no more, *mein tear!*" replied her husband, with a strong German accent.

"Confound their impudence!" exclaimed his wife with a heated countenance, "'ere, send *Monsieur* 'ere at once! I'll soon see if we're not to 'ave enough to eat in 'is beastly hotel!"

All the ladies who understood what she said, looked horrified at such language, but that was of no consequence to Madame Gobelli, who continued to call out at intervals for "*Monsieur*" until she found the dinner was coming to an end without her, and thought it would be more politic to attend to business and postpone her feud till a more convenient occasion. The Baroness Gobelli was a mystery to most people in the hotel. She was an enormous woman of the elephant build, with a large, flat face and clumsy hands and feet. Her skin was coarse, so was her hair, so were her features. The only things which redeemed an otherwise repulsive face, were a pair of good-humoured, though cunning blue eyes and a set of firm, white teeth.

Who the Baroness had originally been, no one could quite make out. It was evident that she must have sprung from some low origin, from her lack of education and breeding, yet she spoke familiarly of aristocratic names, even of royal ones, and appeared to be acquainted with their families and homes. There was a floating rumour that she had been old Mr. Bates's cook before he married her, and when he left her a widow with an only child and a considerable fortune, the little German Baron had thought that her money was a fair equivalent for her personality. She was exceedingly vulgar, and when roused, exceedingly vituperative, but she possessed a rough good humour when pleased, and a large amount of natural shrewdness, which stood her instead of cleverness.

But she was an unscrupulous liar, and rather boasted of the fact than otherwise. Having plenty of money at her command, she was used to take violent fancies to people—taking them up suddenly, loading them with presents and favours for as long as it pleased her, and then dropping them as suddenly, without why or wherefore— even insulting them if she could not shake them off without doing so. The Baron was completely under her thumb; more than that, he was servile in her presence, which astonished those people, who did not know that amongst her other arrogant insistences, the Baroness laid claim to holding intercourse with certain supernatural and invisible beings, who had the power to wreak vengeance on all those who offended her. This fear it was, combined with the fact that she had all the money and kept the strings of the bag pretty close where he was concerned, that made the Baron wait upon his wife's wishes as if he were her slave.

Perhaps the softest spot in the Baroness's heart was kept for her sickly and uninteresting son, Bobby Bates, whom she treated, nevertheless, with the roughness of a tigress for her cub. She kept him still more under her surveillance than she did her husband, and Bobby, though he had attained his nineteenth year, dared not say Bo! to a goose, in presence of his Mamma. As the cheese was handed round, Elinor Leyton rose from her seat with an impatient gesture.

"Do let us get out of this atmosphere, Margaret!" she said in a low voice. "I really cannot stand it any longer!"

The two ladies left the table, and went out beyond the balcony, to where a number of painted iron chairs and tables were placed on the Digue, for the accommodation of passing wayfarers, who might wish to rest awhile and quench their thirst with *limonade* or lager beer.

"I wonder who that girl is!" remarked Mrs. Pullen as soon as they were out of hearing, "I don't know whether I like her or not, but there is something rather distinguished-looking about her!"

"Do you think so?" said Miss Leyton, "I thought she only distinguished herself by eating like a cormorant! I never saw anyone in society, gobble her food in such a manner! She made me positively sick!"

"Was it as bad as that?" replied the more quiet Mrs. Pullen, in an indifferent manner. Her eyes were attracted just then by the perambulator which contained her baby, and she rose to meet it.

"How is she, Nurse?" she asked as anxiously as it she had not parted from the infant an hour before; "Has she been awake all the time?"

"Yes, Ma'am, and looking about her like anything! But she seems inclined to sleep now! I thought it was about time to take her in!"

"O! no! not on such a warm, lovely evening! If she does go to sleep in the open air, it will do her no harm. Leave her with me! I want you to go indoors, and find out the name of the young lady who sat opposite to me at dinner today. Philippe understands English. He will tell you!"

"Why on earth do you want to know?" demanded Miss Leyton, as the servant disappeared.

"O! I don't know! I feel a little curious, that is all! She seems so young to be by herself!"

Elinor Leyton answered nothing, but walked across the Digue and stood, looking out over the sea. She was anticipating the arrival of her *fiancé*, Captain Ralph Pullen of the Limerick Rangers, but he had delayed his coming to join them, and she began to find Heyst rather dull.

The visitors of the Lion d'Or had finished their meal by this time, and were beginning to reassemble on the Digue, preparatory to taking a stroll before they turned into one of the many *cafés chantants*, which were situated at stated intervals in front of the sea. Amongst them, came the Baroness Gobelli, leaning heavily on a thick stick with one hand, and her husband's shoulder with the other. The couple presented an extraordinary appearance, as they perambulated slowly up and down the Digue.

She—with her great height and bulk, towering a head above her companion, whilst he—with a full-sized torso, and short legs—a large hat crammed down upon his forehead, and no neck to speak of, so that the brim appeared to rest upon his shoulders—was a ludicrous figure, as he walked beside his wife, bending under the weight of her support. But yet, she was actually proud of him. Notwithstanding his ill-shaped figure, the Baron possessed one of those mild German

11

faces, with pale watery blue eyes, a long nose, and hair and beard of a reddish-golden colour, which entitled him, in the estimation of some people to be called a handsome man, and the Baroness was never tired of informing the public that his head and face had once been drawn for that of some celebrated saint.

Her own appearance was really comical, for though she had plenty of means, her want of taste, or indifference to dress, made everyone stare at her as she passed. On the present occasion, she wore a silk gown which had cost seventeen shillings a yard, with a costly velvet cloak, a bonnet which might have been rescued from the dustbin, and cotton gloves with all her fingers out. She shook her thick walking stick in Miss Leyton's face as she passed by her, and called out loud enough for everyone to hear: "And when is the handsome captain coming to join you, Miss Leyton, eh? Take care he ain't running after some other gal! 'When pensive I thought on my L.O.V.E.' Ha! Ha! ha!"

Elinor flushed a delicate pink but did not turn her head, nor take any notice of her tormentor. She detested the Baroness with a perfectly bitter hatred, and her proud cold nature revolted from her coarseness and familiarity.

"Tied to your brat again!" cried the Baroness, as she passed Margaret Pullen who was moving the perambulator gently to and fro by the handle, so as to keep her infant asleep; "why didn't you put it in the tub as soon as it was born? It would 'ave saved you a heap of trouble! I often wish I had done so by that devil Bobby! 'Ere, where are you, Bobby?"

"I'm close behind you, Mamma!" replied the simple-looking youth.

"Well! don't you get running away from your father and me, and winking at the gals! There's time enough for that, ain't there, Gustave?" she concluded, addressing the Baron.

"Come along, Robert, and mind what your mother tells you!" said the Herr Baron with his guttural German accent, as the extraordinary trio pursued their way down the Digue, the Baroness making audible remarks on everybody she met, as they went.

Margaret Pullen sat where they had left her, moving about the perambulator, whilst her eyes, like Elinor's, were fixed upon the tranquil water. The August sun had now quite disappeared, and the indescribably faint and unpleasant odour, which is associated with the dunes of Heyst, had begun to make itself apparent. A still languor had crept over everything, and there were indications of a thunderstorm in the air. She was thinking of her husband, Colonel Arthur Pullen, the elder brother of Miss Leyton's *fiancé*, who was toiling out in India for baby and herself. It had been a terrible blow to Margaret, to let him go out alone after only one year of happy wedded life, but the expected advent of her little daughter at the time, had prohibited her undertaking so long a journey and she had been compelled to remain behind. And now baby was six months old, and Colonel Pullen hoped to be home by Christmas, so had advised her to wait for his return. But her thoughts were sad sometimes, notwithstanding.

Events happen so unexpectedly in this world—who could say for certain that she and her husband would ever meet again—that Arthur would ever see his little girl, or that she should live to place her in her father's arms? But such a state of feeling was morbid, she knew, and she generally made an effort to shake it off. The nurse, returning with the information she had sent her to acquire, roused her from her reverie.

"If you please. Ma'am, the young lady's name is Brandt, and Philippe says she came from London!"

"English! I should never have guessed it!" observed Mrs. Pullen, "She speaks French so well.

"Shall I take the baby now, Ma'am?"

"Yes! Wheel her along the Digue. I shall come and meet you by and by!"

As the servant obeyed her orders, she called to Miss Leyton.

"Elinor! come here!"

"What is it?" asked Miss Leyton, seating herself beside her.

"The new girl's name is Brandt and she comes from England! Would you have believed it?"

"I did not take sufficient interest in her to make any speculations on the subject. I only observed that she had a mouth from ear to ear, and ate like a pig! What does it concern us, where she comes from?"

At that moment, a Mrs. Montague, who, with her husband, was conveying a family of nine children over to Brussels, under the mistaken impression that they would be able to live cheaper there than in England, came down the hotel steps with half a dozen of them, clinging to her skirts, and went straight up to Margaret Pullen.

"O! Mrs. Pullen! What is that young lady's name, who sat opposite to you at dinner? Everybody is asking! I hear she is enormously rich, and travelling alone. Did you see the lace on her dress? Real Valenci-

13

ennes, and the diamond rings she wore! Frederick says they must be worth a lot of money. She must be someone of consequence I should imagine!"

"On the contrary, my nurse tells me she is English and her name is Brandt. Has she no friends here?"

"Madame Lament says she arrived in company with another girl, but they are located at different parts of the hotel. It seems very strange, does it not?"

"And it sounds very improper!" interposed Elinor Leyton, "I should say the less we have to say to her, the better! You never know what acquaintances you may make in a place like this! When I look up and down the *table d'hôte* menagerie sometimes, it makes me quite ill!"

"Does it?" rejoined Mrs. Montague, "I think it's so amusing! That Baroness Gobelli, for instance—"

"Don't mention her before me!" cried Miss Leyton, in a tone of disgust, "the woman is not fit for civilized society!"

"She is rather common, certainly, and strange in her behaviour," said Mrs. Montague, "but she is very good-natured. She gave my little Edward a *louis* yesterday. I felt quite ashamed to let him take it!"

"That just proves her vulgarity," exclaimed Elinor Leyton, who had not a sixpence to give away, herself, "it shews that she thinks her money will atone for all her other shortcomings! She gave that Miss Taylor who left last week, a valuable brooch off her own throat. And poor payment too, for all the dirty things she made her do and the ridicule she poured upon her. I daresay this *nouveau riche* will try to curry favour with us by the same means."

At that moment, the girl under discussion, Miss Brandt, appeared on the balcony, which was only raised a few feet above where they sat. She wore the same dress she had at dinner, with the addition of a little fleecy shawl about her shoulders. She stood smiling, and looking at the ladies (who had naturally dropped all discussion about her) for a few moments, and then she ventured to descend the steps between the rampart gilded lions, and almost timidly, as it seemed, took up a position near them. Mrs. Pullen felt that she could not be so discourteous as to take no notice whatever of the newcomer, and so, greatly to Miss Leyton's disgust, she uttered quietly, "Good evening!"

It was quite enough for Miss Brandt. She drew nearer with smiles mantling over her face.

"Good evening! Isn't it lovely here?—so soft and warm, something

14

like the island, but so much fresher!"

She looked up and down the Digue, now crowded with a multitude of visitors and drew in her breath with a long sigh of content.

"How gay and happy they all seem, and how happy I am too! Do you know, if I had my will, what I should like to do?" she said, addressing Mrs. Pullen.

"No! indeed!"

"I should like to tear up and down this road as hard as ever I could, throwing my arms over my head and screaming aloud!"

The ladies exchanged glances of astonishment, but Margaret Pullen could not forbear smiling as she asked their new acquaintance the reason why.

"O! because I am free—free at last, after ten long years of imprisonment! I am telling you the truth, I am indeed, and you would feel just the same if you had been shut up in a horrid convent ever since you were eleven years old!"

At the word "convent", the national Protestant horror immediately spread itself over the faces of the three other ladies; Mrs. Montague gathered her flock about her and took them out of the way of possible contamination, though she would have much preferred to hear the rest of Miss Brandt's story, and Elinor Leyton moved her chair further away. But Margaret Pullen was interested and encouraged the girl to proceed.

"In a convent! I suppose then you are a Roman Catholic!" Harriet Brandt suddenly opened her slumberous eyes.

"I don't think so! I'm not quite sure what I am! Of course, I've had any amount of religion crammed down my throat in the convent, and I had to follow their prayers, whilst there, but I don't believe my parents were Catholics! But it does not signify, I am my own mistress now. I can be what I like!"

"You have been so unfortunate then as to lose your parents!"

"O! yes! years ago, that is why my guardian, Mr. Trawler, placed me in the convent for my education. And I've been there for ten years! Is it not a shame? I'm twenty-one now! That's why I'm free! You see," the girl went on confidentially, "my parents left me everything, and as soon as I came of age I entered into possession of it. My guardian, Mr. Trawler, who lives in Jamaica,—did I tell you that I've come from Jamaica?—thought I should live with him and his wife, when I left the convent, and pay them for my keep, but I refused. They had kept me too tight! I wanted to see the world and life—it was what I had

15

been looking forward to—so as soon as my affairs were settled, I left the West Indies and came over here!"

"They said you came from England in the hotel!"

"So, I did! The steamer came to London and I stayed there a week before I came on here!"

"But you are too young to travel about by yourself, Miss Brandt! English young ladies never do so!" said Mrs. Pullen.

"I'm not by myself, exactly! Olga Brimont, who was in the convent with me, came too. But she is ill, so she's upstairs. She has come to her brother who is in Brussels, and we travelled together. We had the same cabin on board the steamer, and Olga was very ill. One night the doctor thought she was going to die! I stayed with her all the time. I used to sit up with her at night, but it did her no good. We stopped in London because we wanted to buy some dresses and things, but she was not able to go out, and I had to go alone. Her brother is away from Brussels at present so he wrote her to stay in Heyst till he could fetch her, and as I had nowhere particular to go, I came with her! And she is better already! She has been fast asleep all the afternoon.'

"And what will you do when your friend leaves you?" asked Mrs. Pullen.

"O! I don't know! Travel about, I suppose! I shall go wherever it may please me!"

"Are you not going to take a walk this evening?" demanded Elinor Leyton in a low voice of her friend, wishing to put a stop to the conversation.

"Certainly! I told nurse I would join her and baby by and by!"

"Shall I fetch your hat then?" enquired Miss Leyton, as she rose to go up to their apartments.

"Yes! if you will, dear, please, and my velvet cape, in case it should turn chilly!"

"I will fetch mine too!" cried Miss Brandt, jumping up with alacrity, "I may go with you, mayn't I? I'll just tell Olga that I'm going out and be down again in five minutes!" and without waiting for an answer, she was gone.

"See what you have brought upon us!" remarked Elinor in a vexed tone.

"Well! it was not my fault," replied Margaret, "and after all, what does it signify? It is only a little act of courtesy to an unprotected girl. I don't dislike her, Elinor! She is very familiar and communicative, but fancy what it must be like to find herself her own mistress, and with

16

money at her command, after ten years' seclusion within the four walls of a convent! It is enough to turn the head of any girl. I think it would be very churlish to refuse to be friendly with her!"

"Well! I hope it may turn out all right! But you must remember how Ralph cautioned us against making any acquaintances in a foreign hotel."

"But I am not under Ralph's orders, though you may be, and I should not care to go entirely by the advice of so very fastidious and exclusive a gentleman as he is! My Arthur would never find fault with me, I am sure, for being friendly with a young unmarried girl."

"Anyway Margaret, let me entreat you not to discuss my private affairs with this new *protégée* of yours. I don't want to see her saucy eyes goggling over the news of my engagement to your brother-in-law!"

"Certainly, I will not, since you ask it! But you hardly expect to keep it a secret when Ralph comes down here, do you?"

"Why not? Why need anyone know more than that he is your husband's brother?"

"I expect they know a good deal more now," said Margaret, laughing. "The news that you are the Honourable Elinor Leyton and that your father is Baron Walthamstowe, was known all over Heyst the second day we were here. And I have no doubt it has been succeeded by the interesting intelligence that you are engaged to marry Captain Pullen. You cannot keep servants' tongues from wagging, you know!"

"I suppose not!" replied Elinor, with a moue of contempt. "However, they will learn no more through me or Ralph. We are not 'Arry and 'Arriet' to sit on the Digue with our arms round each other's waists."

"Still—there are signs and symptoms," said Margaret, laughing.

"There will be none with us!" rejoined Miss Leyton, indignantly, as Harriet Brandt, with a black lace hat on, trimmed with yellow roses, and a little *fichu* tied carelessly across her bosom, ran lightly down the steps to join them.

CHAPTER 2

The Digue was crowded by that time. All Heyst had turned out to enjoy the evening air and to partake in the gaiety of the place. A band was playing on the movable orchestra, which was towed by three skinny little donkeys, day after day, from one end of the Digue to the other. Tonight, it was its turn to be in the middle, where a large company of people was sitting on green painted chairs that cost ten centimes for hire each, whilst children danced, or ran madly round and round its base. Everyone had changed his, or her, seaside garb for more fashionable array—even the children were robed in white frocks and gala hats—and the whole scene was gay and festive.

Harriet Brandt ran from one side to the other of the Digue, as though she also had been a child. Everything she saw seemed to astonish and delight her. First, she was gazing out over the calm and placid water—and next, she was exclaiming at the bits of rubbish in the shape of embroidered baskets, or painted shells, exhibited in the shop windows, which were side by side with the private houses and hotels, forming a long line of buildings fronting the water.

She kept on declaring that she wanted to buy that or this, and lamenting she had not brought more money with her.

"You will have plenty of opportunities to select and purchase what you want tomorrow," said Mrs. Pullen, "and you will be better able to judge what they are like. They look better under the gas than they do by daylight, I can assure you, Miss Brandt!"

"O! but they are lovely—delightful!" replied the girl, enthusiastically, "I never saw anything so pretty before! Do look at that little doll in a bathing costume, with her cap in one hand, her sponge in the other! She is charming—unique! *Tout ce qu'il ya de plus beau!"*

She spoke French perfectly, and when she spoke English, it was with a slightly foreign accent, that greatly enhanced its charm. It made Mrs. Pullen observe:

"You are more used to speaking French than English, Miss Brandt!"

"Yes! We always spoke French in the convent, and it is in general use in the island. But I thought—I hoped—that I spoke English like an English woman! I *am* an Englishwoman, you know!"

"Are you? I was not quite sure! Brandt sounds rather German!"

"No! my father was English, his name was Henry Brandt, and my mother was a Miss Carey—daughter of one of the Justices of Barbadoes!"

"O! indeed!" replied Mrs. Pullen. She did not know what else to say. The subject was of no interest to her! At that moment, they encountered the nurse and perambulator, and she naturally stopped to speak to her baby.

The sight of the infant seemed to drive Miss Brandt wild.

"O! is that your baby, Mrs. Pullen, is that really your baby?" she exclaimed excitedly, "you never told me you had one. O! the darling! the sweet dear little angel! I love little white babies! I adore them. They

18

are so sweet and fresh and clean—so different from the little niggers who smell so nasty, you can't touch them! We never saw a baby in the convent, and so few English children live to grow up in Jamaica! O! let me hold her! let me carry her! I *must!*"

She was about to seize the infant in her arms, when the mother interposed.

"No, Miss Brandt, please, not this evening! She is but half awake, and has arrived at that age when she is frightened of strangers. Another time perhaps, when she has become used to you, but not now!"

"But I will be so careful of her, pretty dear!" persisted the girl, "I will nurse her so gently, that she will fall to sleep again in my arms. Come! my little love, come!" she continued to the baby who pouted her lips and looked as if she were going to cry.

"Leave her alone!" exclaimed Elinor Leyton in a sharp voice. "Do you not hear what Mrs. Pullen says—that you are not to touch her!"

She spoke so acridly, that gentle Margaret Pullen felt grieved for the look of dismay that darted into Harriet Brandt's face on hearing it.

"O! I am sorry—I didn't mean—" she stammered, with a side-glance at Margaret.

"Of course, you did not mean anything but what was kind," said Mrs. Pullen, "Miss Leyton perfectly understands that, and when baby is used to you, I daresay she will be very grateful for your attentions. But tonight, she is sleepy and tired, and, perhaps, a little cross. Take her home, Nurse," she went on, "and put her to bed! Goodnight, my sweet!" and the perambulator passed them and was gone.

An awkward silence ensued between the three women after this little incident. Elinor Leyton walked somewhat apart from her companions, as if she wished to avoid all further controversy, whilst Margaret Pullen sought some way by which to atone for her friend's rudeness to the young stranger. Presently they came across one of the *cafés chantants* which are attached to the seaside hotels, and which was brilliantly lighted up. A large awning was spread outside, to shelter some dozens of chairs and tables, most of which were already occupied.

The windows of the hotel *salon* had been thrown wide open, to accommodate some singers and musicians, who advanced in turn and stood on the threshold to amuse the audience. As they approached the scene, a tenor in evening dress was singing a love song, whilst the musicians accompanied his voice from the *salon*, and the occupants of the chairs were listening with rapt attention.

"How charming! how delightful!" cried Harriet Brandt, as they

19

reached the spot, "I never saw anything like this in the island!"

"You appear never to have seen anything!" remarked Miss Leyton, with a sneer. Miss Brandt glanced apologetically at Mrs. Pullen.

"How could I see anything, when I was in the convent?" she said, "I know there are places of entertainment in the island, but I was never allowed to go to any. And in London, there was no one for me to go with! I should so much like to go in there," indicating the *café*. "Will you come with me, both of you I mean, and I will pay for everything! I have plenty of money, you know!"

"There is nothing to pay, my dear, unless you call for refreshment," was Margaret's reply.

"Yes, I will go with you certainly, if you so much wish it! Elinor, you won't mind, will you?"

But Miss Leyton was engaged talking to a Monsieur and Mademoiselle Vieuxtemps—an old brother and sister, resident in the Lion d'Or—who had stopped to wish her good-evening! They were dear, good old people, but rather monotonous and dull, and Elinor had more than once ridiculed their manner of talking and voted them the most terrible bores. Mrs. Pullen concluded therefore, that she would get rid of them as soon as courtesy permitted her to do so, and follow her. With a smile and a bow therefore, to the Vieuxtemps, she pushed her way through the crowd, with Harriet Brandt, to where she perceived that three seats were vacant, and took possession of them. They were not good seats for hearing or seeing, being to one side of the salon, and quite in the shadow, but the place was so full that she saw no chance of getting any others. As soon as they were seated, the waiter came round for orders, and it was with difficulty that Mrs. Pullen prevented her companion purchasing sufficient liqueurs and cakes to serve double the number of their company.

"You must allow me to pay for myself, Miss Brandt," she said gravely, "or I will never accompany you anywhere again!"

"But I have lots of money," pleaded the girl, "much more than I know what to do with—it would be a pleasure to me, it would indeed!"

But Mrs. Pullen was resolute, and three *limonades* only were placed upon their table. Elinor Leyton had not yet made her appearance, and Mrs. Pullen kept craning her neck over the other seats to see where she might be, without success.

"She cannot have missed us!" she observed, "I wonder if she can have continued her walk with the Vieuxtemps!"

"O! what does it signify?" said Harriet, drawing her chair closer to that of Mrs. Pullen, "we can do very well without her. I don't think she's very nice, do you?"

"You must not speak of Miss Leyton, like that to me, Miss Brandt," remonstrated Margaret, gently, "because—she is a great friend of our family."

She had been going to say, "Because she will be my sister-in-law before long," but remembered Elinor's request in time, and substituted the other sentence.

"I don't think she's very kind, though," persisted the other.

"It is only her manner, Miss Brandt! She does not mean anything by it!"

"But you are so different," said the girl as she crept still closer, "I could see it when you smiled at me at dinner. I knew I should like you at once. And I want you to like me too—so much! It has been the dream of my life to have some friends. That is why I would not stay in Jamaica. I don't like the people there! I want friends—real friends!"

"But you must have had plenty of friends of your own age in the convent."

"That shews you don't know anything about a convent! It's the very last place where they will let you make a friend—they're afraid lest you should tell each other too much! The convent I was in was an Ursuline order, and even the nuns were obliged to walk three and three, never two, together, lest they should have secrets between them. As for us girls, we were never left alone for a single minute! There was always a sister with us, even at night, walking up and down between the row of beds, pretending to read her prayers, but with her eyes on us the whole time and her ears open to catch what we said. I suppose they were afraid we should talk about lovers. I think girls do talk about them when they can, more in convents than in other places, though they have never had any. It would be so dreadful to be like the poor nuns, and never have a lover to the end of one's days, wouldn't it?"

"You would not fancy being a nun then, Miss Brandt!"

"I—O! dear no! I would rather be dead, twenty times over! But they didn't like my coming out at all. They did try so hard to persuade me to remain with them for ever! One of them, Sister Feodore, told me I must never talk even with gentlemen, if I could avoid it—that they were all wicked and nothing they said was true, and if I trusted them, they would only laugh at me afterwards for my pains. But I don't believe that, do you?"

"Certainly not!" replied Margaret warmly. "The sister who told you so knew nothing about men. My dear husband is more like an angel than a man, and there are many like him. You mustn't believe such nonsense, Miss Brandt! I am sure you never heard your parents say such a silly thing!"

"O! my father and mother! I never remember hearing them say anything!" replied Miss Brandt. She had crept closer and closer to Mrs. Pullen as she spoke, and now encircled her waist with her arm, and leaned her head upon her shoulder. It was not a position that Margaret liked, nor one she would have expected from a woman on so short an acquaintance, but she did not wish to appear unkind by telling Miss Brandt to move further away. The poor girl was evidently quite unused to the ways and customs of Society, she seemed moreover very friendless and dependant—so Margaret laid her solecism down to ignorance and let her head rest where she had placed it, resolving inwardly meanwhile that she would not subject herself to be treated in so familiar a manner again.

"Don't you remember your parents then?" she asked her presently.

"Hardly! I saw so little of them," said Miss Brandt, "my father was a great doctor and scientist, I believe, and I am not quite sure if he knew that he had a daughter!"

"O! my dear, what nonsense!"

"But it is true, Mrs. Pullen! He was always shut up in his laboratory, and I was not allowed to go near that part of the house. I suppose he was very clever and all that—but he was too much engaged in making experiments to take any notice of me, and I am sure I never wanted to see him!"

"How very sad! But you had your mother to turn to for consolation and company, whilst she lived, surely?"

"O! my mother!" echoed Harriet, carelessly. "Yes! my mother! Well! I don't think I knew much more of her either. The ladies in Jamaica get very lazy, you know, and keep a good deal to their own rooms. The person there I loved best of all, was old Pete, the overseer!"

"The overseer!"

"Of the estate and niggers, you know! We had plenty of niggers on the coffee plantation, regular African fellows, with woolly heads and blubber lips, and yellow whites to their eyes. When I was a little thing of four years old, Pete used to let me whip the little niggers for a treat, when they had done anything wrong. It used to make me laugh to see them wriggle their legs under the whip and cry!"

22

"O! don't, Miss Brandt!" exclaimed Margaret Pullen, in a voice of pain.

"It's true, but they deserved it, you know, the little wretches, always thieving or lying or something! I've seen a woman whipped to death, because she wouldn't work. We think nothing of that sort of thing, over there. Still—you can't wonder that I was glad to get out of the island. But I loved old Pete, and if he had been alive when I left, I would have brought him to England with me. He used to carry me for miles through the jungle on his back,—out in the fresh mornings and the cool, dewy eves. I had a pony to ride, but I never went anywhere without his hand upon my bridle rein. He was always so afraid lest I should come to any harm. I don't think anybody else cared. Pete was the only creature who ever loved me, and when I think of Jamaica, I remember my old nigger servant as the one friend I had there!"

"It is very, very sad!" was all that Mrs. Pullen could say.

She had become fainter and fainter, as the girl leaned against her with her head upon her breast. Some sensation which she could not define, nor account for—some feeling which she had never experienced before—had come over her and made her head reel. She felt as if something or someone, were drawing all her life away. She tried to disengage herself from the girl's clasp, but Harriet Brandt seemed to come after her, like a coiling snake, till she could stand it no longer, and faintly exclaiming:

"Miss Brandt! let go of me, please! I feel ill!" she rose and tried to make her way between the crowded tables, towards the open air. As she stumbled along, she came against (to her great relief) her friend, Elinor Leyton.

"O! Elinor!" she gasped, "I don't know what is the matter with me! I feel so strange, so light-headed! Do take me home!"

Miss Leyton dragged her through the audience, and made her sit down on a bench, facing the sea.

"Why! what's the matter?" demanded Harriet Brandt, who had made her way after them, "is Mrs. Pullen ill?"

"So it appears," replied Miss Leyton, coldly, "but how it happened, you should know better than myself! I suppose it is very warm in there!"

"No! no! I do not think so," said Margaret, with a bewildered air, "we had chairs close to the side. And Miss Brandt was telling me of her life in Jamaica, when such an extraordinary sensation came over me! I can't describe it! it was just as if I had been scooped hollow!"

23

At this description, Harriet Brandt burst into a loud laugh, but Elinor frowned her down.

"It may seem a laughing matter to you, Miss Brandt," she said, in the same cold tone, "but it is none to me. Mrs. Pullen is far from strong, and her health is not to be trifled with. However, I shall not let her out of my sight again."

"Don't make a fuss about it, Elinor," pleaded her friend, "it was my own fault, if anyone's. I think there must be a thunderstorm in the air, I have felt so oppressed all the evening. Or is the smell from the dunes worse than usual? Perhaps I ate something at dinner that disagreed with me!"

"I cannot understand it at all," replied Miss Leyton, "you are not used to fainting, or being suddenly attacked in any way. However, if you feel able to walk, let us go back to the hotel. Miss Brandt will doubtless, find someone to finish the evening with!"

Harriet was just about to reply that she knew no one but themselves, and to offer to take Mrs. Pullen's arm on the other side, when Elinor Leyton cut her short.

"No! thank you, Miss Brandt! Mrs. Pullen would, I am sure, prefer to return to the hotel alone with me! You can easily join the Vieux-temps or any other of the visitors to the Lion d'Or. There is not much ceremony observed amongst the English at these foreign places. It would be better perhaps if there were a little more! Come, Margaret, take my arm, and we will walk as slowly as you like! But I shall not be comfortable until I see you safe in your own room!"

So, the two ladies moved off together, leaving Harriet Brandt standing, disconsolately on the Digue, watching their departure. Mrs. Pullen had uttered a faint goodnight to her, but had made no suggestion that she should walk back with them, and it seemed to the girl as if they both in some measure, blamed her for the illness of her companion. What had she done, she asked herself, as she reviewed what had passed between them, that could in any way account for Mrs. Pullen's illness? She liked her so much—so very much—she had so hoped she was going to be her friend—she would have done anything and given anything sooner than put her to inconvenience in any way.

As the two ladies moved slowly out of sight, Harriet turned sadly and walked the other way. She felt lonely and disappointed. She knew no one to speak to, and there was a cold empty feeling in her breast, as though, in losing her hold on Margaret Pullen, she had lost something on which she had depended. Something of her feeling must

24

have communicated itself to Margaret Pullen, for after a minute or two she stopped and said, "I don't half like leaving Miss Brandt by herself, Elinor! She is very young to be wandering about a town by night and alone!"

"Nonsense!" returned Miss Leyton, shortly, "a young lady who can make the voyage from Jamaica to Heyst on her own account, knocking about in London for a week on the way, is surely competent to walk back to the hotel without your assistance. I should say that Miss Brandt was a very independent young woman!"

"Perhaps, by nature, but she has been shut up in a convent for the best part of her life, and that is not considered to be a good preparation for fighting one's way through the world!"

"She'll be able to fight her own battles, never fear!" was Elinor's reply.

Just then they encountered Bobby Bates, who lifted his cap as he hurried past them.

"Where are you going so fast, Mr. Bates?" said Elinor Leyton.

"I am going back to the hotel to fetch Mamma's fur boa!" he answered.

They were passing a lighted lamp at the time, and she noticed that the lad's eyes were red, and his features bore traces of distress.

"Are you ill?" she enquired quickly, "or in any trouble?"

He halted for a minute in his stride.

"No! no! not exactly," he said in a low voice, and then, as if the words came from him against his will, he went on, "But O! I do wish someone would speak to Mamma about the way she treats me. It's cruel—to strike me with her stick before all those people, as if I were a baby, and to call me such names! Even the servant William laughs at me! Do all mothers do the same, Miss Leyton? Ought a man to stand it quietly?"

"Decidedly not!" cried Elinor, without hesitation.

"O! Elinor! remember, she is his mother," remonstrated Margaret, "don't say anything to set him against her!"

"But I was nineteen last birthday," continued the lad, "and sometimes she treats me in such a manner, that I can't bear it! The Baron dare not say a word to her! She swears at him so. Sometimes, I think I will run away and go to sea!"

"No! no! you mustn't do that!" called Miss Leyton after him, as he quickened his footsteps, in the direction of the Lion d'Or.

"What an awful woman!" sighed Mrs. Pullen. "Fancy! Striking her own son in public, and with that thick stick too. I believe he had been crying!"

"I am sure he had," replied her friend, "you can see the poor fellow is half-witted, and very weakly into the bargain. I suppose she has beaten his brains to a pap. What a terrible misfortune to have such a mother! You should hear some of the stories Madame Lamont has to tell of her!"

"But how does she hear them?"

"Through the Baron's servant William, I suppose. He says the Baroness has often taken her stick to him and the other servants, and thinks no more of swearing at them, than a trooper! They all hate her. One day, she took up a kitchen cleaver and advanced upon her coachman with it, but he seized her by both arms and sat her down upon the fire, whence she was only rescued after being somewhat severely burned!"

"It served her right!" exclaimed Margaret, laughing at the ludicrous idea, "but what a picture she must have presented, seated on the kitchen range! Where can the woman have been raised? What sort of a person can she be?"

"Not what she pretends, Margaret, you may be sure of that! All her fine talk of lords and ladies is so much bunkum. But I pity the poor little Baron, who is, at all events, inoffensive. How can he put up with such a wife! He must feel very much ashamed of her sometimes!"

"And yet he seems devoted to her! He never leaves her side for a moment. He is her walking stick, her fetcher and carrier, and her scribe. I don't believe she can write a letter!"

"And yet she was talking at the *table d'hôte* yesterday of the Duke of This and the Earl of That, and hinting at her having stayed at Osborne and Windsor. Of course, they are falsehoods! She has never seen the inside of a palace unless it was in the capacity of a charwoman! Have you observed her hair? It is as coarse as a horse tail? And her hands! Bobby informed me the other day that his Mamma took nines in gloves! She's not a woman, my dear! She's a female elephant!"

Margaret was laughing still, when they reached the steps of the Lion d'Or.

"You are very naughty and very scandalous, Elinor," she said, "but you have done me a world of good. My unpleasant feelings have quite gone. I am quite capable of continuing our walk if you would like to do so."

"No such thing, Madam," replied Miss Leyton, "I am responsible

26

for your well-doing in Arthur's absence. Upstairs and into bed you go, unless you would like a cup of coffee and a *chasse* first. That is the only indulgence I can grant you."

But Mrs. Pullen declined the proffered refreshment, and the two ladies sought their rooms in company.

CHAPTER 3

The next morning dawned upon a perfect August day. The sun streamed brightly over every part of Heyst, turning the loose dry yellow sand (from end to end of which, not a stone or boulder was to be seen), into a veritable cloth of gold. The patient asses, carrying their white-covered saddles, and tied to stakes, were waiting in a row for hire, whilst some dozen Rosinantes, called by courtesy, horses, were also of the company. The sands were already strewn with children, their short petticoats crammed into a pair of bathing drawers, and their heads protected by linen hats or bonnets, digging away at the dry sand as if their lives depended on their efforts. The bathing machines, painted in gay stripes of green, red, blue, or orange, were hauled down, ready for action, and the wooden tents, which can be hired for the season at any foreign watering place, were being swept out and arranged for the day's use.

Some of the more pretentious ones, belonging to private families, were surmounted by a gilt coronet, the proud possession of the Comte Darblaye, or the Herr Baron Grumplestein—sported flags moreover of France or Germany, and were screened from the eyes of the vulgar, by lace or muslin curtains, tied up with blue ribbons. On the balcony of the Lion d'Or, where the visitors always took their breakfast, were arranged tables, piled with dishes of crevettes, fresh from the sea, *pistolets*, and beautiful butter as white and tasteless as cream. It was a delight to breakfast on the open balcony, with the sea breeze blowing in one's face, and in the intervals of eating prawns and bread and butter, or perusing the morning papers, to watch the cheerful scene below.

The Baroness was there, early, of course. She, and her husband, and the ill-used Bobby, occupied a table to themselves, whence she addressed her remarks to whomever she chose, whether they wished to listen or not, and the Baron shelled her crevettes and buttered her *pistolets* for her. Margaret and Elinor were rather later than usual, for Mrs. Pullen had not passed a good night, and Miss Leyton would not have her disturbed.

Harriet Brandt was there as they appeared, and beside her, a pale,

27

unhealthy-looking young woman, whom she introduced as her friend, and travelling companion, Olga Brimont.

"Olga did not wish to come down. She thought she would lie another day in bed, but I made her get up and dress, and I was right, wasn't I, Mrs. Pullen?"

"I think the fresh air will do Mademoiselle Brimont more good than the close bedroom, if she is strong enough to stand it!" replied Margaret, with a smile. "I am afraid you are still feeling weak," she continued, to the newcomer.

"I feel better than I did on board the steamer, or in London," said Mademoiselle Brimont. She was an undersized girl with plain features, and did not shew off to advantage beside her travelling companion.

"Did you suffer so much from sea-sickness? I can sympathise with you, as I am a very bad sailor myself!"

"O! no! *Madame*, it was not the *mal de mer*. I can hardly tell you what it was. Miss Brandt and I occupied a small cabin together, and perhaps, it was because it was so small, but I did not feel as if I could breathe there—such a terrible oppression as though someone were sitting on my chest—and such a general feeling of emptiness It was the same in London, though Miss Brandt did all she could for me, indeed she sat up with me all night, till I feared she would be ill herself—but I feel better now! Last night I slept for the first time since leaving Jamaica!"

"That is right! You will soon get well in this lovely air!"

They all sat down at the same table, and commenced to discuss their rolls and coffee. Margaret Pullen, glancing up once was struck by the look with which Harriet Brandt was regarding her—it was so full of yearning affection—almost of longing to approach her nearer, to hear her speak, to touch her hand! It amused her to observe it! She had heard of cases, in which young unsophisticated girls had taken unaccountable affections for members of their own sex, and trusted she was not going to form the subject for some such experience on Miss Brandt's part. The idea made her address her conversation more to Mademoiselle Brimont, than to her companion of the evening before.

"I suppose you and Miss Brandt were great friends in the convent," she said.

"O! no, *Madame*, we hardly ever saw each other whilst there, except in chapel. There is so much difference in our ages, I am only seventeen, and was in the lower school, whilst Miss Brandt did hardly any lessons during the last two years she spent there. But I was very glad to have her company across to England. My brother would have sent for me last year, if he could have heard of a lady to travel with me!"

"Are you going on to join your brother soon?"

"He says he will fetch me, *Madame*, as soon as he can be spared from his business. He is my only relation. My parents died, like Miss Brandt's, in the West Indies."

"Well! you must be sure and get your looks back before he arrives!" said Margaret, kindly.

The headwaiter now appeared with the letters from England, amongst which was one for Miss Leyton in a firm, manly handwriting, with a regimental crest in blue and gold upon the envelope. Her face did not change in the least as she broke the seal, although it came from her *fiancé*, Captain Ralph Pullen.

Elinor Leyton's was an exceptionally cold face, and it matched her disposition. She had attractive features;—a delicate nose, carved as if in ivory—brown eyes, a fair rose-tinted complexion, and a small mouth with thin, firmly closed lips. Her hair was bronze-coloured, and it was always dressed to perfection. She had a good figure too, with small hands and feet—and she was robed in excellent taste. She was pre-eminently a woman for a man to be proud of as the mistress of his house, and the head of his table. She might be trusted never to say or do an unladylike thing—before all, she was cognisant of the obligations which devolved upon her as the daughter of Lord Walthamstowe and a member of the British aristocracy.

But in disposition she was undoubtedly cold, and her *fiancé* had already begun to find it out. Their engagement had come about neither of them quite knew how, but he liked the idea of being connected with an aristocratic family, and she was proud of having won a man, for whom many caps had been pulled in vain. He was considered to be one of the handsomest men of his generation, and she was what people called an unexceptional match for him. She was fond of him in her way, but her way was a strange one. She called the attitude she assumed towards him, a proper and ladylike reserve, but impartial spectators, with stronger feelings, would have deemed it indifference.

However, like the proverbial dog in the manger, whether she valued her rights in Captain Pullen or not, Miss Leyton had no intention of permitting them to be interfered with. She would have died sooner than admit that he was necessary to her happiness,—at the same time she considered it due to her dignity as a woman, never to give in to his wishes, when they opposed her own, and often when they did not.

She displayed no particular enthusiasm when they met, nor distress when they parted—neither was she ever troubled by any qualms lest during their frequent separations, he should meet some woman whom he might perchance prefer to herself. They were engaged and when the proper time came they would marry—meanwhile their private affairs concerned no one but themselves. In short Elinor Leyton was not, what is termed, "a man's woman"—all her friends (if she had any) were of her own sex.

Having perused her letter, she refolded and replaced it in its envelope without a glance in the direction of Mrs. Pullen. Margaret thought she had a right to be informed of her brother-in-law's movements. She had invited Miss Leyton to accompany her to Heyst at his request, and any preparations which might be requisite before he joined them, would have to be made by herself.

"Is that from Ralph? What does he say?" she enquired in a low voice.

'Nothing in particular!"

"But when may we expect him at Heyst?"

"Next week, he says, in time for the *Bataille des Fleurs!*"

"Are you not pleased?"

"Of course, I am!" replied Elinor, but without a sparkle or blush

"O! if it were only my Arthur that were coming!" exclaimed Margaret, fervently, "I should go mad with joy!"

"Then it is just as well perhaps that it is *not* your Arthur!" rejoined her companion, as she put the letter into her pocket.

"Now, Bobby," announced the strident tones of the Baroness Gobelli from the other side of the balcony, "leave off picking the shrimps! You've 'ad more than enough! Ain't bread and butter good enough for you? What'll you want next?"

"But, Mamma," pleaded the youth, "I've only had a few! I've been shelling Papa's all this time!"

"Put 'm down at once, I say!" reiterated the Baroness, "ere William, take Bobby's plate away! He's 'ad plenty for this morning!"

"But I haven't begun yet. I'm hungry!" remonstrated Bobby.

"Take 'is plate away!" roared the Baroness. "Ang it all! Can't you 'ear what I say?"

"*Mein tear! mein tear!*" ejaculated the Herr Baron in a subdued voice.

"Leave me alone, Gustave! Do you suppose I can't manage my own son? He ain't yours! 'E'd make 'imself ill if I didn't look after him.

30

Take 'is plate away, at once!"

The man-servant William lifted the plate of peeled shrimps and bread and butter from the table, whilst Bobby with a very red face rose from his seat and rushed down the steps to the beach.

"He! he! he!" cackled the Baroness, "that'll teach 'im not to fiddle with 'is food another time! Bobby don't care for an empty belly!"

"What a shame!" murmured Margaret, who was nothing if she was not a mother, "now the poor boy will go without his breakfast."

Presently, William was to be seen sneaking past the hotel with a parcel in his hands. The Baroness pounced upon him like a cat upon a mouse.

"William!" she cried from the balcony, "what 'ave you got in your 'and?"

"Summat of my own, my lady!"

"Bring it 'ere!"

The man mounted the steps and stood before his mistress. He held a parcel in his hands, wrapped up in a table napkin.

"Open that parcel!" said the Baroness.

"Indeed, my lady, it's only the shrimps as Master Robert left behind him and I thought they would make me a little relish on the sands, my lady!"

"Open that parcel!"

William obeyed, and disclosed the rolls and butter and peeled shrimps just as Bobby had left them.

"You were going to take 'em down to Bobby on the beach!"

"No, indeed, my lady!"

"Confound you, Sir, don't you lie to me!" exclaimed the Baroness, shaking her stick in his face, "I've ways and means of finding out things that you know nothing of! Throw that stuff into the road!"

"But, my lady—"

"Throw it into the road at once, or you may take your month's warning! 'Ang it all! are you the mistress, or am I?"

The servant threw a glance of enquiry in the direction of the Herr Baron, but the Herr Baron kept his face well down in his plate, so after a pause, he walked to the side, and shook the contents of the napkin upon the Digue.

"And now don't you try any more of your tricks upon me or I'll thrash you till your own mother won't know you! You leave Bobby alone for the future, or it'll be the worst day's work you ever did! Remember that!"

31

"Very good, my lady!" replied William, but as he left the balcony he gave a look at the other occupants, which well conveyed his feelings on the subject.

"I should not be surprised to hear that that woman had been murdered by her servants some day!" said Margaret to Elinor Leyton.

"No! and I should not be sorry! I feel rather like murdering her myself. But let us go down to the sands, Margaret, and try to find the disconsolate Bobby! I'm not afraid of his mother if William is, and if he wants something to eat, I shall give it him!"

They fetched their hats and parasols, and having left the hotel by a side entrance, found their way down to the sands. It was a pretty sight there, and in some cases, a comical one. The bathing machines were placed some sixty or more feet from the water, according to the tide, and their occupants, clad in bathing costumes, had to run the gauntlet of all the eyes upon the beach, as they traversed that distance in order to reach the sea. To some visitors, especially the English ones, this ordeal was rather trying. To watch them open a crevice of the machine door, and regard the expectant crowd with horror;—then after some hesitation, goaded on by the cries of the bathing women that the time was passing, to see them emerge with reluctant feet, sadly conscious of their unclothed condition, and of the unsightly corns and bunions which disfigured their feet—to say nothing of the red and blue tint which their skin had suddenly assumed—was to find it almost impossible to refrain from laughter.

The very skinny and knuckle-kneed ones; the very fat and bulging ones; the little fair men who looked like Bobby's peeled shrimps, and the muscular black and hairy ones who looked like bears escaped from a menagerie,—these types and many others, our ladies could not help being amused at, though they told each other it was very improper all the time. But everybody had to pass through the same ordeal and everybody submitted to it, and tried to laugh off their own humiliation by ridiculing the appearance of their neighbours.

Margaret and Elinor were never tired of watching the antics of the Belgians and Germans whilst they were (what they called) bathing. The fuss they made over entering two feet of water—the way in which they gasped and puffed as they caught it up in their hands and rubbed their backs and chests with it—the reluctance with which the ladies were dragged by their masculine partners into the briny, as if they expected to be overwhelmed and drowned by the tiny waves which rippled over their toes, and made them catch their breath. And lastly, when they were convinced there was no danger, to see them, men and women, fat and thin, take hands and dance round in a ring as if they were playing at "Mulberry Bush" was too delightful. But if one bather, generally an Englishman, more daring than his fellows, went in for a good swim, the coast-guardsmen ran along the breakwater, shouting "*Gare, gare!*" until he came out again.

"They are funnier than ever today," remarked Margaret, after a while, "I wonder what they will say when they see Ralph swimming out next week. They will be frightened to death. All the Pullers are wonderful swimmers. I have seen Anthony Pennell perform feats in the water that made my blood run cold! And Ralph is famous for his diving!"

The topic did not appear to interest Elinor. She reverted to the subject of Anthony.

"Is that the literary man—the cousin?"

"Yes! Have you not met him?"

"Never!"

"I am sure you would like him! He is such a fine fellow! Not such a 'beauty man' as Ralph, perhaps, but quite as tall and stalwart! His last book was a tremendous success!"

"Ralph has never mentioned him to me, though I knew he had a cousin of that name!"

"Well!—if you won't be offended at my saying so—Ralph has always been a little jealous of Anthony, at least so Arthur says. He outstripped him at school and college, and the feeling had its foundation there. And anyone might be jealous of him now! He has shewn himself to be a genius!"

"I don't like geniuses as a rule," replied Elinor, "they are so conceited. I believe that is Bobby Bates sitting out there on the breakwater! I will go and see if he is still hungry!"

"Give the poor boy a couple of *francs* to get himself a breakfast in one of the restaurants," said Margaret, "he will enjoy having a little secret from his terrible Mamma!"

She had not been alone long before the nurse came up to her, with the perambulator, piled up with toys, but no baby. Margaret's tears were excited at once.

"Nurse! nurse, what is the matter? Where is the baby?" she exclaimed in tones of alarm.

"Nothing's the matter, Ma'am! pray don't frighten yourself!" replied the servant, "it's only that the young ladies have got baby, and they've bought her all these toys, and sent me on to tell you that they would be here directly!

The perambulator was filled with expensive playthings useless for an infant of six months old. Dolls, woolly sheep, fur cats, and gaily coloured balls with a huge box of chocolates and caramels, were piled one on the top of the other. But Mrs. Pullen's face expressed nothing but annoyance.

"You had no right to let them take her, Nurse—you had no right to let the child out of your sight! Go back at once and bring her here to me! I am exceedingly annoyed about it!"

"Here are the young ladies, Ma'am, and you had better lay your orders on them, yourself, for they wouldn't mind me," said the nurse, somewhat sullenly.

In another minute, Harriet Brandt, and Olga Brimont had reached her side, the former panting under the weight of the heavy infant, but with her face scarlet with the excitement of having captured her.

"O! Miss Brandt!" cried Margaret, "you have given me such a fright! You must never take baby away from her nurse again, please! As I told you last night, she is afraid of strangers, and generally cries when they try to take her! Come to me, my little one!" she continued, holding out her arms to the child, "come to mother and tell her all about it!"

But the baby seemed to take no notice of the fond appeal. It had its big eyes fixed upon Miss Brandt's face with a half-awed, half-interested expression.

"O! no! don't take her away!" said Harriet, eagerly, "she is so good with me! I assure you she is not frightened in the least bit, are you, my little love?" she added, addressing the infant. "And nurse tells me her name is Ethel, so I have ordered them to make her a little gold bangle with 'Ethel' on it, and she must wear it for my sake, darling little creature!"

"But, Miss Brandt, you must not buy such expensive things for her, indeed. She is too young to appreciate them; besides I do not like you to spend so much money on her!"

"But, why shouldn't I? What am I to do with my money, if I may not spend it on others?"

"But, such a quantity of toys! Surely, you have not bought all these for my baby!"

"Of course, I have! I would have bought the whole shop if it would have pleased her! She likes the colours! Little darling! look

34

how earnestly she gazes at me with her lovely grey eyes, as if she knew what a little beauty I think her! O! you pretty dear! you sweet pink and white baby!"

Mrs. Pullen felt somewhat annoyed as she saw the dolls and furry animals which were strewn upon the sands, at the same time she was flattered by the admiration exhibited of her little daughter, and the endearments lavished upon her. She considered them all well-deserved (as what mother would not?)—and it struck her that Harriet Brandt must be a kind-hearted, as well as a generous girl to spend so much money on a stranger's child.

"She certainly does seem wonderfully good with you," she observed presently, "I never knew her so quiet with anybody but her nurse or me, before. Isn't it marvellous, Nurse?"

"It is, Ma'am! Baby do seem to take surprisingly to the young lady! And perhaps I might go into the town, as she is so quiet, and get the darning wool for your stockings!"

"O! no! no! We must not let Miss Brandt get tired of holding her. She is too heavy to be nursed for long!"

"Indeed, indeed she is not!" cried Harriet, "do let me keep her, Mrs. Pullen, whilst nurse goes on her errand. It is the greatest pleasure to me to hold her. I should like never to give her up again!"

Margaret smiled.

"Very well, Nurse, since Miss Brandt is so kind, you can go!"

As the servant disappeared, she said to Harriet,

"Mind! you give her to me directly she makes your arm ache! I am more used to the little torment than you are."

"How can you call her by such a name, even in fun? What would I not give to have a baby of my very own to do what I liked with? I would never part with it, night nor day, I would teach it to love me so much, that it should never be happy out of my sight!"

"But that would be cruel, my dear! Your baby might have to part with you, as you have had to part with your mother!"

At the mention of her mother, something came into Miss Brandt's eyes, which Margaret could not define. It was not anger, nor sorrow, nor remorse. It was a kind of sullen contempt. It was something that made Mrs. Pullen resolve not to allude to the subject again. The incident made her examine Harriet's eyes more closely than she had done before. They were beautiful in shape and colour, but they did not look like the eyes of a young girl. They were deeply, impenetrably black—with large pellucid pupils, but there was no sparkle nor brightness in them, though they were underlaid by smouldering fires which might burst forth into flame at any moment, and which seemed to stir and kindle and then go out again, when she spoke of anything that interested her.

There was an attraction about the girl, which Mrs. Pullen acknowledged, without wishing to give in to. She could not keep her eyes off her! She seemed to hypnotise her as the snake is said to hypnotise the bird, but it was an unpleasant feeling, as if the next moment, the smouldering fire would burst forth into flame and overwhelm her. But watching her play with, and hearing her talk to, her baby, Margaret put the idea away from her, and only thought how kindly natured she must be, to take so much trouble for another woman's child. It was not long before Miss Leyton found her way back to them, and as her glance fell upon Harriet Brandt and the baby, she elevated her eyebrows.

"Where is the nurse?" she demanded, curtly

"She has gone to the shops to see if she can get some darning wool, and Miss Brandt was kind enough to offer to keep baby for her till she returns. And O! Elinor, look what beautiful toys Miss Brandt has bought her! Isn't she too kind?"

"Altogether too kind!" responded Elinor. "By the way, Margaret, I found our friend and transacted the little business we spoke of! But he says his Mamma has ordered him to remain here, till she comes down to see him bathe, and dry him, I suppose, with her own hands! And do I not descry her fairy feet indenting the sands at this very moment, and bearing down in our direction?"

"You could hardly mistake her for anybody else!" replied Mrs. Pullen.

In another minute the Baroness was upon them.

"Hullo," she called out, "you're just in time to see Gustave bathe! He looks lovely in his bathing costume! His legs are as white as your baby's, Mrs. Pullen, and twice as well worth looking at!"

"*Mein tear! mein tear!*" remonstrated the Baron.

"Don't be a fool, Gustave! You know it's the truth! And the loveliest feet, Miss Leyton! Smaller than yours, I bet. Where's that devil, Bobby? I'm going to give 'im a dousing for his villainy this morning I can tell you! Once I get 'is 'ead under water, it won't come up again in a hurry! I expect 'e's pretty 'ungry by this time! But 'e don't get a *centime* out of me for cakes today. I'll teach 'im not to stuff 'imself like a pig again. Come, Gustave! 'ere's a machine for you! Get me a chair that I may sit outside it! Now, we'll 'ave some fun," she added, with a wink at Mrs. Pullen.

"Let us move on to the breakwater!" said Margaret to Elinor Leyton, and the whole party got up and walked some little distance off.

"Ah! you don't hoodwink me!" screamed the Baroness after them. "You've got glasses with you, and you're going to 'ave a good squint at Gustave's legs through 'em, I know! You'd better 'ave stayed 'ere, like honest women, and said you enjoyed the sight!"

"O! Margaret!" said Miss Leyton, with a look of horror, "if it had not been for the *Bataille des Fleurs* and ....the other thing.... I should have said, for goodness' sake, let us move on to Ostende or Blankenburghe, with the least possible delay. That woman will be the death of me yet! I'm sure she will!"

Notwithstanding which, they could not help laughing in concert, a little later on, to see the unwilling Bobby dragged down by William to bathe, and as he emerged from his machine, helpless and half naked, to watch his elephantine mother chase him with her stout stick in hand, and failing to catch him in time, slip on the wet sand and flounder in the waves herself, from which plight, it looked very much as though her servant instead of rescuing her, did his best to push her further in, before he dragged her, drenched and disordered, on dry land again.

CHAPTER 4

The Baroness Gobelli's temperament was as inconsistent as her dress. Under the garb of jocose good-humour, which often degenerated to horseplay, she concealed a jealous and vindictive disposition, which would go any lengths, when offended, to revenge itself. She was wont to say that she never forgot, nor forgave an injury, and that when she had her knife (as she termed it) in a man, she knew how to bide her time, but that when the time came, she turned it. These bloodthirsty sentiments, coupled with an asseveration which was constantly on her lips, that when she willed the death of anyone, he died, and that she had powers at her command of which no one was aware but herself, frightened many timid and ignorant people into trying to propitiate so apparently potent a mortal, and generally kowtowing before her. To such votaries, so long as they pleased her, Madame Gobelli was used to shew her favour by various gifts of dresses, jewellery, or money, according to their circumstances, for in some cases she was lavishly generous, but she soon tired of her acquaintances and replaced them by fresh favourites.

The hints that she gave forth, regarding herself and her antecedents, were too extraordinary to gain credence except from the most
ignorant of her auditors, but the Baroness always spoke in parables,
and left no proof of what she meant, to be brought up against her.
This proved that if she were clever, she was still more cunning. The
hints she occasionally gave of being descended from Royal blood,
though on the wrong side of the blanket, and of the connection being
acknowledged privately, if not publicly, by the existing members of
the reigning family, were received with open mouths by people of her
own class, but rejected with scorn by such as were acquainted with
those whom she affected to know. It was remarkable also, and only another proof that, whatever her real birth and antecedents, the Baroness
Gobelli was unique, that, notwithstanding her desire to be considered
noble by birth if not by law, she never shirked the fact that the Baron
was in trade—on the contrary she rather made a boast of it, and used
to relate stories bringing it into ridicule with the greatest gusto.

The fact being that Baron Gobelli was the head of a large firm of
export bootmakers, trading in London under the name of Fantaisie et
Cie, the boots and shoes of which, though professedly French, were all
manufactured in Germany, where the firm maintained an enormous
factory. The Baroness could seldom be in the company of anyone
for more than five minutes, without asking them where they bought
their boots and shoes, and recommending them to Fantaisie et Cie as
the best makers in London. She wanted to be first in everything—in
popularity, in notice, and in conversation—if she could not attract attention by her personality, she startled people by her vulgarity—if she
could not reign supreme by reason of her supposed birth, she would
do so by boots and shoes, if nothing else—and if anybody slighted her
or appeared to discredit her statements, he or she was immediately
marked down for retaliation.

Harriet Brandt had not been many days in Heyst before the Baroness had become jealous of the attention which she paid Mrs. Pullen
and her child. She saw that the girl was attractive, she heard that she
was rich, and she liked to have pretty and pleasant young people about
her when at home—they drew men to the house and reflected a sort
of credit upon herself—and she determined to get Harriet away from
Margaret Pullen and chain her to her own side instead. The Baroness
hated Miss Leyton quite as much as Elinor hated her. She was quick
of hearing and very intuitive—she had caught more than one of the
young lady's uncomplimentary remarks upon herself, and had divined

38

still more than she had heard. She had observed her sympathy with Bobby also, and that she encouraged him in his boyish rebellion. For all these reasons, she "had her knife" into Miss Leyton, and was waiting her opportunity to turn it. And she foresaw—with the assistance perhaps of the Powers of Darkness, of whose acquaintance she was so proud—that she would be enabled to take her revenge on Elinor Leyton through Harriet Brandt.

But her first advances to the latter were suavity itself. She was not going to frighten the girl by shewing her claws, until she had stroked her down the right way with her *pattes de velours.*

She came upon her one morning, as she sat upon the sands, with little Ethel in her arms. The nurse was within speaking distance, busy with her needlework, and the infant seemed so quiet with Miss Brandt and she took such evident pleasure in nursing it, that Mrs. Pullen no longer minded leaving them together, and had gone for a stroll with Miss Leyton along the Digue. So, the Baroness found Harriet, comparatively speaking, alone.

"So you're playing at nursemaid again!" she commenced in her abrupt manner. "You seem to have taken a wonderful fancy to that child!"

"She is such a good little creature," replied Harriet, "she is no trouble whatever. She sleeps half the day!"

Miss Brandt had a large box of chocolates beside her, into which she continually dipped her hand. Her mouth, too, was stained with the delicate sweetmeat—she was always eating, either fruit or bonbons. She handed the box now, with a timid air, to the Baroness. "Do you care for chocolate, *Madame?*" she asked. The Baroness did not like to be called "*Madame*" according to the French fashion. She thought it derogated from her dignity. She wished everyone to address her as "my lady," and considered she was cheated out of her rights when it was omitted. But she liked chocolate almost as well as Harriet did.

"Thank you! I'll 'ave a few!" she said, grabbing about a dozen in her huge hand at the first venture. "What a liking for candies the Amurricans seem to 'ave introduced into England! I can remember the time when you never saw such a thing as sweets in the palace—I don't think they were allowed—and now they're all over the place. I shouldn't wonder if Her Majesty hasn't a box or two in her private apartments, and as for the princesses, well—!"

"The palace!—Her Majesty!"—echoed Miss Brandt, opening her dark eyes very wide.

"As I tell 'em," continued the Baroness, "they won't 'ave a tooth left amongst the lot of 'em soon! What are you staring at?"

"But—but—do you go to the queen's palace?" demanded Harriet, incredulously, as well she might.

"Not unless I'm sent for, you may take your oath! I ain't fond enough of 'em for all that; besides, Windsor's 'orribly damp and don't suit me at all. But you mustn't go and repeat what I tell you, in the hotel. It might give offence in high places if I was known to talk of it. You see there's some of 'em has never seen me since I married the Baron! Being in trade, they thought 'e wasn't good enough for me! I've 'eard that when Lady Morton—the dowager countess, you know—was asked if she 'ad seen me lately, she called out loud enough for the whole room to 'ear, 'Do you mean the woman that married the boot man? No! I 'aven't seen 'er, and I don't mean to either!' Ha! ha! ha! But I can afford to laugh at all that, my dear!"

"But—I don't quite understand!" said Harriet Brandt, with a bewildered look.

"Why! the Baron deals in shoe-leather! 'Aven't you 'eard it? I suppose we've got the largest manufactory in Germany! Covers four acres of ground, I give you my word!"

"Shoe-leather!" again ejaculated Harriet Brandt, not knowing what to say.

"Why, yes! of course all the aristocracy go in for trade now-a-days! It's the fashion! There's the Viscountess Gormsby keeps a bonnet shop, and Lord Charles Snowe 'as a bakery, and Lady Harrison 'as an old curiosity shop, and stands about it, dusting tables and chairs, all day! But how can you know anything about it, just coming from the West Indies, and all those 'orrid blacks! Ain't you glad to find yourself amongst Christians again?"

"This is the first time I ever left Jamaica," said Miss Brandt, "I was born there."

"But you won't die there, or I'm much mistaken! You're too good to be wasted on Jamaica! When are you going back to England?"

"O! I don't know! I've hardly thought about it yet! Not while Mrs. Pullen stays here, though!"

"Why! you're not tied to 'er apron-string, surely! What's she to you?"

"She is very kind, and I have no friends!" replied Miss Brandt.

The Baroness burst into a coarse laugh.

"You won't want for friends, once you shew your face in England,

I can tell you. I'd like to 'ave you at our 'ouse, the Red 'Ouse, we call it. Princess—but there, I mustn't tell you 'er name or it'll go through the hotel, and she says things to me that she never means to go further—but she said the other day that she preferred the Red 'Ouse to Windsor! And for comfort, and cheerfulness, so she may!"

"I suppose it is very beautiful then!" observed Harriet.

"You must judge for yourself," replied the Baroness, with a broad smile, "when you come to London. You'll be your own mistress there, I suppose, and not so tied as you are here! I call it a shame to keep you dancing attendance on that brat, when there's a nurse whose business it is to look after 'er!"

"O! but indeed it is my own wish!" said the girl, as she cuddled the sleeping baby to her bosom, and laid her lips in a long kiss upon its little mouth. "I asked leave to nurse her! She loves me and even Nurse cannot get her off to sleep as I can! And it is so beautiful to have something to love you, Madame Gobelli! In the convent, I felt so cold—so lonely! If ever I took a liking to a girl, we were placed in separate rooms! It is what I have longed for—to come out into the world and find someone to be a friend, and to love me, only me, and all for myself!"

Madame Gobelli laughed again.

"Well! you've only got to shew those eyes of yours, to get plenty of people to love you, and let you love them in return—that is, if the men count in your estimation of what's beautiful!"

Harriet raised her eyes and looked at the woman who addressed her!

There was the innocence of ignorance in them as yet, but the slumbering fire in their depths proved of what her nature would be capable, when it was given the opportunity to shew itself. Hers was a passionate temperament, yearning to express itself—panting for the love which it had never known—and ready to burst forth like a tree into blossom, directly the sun of Desire and Reciprocity shone upon it. The elder woman, who had not been without her little experiences in her day, recognised the feeling at once, and thought that she would not give a fig for the virtue of any man who was subjected to its influence.

"I don't think that you'll confine your attentions to babies long!" quoth the Baroness, as she encountered that glance.

"How do you know?" said her young companion.

"Ah! it's enough that I *do* know, my dear! I 'ave ways and means of knowing things that I keep to myself! I 'ave friends about me too, who can tell me everything—who can 'elp me, if I choose, to give Life and Fortune to one person, and Trouble and Death to another—and woe to them that offend me, that's all!"

But if the Baroness expected to impress Miss Brandt with her hints of terror, she was mistaken. Harriet did not seem in the least astonished. She had been brought up by old Pete and the servants on her father's plantation, to believe in witches, and the evil eye, and "*Obeah*" and the whole cult of Devil worship.

"I know all about that," she remarked presently, "but you can't do me either good or harm. I want nothing from you and I never shall!"

"Don't you be too sure of that!" replied Madame Gobelli, nodding her head. "I've brought young women more luck than enough with their lovers before now—yes! and married women into the bargain! If it 'adn't been for me, Lady—there! it nearly slipped out, didn't it?—but there's a certain countess who would never 'ave been a widow and married for the second time to the man of 'er 'eart, if I 'adn't 'elped 'er and she knows it too! By the way, 'ow do you like Miss Leyton?"

"Not at all," replied Harriet, quickly, "she is not a bit like Mrs. Pullen—so cold and stiff and disagreeable! She hardly ever speaks to me! Is it true that she's the daughter of a lord, as Madame Lamont says, and is it that, makes her so proud?"

"She's the daughter of Lord Walthamstowe, but that's nothing. They've got no money. 'Er people live down in the country, quite in a beggarly manner. A gal with a fortune of 'er own, would rank 'eads and 'eads above 'er in Society. There's not much thought of beside money, now-a-days, I can tell you!"

"Why does she stay with Mrs. Pullen then? Are they any relation to each other?" demanded Harriet.

"Relation, no! I expect she's just brought 'er 'ere out of charity, and because she couldn't afford to go to the seaside by 'erself!"

She had been about to announce the projected relationship between the two ladies, when a sudden thought struck her. Captain Ralph Pullen was expected to arrive in Heyst in a few days—thus much she had ascertained through the landlady of the Lion d'Or. She knew by repute that he was considered to be one of the handsomest and most conceited men in the Limerick Rangers, a corps which was noted for its good-looking officers. It might be better for the furtherance of her plans against the peace of Miss Leyton's mind, she thought, to keep her engagement to Captain Pullen a secret—at all events, no one could say it was her business to make it public. She looked in Harriet Brandt's yearning, passionate eyes, and decided that it would be strange if any impressionable young man could be thrown within their influence, without having his fidelity a little shaken, especially if affianced to such a cold, uninteresting "bit of goods" as Elinor Leyton. Like the parrot in the story, though she said nothing, she "thought a deal" and inwardly rumbled with half-suppressed laughter, as she pictured the discomfiture of the latter young lady, if by any chance, she should find her *fiancé's* attentions transferred from herself to the little West Indian.

"You seem amused, *Madame!*" said Harriet presently.

"I was thinking of you, and all the young men who are doomed to be slaughtered by those eyes of yours," said the Baroness. "You'd make mischief enough amongst *my* friends, I bet, if I 'ad you at the Red 'Ouse!"

Harriet felt flattered and consciously pleased. She had never received a compliment in the Convent—no one had ever hinted that she was pretty and she had had no opportunity of hearing it since.

"Do you think I am handsome then?" she enquired with a heightened colour.

"I think you're a deal worse! I think you're dangerous!" replied her new friend, "and I wouldn't trust you with the Baron any further than I could see you!"

"O! how can you say so?" exclaimed the girl, though she was pleased all the same to hear it said.

"I wouldn't, and that's the truth! Gustave's an awful fellow after the gals. I 'ave to keep a tight old on 'im, I can tell you, and the more you keep out of 'is way, the better I shall be pleased! You'll make a grand match someday, if you're only sharp and keep your eyes open."

"What do you call a grand match?" asked Harriet, as she let the nurse take the sleeping child from her arms without remonstrance.

"Why! a Lord or an Honourable at the very least! since you 'ave money of your own. It's money they're all after in these times, you know—why! we 'ave dooks and markisses marrying all sorts of gals from Amurrica—gals whose fathers made their money in oil, or medicine, or electricity, or any other dodge, so long as they made it! And why shouldn't you do the same as the Amurrican gals? You have money, I know—and a goodish lot, I fancy—" added the Baroness, with her cunning eyes fixed upon the girl as if to read her thoughts.

"O! yes!" replied Harriet, "Mr. Trawler, my trustee, said it was too much for a young woman to have under her own control, but I don't know anything about the value of money, never having had it to spend before. I am to have fifteen hundred pounds every year. Is that a good deal?"

"Quite enough to settle you in life, my dear!" exclaimed the Baroness, who immediately thought what a good thing it would be if Miss Brandt could be persuaded to sink her capital in the boot trade, "and all under your own control too! You are a lucky young woman! I know 'alf a dozen lords,—not to say princes—who would jump at you!"

"Princes!" cried Harriet, unable to believe her ears.

"Certainly! Not English ones of course, but German, which are quite as good after all, for a prince is a prince any day! There's Prince Adalbert of Waxsquiemer, and Prince Harold of Muddlesheim, and Prince Loris of Taxelmein, and ever so many more, and they're in and out of the Red 'Ouse, twenty times a day! But don't you be in an 'urry! Don't take the first that offers, Miss Brandt! Pick and choose! Flirt with whom you like and 'ave your fun, but wait and look about you a bit before you decide!"

The prospect was too dazzling! Harriet Brandt's magnificent eyes were opened to their widest extent—her cheeks flushed with expectation—both life and light had flashed into her countenance. Her soul was expanding, her nature was awakening—it shone through every feature—the Baroness had had no idea she was so beautiful! And the hungry, yearning look was more accentuated than before—it seemed as if she were on the alert, watching for something, like a panther awaiting the advent of its prey. It was a look that women would have shrunk from, and men welcomed and eagerly responded to.

"I should like to go and see you when I go to England—very much!" she articulated slowly.

"And so you shall, my dear! The Baron and me will be very glad to 'ave you on a visit. And you mustn't let that capital of yours lie idle, you know! If it's in your own 'ands, you must make it yield double to what it does now! You consult Gustave! 'E's a regular business man and knows 'ow many beans make five! 'E'll tell you what's best to be done with it—'e'll be a good friend to you, and you can trust 'im with everything!"

"Thank you!" replied the girl, but she still seemed to be lost in a kind of reverie. Her gaze was fixed—her full crimson lips were slightly parted—her slender hands kept nervously clasping and unclasping each other.

"Well, you are 'andsome and no mistake!" exclaimed the Baroness. "You remind me a little of the Duchess of Bewlay before she was married! The first wife, I mean—the second is a poor, pale-faced, sandy-'aired creature. ('Ow the dook can stomach 'er after the other, I can't make out!) The first duchess's mother was a great flame of my grandfather, the Dook of—however, I mustn't tell you that! It's a State secret, and I might get into trouble at court! You'd better not say I mentioned it."

But Harriet Brandt was not in a condition to remember or repeat anything. She was lost in a dream of the possibilities of the Future.

The bell for *dejeuner* roused them at last, and brought them to their feet. They resembled each other in one particular . . . . . they were equally fond of the pleasures of the table.

The little Baron appeared dutifully to afford his clumsy spouse the benefit of his support in climbing the hillocks of shifting sand, which lay between them and the hotel, and Miss Brandt sped swiftly on her way alone.

"I've been 'aving a talk with that gal Brandt," chuckled the Baroness to her husband, "she's a regular green-'orn and swallows everything you tell 'er. I've been stuffing 'er up, that she ought to marry a prince, with 'er looks and money, and she quite believes it. But she ain't bad-looking when she colours up, and I expect she's rather a warm customer, and if she takes a fancy to a man, 'e won't well know 'ow to get out of it! And if he tries to, she'll make the fur fly. Ha! ha! ha!"

"Better leave it alone, better leave it alone!" said the stolid German, who had had more than one battle to fight already, on account of his wife's matchmaking propensities, and considered her quite too clumsy an artificer to engage in so delicate a game.

CHAPTER 5

There was a marked difference observable in the manner of Harriet Brandt after her conversation with the Baroness. Thitherto she had been shy and somewhat diffident—the seclusion of her conventual life and its religious teachings had cast a veil, as it were, between her and the outer world, and she had not known how to behave, nor how much she might venture to do, on being first cast upon it. But Madame Gobelli's revelations concerning her beauty and her prospects, had torn the veil aside, and placed a talisman in her hands, against her

45

secret fear.

She was beautiful and dangerous—she might become a princess if she played her cards well—the knowledge changed the whole face of Nature for her. She became assured, confident, and anticipatory. She began to frequent the company of the Baroness, and without neglecting her first acquaintances, Mrs. Pullen and her baby, spent more time in the Gobellis' private sitting-room than in the balcony, or public *salon*, a fact for which Margaret did not hesitate to declare herself grateful.

"I do not know how it is," she confided to Elinor Leyton, "I rather like the girl, and I would not be unkind to her for all the world, but there is something about her that oppresses me. I seem never to have quite lost the sensation she gave me the first evening that she came here. Her company enervates me—I get neuralgia whenever we have been a short time together—and she leaves me in low spirits and more disposed to cry than laugh!"

"And no wonder," said her friend, "considering that she has that detestable schoolgirl habit of hanging upon one's arm and dragging one down almost to the earth! How you have stood it so long, beats me! Such a delicate woman as you are too. It proves how selfish Miss Brandt must be, not to have seen that she was distressing you!"

"Well! it will take a large amount of expended force to drag Madame Gobelli to the ground," said Margaret, laughing, "so I hope Miss Brandt will direct that portion of her attention to her, and leave me only the residue. Poor girl! she seems to have had so few people to love, or to love her, during her lifetime, that she is glad to practise on anyone who will reciprocate her affection. Did you see the Baroness kissing her this morning?"

"I saw the Baroness scrubbing her beard against Miss Brandt's cheek, if you call that 'kissing'?" replied Elinor. "The Baroness never kisses! I have noticed her salute poor Bobby in the morning exactly in the same manner. I have a curiosity to know if it hurts."

"Why don't you try it?" said Margaret.

"No, thank you! I am not so curious as all that! But the Gobellis and Miss Brandt have evidently struck up a great friendship. She will be the recipient of the Baroness's cast-off trinkets and laces next!"

"She is too well off for that, Elinor! Madame Lamont told me she has a fortune in her own right, of fifteen hundred a year!"

"She will want it all to gild herself with!" said Elinor. Margaret Pullen looked at Miss Leyton thoughtfully. Did she really mean what she said, or did her jealousy of the West Indian heiress, render her capable of uttering untruths? Surely, she must see that Harriet Brandt was handsome—growing handsomer indeed, every day, with the pure sea air tinting her cheeks with a delicate flush like the inside of a shell—and that her beauty, joined to her money, would render her a tempting morsel for the men, and a formidable rival for the women.

"I do not think you would find many people to agree with your opinion, Elinor!" she said after a pause, in answer to Miss Leyton's last remark.

"Well! I think she's altogether odious," replied her friend with a toss of her head, "I thought it the first time I saw her, and I shall think it to the last!"

It was the day that Captain Ralph Pullen was expected to arrive in Heyst and the two ladies were preparing to go to the station to meet him.

"The Baroness has at all events done you one good turn," continued Miss Leyton, "she has delivered you for a few hours, from your 'Old Man of the Sea.' What have you been doing with yourself all the morning! I expected you to meet me on the sands, after I had done bathing!"

"I have not stirred out, Elinor. I am uneasy about baby! She does not seem at all well. I have been waiting your return to ask you whether I had not better send for a doctor to see her. But I am not sure if there is such a thing in Heyst!"

"Sure to be, but don't send unless it is absolutely necessary. What is the matter with her?"

The nurse was sitting by the open window with little Ethel on her lap. The infant looked much the same as usual—a little paler perhaps, but in a sound sleep and apparently enjoying it.

"She does not seem ill to me," continued Elinor, "is she in any pain?"

"Not at all, Miss," said the nurse, "and begging the mistress's pardon, I am sure she is frightening herself without cause. Baby is cutting two more teeth, and she feels the heat. That's all!"

"Why are you frightened, Margaret?" asked Miss Leyton.

"Because her sleep is unnatural, I am sure of it," replied Mrs. Pullen, "she slept all yesterday, and has hardly opened her eyes today. It is more like torpor than sleep. We can hardly rouse her to take her bottle and you know what a lively, restless little creature she has always been."

"But her teeth," argued Elinor Leyton, "surely her teeth account for everything! I know my sister, Lady Armisdale, says that nothing varies so quickly as teething children—that they're at the point of death one hour and quite well the next, and she has five, so she ought to know!"

"That's quite right, Miss," interposed the nurse, respectfully, "and you can hardly expect the dear child to be lively when she's in pain. She has a little fever on her too! If she were awake, she would only be fretful! I am sure that the best medicine for her is sleep!"

"You hear what Nurse says, Margaret, but if you are nervous, why not send for a doctor to see her! We can ask Madame Lamont as we go downstairs who is the best here, and call on him as we go to the station, or we can telegraph to Bruges for one, if you think it would be better!"

"O! no! no! I will not be foolish! I will try and believe that you and Nurse know better than myself. I will wait at all events until to-morrow."

"Where has baby been this morning?"

"She was with Miss Brandt on the sands, Miss!" replied the nurse.

"Since you are so anxious about Ethel, Margaret, I really wonder that you should trust her with a stranger like Miss Brandt! Perhaps she let the sun beat on her head."

"O! no, Elinor, Nurse was with them all the time. I would not let Miss Brandt or anyone take baby away alone. But she is so good-natured and so anxious to have her, that I don't quite know how to refuse."

"Perhaps she has been stuffing the child with some of her horrid chocolates or caramels. She is gorging them all day long herself!"

"I know my duty too well for that, Miss!" said the nurse resentfully, 'I wouldn't have allowed it! The dear baby did not have anything to eat at all.

"Well! you're both on *her* side evidently, so I will say no more," concluded Miss Leyton. "At the same time if *I* had a child, I'd sooner trust it to a wild beast than the tender mercies of Miss Brandt. But it's past four o'clock, Margaret! If we are to reach the *entrepôt* in time we must be going!'

Mrs. Pullen hastily assumed her hat and mantle, and prepared to accompany her friend. They had opened the door, and were about to leave the room when a flood of melody suddenly poured into the apartment. It proceeded from a room at the other end of the corridor and was produced by a *mandolin* most skilfully played. The silvery notes in rills and trills and chords, such as might have been evolved from a fairy harp, arrested the attention of both Miss Leyton and Mrs. Pullen. They had scarcely expressed their wonder and admiration to each other, at the skilful manipulation of the instrument (which evinced such art as they had never heard before except in public) when the strings of the *mandolin* were accompanied by a young, fresh *contralto* voice.

"O! hush! hush!" cried Elinor, with her finger on her lip, as the rich mellow strains floated through the corridor, "I don't think I ever heard such a lovely voice before. Whose on earth can it be?"

The words of the song were in Spanish, and the only one they could recognise was the refrain of, "*Seralie! Seralie!*" But the melody was wild, pathetic, and passionate, and the singer's voice was touching beyond description.

"Some professional must have arrived at the hotel," said Margaret, "I am sure that is not the singing of an amateur. But I hope she will not practise at night, and keep baby awake!"

Elinor laughed.

"O! you mother!" she said, "I thought you were lamenting just now that your ewe lamb slept too much! For my part, I should like to be lulled to sleep each night by just such strains as those. Listen, Margaret! She has commenced another song. Ah! Gounod's delicious *Ave Maria*. How beautiful!"

"I don't profess to know much about music," said Margaret, "but it strikes me that the charm of that singing lies more in the voice than the actual delivery. Whoever it is, must be very young!"

"Whoever it proceeds from, it is charming," repeated Elinor. 'How Ralph would revel in it! Nothing affects him like music. It is the only thing which makes me regret my inability to play or sing. But I am most curious to learn who the new arrival is. Ah! here is Mademoiselle Brimont! she continued, as she caught sight of Olga Brimont, slowly mounting the steep staircase, "*Mademoiselle*, do you happen to know who it is who owns that lovely voice? Mrs. Pullen and I are perfectly enchanted with it!"

Olga Brimont coloured a little. She had never got over her shyness of the English ladies, particularly of the one who spoke so sharply. But she answered at once,

"It is Harriet Brandt! Didn't you know that she sung?"

Miss Leyton took a step backward. Her face expressed the intensest surprise—not to say incredulity.

"Harriet Brandt! Impossible!" she ejaculated.

"Indeed, it is her," repeated Olga, "she always sung the solos in the convent choir. They used to say she had the finest voice in the island. O! yes, it is Harriet, really."

And she passed on to her own apartment.

"Do *you* believe it?" said Elinor Leyton, turning almost fiercely upon Mrs. Pullen.

"How can I do otherwise," replied Margaret, "in the face of Mademoiselle Brimont's assertion? But it is strange that we have heard nothing of Miss Brandt's talent before!"

"Has she ever mentioned the fact to you, that she could sing?"

"Never! but there has been no opportunity. There is no instrument here, and we have never talked of such a thing! Only fancy her possessing so magnificent a voice! What a gift! She might make her fortune by it if she needed to do so."

"Well! she ought to be able to sing with that mouth of hers," remarked Miss Leyton almost bitterly, as she walked into the corridor. She was unwilling to accord Harriet Brandt the possession of a single good attribute. As the ladies traversed the corridor, they perceived that others had been attracted by the singing as well as themselves, and most of the bedroom doors were open. Mrs. Montague caught Margaret by the sleeve as she passed.

"O! Mrs. Pullen, what a heavenly voice! Whose is it? Fred is just mad to know!"

"It's only that girl Brandt!" replied Elinor roughly, as she tried to escape further questioning.

"Miss Brandt! what, the little West Indian! Mrs. Pullen, is Miss Leyton jesting?"

"No, indeed, Mrs. Montague! Mademoiselle Brimont was our informant," said Margaret.

But at that moment their attention was diverted by the appearance of Harriet Brandt herself. She looked brilliant. In one hand she carried her *mandolin*, a lovely little instrument, of sandalwood inlaid with mother-o'-pearl,—her face was flushed with the exertion she had gone through and her abundant hair was somewhat in disorder. Mrs. Montague pounced on her at once.

"O! Miss Brandt! you are a sly puss! We have all been delighted— enchanted! What do you mean by hiding your light under a bushel in this way? Do come in here for a minute and sing us another song! Major Montague is in ecstasies over your voice!"

50

"I can't stop, I can't indeed!" replied Miss Brandt, evidently pleased with the effect she had produced, "because I am on my way down to dear Madame Gobelli. I promised to sing for her this afternoon. I was only trying my voice to see if it was fit for anything!"

She smiled at Mrs. Pullen as she spoke and added,

"I hope I have not disturbed the darling baby! I thought she would be out this lovely afternoon!"

"O! no! you did not disturb her. We have all been much pleased, and surprised to think that you have never told us that you could sing!"

"How could I tell that anyone would care about it?" replied Harriet, indifferently, with a shrug of her shoulders. "But the Baron is very musical! He has a charming tenor voice. I have promised to accompany him! I mustn't delay any longer! Good afternoon!"

And she flew down the stairs with her *mandolin*.

"It is all the dear Baroness and the dear Baron now, you perceive," remarked Elinor to Mrs. Pullen, as they walked together to the railway station, "you and the baby are at a discount. Miss Brandt is the sort of young lady, I fancy, who will follow her own interests wherever they may lead her!"

"You should be the last to complain of her for that, Elinor, since you have tried to get rid of her at any cost," replied her friend.

Captain Ralph Pullen arrived punctually by the train which he had appointed, and greeted his sister-in-law and *fiancée* with marked cordiality.

He was certainly a man to be proud of, as far as outward appearance went. He was acknowledged, by general consent, to be one of the handsomest men in the British Army, and he was fully aware of the fact. He was tall and well built, with good features, almost golden hair; womanish blue eyes, and a long drooping moustache, which he was always caressing with his left hand. He regarded all women with the same languishing, tired-to-death glance, as if the attentions shewn him by the *beau sexe* had been altogether too much for him, and the most he could do now was to regard them with an indolent, worn-out favour, which had had all the excitement, and freshness, and flavour taken out of it long before.

Most women would have considered his method of treatment as savouring little short of insult, but Elinor Leyton's nature did not make extravagant demands upon her lover, and so long as he dressed and looked well and paid her the courtesies due from a gentleman to a gentlewoman, she was quite satisfied. Margaret, on the other hand, had seen through her brother-in-law's affectations from the first, and despised him for them. She thought him foolish, vain, and uncompanionable, but she bore with him for Arthur's sake. She would have welcomed his cousin Anthony Pennell, though, with twice the fervour.

Ralph was looking remarkably well. His light grey suit of tweed, was fresh and youthful looking, and the yellow rose in his buttonhole was as dainty as if he had just walked out of his Piccadilly club.

He was quite animated (for him) at the idea of spending a short time in Heyst, and actually went the length of informing Elinor that she looked "very fit" and if it was not so public a place he should kiss her. Miss Leyton coloured faintly at the remark, but she turned her head away and would not let him see that she was sorry the place was so public.

"Heyst seems to have done you both a lot of good," Captain Pullen went on presently, "I am sure you are fatter, Margaret, than when you were in town. And, how is the daughter?"

"Not very well, I am sorry to say, Ralph! She is cutting more teeth. Elinor and I were consulting whether we should send for a doctor to see her, only this afternoon."

"By the way, I have good news for you, or you will consider it so. Old Phillips is coming over to join us next week."

"Doctor Phillips, my dear old godfather!" exclaimed Margaret, "O! I *am* glad to hear it! He will set baby to rights at once. But who told you so, Ralph?"

"The old gentleman himself! I met him coming out of his club the other day and told him I was coming over here, and he said he should follow suit as soon as ever he could get away, and I was to tell you to get a room for him by next Monday!"

"I shall feel quite happy about my baby now," said Mrs. Pullen, "I have not much faith in Belgian doctors. Their *pharmacopoeia* is quite different from ours, but Doctor Phillips will see if there is anything wrong with her at once!"

"I hope you will not be disappointed with the hotel visitors, Ralph," said Elinor, "but they are a terrible set of riffraff. It is impossible to make friends with any one of them. They are such dreadful people!"

"O! you mustn't class them all together, Elinor," interposed Margaret, "I am sure the Montagues and the Vieuxtemps are nice enough! And *du reste*, there is no occasion for Ralph even to speak to them."

"Of course not," said Captain Pullen, "I have come over for the sake of your company and Margaret's, and have no intention of making the acquaintance of any strangers. When is the *Bataille des Fleurs?* Next week! that's jolly. Old Phillips will be here by that time, and he and Margaret can flirt together, whilst you and I are billing and cooing, eh Elinor?"

"Don't be vulgar, Ralph," she answered, "you know how I dislike that sort of thing! And we have had so much of it here!"

"What, billing and cooing?" he questioned. But Elinor disdained to make any further remark on the subject.

The appearance of Ralph Pullen at the *table d'hôte* dinner, naturally excited a good deal of speculation. The English knew that Mrs. Pullen expected her brother-in-law to stay with her, but the foreigners were all curious to ascertain who the handsome, well-groomed, military looking stranger might be, who was so familiar with Mrs. Pullen and her friend. The Baroness was not behind the rest in curiosity and admiration. She was much before them in her determination to gratify her curiosity and make the acquaintance of the newcomer, whose name she guessed, though no introduction had passed between them. She waited through two courses to see if Margaret Pullen would take the initiative, but finding that she addressed all her conversation to Captain Pullen, keeping her face, meanwhile, pertinaciously turned from the party sitting opposite to her, she determined to force her hand.

"Mrs. Pullen!" she cried, in her coarse voice, "when are you going to introduce me to your 'andsome friend?"

Margaret coloured uneasily and murmured,

"My brother-in-law, Captain Pullen—Madame Gobelli."

"Very glad to see you. Captain," said the Baroness, as Ralph bowed to her in his most approved fashion, "your sister thought she'd keep you all to 'erself, I suppose! But the young ladies of Heyst would soon make mincemeat of Mrs. Pullen if she tried that little game on them. We 'aven't got too many good-looking young men 'ereabouts, I can tell you. Are you going to stay long?"

Captain Pullen murmured something about "uncertain" and "not being quite sure," whilst the Baroness regarded him full in the face with a broad smile on her own. She always had a keen eye for a handsome young man!

"Ah! you'll stay as long as it suits your purpose, won't you? I expect you 'ave your own little game to play, same as most of us! And it's a pretty little game, too, isn't it, especially when a fellow's young and good-looking and 'as the chink-a-chink, eh?

"I fancy I know some of your brother officers, Mr. Naggett, and Lord Menzies, they belong to the Rangers, don't they?" continued Madame Gobelli, "Prince Adalbert of Waxsquiemer used to bring 'em to the Red 'Ouse! By the way I 'aven't introduced you to my 'usband, Baron Gobelli! Gustave, this is Captain Ralph Pullen, the colonel's brother, you know. You must 'ave a talk with 'im after dinner! You two would 'it it off first-rate together! Gustave's in the boot trade, you know, Captain Pullen! We trade under the name of Fantaisie et Cie! The best boots and shoes in London, and the largest manufactory, I give you my word! You should get your boots from us. I know you dandy officers are awfully particular about your tootsies. If you'll come and see me in London, I'll take you over the manufactory, and give you a pair. You'll never buy any others, once you've tried 'em!"

Ralph Pullen bowed again, and said he felt certain that *Madame* was right and he looked forward to the fulfilment of her promise with the keenest anticipation.

Harriet Brandt meanwhile, sitting almost opposite to the stranger, was regarding him from under the thick lashes of her slumberous eyes, like a lynx watching its prey. She had never seen so good-looking and aristocratic a young man before. His crisp golden hair and drooping moustaches, his fair complexion, blue eyes and chiselled features, were a revelation to her. Would the princes whom Madame Gobelli had promised she should meet at her house, be anything like him, she wondered—*could* they be as handsome, as perfectly dressed, as fashionable, as completely at their ease, as the man before her? Every other moment, she was stealing a veiled glance at him—and Captain Pullen was quite aware of the fact. What young man, or woman, is not aware when they are being furtively admired?

Ralph Pullen was one of the most conceited of his sex, which is not saying a little—he was *accablé* with female attentions wherever he went, yet he was not *blasé* with them, so long as he was not called upon to reciprocate in kind. Each time that Harriet's magnetic gaze sought his face, his eyes by some mystical chance were lifted to meet it, and though all four lids were modestly dropped again, their owners did not forget the effect their encounter had left behind it.

"'Ave you been round Heyst yet, Captain Pullen," vociferated Madame Gobelli, "and met the procession? I never saw such rubbish in my life. I laughed fit to burst myself! A lot of children rigged out in blue and white, carrying a doll on a stick, and a crowd of fools following and singing 'ymns. Call that Religion? It's all tommy rot. Don't you agree with me, Mrs. Pullen?"

"I cannot say that I do, *Madame!* I have been taught to respect every religion that is followed with sincerity, whether I agree with its doctrine or not. Besides, I thought the procession you allude to, a very pretty sight. Some of the children with their fair hair and wreaths of flowers looked like little angels!"

"O! you're an 'umbug!" exclaimed the Baroness, "you say that just to please these Papists. Not that I wouldn't just as soon be a Papist as a Protestant, but I 'ate cant. I wouldn't 'ave Bobby 'ere, brought up in any religion. Let 'im choose for 'imself when 'e's a man, I said, but no cant, no 'umbug! I 'ad a governess for 'im once, a dirty little sneak, who thought she'd get the better of me, so she made the boy kneel down each night and say, 'God bless father and mother and all kind friends, and God bless my enemies.' I came on 'em one evening and I 'ad 'im up on his legs in a moment. I won't 'ave it, Bobby, I said, I won't 'ave you telling lies for anyone, and I made 'im repeat after me, 'God bless father and mother and all kind friends, and d——n my enemies.' The governess was so angry with me, that she gave warning, he! he! he! But I 'ad my way, and Bobby 'asn't said a prayer since, 'ave you, Bobby?"

"Sometimes, Mamma!" replied the lad in a low voice. Margaret Pullen's kind eyes sought his at once with an encouraging smile.

"Well! you'd better not let me 'ear you, or I'll give you 'what for.' I 'ate 'umbug, don't you. Captain Pullen?"

"Unreservedly, *Madame!*" replied Ralph in a stifled voice and with an inflamed countenance. He had been trying to conceal his amusement for some time past, greatly to the disgust of Miss Leyton, who would have had him pass by his opposite neighbour's remarks in silent contempt, and the effort had been rather trying. As he spoke, his eyes sought those of Harriet Brandt again, and discovered the sympathy with his distress, lurking in them, coupled with a very evident look of admiration for himself. He looked at her back again—only one look, but it spoke volumes! Captain Pullen had never given such a glance at his *fiancée*, nor received one from her! It is problematical if Elinor Leyton *could* make a telegraph of her calm brown eyes—if her soul (if indeed she had in that sense a soul at all) ever pierced the bounds of its dwelling-place to look through its windows. As the dessert appeared, Margaret whispered to her brother-in-law,

"If we do not make our escape now, we may not get rid of her all the evening," at which hint he rose from table, and the trio left the *salle à manger* together. As Margaret descended again, equipped for their evening stroll, she perceived Harriet Brandt in the corridor also ready, and waiting apparently for her. She took her aside at once.

"I cannot ask you to join us in our walk this evening, Miss Brandt," she said, "because, as it is the first day of my brother's arrival, we shall naturally have many family topics to discuss together!"

For the first time since their acquaintance, she observed a sullen look creep over Harriet Brandt's features.

"I am going to walk with the Baron and Baroness, thank you all the same!" she replied to Margaret's remark, and turning on her heel, she re-entered her room. Margaret did not believe her statement, but she was glad she had had the courage to warn her—she knew it would have greatly annoyed Elinor if the girl she detested had accompanied them on that first evening. The walk proved after all to be a very ordinary one. They paraded up and down the Digue, until they were tired and then they sat down on green chairs and listened to the orchestra whilst Ralph smoked his cigarettes. Elinor was looking her best. She was pleased and mildly excited—her costume became her—and she was presumably enjoying herself, but as far as her joy in Captain Pullen went, she might have been walking with her father or her brother. The conscious looks that had passed between him and Harriet Brandt, were utterly wanting.

They began by talking of home, of Elinor's family, and the last news that Margaret had received from Arthur—and then went on to discuss the visitors to the Hotel. Miss Leyton waxed loud in her denunciation of the Baroness and her familiar vulgarity—she deplored the ill fate that had placed them in such close proximity at the *table d'hôte*, and hoped that Ralph would not hesitate to change his seat if the annoyance became too great. She had warned him, she said, of what he might expect by joining them at Heyst.

"My dear girl," he replied, "pray don't distress yourself! In the first place I know a great deal more about foreign hotels than you do, and knew exactly what I might expect to encounter, and in the second, I don't mind it in the least—in fact, I like it, it amuses me, I think the Baroness is quite a character, and look forward to cultivating her acquaintance with the keenest anticipations."

"O! *don't*, Ralph, pray don't!" exclaimed Miss Leyton, fastidiously, "the woman is beneath contempt! I should be exceedingly annoyed if you permitted her to get at all intimate with you."

"Why not, if it amuses him?" demanded Margaret, laughing, "for my part, I agree with Ralph, that her very vulgarity makes her most amusing as a change, and it is not as if we were likely to be thrown in her way when we return to England!"

"She is a *rara avis*," cried Captain Pullen enthusiastically, "she certainly must know some good people if men like Naggett and Menzies have been at her house, and yet the way she advertises her boots and shoes is too delicious! O! dear yes! I cannot consent to cut the Baroness Gobelli! I am half in love with her already!"

Elinor Leyton made a gesture of disgust.

"And you—who are considered to be one of the most select and fastidious men in Town," she said, "I wonder at you!"

Then he made a bad matter worse, by saying,

"By the way, Margaret, who was that beautiful girl who sat on the opposite side of the table?"

"The *what,*" exclaimed Elinor Leyton, ungrammatically, as she turned round upon the Digue and confronted him.

"He means Miss Brandt!" interposed Margaret, hastily, "many people think that she is handsome!"

"No one could think otherwise," responded Ralph. "Is she Spanish?"

"O! no; her parents were English. She comes from Jamaica!"

"Ah! a drop of Creole blood in her then, I daresay! You never see such eyes in an English face!"

"What's the matter with her eyes?" asked Elinor sharply.

"They're very large and dark, you know, Elinor!" said Mrs. Pullen, observing the cloud which was settling down upon the girl's face, "but it is not everybody who admires dark eyes, or you and I would come off badly!"

"Well, with all due deference to you, my fair sister-in-law," replied Ralph, with the stupidity of a selfish man who never knows when he is wounding his hearers, "most people give the preference to dark eyes in women. Anyway, Miss Brandt (if that is her name) is a beauty and no mistake!"

"I can't say that I admire your taste," said Elinor, "and I sincerely hope that Miss Brandt will not force her company upon us whilst you are here. Margaret and I have suffered more than enough already in that respect! She is only half educated and knows nothing of the world, and is altogether, a most uninteresting companion. I dislike her exceedingly!"

"Ah! don't forget her singing!" cried Margaret, unwittingly.

"Does she sing?" demanded the captain.

"Yes! and wonderfully well for an amateur! She plays the *mandolin* also. I think Elinor is a little hard on her! Of course she is very young and unformed, but she has only just come out of a convent where she has been educated for the last ten years. What can you expect of a girl who has never been out in Society? I know that she is very good-natured, and has waited on baby as if she had been her servant!"

"Don't you think we have had about enough of Miss Harriet Brandt?" said Elinor, "I want to hear what Ralph thinks of Heyst, or if he advises our going on to Ostende. I believe Ostende is much gayer and brighter than Heyst!"

"But we must wait now till Doctor Phillips joins us," interposed Margaret.

"He could come after us, if Ralph preferred Ostende or Blanken-burghe," said Elinor eagerly.

"My dear ladies," exclaimed Captain Pullen, "allow me to form an opinion of Heyst first, and then we will talk about other places. This seems pleasant enough in all conscience to me now!"

"O! you two are bound to think any place pleasant," laughed Margaret, "but I think I must go in to my baby! I do not feel easy to be away from her too long, now that she is ailing. But there is no need for you to come in, Elinor! It is only just nine o'clock!"

"I would rather accompany you," replied Miss Leyton, primly.

"No! no! Elinor, stay with me! If you are tired we can sit in the balcony. I have seen nothing of you yet!" remonstrated her lover.

She consented to sit in the balcony with him for a few minutes, but she would not permit his chair to be placed too close to hers.

"The waiters pass backward and forward," she said, "and what would they think?"

"The deuce take what they think," replied Captain Pullen, "I haven't seen you for two months, and you keep me at arms' length as if I should poison you! What do you suppose a man is made of?"

"My dear Ralph, you know it is nothing of the kind, but it is quite impossible that we can sit side by side like a pair of turtle doves in a public hotel like this!"

"Let us go up to your room then?"

"To my bedroom?" she ejaculated with horror.

"To Margaret's room then! she won't be so prudish, I'm sure! Any-where where I can speak to you alone!"

"The nurse will be in Margaret's room, with little Ethel!"

"Hang it all, then, come for another walk! Let us go away from the town, out on those sand hills. I'm sure no one will see us there!"

"Dear Ralph, you must be reasonable! If I were seen walking about Heyst alone with you at night, it would be all over the town tomorrow."

"Let it be! Where's the harm?"

"But I have kept our engagement most scrupulously secret! No one knows anything, but that you are Margaret's brother-in-law! You don't know how they gossip and chatter in a place like this. I could never consent to appear at the public *table d'hôte* again, if I thought that all those vulgarians had been discussing my most private affairs!"

"O! well! just as you choose!" replied Ralph Pullen discontentedly, "but I suppose you will not object to *my* taking another turn along the Digue before I go to bed! Here, *garçon*, bring me a chasse! Goodnight, then, if you will not stay!"

"It is not that I *will* not—it is that I *cannot,* Ralph!" said Miss Leyton, as she gave him her hand. "Goodnight! I hope you will find your room comfortable, and if it is fine tomorrow, we will have a nice walk in whichever direction you prefer!"

"And much good that will be!" grumbled the young man, as he lighted his cigarette and strolled out again upon the Digue.

As he stood for a moment looking out upon the sea, which was one mass of silvery ripples, he heard himself called by name. He looked up. The Gobellis had a private sitting-room facing the Digue on the ground floor, and the Baroness was leaning out of the open window, and beckoning to him.

"Won't you come in and 'ave a whiskey and soda?" she asked.

"The Baron 'as 'is own whiskey 'ere, real Scotch, none of your nasty Belgian stuff, 'alf spirits of wine and 'alf varnish! Come along! We've got a jolly little parlour, and my little friend 'Arriet Brandt shall sing to you! Unless you're off on some lark of your own, eh?"

"No! indeed," replied Ralph, "I was only wondering what I should do with myself for the next hour. Thank you so much! I'll come with pleasure."

And in another minute, he was seated in the company of the Baron and Baroness and Harriet Brandt.

CHAPTER 6

The day had heralded in the *Bataille des Fleurs* and all Heyst was *en fête.* The little furnished villas, hired for the season, were all built alike, with a balcony on the ground floor, which was transformed into a veritable bower for the occasion. Villa Imperatrice vied with Villa Mentone and Villa Sebastien, as to which decoration should be the most beautiful and effective, and the result was a long line of arbours garlanded with every sort of blossom.

From early morning, the occupants were busy, entwining their pillars with evergreens, interspersed with flags and knots of ribbon, whilst the balustrades were laden with growing flowers and the tables inside bore vases of severed blooms. One balcony was decorated with corn, poppies and bluets, whilst the next would display pink roses mixed with the delicate blue of the sea-nettle, and the third would be all yellow silk and white marguerites. The procession of *charettes*, and the *Bataille* itself was not to commence till the afternoon, so the visitors crowded the sands as usual in the morning, leaving the temporary owners of the various villas, to toil for their gratification, during their absence.

Margaret Pullen felt sad as she sat in the hotel balcony, watching the proceedings on each side of her. She had intended her baby's perambulator to take part in the procession of *charettes*, and had ordered a quantity of white field lilies with which to decorate it. It was to be a veritable triumph—so she and Miss Leyton had decided between themselves—and she had fondly pictured how lovely little Ethel would look with her fluffy yellow hair, lying amongst the blossoms, but now baby was too languid and ill to be taken out of doors, and Margaret had given all the flowers to the little Montagues, who were trimming their mail-cart with them, in their own fashion.

As she sat there, with a pensive, thoughtful look upon her face, Harriet Brandt, dressed in a costume of grass-cloth, with a broad-brimmed hat, nodding with poppies and green leaves, that wonderfully became her, on her head, entered the balcony with an eager, excited appearance. "O! Mrs. Pullen! have you seen the Baroness?" she exclaimed. "We are going to bathe this morning. Aren't you coming down to the sands?"

"No! Miss Brandt, not today. I am unhappy about my dear baby! I am sure you will be sorry to hear that she has been quite ill all night— so restless and feverish!"

"O! she'll be all right directly her teeth come through!" replied Harriet indifferently, as her eyes scanned the scene before them. "There's the Baroness! She's beckoning to me! Goodbye!" and without a word of sympathy or comfort, she rushed away to join her friends.

"Like the way of the world!" thought Margaret, as she watched the girl skimming over the sands, "but somehow—I didn't think she would be so heartless!

Miss Leyton and her *fiancé* had strolled off after breakfast to take a walk, and Mrs. Pullen went back to her own room, and sat down quietly to needlework. She was becoming very anxious for Doctor Phillips' arrival; had even written to England to ask him to hurry it if possible—for her infant, though not positively ill, rejected her food so often, that she was palpably thinner and weaker.

After she had sat there for some time, she took up her field-glasses, to survey the bathers on the beach. She had often done so before, when confined to the hotel—it afforded her amusement to watch their faces and antics. On the present occasion, she had no difficulty in distinguishing the form of the Baroness Gobelli, looking enormous as, clad in a most conspicuous bathing costume, she waddled from her machine into the water, loudly calling attention to her appearance, from all assembled on the sands, as she went. The Baron, looking little less comical, advanced to conduct his spouse down to the water, whilst after them flew a slight boyish figure in yellow, with a mane of dark hair hanging down her back, which Margaret immediately recognised as that of Harriet Brandt.

She was dancing about in the shallow water, shrieking whenever she made a false step, and clinging hold of the Baron's hand, when Margaret saw another gentleman come up to them, and join in the ring. She turned the glasses upon him and saw to her amazement that it was her brother-in-law. Her first feeling was that of annoyance. There was nothing extraordinary or improper, in his joining the Baroness's party—men and women bathed promiscuously in Heyst, and no one thought anything of it. But that Ralph should voluntarily mix himself up with the Gobellis, after Elinor's particular request that he should keep aloof from them, was a much more serious matter. And by the way, that reminded her, where was Elinor the while? Margaret could not discern her anywhere upon the sands, and wondered if she had also been persuaded to bathe.

She watched Captain Pullen evidently trying to induce Miss Brandt to venture further into the water, holding out both hands for her protection,—she also saw her yield to his persuasion, and leaving go of her hold on the Herr Baron, trust herself entirely to the stranger's care. Mrs. Pullen turned from the window with a sigh. She hoped there were not going to be any "ructions" between Ralph and Elinor—but she would not have liked her to see him at that moment. She bestowed a silent benediction, "not loud but deep" on the foreign fashion of promiscuous bathing, and walked across the corridor to her friend's room, to see if she had returned to the hotel. To her surprise, she found Miss Leyton dismantled of her walking attire, soberly seated at her table, writing letters.

"Why! Elinor," she said, "I thought you were out with Ralph!"

The young lady was quite composed.

"So I was," she answered, "until half an hour ago! But as he then expressed his determination to bathe, I left him to his own devices and came back to write my letters."

"Would he not have preferred your waiting on the sands till he could join you again?"

"I did not ask him! I should think he would hardly care for me to watch him whilst bathing, and I am sure I should not consent to do so!"

"But everybody does it here, Elinor, and if you did not care to go down to the beach, you might have waited for him on the Digue."

"My dear Margaret, I am not in the habit of dancing attendance upon men. It is their business to come after me! If Ralph is eager for another walk after his dip, he can easily call for me here!"

"True! and he can as easily go for his walk with any stray acquaintance he may pick up on the sands!"

"O! if he should prefer it, he is welcome to do so," replied Elinor, resuming her scribbling.

"My dear Elinor, I don't think you quite understand Ralph! He has been terribly spoilt, you know, and when men have been accustomed to attention they will take it wherever they can get it! He has come over here expressly to be with you, so I think you should give him every minute of your time. Men are fickle creatures, my dear! It will take some time yet to despoil them of the idea that women were made for their convenience."

"I am afraid the man is not born yet for whose convenience I was made!"

"Well! you know the old saying: '*Most women can catch a man, but it takes a clever woman to keep him.*' I don't mean to insinuate that you are in any danger of losing Ralph, but I think he's quite worth keeping, and, I believe, you think so too!"

"And I mean to keep him!" replied Miss Leyton, as she went on writing.

Margaret did not venture to give her any further hints, but returned to her own room, and took another look through her spyglass. The bathers in whom she was interested, had returned to their machines by this time, and presently emerged, "clothed and in their right minds." Miss Brandt looking more attractive than before, with her long hair hanging down her back to dry. And then, that occurred which she had been anticipating. Captain Pullen, having taken a survey of the beach, and seeing none of his own party there, climbed with Harriet Brandt to where they were high and dry above the tide, and threw himself down on the hot, loose sand by her side, whilst the Baron and Baroness with a laughing injunction to the two young people, to take care of themselves, toiled up to the Digue and walked off in another direction.

When they all met at *dejeuner*, she attacked her brother-in-law on the subject.

"Have you been bathing all this while?" she said to him, "you must have stayed very long in the water!"

"O! dear no!" he replied, "I wasn't in above a quarter of an hour!"

'And what have you been doing since?"

"Strolling about, looking for you and Elinor!" said Captain Pullen. "Why the dickens didn't you come out this lovely morning?"

"I could not leave baby!" said Margaret shortly.

"And I was writing," chimed in Elinor.

"Very well, ladies, if you prefer your own company to mine, of course I have nothing to say against it! But I suppose you are not going to shut yourselves up this afternoon!"

"O! no. It is a public duty to attend the *Bataille des Fleurs*. Have you bought any confetti, Ralph?"

"I have! Miss Brandt was good enough to shew me where to get them, and we are well provided. There is to be a race between lady jockeys at the end of the Digue too, I perceive!"

"What, with horses?"

"I conclude so. I see they have railed in a portion of ground for the purpose," replied Captain Pullen.

"'Ow could they race without 'orses?" called out the Baroness.

Harriet Brandt did not join in the conversation, but she was gazing all the while at Ralph Pullen—not furtively as she had done the day before, but openly, and unabashedly, as though she held a proprietary right in him. Margaret noticed her manner at once and interpreted it aright, but Miss Leyton, true to her principles, never raised her eyes in her direction and ignored everything that came from that side of the table.

Mrs. Pullen was annoyed; she knew how angry Elinor would be if she intercepted any telegraphic communication between her lover and Miss Brandt; and she rose from the table as soon as possible, in order to avert such a catastrophe. She had never considered her brother-in-law a very warm wooer, and she fancied that his manner towards Miss Leyton was more indifferent than usual. She took one turn with them along the Digue to admire the flower-bedecked villas, which were in full beauty, and then returned to her nursery, glad of an excuse to leave them together, and give Elinor a chance of becoming more cordial and affectionate to Ralph, than she had yet appeared to be. The lovers had not been alone long, however, before they were waylaid, to the intense disgust of Elinor, by Harriet Brandt and her friend, Olga Brimont.

Still further to her annoyance, Captain Pullen seemed almost to welcome the impertinent interference of the two girls, who could scarcely have had the audacity to join their company, unless he had invited them to do so.

"The *charettes* are just about to start!" exclaimed Harriet, "O! they are lovely, and such dear little children! I am so glad that the *Bataille des Fleurs* takes place today, because my friend's brother, Alfred Brimont, is coming to take her to Brussels the day after tomorrow!"

"Brussels is a jolly place. Mademoiselle Brimont will enjoy herself there," said Ralph. "There are theatres, and balls and picture-galleries, and every pleasure that a young lady's heart can desire!"

"Have you been to Brussels?" asked Harriet.

"Yes! when I was a nasty little boy in jacket and trousers. I was placed at Mr. Jackson's English school there, in order that I might learn French, but I'm afraid that was the last thing I acquired. The Jackson boys were known all over the town for the greatest nuisances in it!"

"What did you do?"

"What did we *not* do? We tore up and down the rue Montague de la Cour at all hours of the day, shouting and screaming and getting into scrapes. We ran up bills at the shops which we had no money to pay—we appeared at every place of amusement—and we made love to all the schoolgirls, till we had become a terror to the schoolmistresses."

"What naughty boys!" remarked Miss Brandt, with a side-glance at Miss Leyton. She did not like to say all she thought before this very stiff and proper young English lady. "But Captain Pullen," she continued, "where are the confetti? Have you forgotten them? Shall I go and buy some more?"

"No! no! my pockets are stuffed with them," he said, producing two bags, of which he handed Harriet one. Her thanks were conveyed by throwing a large handful of tiny pieces of blue and white and pink paper (which do duty for the more dangerous chalk sugarplums) at him and which covered his tweed suit and sprinkled his fair hair and moustaches. He returned the compliment by flying after her retreating figure, and liberally showering confetti upon her.

"O! Ralph! I do hope you are not going to engage in this horse-play," exclaimed Elinor Leyton, "because if so I would rather return to the hotel. Surely, we may leave such vulgarities to the common people, and—Miss Harriet Brandt!"

"What nonsense!" he replied. "It's evident you've never been in Rome during the carnival! Why, everyone does it! It's the national custom. If you imagine I'm going to stand by, like a British tourist, and stare at everything, without joining in the fun, you're very much mistaken!"

"But is it fun?" questioned Miss Leyton.

"To me it is! Here goes!" he cried, as he threw a handful of paper into the face of a passing stranger, who gave him as good as she had got, in return.

"I call it low—positively vulgar," said Miss Leyton, "to behave so familiarly with people one has never seen before—of whose antecedents one knows nothing! I should be very much surprised if the mob behaved in such a manner towards me. Oh!"

The exclamation was induced by the action of some young *épicier*, or hotel *garçon*, who threw a mass of confetti into her face with such violence as almost for the moment to blind her.

"Ha! ha! ha!" roared Ralph Pullen with his healthy British lungs, as he saw her outraged feelings depicted in her countenance.

"I thought you'd get it before long!" he said, as she attempted to brush the offending paper off her mantle.

"It has not altered my opinion of the indecency of the custom!" she replied.

"Never mind!" he returned soothingly. "Here come the *charettes*."

They were really a charming sight. On one cart was drawn a boat, with little children dressed as fishermen and women—another represented a harvest field, with the tiny haymakers and reapers—whilst a third was piled with wool to represent snow, on the top of which were seated three little girls attired as Esquimaux. The mail-carts, and perambulators belonging to the visitors to Heyst were also well represented, and beautifully trimmed with flowers. The first prize was embowered in lilies and white roses, whilst its tiny inmate was seated in state as the Goddess Flora, with a wreath twined in her golden curls. The second was taken by a gallant Neapolitan fisherman of about four years old, who wheeled a mail-cart of pink roses, in which sat his little sisters, dressed as angels with large white wings. The third was a wheelbarrow hidden in moss and narcissi, on which reposed a Sleeping Beauty robed in white tissue, with a coronal of forget-me-nots.

Harriet Brandt fell into ecstasies over everything she saw. When pleased and surprised, she expressed herself more like a child than a young woman, and became extravagant and ungovernable. She tried to kiss each baby that took part in the procession, and thrust coins into their chubby hands to buy bonbons and confetti with. Captain Pullen thought her conduct most natural and unaffected; but Miss Leyton insisted that it was all put on for effect. Olga Brimont tried to put in a good word for her friend.

"Harriet is very fond of children," she said, "but she has never seen any—there were no children at the convent under ten years of age, so she does not know how to make enough of them when she meets them. She wants to kiss everyone. Sometimes, I tell her I think she would like to eat them. But she only means to be kind!"

"I am sure of that!" said Captain Pullen.

"But she should be told," interposed Elinor, "that it is not the custom in civilized countries for strangers to kiss every child they meet, any more than it is to speak before being introduced, or to bestow their company where it is not desired. Miss Brandt has a great deal to learn in that respect before she can enter English Society!"

As is often the case when a woman becomes unjust in abusing another, Miss Leyton made Captain Pullen say more to cover her discourtesy, than, in other circumstances, he would have done.

"Miss Brandt," he said slowly, "is so beautiful, that she will have a great deal forgiven her, that would not be overlooked in a plainer woman."

"That may be *your* opinion, but it is not mine," replied Miss Leyton.

Her tone was so acid, that it sent him flying from her side, to battle with his confetti against the tribe of Montagues, who fortunately for the peace of all parties, joined their forces to theirs, and after some time spent on the Digue, they returned, a large party, to the hotel.

It was not until they had sat down to dinner, that they remembered they had never been to see the lady jockey race.

"He! he! he!" laughed Madame Gobelli, "but I did, and you lost something, I can tell you! We ''ad great difficulty to get seats, but when we did, it was worth it, wasn't it, Gustave?"

"You said so, *mein tear!"* replied the Baron, gravely.

"And you *thought* so, you old rascal! don't you tell me! I saw your wicked eyes glozing at the gals in their breeches and boots! There weren't any 'orses, after all, Captain Pullen, but sixteen gals with different coloured jackets on and top boots and tight white breeches, such a sight you never saw, Gustave 'ere, *did* 'ave a treat! As for Bobby, when I found we couldn't get out again, because of the crowd, I tied my 'andkerchief over 'is eyes, and made him put 'is 'ead in my lap!"

"Dear! dear!" cried Ralph, laughing, "was it as bad as that, *Madame?"*

"Bad! my dear boy! It was as bad as it could be! It's a mercy you weren't there, or we shouldn't 'ave seen you 'ome again so soon! There were the sixteen gals, with their tight breeches and their short racing jackets, and a fat fellow dressed like a huntsman whipping 'em round and round the ring, as if they were so much cattle! You should 'ave seen them 'op, when he touched 'em up with the lash of 'is whip. I expect they've never 'ad such a tingling since the time their mothers smacked 'em! There was a little fat one, there! I wish you could 'ave seen 'er, when 'e whipped 'er to make 'er 'urry! It was comical! She 'opped like a kangaroo!"

"And what was the upshot of it all? Who won?" asked Ralph.

"O! I don't know! I got Gustave out as soon as I could! I wasn't going to let 'im spend the whole afternoon, watching those gals 'opping. There were 'is eyes goggling out of 'is 'ead, and his lips licking each other, as if 'e was sucking a sugar-stick—"

"Mein tear! mein tear!" interposed the unfortunate Baron.

"You go on with your dinner, Gustave, and leave me alone! *I* saw you! And no more lady jockey races do you attend, whilst we're in this Popish country. They ain't good for you."

"I'm very thankful that I have been saved such a dangerous experiment," said Captain Pullen, "though if I thought that you would tie your handkerchief over my eyes, and put my head in your lap, *Madame*, I should feel tempted to try it as soon as dinner is over!"

"Go along with you, you bad boy!" chuckled the Baroness, "there's something else to see this evening! They are going to 'ave a procession of lanterns as soon as it's dark!"

"And it is to stop in front of every hotel," added Harriet, "and the landlords are going to distribute bonbons and *gateaux* amongst the lantern bearers."

"O! we must not miss that on any account!" replied Captain Pullen, addressing himself to her in reply.

Margaret and Elinor thought, when the time came, that they should be able to see the procession of lanterns just as well from the balcony as when mingled with the crowd, so they brought their work and books down there, and sat with Ralph, drinking coffee and conversing of all that had occurred. The Baroness had disappeared, and Harriet Brandt had apparently gone with her—a fact for which both ladies were inwardly thankful.

Presently, as the dusk fell, the procession of lanterns could be seen wending its way from the further end of the Digue. It was a very pretty and fantastical sight. The bearers were not only children—many grown men and women took part in it, and the devices into which the Chinese lanterns had been formed were quaint and clever. Some held a ring around them, as milkmaids carry their pails—others held crosses and banners designed in tiny lanterns, far above their heads. One, which could be seen topping all the rest, was poised like a skipping rope over the bearer's shoulders, whilst the coloured lanterns swung inside it, like a row of bells. The members of the procession shouted, or sung, or danced, or walked steadily, as suited their temperaments, and came along, a merry crowd up and down the Digue, stopping at the various hotels for largesse in the shape of cakes and sugar-plums.

Ralph Pullen found his eyes wandering more than once in the direction of the Baroness's sitting-room, to see if he could catch a glimpse of her or her *protégée* (as Harriet Brandt seemed now universally acknowledged to be), but he heard no sound, nor caught a glimpse of them, and concluded in consequence that they had left the hotel again.

"Whoever is carrying that skipping rope of lanterns, seems to be in a merry mood," observed Margaret after a while, "for it is jumping up and down in the most extravagant manner! She must be dancing!

Do look, Elinor!"

"I see! I suppose this sort of childish performance amuses a childish people, but for my own part, I think once of it is quite enough, and am thankful that we are not called upon to admire it in England!"

"O! I think it is rather interesting," remarked Margaret, "I only wish my dear baby had been well enough to enjoy it! How she would have screamed and cooed at those bright coloured lanterns! But when I tried to attract her attention to them just now, she only whined to be put into her cot again. How thankful I shall be to see dear Doctor Phillips tomorrow!"

The procession had reached the front of the hotel by this time, and halted there for refreshment. The waiters, Jules and Phillippe and Henri, appeared with plates of dessert and cakes and threw them indiscriminately amongst the people. One of the foremost to jump and scramble to catch the falling sweetmeats was the girl who carried the lantern skipping rope above her head, and in whom Ralph Pullen, to his astonishment, recognised Harriet Brandt. There she was, fantastically dressed in a white frock, and a broad yellow sash, with her magnificent hair loose and wreathed with scarlet flowers. She looked amazingly handsome, like a Bacchante, and her appearance and air of abandon, sent the young man's blood into his face and up to the roots of his fair hair.

"Surely!" exclaimed Margaret, "that is never Miss Brandt!"

"Yes! it is," cried Harriet, "I'm having the most awful fun! Why don't you come too? I've danced the whole way up the Digue, and it is so warm! I wish the waiters would give us something to drink! I've eaten so many bonbons I feel quite sick!"

"What will you take, Miss Brandt?" asked Captain Pullen eagerly, "*limonade* or soda water?"

"A *limonade*, please! You *are* good!" she replied, as he handed her the tumbler over the balcony balustrades. "Come along and dance with me!"

"I cannot! I am with my sister and Miss Leyton!" he replied.

"O! pray do not let *us* prevent you," said Elinor in her coldest voice, "Margaret was just going upstairs and I am quite ready to accompany her!"

"No, no, Elinor," whispered Mrs. Pullen with a shake of her head, "stay here, and keep Ralph company!"

"But it is nearly ten o'clock," replied Miss Leyton, consulting her watch, "and I have been on my feet all day! and feel quite ready for bed. Goodnight Ralph!" she continued, offering him her hand.

"Well! if you two are really going to bed, I shall go too," said Captain Pullen, rising, "for there will be nothing for me to do here after you're gone!"

"Not even to follow the procession?" suggested Miss Leyton, with a smile.

"Don't talk nonsense!" he rejoined crossly. "Am I the sort of man to go bobbing up and down the Digue amongst a parcel of children?"

He shook hands with them both, and walked away rather sulkily to his own quarter of the hotel. But he did not go to bed. He waited until some fifteen minutes had elapsed, and then telling himself that it was impossible to sleep at that hour, and that if Elinor chose to behave like a bear, it was not his fault, he came downstairs again and sauntered out on the sea front.

It was very lonely there at that moment. The procession had turned and gone down to the other end again, where its lights and banners could be seen, waving about in the still summer air.

"Why shouldn't the girl jump about and enjoy herself if she chooses," thought Ralph Pullen, "Elinor makes no allowances for condition or age, but would have everyone as prim and old-maidish as herself. I declare she gets worse each time I see her! A nice sort of wife she will make if this kind of thing goes on! But by Jingo! if we are ever married, I'll take her prudery out of her, and make her—what? The woman who commences by pursing her mouth up at everything, ends by opening it wider than anybody else! There's twice as much harm in a prude as in one of these frank openhearted girls, whose eyes tell you what they're thinking of, the first time you see them!"

He had been strolling down the Digue as he pondered thus, and now found himself meeting the procession again.

"Come and dance with me," cried Harriet Brandt, who, apparently as fresh as ever, was still waving her branch of lanterns to the measure of her steps. He took her hand and tried to stop her.

"Haven't you had about enough of this?" he said, "I'm sure you must be tired. Here's a little boy without a lantern! Give him yours to hold, and come for a little walk with me!"

The touch of his cool hand upon her heated palm, seemed to rouse all the animal in Harriet Brandt's blood. Her hand, very slight and lissom, clung to his with a force of which he had not thought it capable, and he felt it trembling in his clasp.

"Come!" he repeated coaxingly, "you mustn't dance any more or you will overtire yourself! Come with me and get cool and rest!"

She threw her branch of lanterns to the boy beside her impetuously.

"Here!" she cried, "take them! I don't want them anymore! And take me away," she continued to Ralph, but without letting go of his hand, "You are right! I want—I want—rest!"

Her slight figure swayed towards him as he led her out of the crowd, and across a narrow street, to where the road ran behind all the houses and hotels, and was dark and empty and void. The din of the voices, and the trampling of feet, and the echo of the songs still reached them, but they could see nothing—the world was on the Digue, and they were in the dusk and quietude together—and alone.

Ralph felt the slight form beside him lean upon his shoulder till their faces almost touched. He threw his arm about her waist. Her hot breath fanned his cheek.

"Kiss me!" she murmured in a dreamy voice. Captain Pullen was not slow to accept the invitation so confidingly extended. What Englishman would be? He turned his face to Harriet Brandt's, and her full red lips met his own, in a long-drawn kiss, that seemed to sap his vitality. As he raised his head again, he felt faint and sick, but quickly recovering himself, he gave her a second kiss more passionate, if possible, than the first. Then the following whispered conversation ensued between them. "Do you know," he commenced, with his head close to hers, "that you are the very jolliest little girl that I have ever met!"

"And you—you are the man I have dreamt of, but never seen till now!"

"How is that? Am I so different from the rest of my sex?"

"Very—very different! So strong and brave and beautiful!"

"Dear little girl! And so you really like me?"

"I love you," said Harriet feverishly, "I loved you the first minute we met.

"And I love you! You're awfully sweet and pretty, you know!"

"Do you really think so? What would Mrs. Pullen say if she heard you?"

"Mrs. Pullen is not the keeper of my conscience. But she must not hear it."

"O! no! nor Miss Leyton either!"

"Most certainly not Miss Leyton. She is a terrible prude! She would be awfully shocked!"

"It must be a secret,—just between you and me!" murmured the girl.

"Just so! A sweet little secret, all our own, and nobody else's!" And then the fair head and the dark one came again in juxtaposition, and the rest was lost in—Silence!

CHAPTER 7

Doctor Phillips had not been in the Hotel Lion d'Or five minutes before Margaret Pullen took him upstairs to see her baby. She was becoming terribly anxious about her. They encountered Captain Ralph Pullen on the staircase.

"Hullo! young man, and what have *you* been doing to yourself?" exclaimed the doctor.

He was certainly looking ill. His face was chalky white, and his eyes seemed to have lost their brightness and colour.

"Been up racketing late at night?" continued Doctor Phillips. 'What is Miss Leyton about, not to look after you better?"

"No, indeed, Doctor," replied the young man with a smile, "I am sure my sister-in-law will testify to the good hours I have kept since here. But I have a headache this morning—a rather bad one," he added, with his hand to the nape of his neck.

"Perhaps this place doesn't agree with you—it was always rather famous for its smells, if I remember aright! However, I am going to see Miss Ethel Pullen now, and when I have finished with her, I will look after you!"

"No, thank you, Doctor," said Ralph laughing, as he descended the stairs. "None of your nostrums for me! Keep them for the baby!"

"He is not looking well," observed Doctor Phillips to Margaret, as they walked on together.

"I don't think he is, now you point it out to me, but I have not noticed it before," replied Margaret. "I am sure he has been living quietly enough whilst here!"

The infant was lying as she had now done for several days past—quite tranquil and free from pain, but inert and half asleep. The doctor raised her eyelids and examined her eyeballs—felt her pulse and listened to her heart—but he did not seem to be satisfied.

"What has this child been having?" he asked abruptly.

"Having, Doctor? Why! nothing, of course, but her milk, and I have always that from the same cow!"

"No opium—no soothing syrup, nor quackeries of any kind?"

"Certainly not! You know how often you have warned me against anything of the sort!"

"And no one has had the charge of her, except you and the nurse here? You can both swear she has never been tampered with?"

"O! I think so, certainly, yes! Baby has never been from under the eye of one or the other of us. A young lady resident in the hotel—a Miss Brandt—has often nursed her and played with her, but one of us has always been there at the time."

"A Miss—what did you say?" demanded the doctor, sharply.

"A Miss Brandt—a very good-natured girl, who is fond of children!"

"Very well then! I will go at once to the *pharmacien's*, and get a prescription made up for your baby, and I hope that your anxiety may soon be relieved!"

"O! thank you, Doctor, so much!" exclaimed Margaret, "I knew you would do her good, as soon as you saw her!"

But the doctor was not so sure of himself. He turned the case over and over in his mind as he walked to the chemist's shop, wondering how such a state of exhaustion and collapse could have been brought about.

The baby had her first dose and the doctor had just time to wash and change his travelling suit before they all met at the dinner table.

Here they found the party opposite augmented by the arrival of Monsieur Alfred Brimont, a young Brussels tradesman, who had come over to Heyst to conduct his sister home. He was trying to persuade Harriet Brandt to accompany Olga and stay a few days with them, but the girl—with a long look in the direction of Captain Pullen—shook her head determinately.

"O! you might come, Harriet, just for a few days," argued Olga, "now that the *Bataille des Fleurs* is over, there is nothing left to stay for in Heyst, and Alfred says that Brussels is such a beautiful place."

"There are the theatres, and the Parc, and the Quinconce, and Wauxhall!" said young Brimont, persuasively, "*Mademoiselle* would enjoy herself, I have no doubt!"

But Harriet still negatived the proposal.

"Why shouldn't we make up a party and all go together," suggested the Baroness, "me and the Baron and Bobby and 'Arriet? You would like it then, my dear, wouldn't you?" she said to the girl, "and you really should see Brussels before we go 'ome! What do you say, Gustave? We'd go to the Hotel de Saxe, and see everything! It wouldn't take us more than a week or ten days."

"Do as you like, *mein tear*," acquiesced the Baron.

"And why shouldn't you come with us, Captain?" continued Madame Gobelli to Ralph. "You don't look quite the thing to me! A little change would do you good. All work and no play makes Jack a dull boy! 'Ave you been to Brussels?"

"I lived there for years, *Madame*, and know every part of it!" he replied.

"Come and renew your acquaintance then, and take me and 'Arriet about! The Baron isn't much good when it comes to sightseeing, are you, Gustave? 'E likes 'is pipe and 'is slippers too well! But you're young and spry! Well! is it a bargain?"

"I really could not decide in such a hurry," said Ralph, with a glance at Margaret and Elinor, "but we might all go to Brussels perhaps, a little later on."

"I don't think you must buoy up the hopes of the Baroness and Miss Brandt with that idea," remarked Miss Leyton, coldly, "because I am sure that Mrs. Pullen has no intention of doing anything of the sort. If you wish to accompany Madame Gobelli's party, you had better make your arrangements without any reference to us!"

"All right! If you prefer it, I will," he answered in the same indifferent tone.

"*Who* is that young lady sitting opposite, with the dark eyes?" demanded Doctor Phillips of Mrs. Pullen.

"The same I spoke to you of, upstairs, as having been kind to baby—Miss Harriet Brandt!"

"I knew a Brandt once," he answered. "Has she anything to do with the West Indies?"

"O! yes! she comes from Jamaica! She is an orphan, the daughter of Doctor Henry Brandt, and has been educated in the Ursuline Convent there! She is a young lady with an independent fortune, and considered to be quite a catch in Heyst!"

'And you and Miss Leyton are intimate with her?"

"She has attached herself very much to us since coming here. She has few friends, poor girl!"

"Will you introduce me?"

"Miss Brandt, my friend, Doctor Phillips, wishes for an introduction to you.'

The usual courtesies passed between them, and then the doctor said, "I fancy I knew your father. Miss Brandt, when I was quartered in Jamaica with the Thirteenth Lances. Did he not live on the top of the hill, on a plantation called Helvetia?"

"That was the name of our place," replied Harriet, "but I left it when I was only eleven. My trustee Mr. Trawler lives there now!"

"Ah! Trawler the attorney! I have no doubt he made as much out of the property as he could squeeze."

"Do you mean that he cheated me?" asked Harriet, naively.

"God forbid! my dear young lady. But he was a great crony of your father's, and a d—d sharp lawyer, and those sort of gentry generally feather their own nest pretty well, in payment of their friendship."

"He can't do me any harm now," said Harriet, "for I have my property in my own hands!"

"Quite right! quite right! that is, if you're a business woman," rejoined the doctor. "And are you travelling all by yourself?"

Harriet was about to answer in the affirmative, when the Baroness took the words out of her mouth.

"No, Sir, she ain't! She came over with her friend, Mademoiselle Brimont, and now she's under my chaperonage. She's a deal too 'andsome, ain't she? to be travelling about the world alone, with her money-bags under her arm. My name's the Baroness Gobelli,— this is my 'usband, Baron Gustave Gobelli, and this is my little boy, Bobby Bates—by my first 'usband, you'll understand—and when you return to London, if you like to come and see Miss Brandt at our 'ouse—the Red 'Ouse, 'Olloway, we shall be very pleased to see you!"

"I am sure, *Madame*, you are infinitely kind," replied Doctor Phillips gravely.

"Not at all! You'll meet no end of swells there, Prince Loris of Taxelmein, and Prince Adalbert of Waxsquiemer, and 'caps of others. But all the same we're in trade, the Baron and I—and we're not ashamed of it either. We make boots and shoes! Our firm is Fantaisie et Cie, of Oxford Street, and though I say it, you won't find better boots and shoes in all London than ours. No brown paper soles, and rotten uppers! Not a bit of it! It's all genuine stuff with us. You can take any boot out of the shop and rip it to pieces, and prove what I say! The best materials, and the best workmen, that's our principle, and it answers. We can't make 'em fast enough!"

"I have no doubt of it," again gravely responded the old doctor.

"Ah! you might send some of your patients to us, Doctor, and we'll pay back, by recommending you to our friends. Are you a gout man? Prince Adalbert 'as the gout awfully! I've rubbed 'is feet with Elliman's Embrocation, by the hour together, but nothing gives 'im relief!

Now if you could cure 'im your fortune would be made! 'L says it's all the English climate, but *I* say it's over eating, and 'e'd attend more to a medical man, if 'e told 'im to diet, than 'e will to me!"

"Doubtless, doubtless!" said the doctor, in a dreamy manner. He seemed to be lost in a reverie, and Margaret had to touch his arm to remind him that the meal was concluded.

She wanted him to join the others in a promenade and see the beauties of Heyst, but he was strangely eager in declining it.

"No! no! let the youngsters go and enjoy themselves, but I want to speak to you, *alone.*"

"My dear doctor, you frighten me! Nothing about baby, I hope!"

"Not at all! Don't be foolish! But I want to talk to you where we cannot be overheard."

"I think we had better wait till the rest have dispersed then, and go down upon the sands. It is almost impossible to be private in a hotel like this!"

"All right! Get your hat and we will stroll off together."

As soon as they were out of earshot, he commenced abruptly,

"It is about that Miss Brandt! You seem pretty intimate with her! You must stop it at once. You must have nothing more to do with her.'

Margaret's eyes opened wide with distress.

"But, Doctor Phillips, for what reason? I don't see how we could give her up now, unless we leave the place."

"Then leave the place! You mustn't know her, neither must Miss Leyton. She comes of a terrible parentage. No good can ever ensue of association with her."

"You must tell me more than this, Doctor, if you wish me to follow your advice!"

"I will tell you all I know myself! Some twelve or thirteen years ago I was quartered in medical charge of the Thirteenth Lances, and stationed in Jamaica, where I knew of, rather than knew, the father of this girl, Henry Brandt. You called him a doctor—he was not worthy of the name. He was a scientist perhaps—a murderer certainly!"

"How horrible! Do you really mean it?"

"Listen to me! This man Brandt matriculated in the Swiss hospitals, whence he was expelled for having caused the death of more than one patient by trying his scientific experiments upon them. The Swiss laboratories are renowned for being the most foremost in Vivisection and other branches of science that gratify the curiosity and harden the heart of man more than they confer any lasting benefit on humanity.

Even there, Henry Brandt's barbarity was considered to render him unfit for association with civilized practitioners, and he was expelled with ignominy. Having a private fortune he settled in Jamaica, and set up his laboratory there, and I would not shock your ears by detailing one hundredth part of the atrocities that were said to take place under his supervision, and in company of this man Trawler, whom the girl calls her trustee, and who is one of the greatest brutes unhung."

"Are you not a little prejudiced, dear Doctor?"

"Not at all! If when you have heard all, you still say so, you are not the woman I have taken you for. Brandt did not confine his scientific investigations to the poor dumb creation. He was known to have decoyed natives into his Pandemonium, who were never heard of again, which raised, at last the public feeling so much against him, that I am glad to say that his negroes revolted, and after having murdered him with appropriate atrocity, set fire to his house and burned it and all his property to the ground. Don't look so shocked! I repeat that I *am glad* to say it, for he richly deserved his fate, and no torture could be too severe for one who spent his worthless life in torturing God's helpless animals!"

"And his wife—" commenced Margaret.

"He had no wife! He was never married!"

"Never married! But this girl Harriet Brandt—"

"Has no more right to the name than you have! Henry Brandt was not the man to regard the laws, either of God or man. There was no reason why he should not have married—for that very cause, I suppose, he preferred to live in concubinage."

"Poor Harriet! Poor child! And her mother, did you know her?"

"Don't speak to me of her mother. She was not a woman, she was a fiend, a fitting match for Henry Brandt! To my mind she was a revolting creature. A fat, flabby half caste, who hardly ever moved out of her chair but sat eating all day long, until the power to move had almost left her! I can see her now, with her sensual mouth, her greedy eyes, her low forehead and half-formed brain, and her lust for blood. It was said that the only thing which made her laugh, was to watch the dying agonies of the poor creatures her brutal protector slaughtered. But she thirsted for blood, she loved the sight and smell of it, she would taste it on the tip of her finger when it came in her way. Her servants had some story amongst themselves to account for this lust. They declared that when her slave mother was pregnant with her, she was bitten by a Vampire bat, which are formidable creatures in the West Indies, and are said to fan their victims to sleep with their enormous wings, whilst they suck their blood. Anyway, the slave woman did not survive her delivery, and her fellows prophesied that the child would grow up to be a murderess. Which doubtless she was in heart, if not in deed!"

"What an awful description! And what became of her?"

"She was killed at the same time as Brandt, indeed the natives would have killed her in preference to him, had they been obliged to choose, for they attributed all the atrocities that went on in the laboratory to her influence. They said she was '*Obeah*' which means diabolical witchcraft in their language. And doubtless their unfortunate child would have been slaughtered also, had not the overseer of the plantation carried her off to his cabin, and afterwards, when the disturbance was quelled, to the convent, where, you say, she has been educated."

"But terrible as all this is, dear Doctor, it is not the poor girl's fault. Why should we give up her acquaintance for that?"

"My dear Margaret, are you so ignorant as not to see that a child born under such conditions cannot turn out well? The bastard of a man like Henry Brandt, cruel, dastardly, godless, and a woman like her terrible mother, a sensual, self-loving, crafty and bloodthirsty half-caste—what do you expect their daughter to become? She may seem harmless enough at present, so does the tiger cub as it suckles its dam, but that which is bred in her will come out sooner or later, and curse those with whom she may be associated. I beg and pray of you, Margaret, not to let that girl come near you, or your child, any more. There is a curse upon her, and it will affect all within her influence!"

"You have made me feel very uncomfortable, Doctor," replied Mrs. Pullen. "Of course if I had known all this previously, I would not have cultivated Miss Brandt's acquaintance, and now I shall take your advice and drop her as soon as possible! There will be no difficulty with Miss Leyton, for she has had a strange dislike to the girl ever since we met, but she has certainly been very kind to my baby—"

"For Heaven's sake don't let her come near your baby anymore!" cried Doctor Phillips, quickly.

"Certainly, I will not, and perhaps it would be as well if we moved on to Ostende or Blankenburghe, as we have sometimes talked of doing. It would sever the acquaintance in the most effectual way!"

"By all means do so, particularly if the young lady does not go to Brussels, as that stout party was proposing, at dinner time. What an extraordinary person she appears to be! Quite a character!"

"That is just what she is! But, Doctor, there is another thing I should like to speak to you about, concerning Miss Brandt, and I am sure I may trust you to receive it in the strictest confidence. It is regarding my brother-in-law, Ralph Pullen. I am rather afraid, from one or two things I have observed, that he likes Miss Brandt—O! I don't mean anything particular, for (as you know) he is engaged to be married to Elinor Leyton and I don't suspect him of wronging her, only—young men are rather headstrong you know and fond of their own way, and perhaps if you were to speak to Ralph—"

"Tell me plainly, has he been carrying on with this girl?"

"Not in the sense you would take it, Doctor, but he affects her company and that of the Gobellis a good deal. Miss Brandt sings beautifully, and Ralph loves music, but his action annoys Elinor, I can see that, and since you think we should break off the intimacy—"

"I consider it most imperatively necessary, for many reasons, and especially in the case of a susceptible young man like Captain Pullen. She has money you say—"

"Fifteen hundred a year! So I am told!"

"And Miss Leyton has nothing, and Ralph only his pay! O! yes! you are quite right, such an acquaintanceship is dangerous for him. The sense of honour is not so strong now, as it was when I was a boy, and gold is a powerful bait with the rising generation. I will take an early opportunity of talking to Captain Pullen on the subject."

"You will not wound his feelings, Doctor, nor betray me?"

"Trust me for doing neither! I shall speak from my own experience, as I have done to you. If he will not take my advice, you must get someone with more influence to caution him about it. I hardly know how to make my meaning clear to you, Margaret, but Miss Brandt is a *dangerous* acquaintance, for all of you. We medical men know the consequences of heredity, better than outsiders can do. A woman born in such circumstances—bred of sensuality, cruelty, and heartlessness—cannot in the order of things, be modest, kind, or sympathetic. And she probably carries unknown dangers in her train. Whatever her fascinations or her position may be, I beg of you to drop her at once and for ever!"

"Of course I will, but it seems hard upon her! She has seemed to crave so for affection and companionship."

"As her mother craved for food and blood; as her father craved for inflicting needless agony on innocent creatures, and sneered meanwhile at their sufferings! I am afraid I should have little faith in Miss Brandt craving for anything, except the gratification of her own senses!"

They were seated on the lower step of the wooden flight that led from the Digue to the sands, so that whilst they could see what went on above them, they were concealed from view themselves.

Just then, Harriet Brandt's beautiful voice, accompanied by the silvery strains of the *mandolin*, was heard to warble Gounod's *Marguerite* from the open window of the Baroness's sitting-room. Margaret glanced up. The apartment was brilliantly lighted—on the table were bottles of wine and spirits, with cakes and fruit, and Madame Gobelli's bulky form might be seen leaning over the dishes. She had assembled quite a little party there that night.

The two Brimonts were present, and Captain Pullen's tall figure was distinctly visible under the lamplight. Harriet was seated on the sofa, and her full voice filled the atmosphere with melody.

"There's something like a voice!" remarked the old doctor.

"That is the very girl we have been talking of!" replied Mrs. Pullen. "I told you she had a lovely voice, and was an accomplished musician."

"Is that so?" said Doctor Phillips, "then she is still more dangerous than I imagined her to be! Those tones would be enough to drag any man down to perdition, especially if accompanied by such a nature as I cannot but believe she must have inherited from her progenitors!"

"And see, Doctor, there is Ralph," continued Margaret, pointing out her brother-in-law. "I left him with Miss Leyton. He must have got rid of her by some means and crept up to the Gobellis. He cannot care for *them*. He is so refined, so fastidious with regard to people in general, that a woman like the Baroness, must grate upon his feelings every time she opens her mouth, and the Baron never opens his at all. He can only frequent their company for the sake of Harriet Brandt! I have seen it for some time past and it has made me very uneasy."

"He shall know everything about her tomorrow, and then if he will not hear reason—" Doctor Phillips shrugged his shoulders and said no more.

"But surely," said his companion, "you do not think for a moment that Ralph could ever seriously contemplate breaking his engagement with Elinor Leyton for the sake of this girl! O! how angry Arthur would be if he suspected his brother could be guilty of such a thing—*he,* who considers that a man's word should be his bond!"

"It is impossible to say, Margaret—I should not like to give an opinion on the subject. When young men are led away by their passions, they lose sight of everything else—and if this girl is anything like her mother, she must be an epitome of lust!"

"O! you will speak to Ralph as soon as ever you can," cried Margaret, in a tone of distress. "You will put the matter as strongly before him as possible, will you not?"

"You may depend on my doing all I can, Margaret, but as there seems no likelihood of my being able to interview the young gentleman tonight, suppose you and I go to bed! I feel rather tired after my passage over, and you must want to go back to your baby!"

"Doctor," said Margaret, in a timid voice, as they ascended the hotel staircase together, "you don't think baby *very* ill, do you?"

"I think she requires a great deal of care, Margaret!"

"But she has always had that!"

"I don't doubt it, but I can't deny that there are symptoms about her case that I do not understand. She seems to have had all her strength drawn out of her. She is in the condition of a child who has been exercised and excited and hurried from place to place, far beyond what she is able to bear. But it may arise from internal causes. I shall be better able to judge tomorrow when my medicine has had its effect. Goodnight, my dear, and don't worry. Please God, we will have the little one all right again in a couple of days."

But he only said the words out of compassion. In his own opinion, the infant was dying.

Meanwhile, Harriet having finished her songs, was leaning out of the window with Ralph Pullen by her side. She wore an open sleeve and as he placed his hand upon her bare arm, the girl thrilled from head to foot

"And so you are determined not to go to Brussels," he whispered in her ear.

"Why should I go? You will not be there! The Baroness wants to stay for a week! What would become of me all that time, moping after you?"

"Are you sure that you *would* mope? Monsieur Brimont is a nice young man, and seems quite ready to throw himself at your feet! Would he not do as well, *pro tem?*"

Harriet's only answer was to cast her large eyes upwards to meet his own.

"Does that mean, 'No'," continued Captain Pullen, "then how would it do, if *I* joined you there, after a couple of days? Would the Baroness be complaisant do you think, and a little short-sighted, and let us go about together, and shew each other the sights of the town?"

"O! I'm sure she would!" cried Harriet, all the blood in her body flying into her face, "she is so very kind to me! Madame Gobelli!" she continued, turning from the window to the light, "Captain Pullen says that if you will allow him to shew us the lions of Brussels, he will come and join us there in a couple of days—"

"If I find I can manage it!" interposed Ralph, cautiously.

"Manage it! Why, of course you can manage it," said the Baroness. "What's to 'inder a young man like you doing as 'e chooses? You're not tied to your sister's apron-string, are you? Now mind! we shall 'old you to it, for I believe it's the only thing that will make 'Arriet come, and I think a week in Brussels will do us all good! You're not looking well yourself, you know, Captain Pullen! You're as white as ashes this evening, and if I didn't know you were such a good boy, I should say you'd been dissipating a bit lately! He! he! he!"

"The only dissipation I have indulged in, is basking in the sunshine of your eyes, *Madame!*" replied Ralph gallantly.

"That's a good 'un!" retorted the Baroness, "it is more likely you've been looking too much in the eyes of my little friend 'ere. You're a couple of foxes, that's what you are, and I expect it would take all my time to be looking after you both! And so, I suppose it's settled, Miss 'Arriet, and you'll come with us to Brussels after all!"

"Yes, *Madame*, if you'll take charge of me!" said Miss Brandt.

"We'll do that for a couple of days, and then we'll give over charge. Are we to engage a room for you, Captain, at the Hotel de Saxe?"

"I had better see after that myself, *Madame*, as the date of my coming is uncertain," replied Ralph.

"But you will come!" whispered Harriet.

"Need you ask? Would I not run over the whole world, only to find myself by your side? Haven't you taken the taste out of everything else for me, Harriet?"

CHAPTER 8

Doctor Phillips was a man of sixty, and a bachelor. He had never made any home ties for himself, and was therefore more interested in Margaret Pullen (whose father had been one of his dearest friends) than he might otherwise have been. He feared that a heavy trial lay before her and he was unwilling to see it aggravated by any misconduct on the part of her brother-in-law. He could see that the young man was (to say the least of it) not behaving fairly towards his *fiancée*, Elinor Leyton, and he was determined to open his eyes to the true state of affairs, with regard to Harriet Brandt. He spent a sleepless night, his last visit to Margaret's suffering child having strengthened his opinion as to her hopeless condition, and he lay awake wondering how he should break the news to the poor young mother.

He rose with the intention of speaking to Ralph without delay, but he found it more difficult to get a word with him than he had anticipated. The Gobelli party had decided to start with the Brimonts that afternoon, and Captain Pullen stuck to them the entire morning, ostensibly to assist the Baroness in her preparations for departure, but in reality, as anyone could see, to linger by the side of Miss Brandt. Miss Leyton perceived her lover's defalcation as plainly as the rest, but she was too proud to make a hint upon the subject, even to Margaret Pullen. She sat alone in the balcony, reading a book, and gave no sign of annoyance, or discomfiture. But a close observer might have seen the trembling of her lip when she attempted to speak, and the fixed, white look upon her face, which betrayed her inward anxiety. It made Margaret's kind heart ache to see her, and Doctor Phillips more indignant with Ralph Pullen than before.

The party for Brussels had arranged to travel by the three o'clock train, and at the appointed time the doctor was ready in the balcony to accompany them to the *entrepôt*. There were no cabs in Heyst, the station being in the town. Luggage was conveyed backwards and forwards in hand carts drawn by the porters, and travellers invariably walked to their destination. The Baroness appeared dressed for her journey, in an amazing gown of blue velvet, trimmed with rare Maltese lace, with a heavy mantle over it, and a small hat on her head, which made her round, flat, unmeaning face, look coarser than before. She used the Herr Baron as a walking stick as usual, whilst Harriet Brandt, in a white frock and large hat shading her glowing eyes under a scarlet parasol, looked like a tropical bird skimming by her side, with Captain Pullen in close attendance, carrying a flimsy wrap in case she should require it before she reached her journey's end. The Brimonts, following in the rear, were of no account beside their more brilliant and important friends.

Ralph Pullen did not look pleased when he saw Doctor Phillips join the party.

'Are you also going to the *entrepôt?*' he exclaimed, "what can you find to interest you there?—a dirty little smutty place! I am going just to help the ladies over the line, as there is no bridge for crossing."

"Perhaps I am bent on the same errand," replied the doctor, "do you give me credit for less gallantry than yourself, Pullen?"

"That's right, Doctor," said the Baroness, "and I've no doubt you'll be very useful! My Bobby ain't any manner of good, and the Baron 'as so many traps to carry that 'e 'asn't got an arm to spare. I only wish you were coming with us! Why don't you make up your mind to come over with Captain Pullen the day after tomorrow, and 'ave a little 'oliday?"

"I was not aware that Captain Pullen *was* going to Brussels, *Madame!* I fancy he will have to get Miss Leyton's consent first!"

At the mention of Miss Leyton's name in connection with himself, Ralph Pullen flushed uneasily, and Harriet Brandt turned a look of startled enquiry upon the speaker.

"O! 'ang Miss Leyton!" retorted the Baroness, graphically, "she surely wouldn't stop Captain Pullen's fun, just because 'e's staying with 'is sister-in-law! I should call that very 'ard. You can't always tie a young man to 'is relations' apron-strings, Doctor!"

"Not always, *Madame!*" he replied, and dropped the subject.

"You wouldn't let Miss Leyton or Mrs. Pullen keep you from me!" whispered Harriet, to her cavalier.

"Never!" he answered emphatically.

They had reached the little station by this time, and the porters were calling out vociferously, that the train was about to start for Brussels, so that in the hurry of procuring their tickets, and conveying the ladies and the luggage across the cinder-besprinkled line, to where the train stood puffing to be off, there was no more time to exchange sentimentalities, or excite suspicion. The party being safely stowed away in their carriage, Ralph Pullen and Doctor Phillips stood on the wooden platform with their hats off, bowing their farewells.

"Mind you don't put off your coming after Thursday!" screamed the Baroness to Ralph, as she filled up the entire window with her bulky person, "we shall expect you by dinner-time! And I shall bespeak a room for you, whether you will or no! 'Arriet 'ere will break 'er 'eart if you don't turn up, and I don't want the responsibility of 'er committing suicide on my 'ands!"

"All right! all right!" responded Ralph, pretending to turn it off as a joke, "None of you shall do that on my account, I promise you!"

"O! well! I 'ope you're going to keep your word, or we shall come back to 'Eyst in double quick time. Goodbye! Goodbye!" and kissing her fat hand to the two gentlemen, the Baroness was whisked out of Heyst.

Ralph looked longingly after the departing line of carriages for a minute, and then crossed the line again to the road beyond.

Doctor Phillips did not say a word till they were well clear of the station, and then he commenced,

"Of course you're not in earnest about following these people to Brussels."

"Why should I not be? I knew Brussels well as a lad, and I should enjoy renewing my acquaintance with the old town."

"In proper company perhaps, but you can hardly call that party a fit one for you to associate with!"

"You're alluding to the Baron and Baroness being in trade. Well! as a rule I confess that I do not care to associate intimately with boot-makers and their friends, but one does things abroad that one would not dream of doing in England. And for all her vulgarity, Madame Gobelli is very good-natured and generous, and I really don't see that I lower my dignity by being on friendly terms with her whilst here!"

"I was not alluding to Madame Gobelli, though I do not think that either she or the Brimonts are fit companions for a man who be-longs to the Limerick Rangers, and is engaged to marry the daughter of Lord Walthamstowe. Neither do I admire the spirit which would induce you to hobnob with them in Heyst, when you would cut them in Bond Street, But as far as I know the Baron and his wife are harmless. It is Miss Harriet Brandt that I would caution you against!"

A quick resentment appeared on Ralph Pullen's features. His eyes darkened, and an ominous wrinkle stood out on his brow.

"And what may you have to say of Miss Brandt?" he demanded, coldly.

"A great deal more than you know, or can possibly imagine! She is not a fit person for Elinor Leyton to associate with, and consequently, one whom it is your duty to avoid, instead of cultivating."

"I think you exceed *your* duty. Doctor, in speaking to me thus!"

"I am sorry you should think so, Pullen, but your anger will not deter me from telling you what is in my mind. You must not forget how old a friend I am of both sides of your family. Your brother Ar-thur is one of my greatest chums, and his wife's father was, without exception, my dearest friend—added to this, I am on intimate terms with the Walthamstowes. Knowing what I do, therefore, I should hold myself criminal if I left you in ignorance of the truth concerning this young woman."

"Are you alluding, may I ask, to Miss Brandt?"

"I am alluding to the girl who calls herself by that name, but who is in reality only the bastard daughter of Henry Brandt, one of the most infamous men whom God ever permitted to desecrate this earth, and his half-caste mistress,"

"Be careful what you say, Doctor Phillips!" said Ralph Pullen, with ill-suppressed wrath gleaming in his blue eyes.

"There is no need to be, my dear fellow, I can verify everything I say, and I fear no man's resentment. I was stationed in Jamaica with my regiment, some fifteen years ago, when this girl was a child of six years old, running half naked about her father's plantation, uncared for by either parent, and associating solely with the negro servants. Brandt was a brute—the perpetrator of such atrocities in vivisection and other scientific experiments, that he was finally slaughtered on his own plantation by his servants, and everyone said it served him right. The mother was the most awful woman I have ever seen, and my experience of the sex in back slums and alleys has not been small.

"She was the daughter of a certain Judge Carey of Barbadoes by one of his slave girls, and Brandt took her as his mistress before she was fourteen. At thirty, when I saw her she was a revolting spectacle. Gluttonous and obese—her large eyes rolling and her sensual lips protruding as if she were always licking them in anticipation of her prey. She was said to be 'Obeah' too by the natives and they ascribed all the deaths and diseases that took place on the plantation, to her malign influence. Consequently, when they got her in their clutches, I have heard that they did not spare her, but killed her in the most torturing fashion they could devise."

"And did the British Government take no notice of the massacre?"

"There was an enquiry, of course, but the actual perpetrator of the murders could not be traced, and so the matter died out. The hatred and suspicion in which Brandt had been held for some time, had a great effect upon the verdict, for in addition to his terrible experiments upon animals—experiments which he performed simply for his own gratification and for no use that he made of them in treating his fellow creatures—he had been known to decoy diseased and old natives into his laboratory, after which they were never seen again, and it was the digging up of human bones on the plantation, which finally roused the negroes to such a pitch of indignation that they rose *en masse,* and after murdering both Brandt and his abominable mistress, they set fire to the house and burned it to the ground.

"There is no doubt but that, if the overseer of the plantation, an

86

African negro named Pete, had not carried off the little girl, she would have shared the fate of her parents. And who can say if it would not have been as well if she had!"

"I really cannot see what right you have to give vent to such a sentiment!" exclaimed Captain Pullen. "What has this terrible story got to do with Miss Brandt?"

"Everything! '*When the cat is black, the kitten is black too!*' It's the law of Nature!"

"I don't believe it! Miss Brandt bears no trace in feature or character of the parentage you ascribe to her!"

"Does she not? Your assertion only proves your ignorance of character, or characteristics. The girl is a quadroon, and she shews it distinctly in her long-shaped eyes with their blue whites and her wide mouth and blood-red lips! Also in her supple figure and apparently boneless hands and feet. Of her personal character, I have naturally had no opportunity of judging, but I can tell you by the way she eats her food, and the way in which she uses her eyes, that she has inherited her half-caste mother's greedy and sensual disposition. And in ten years' time she will in all probability have no figure at all! She will run to fat. I could tell that also at a glance!"

"And have you any more compliments to pay the young lady?" enquired Captain Pullen, sarcastically.

"I have this still to say, Pullen—that she is a woman whom you must never introduce to your wife, and that it is your bounden duty to separate her, as soon as possible, from your *fiancée* and your sister-in-law!"

"And what if I refuse to interfere in a matter which, as far as I can see, concerns no one but Miss Brandt herself?"

"In that case, I regret to say that I shall feel it *my* duty, to inform your brother Colonel Pullen and your future father-in-law, Lord Walthamstowe of what I have told you! Come, my dear boy, be reasonable! This girl has attracted you, I suppose! We are all subject to a woman's influence at times, but you must not let it go further. You must break it off, and this is an excellent opportunity to do so! Your sister's infant is, I fear, seriously ill. Take your party on to Ostende, and send the Baroness a polite note to say that you are prevented from going to Brussels, and all will be right! You will take my advice—will you not?"

"No! I'll be hanged if I will," exclaimed the young man, "I am not a boy to be ordered here and there, as if I were not fit to take care of myself. I've pledged my word to go to Brussels and to Brussels I shall go. If Miss Leyton doesn't like it, she must do the other thing! She does not shew me such a superfluity of affection as to prevent the necessity of my seeking for sympathy and friendship elsewhere."

"I am sorry to hear you speak like that, Pullen. It does not augur well for the happiness of your married life!"

"I have thought more than once lately, that I shall not be married at all—that is to Miss Leyton!"

"No! no! don't say so. It is only a passing infidelity, engendered by the attraction of this other girl. Consider what your brother would say, and what Lord Walthamstowe would think, if you committed the great mistake at this late hour, of breaking off your engagement!"

"I cannot see why my brother's opinion, or Lord Walthamstowe's thoughts, should interfere with the happiness of my whole life," rejoined Ralph, sullenly. "However, let that pass! The question on the tapis is, my acquaintance with Miss Brandt, and which you consider should be put a stop to. For what reason? If what you bring against her is true, it appears to me that she has all the more need of the protection and loyalty of her friends. It would be cowardly to desert a girl, just because her father and mother happened to be brutes. It is not *her* fault!"

"I quite allow that! Neither is it the fault of a madman that his progenitors had lunacy in their blood, nor of a consumptive, that his were strumous. All the same the facts affect their lives and the lives of those with whom they come in contact. It is the curse of heredity!"

"Well! and if so, how can it concern anyone but the poor child herself?"

"O! yes, it can and it will! And if I am not greatly mistaken, Harriet Brandt carries a worse curse with her even than that! She possesses the fatal attributes of the Vampire that affected her mother's birth—that endued her with the thirst for blood, which characterised her life—that will make Harriet draw upon the health and strength of all with whom she may be intimately associated—that may render her love fatal to such as she may cling to! I must tell you, Pullen, that I fear we have already proofs of this in the illness of your little niece, whom, her mother tells me, was at one time scarcely ever out of Miss Brandt's arms. I have no other means of accounting for her sudden failure of strength and vitality. You need not stare at me, as if you thought I do not know what I am talking about! There are many cases like it in the world. Cases of persons who actually feed upon the lives of others, as the deadly upas tree sucks the life of its victim, by lulling him into a sleep from which he never wakens!"

"Phillips, you must be mad! Do you know that you are accusing Miss Brandt of murder—of killing the child to whom she never shewed anything but the greatest kindness. Why! I have known her carry little Ethel about the sands for a whole afternoon."

"All the worse for poor little Ethel! I do not say she does harm intentionally or even consciously, but that the deadly attributes of her bloodthirsty parents have descended on her in this respect, I have not a shadow of doubt! If you watch that young woman's career through life, you will see that those she apparently cares for most, and clings to most, will soonest fade out of existence, whilst she continues to live all the stronger that her victims die!"

"Rubbish! I don't believe it!" replied Ralph sturdily. "You medical men generally have some crotchet in your brains, but this is the most wonderful bee that ever buzzed in a bonnet! And all I can say is, that I should be quite willing to try the experiment!"

"You *have* tried it, Pullen, in a mild form, and it has had its effect on you! You are not the same fellow who came over to Heyst, though by all rules, you should be looking better and stronger for the change. And Margaret has already complained to me of the strange effect this girl has had upon her! But you must not breathe a suspicion to her concerning the child's illness, or I verily believe she would murder Miss Brandt!"

"Putting all this nonsense aside," said Ralph, "do you consider Margaret's baby to be seriously ill?"

"Very seriously. My medicines have not had the slightest effect upon her condition, which is inexplicable. Her little life is being slowly sapped. She may cease to breathe at any moment. But I have not yet had the courage to tell your sister the truth!"

"How disappointed poor Arthur will be!"

"Yes! but his grief will be nothing to the mother's. She is quite devoted to her child!"

By mutual consent, they had dropped the subject of Harriet Brandt, and now spoke only of family affairs. Ralph was a kind-hearted fellow under all his conceit, and felt very grave at the prospect held out in regard to his baby niece.

The fulfilment of the prophecy came sooner than even Doctor Phillips had anticipated. As they were all sitting at dinner that evening, Madame Lamont, her eyes over-brimming with tears, rushed unceremoniously into the *salle à manger*, calling to Margaret.

"*Madame! Madame!* please come up to your room at once! The dear baby is worse!"

Margaret threw one agonised glance at Doctor Phillips and rushed from the room, followed by himself and Elinor Leyton. The high staircase seemed interminable—more than once Margaret's legs failed under her and she thought she should never reach the top. But she did so all too soon. On the bed was laid the infant form, limp and lifeless, and Martin the nurse met them at the door, bathed in tears.

"O! Ma'am!" she cried, "it happened all of a minute! She was lying on my lap, pretty dear, just as usual, when she went off in a convulsion and died."

"Died, died!" echoed Margaret in a bewildered voice, "Doctor Phillips! *who* is it that has died?"

"The baby, Ma'am, the dear baby! She went off like a lamb, without a struggle! O! dear mistress, do try to bear it!"

"Is my baby—*dead?*" said Margaret in the same dazed voice, turning to the doctor who had already satisfied himself that the tiny heart and pulse had ceased to beat.

"No! my dear child, she is not dead—she is living—with God! Try to think of her as quite happy and free from this world's ill."

"O! but I *wanted* her so—I *wanted* her," exclaimed the bereaved mother, as she clasped the senseless form in her arms, "O! baby! baby! why did you go, before you had seen your father?"

And then she slid, rather than sank, from the bedside, in a tumbled heap upon the floor.

"It is better so—it will help her through it," said Doctor Phillips, as he directed the nurse to carry the dead child into Elinor Leyton's room, and placed Margaret on her own bed. "You will not object, Miss Leyton, I am sure, and you must not leave Mrs. Pullen tonight!"

"Of course I shall not," replied Elinor, "I have been afraid for days past that this would happen, but poor Margaret would not take any hints." She spoke sympathetically, but there were no tears in her eyes, and she did not caress, nor attempt to console her friend. She did all that was required of her, but there was no spontaneous suggestion on her part, with regard either to the mother, or the dead child, and as Doctor Phillips noted her coolness, he did not wonder so much at Ralph's being attracted by the fervour and warmth of Harriet Brandt.

As soon as poor Margaret had revived and had her cry out, he administered a sleeping draught to her, and leaving her in charge of

Elinor Leyton, *he* went downstairs again to consult Captain Pullen as to what would be the best thing for them to do.

Ralph was very much shocked to hear of the baby's sudden death, and eager to do all in his power for his brother's wife. There was no Protestant cemetery in Heyst, and Doctor Phillips proposed that they should at once order a little shell, and convey the child's body either to Ostende or England, as Margaret might desire, for burial. The sooner she left the place where she had lost her child, he said, the better, and his idea was that she would wish the body to be taken to Devonshire and buried in the quiet country churchyard, where her husband's father and mother were laid to sleep. He left Ralph to telegraph to his brother in India and to anyone the news might concern in England— also to settle all hotel claims and give notice to the Lamonts that they would leave on the morrow.

"But supposing Margaret should object," suggested Ralph.

"She will not object!" replied the doctor, "she might if we were not taking the child's body with us, but as it is, she will be grateful to be thought, and acted for. She is a true woman, God bless her! I only wish He had not seen fit to bring this heavy trial on her head!"

Not a word was exchanged between the two men about Harriet Brandt. Ralph, remembering the hint the doctor had thrown out respecting her being the ultimate cause of the baby's illness, did not like to bring up her name again—felt rather guilty with respect to it, indeed—and Doctor Phillips was only too glad to see the young man bestirring himself to be useful, and losing sight of his own worry in the trouble of his sister-in-law.

Of course, he could not have refused, or even demurred, at accompanying his party to England on so mournful an errand—and to do him justice, he did not wish it to be otherwise. Brussels and its anticipated pleasures, had been driven clean out of his head by the little tragedy that had occurred in Heyst, and his attitude towards Margaret when they met again, was so quietly affectionate and brotherly that he was of infinite comfort to her. She quite acquiesced in Doctor Phillips' decision that her child should be buried with her father's family, and the mournful group with the little coffin in their midst, set out without delay for Devonshire.

Chapter 9

Harriet Brandt set off for Brussels in the best of spirits. Captain Pullen had pledged himself to follow her in a couple of days, and had sketched with a free hand, the pleasure they would mutually enjoy in each other's company, without the fear of Mrs. Pullen, or Miss Leyton, popping on them round the corner. Madame Gobelli also much flattered her vanity by speaking of Ralph as if he were her confessed lover, and prospective *fiancé*, so that, what with the new scenes she was passing through, and her anticipated good fortune, Harriet was half delirious with delight, and looked as "handsome as paint" in consequence.

Olga Brimont, on the contrary, although quietly happy in the prospect of keeping house for her brother, did not share in the transports of her convent companion. Alfred Brimont, observed, more than once, that she seemed to visibly shrink from Miss Brandt, and took an early opportunity of asking her the reason why. But all her answer was conveyed in a shrug of the shoulders, and a request that he would not leave her at the Hotel de Saxe with the rest of the party, but take her home at once to the rooms over which she was to preside for him. In consequence, the two Brimonts said goodbye to the Gobellis and Harriet Brandt at the Brussels station, and drove to their apartments in the rue de Vienne, after which the others saw no more of them.

The Baroness declared they were "a good riddance of bad rubbish," and that she had never liked that pasty-faced Mademoiselle Brimont, and believed that she was jealous of the brilliancy and beauty of her dear 'Arriet. The Baroness had conceived one of her violent, and generally short-lived, fancies for the girl, and nothing, for the time being, was too good for her. She praised her looks and her talents in the most extravagant manner, and told everyone at the hotel that the Baron and she had known her from infancy—that she was their ward—and that they regarded her as the daughter of the house, with various other falsehoods that made Harriet open her dark eyes with amazement, whilst she felt that she could not afford to put a sudden end to her friendship with Madame Gobelli, by denying them. Brussels is a very pretty town, full of modern and ancient interest, and there was plenty for them to see and hear during their first days there. But Harriet was resolved to defer visiting the best sights until Captain Pullen had joined them.

She went to the concerts at the Quinconce and Wauxhall, and visited the Zoological Gardens, but she would not go to the Musee nor the Academic des Beaux Arts, nor the Cathedral of Sainte Gudule, whilst Ralph remained in Heyst. Madame Gobelli laughed at her for her reticence—called her a sly cat—said she supposed they must make up their minds to see nothing of her when the handsome captain came to Brussels—finally sending her off in company of Bobby to walk in the Pare, or visit the Wiertz Museum. The Baroness was not equal to much walking at the best of times, and had been suffering from rheumatism lately, so that she and the Baron did most of their sight-seeing in a carriage, and left the young people to amuse themselves. Bobby was very proud to be elected Miss Brandt's cavalier, and get out of the way of his formidable Mamma, who made his *table d'hôte* life a terror to him.

He was a well-grown lad and not bad-looking. In his blue eyes and white teeth, he took after his mother but his hair, and his complexion were fair. He was an anaemic young fellow and very delicate, being never without a husky cough, which, however, the Baroness seemed to consider of no consequence. He hardly ever opened his mouth in the presence of his parents, unless it were to remonstrate against the Baroness's strictures on his appearance, or his conduct, but Harriet Brandt found he could be communicative enough, when he was alone with her. He gave her lengthy descriptions of the Red House, and the treasures which it contained—of his Mamma's *barouche* lined with satin—of the large garden which they had at Holloway, with its greenhouses and hothouses, and the numbers of people who came to visit them there.

"O! yes!" rejoined Harriet, "the Baroness has told me about them, Prince Adalbert and Prince Loris and others! She said they often came to the Red House! I should like to know them very much!"

The youth looked at her in a mysterious manner.

"Yes! they do come, very often, and plenty of other people with them; the Earl of Waterhouse and Lord Drinkwater, and Lady Mountacue, and more than I know the names of. But—but—did Mamma tell you *why* they come?"

"No! not exactly! To see her and the Baron, I suppose!"

"Well! yes! for that too perhaps," stammered Bobby. "But there is another reason. Mamma is very wonderful, you know! She can tell people things they never knew before. And she has a room where— but I had better not say any more. You might repeat it to her and then she would be so angry." The two were on their way to the Wiertz Museum at the time, and Harriet's curiosity was excited.

"I will not, I promise you, Bobby," she said, "what has the Baroness in that room?"

Bobby drew near enough to whisper, as he replied,

"O! I don't know, I daren't say, but horrible things go on there! Mamma has threatened sometimes to make me go in with her, but I wouldn't for all the world. Our servants will never stay with us long. One girl told me before she left that Mamma was a witch, and could raise up the dead. Do you think it can be true—that it is possible?"

"I don't know," said Harriet, "and I don't want to know! There are no dead that *I* want to see back again, unless indeed it were dear old Pete, our overseer. He was the best friend I ever had. One night our house was burned to the ground and lots of the things in it, and old Pete wrapped me up in a blanket and carried me to his cabin in the jungle, and kept me safe until my friends were able to send me to the convent. I shall never forget that. I should like to see old Pete again, but I don't believe the Baroness could bring him back. It wants '*Obeah*' to do that!"

"What is '*Obeah*,' Miss Brandt?"

"Witchcraft, Bobby!"

"Is it wicked?"

"I don't know. I know nothing about it! But let us talk of something else. I don't believe your Mamma can do anything more than other people, and she only says it to frighten you. But you mustn't tell her I said so. Is this the Wiertz Museum? I thought it would be a much grander place!"

"I heard father say that it is the house Wiertz lived in, and he left it with all his pictures to the Belgian Government on condition they kept it just as it was."

They entered the gallery, and Harriet Brandt, although not a great lover of painting in general, stood enwrapt before most of the pictures. She passed over the "*Bouton de Rose*" and the sacred paintings with a cursory glance, but the representation of Napoleon in Hell, being fed with the blood and bones of his victims—of the mother in a time of famine devouring her child—and of the Suicide between his good and evil angels, appeared to absorb all her senses. Her eyes fixed themselves upon the canvasses, she stood before them, entranced, enraptured, and when Bobby touched her arm as a hint to come and look at something else, she drew a long breath as though she had been suddenly aroused from sleep. Again, and again she returned to the same spot, the pictures holding her with a strange fascination, which she could not shake off, and when she returned to the hotel, she declared that first thing she should do on the following morning, would be to go back to the Wiertz Museum and gaze once more upon those inimitable figures.

"But such 'orrid subjects my dear," said the Baroness, "Bobby says they were all blood and bones!"

"But I like them—I *like* them!" replied Harriet, moving her tongue slowly over her lips, "they interest me! They are so life-like!"

"Well! tomorrow will be Thursday you know, so I expect you will have somebody's else's wishes to consult! You will 'ave a letter by the early post, you may depend upon it, to say that the Captain will be with us by dinner-time!"

Harriet Brandt flushed a deep rose. It was when the colour came into her usually pale cheeks, and her eyes awaked from their slumbers and sparkled that she looked beautiful. On the present occasion as she glanced up to see Bobby Bates regarding her with steadfast surprise and curiosity, she blushed still more.

"You'll be 'aving a fine time of it, together, you two, I expect," continued the Baroness facetiously, "and Bobby, 'ere, will 'ave to content 'imself with me and his Papa! But we'll all go to the theatre together tomorrow night. I've taken five seats for the Alcazar, which the captain said was the house he liked best in Brussels."

"How good you are to me!" exclaimed Harriet, as she wound her slight arms about the uncouth form of the Baroness.

"Good! Nonsense! Why! Gustave and I look upon you as our daughter, and you're welcome to share everything that is ours. You can come and live altogether at the Red 'Ouse, if you like! But I don't expect we shall keep you long, though I must say I should be vexed to see you throw yourself away upon an army captain before you have seen the world a bit!"

"O! don't talk of such a thing, pray don't!" said the girl, hiding her face in the Baroness's ample bosom, "you know there is nothing as yet—only a pleasant friendship."

"He! he! he!" chuckled Madame Gobelli, "so that's what you call a pleasant friendship, eh? I wonder what Captain Pullen calls it! I expect we shall 'ear in a few days. But what 'e thinks is of no consequence, so long as *you* don't commit yourself, till you've looked about you a little. I do want you to meet Prince Adalbert! 'Is 'air's like flax—such a nice contrast to yours. And you speaking French so well! You would get on first-rate together!"

Bobby did not appear to like this conversation at all.

"I call Prince Adalbert hideous," he interposed. "Why! his face is as red as a tomato, and he drinks too much. I've heard Papa say so! I am

95

sure Miss Brandt wouldn't like him."

"'Old your tongue," exclaimed the Baroness, angrily, "'Ow dare you interrupt when I'm speaking to Miss Brandt? A child like you! What next, I wonder! Just mind your own business, Bobby, or I'll send you out of the room. Go away now, do, and amuse yourself! We don't want any boys 'ere!"

"Miss Brandt is going into the Parc with me," said Bobby sturdily.

'Ah! well, if she is going to be so good, I 'ope you won't worry 'er, that all! But if you would prefer to come out in the carriage with the Baron and me, my dear, we'll take a drive to the Bois de Cambres."

"All right, if Bobby can come too," acquiesced Harriet.

"Lor! whatever do you want that boy to come with us for? 'E'll only take up all the room with 'is long legs."

"But we mustn't leave him alone," said the girl, kindly, "I shouldn't enjoy my drive if we were to do so!"

The lad gave her a grateful glance through eyes that were already moist with the prospect of disappointment.

"Very well then," said Madame Gobelli, "if you will 'ave your own way, 'e may come, but you must take all the trouble of 'im, 'Arriet, mind that!"

Bobby was only too happy to accompany the party, even in these humiliating circumstances, and they all set out together for the Bois de Cambres. The next day was looked forward to by Harriet Brandt as one of certain happiness, but the morning post arrived without bringing the anticipated notice from Ralph Pullen that he should join them as arranged in the afternoon. The piteous eyes that she lifted to the Baroness's face as she discovered the defalcation, were enough to excite the compassion of anyone.

"It's all right!" said her friend, across the breakfast table, "'E said 'e would come, so there's no need of writing. Besides, it was much safer not! 'E couldn't stir, I daresay, without one of those two cats, Mrs. Pullen or Miss Leyton, at 'is elbow, so 'e thought they might find out what 'e was after, and prevent 'is starting. Say they wanted to leave 'Eyst or something, just to keep 'im at their side! You mark my words, I've means of finding out things that you know nothing of, and I've just seen it written over your 'ead that 'e'll be 'ere by dinnertime, so you can go out for your morning's jaunt in perfect comfort!"

Harriet brightened up at this prophecy, and Bobby had never had a merrier time with her than he had that morning.

But the prophecy was not fulfilled. Ralph Pullen was by that time in England with his bereaved sister-in-law, and the night arrived without the people in Brussels hearing anything of him. He had not even written a line to account for his failure to keep his engagement with them. The fact is that Captain Pullen, although as a rule most punctilious in all matters of courtesy, felt so ashamed of himself and the folly into which he had been led, that he felt that silence would be the best explanation that he had decided to break off the acquaintanceship. He had no real feeling for Harriet Brandt or anybody (except himself)—with him "out of sight, was out of mind"—and the sad occurrence which had forced him to return to England seemed an excellent opportunity to rid himself of an undesirable entanglement.

But Harriet became frantic at the nonfulfillment of his promise. Her strong feelings could not brook delay. She wanted to rush back to Heyst to demand the reason of his defalcation—and in default of that, to write, or wire to him at once and ascertain what he intended to do. But the Baroness prevented her doing either. "Look 'ere, 'Arriet!" she said to the girl, who was working herself up into a fever, "it's no use going on like this! 'E'll come or 'e won't come! Most likely you'll see 'im tomorrow or next day, and if not, it'll be because 'is sister won't let 'im leave 'er, and the poor young man doesn't know what excuse to make! Couldn't you see "ow that Doctor Phillips was set against the captain joining us? 'E went most likely and told Mrs. Pullen, and she 'as dissuaded her brother from coming to Brussels. It's 'ard for a man to go against 'is own relations, you know!"

"But he should have written," pleaded Harriet, "it makes me look a fool!"

"Not a bit of it! Captain Pullen thinks you no fool. 'E's more likely to be thinking 'imself one. And, after all, you know, we shall be going back to 'Eyst in a couple more days, and then you can 'ave 'im all to yourself in the evenings and scold 'im to your 'eart's content!"

But the girl was not made of the stuff that is amenable to reason. She pouted and raved and denounced Ralph Pullen like a fury, declaring she would not speak to him when they met again,—yet lay awake at night all the same, wondering what had detained him from her side, and longing with the fierceness of a tigress for blood, to feel his lips against her own and to hear him say that he adored her. Bobby Bates stood by during this tempestuous time, very sorrowful and rather perplexed. He was not admitted to the confidence of his mother and her young friend, so that he did not quite understand why Harriet Brandt should have so suddenly changed from gay to grave, just because Captain Pullen was unable to keep his promise to join them at Brussels. He had so enjoyed her company thitherto and she had seemed to enjoy his, but now she bore the gloomiest face possible, and it was no pleasure to go out with her at all.

He wondered if all girls were so—as capricious and changeable! Bobby had not seen much of women. He had been kept in the school-room for the better part of his life, and his Mamma had not impressed him with a great admiration for the sex. So, naturally, he thought Harriet Brandt to be the most charming and beautiful creature he had ever seen, though he was too shy to whisper the truth, even to himself. He tried to bring back the smiles to her face in his boyish way, and the gift of an abnormally large and long *sucre de pomme* really did achieve that object better than anything else. But the defalcation of Captain Pullen made them all lose their interest in Brussels, and they returned to Heyst a day sooner than they had intended.

As the train neared the station, Harriet's forgotten smiles began to dimple her face again, and she peered eagerly from the windows of the carriage, as if she expected Ralph Pullen to be on the platform to meet them. But from end to end, she saw only cinders, Flemish country women with huge baskets of fish or poultry on their arms, priests in their soutanes and broad-brimmed hats, and Belgians chattering and screaming to each other and their children, as they crossed the line. Still, she alighted with her party, expectant and happy, and traversed the little distance between the *entrepôt* and the hotel, far quicker than the Baroness and her husband could keep up with her. She rushed into the balcony and almost fell into the arms of the *proprietaire* Madame Lamont.

"Ah! *Mademoiselle!*" she cried, "welcome back to Heyst, but have you heard the desolating news?"

"What news?" exclaimed Harriet with staring eyes and a blanched cheek.

"Why! that the English lady, *cette Madame, si tranquille, si charmante,* lost her dear *bébé* the very day that *Mademoiselle* and *Madame la Baronne* left the hotel!"

"Lost," repeated Harriet, "do you mean that the child is *dead?*"

"Ah! yes, I do indeed," replied Madame Lamont, "the dear *bébé* was taken with a fit whilst they were all at dinner, and never recovered again. *C'etait une perte irreparable! Madame* was like a creature distracted whilst she remained here!"

"Where is she then? Where has she gone?" cried Harriet, excitedly.

"Ah! that I cannot tell *Mademoiselle*. The dear *bébé* was taken away to England to be buried. Madame Pullen and Mademoiselle Leyton and Monsieur Phillippe and *le beau Capitaine* all left Heyst on the following day, that is Wednesday, and went to Ostende to take the boat for Dover. I know no more!"

"Captain Pullen has gone away—he is not here?" exclaimed Miss Brandt, betraying herself in her disappointment. "O! I don't believe it! It cannot be true! He has gone to Ostende to see them on board the steamer, but he will return—I am sure he will?"

Madame Lamont shrugged her shoulders.

"*Monsieur* paid everything before he went and gave *douceurs* to all the servants—I do not think he has any intention of returning!"

At that juncture, the Baron and Baroness reached the hotel. Harriet flew to her friend for consolation. "I cannot believe what Madame Lamont says," she exclaimed; "she declares that they are all gone for good, Mrs. Pullen and Miss Leyton and Captain Pullen and the doctor! They have returned to England. But he is sure to come back, isn't he? after all his promises to meet us in Brussels! He couldn't be so mean as to run off to England, without a word, or a line, unless he intended to come back."

She clung to Madame Gobelli with her eyes wide open and her large mouth trembling with agitation, until even the coarse fibre of the Baroness's propriety made her feel ashamed of the exhibition.

"'Old up, 'Arriet!" she said, "you don't want the 'ole 'ouse to 'ear what you're thinking of, surely! Let me speak to Madame Lamont! What is all the row about, *Madame?*" she continued, turning to the *proprietaire*.

"There is no 'row' at all, *Madame*," was the reply, "I was only telling Mademoiselle Brandt of the sad event that has taken place here during your absence—that that *chère* Madame Pullen had the great misfortune to lose her sweet *bébé*, the very day you left Heyst, and that the whole party have quitted in consequence and crossed to England. I thought since *Mademoiselle* seemed so intimate with Madame Pullen and so fond of the dear child, that she would be *desolée* to hear the sad news, but she appears to have forgotten all about it, in her grief at hearing that the *beau capitaine* accompanied his family to England where they go to bury the *petite*."

And with rather a contemptuous smile upon her face, Madame Lamont re-entered the *salle à manger*.

"Now, 'Arriet, don't make a fool of yourself!" said the Baroness.

"You 'eard what that woman said—she's laughing at you and your captain, and the story will be all over the hotel in half an hour. Don't make any more fuss about it! If 'e's gone, crying won't bring 'im back. It's much 'arder for Mrs. Pullen, losing her baby so suddenly! I'm sorry for 'er, poor woman, but as for the other, there's as good fish in the sea as ever came out of it!"

But Harriet Brandt only answered her appeal by rushing away down the corridor and up the staircase to her bedroom like a whirlwind. The girl had not the slightest control over her passions. She would listen to no persuasion, and argument only drove her mad. She tumbled headlong up the stairs, and dashing into her room, which had been reserved for her, threw herself tumultuously upon the bed. How lonely and horrible the corridor on which her apartment opened, seemed. Olga Brimont, Mrs. Pullen, Miss Leyton, and Ralph, all gone! No one to talk to—no one to walk with—except the Baroness and her stupid husband! Of course this interpreted, simply meant that Captain Pullen had left the place without leaving a word behind him, to say the why or wherefore, or hold out any prospect of their meeting again. Of course it was impossible but that they must meet again—they *should* meet again, Harriet Brandt said to herself between her closed teeth—but meanwhile, what a wilderness, what a barren, dreary place this detestable Heyst would seem without him!

The girl put her head down on the pillow, and taking the corner of the linen case between her strong, white teeth, shook it and bit it, as a terrier worries a rat! But that did not relieve her feelings sufficiently, and she took to a violent fit of sobbing, hot, angry tears coursing each other down her cheeks, until they were blurred and stained, and she lay back upon the pillow utterly exhausted.

The first dinner bell rang without her taking any notice of it, and the second was just about to sound, when there came a low tap at her bedroom door. At first she did not reply, but when it was repeated, though rather timidly, she called out,

"Who is it? I am ill. I don't want any dinner! I cannot come down!"

A low voice answered,

"It is *I*, dear Miss Brandt, Bobby! May I come in? Mamma has sent me to you with a message!"

"Very well! You can enter, but I have a terrible headache!" said Harriet.

The door opened softly, and the tall lanky form of Bobby Bates crept silently into the room. He held a small bunch of pink roses in his hand, and he advanced to the bedside and laid them without a word on the pillow beside her hot, inflamed cheek. They felt deliciously cool and refreshing. Harriet turned her face towards them, and in doing so, met the anxious, perturbed eyes of Bobby.

"Well!" she said smiling faintly, "and what is your Mamma's message?"

"She wishes to know if you are coming down to dinner. It is nearly ready!"

"No! no! I cannot! I am not hungry, and my eyes are painful," replied Harriet, turning her face slightly away.

The lad rose and drew down the blind of her window, through which the setting sun was casting a stream of light, and then captured a flacon of *eau de Cologne* from her toilet table, and brought it to her in his hand.

"May I sit beside you a little while in case you need anything?" he asked.

"No! no! Bobby! You will want your dinner, and your Mamma will want you. You had better go down again at once, and tell her that if my head is better, I will meet her on the Digue this evening!"

"I don't want any dinner, I could not eat it whilst you lie here sick and unhappy. I want to stay, to see if I can help you, or do you any good. I wish—I *wish* I could!" murmured the lad.

"Your roses have done me good already," replied Harriet, more brightly. "It was sweet of you to bring them to me, Bobby."

"I wish I had ten thousand pounds a year," said Bobby feverishly, "that I might bring you roses, and everything that you like best!"

He laid his blonde head on the pillow by the side of hers and Harriet turned her face to his and kissed him.

The blood rushed into his face, and he trembled. It was the first time that any woman had kissed him. And all the feelings of his manhood rushed forth in a body to greet the creature who had awakened them.

As for Harriet Brandt, the boy's evident admiration flattered and pleased her. The tigress deprived of blood, will sometimes condescend to milder food. And the feelings with which she regarded Captain Pullen were such as could be easily replaced by anyone who evinced the same reciprocity. Bobby Bates was not a *beau sabreur*, but he was a male creature whom she had vanquished by her charms, and it interested her to watch his rising passion, and to know that he could never possibly expect it to be requited. She kissed and fondled him as he sat beside her with his head on the pillow—calling him every nice name she could think of, and caressing him as if he had been what the Baroness chose to consider him—a child of ten years old.

His sympathy and entreaties that she would make an effort to join them on the Digue, added to his lovelorn eyes, the clear childish blue of which was already becoming blurred with the heat of passion, convinced her that all was not lost, although Ralph Pullen *had* been ungrateful and impolite enough to leave Heyst without sending her notice, and presently she persuaded the lad to go down to his dinner, and inform the Baroness that she had ordered a cup of tea to be sent up to her bedroom, and would try to rise after she had taken it, and join them on the Digue.

"But you will keep a look-out for me, Bobby, won't you?" she said in parting. "You will not let me miss your party, or I shall feel so lonely that I shall come straight back to bed!"

"Miss you! as if I would!" exclaimed the boy fervently, "why! I shall not stir from the balcony until you appear! O! Miss Brandt! I love you so. You cannot tell—you will never know—but you seem like part of my life!"

"Silly boy!" replied Harriet, reproachfully, as she gave him another kiss. "There, run away at once, and don't tell your mother what we've been about, or she will never let me speak to you again."

Bobby's eyes answered for him, that he would be torn to pieces before he let their precious secret out of his grasp, as he took his unwilling way down to the *table d'hôte*.

"Well! you *have* made a little fool of yourself, and no mistake," was the Baroness's greeting, as Harriet joined her in the balcony an hour later, "and a nice lot of lies I've 'ad to tell about you to Mrs. Montague and the rest. But luckily, they're all so full of the poor child's death, and the coffin of white cloth studded with silver nails that was brought from Bruges to carry the body to England in, that they 'ad no time to spare for your tantrums. Lor! that poor young man must 'ave 'ad enough to do, I can tell you, from all accounts, without writing to you! Everything was on 'is 'ands, for Mrs. Pullen wouldn't let the doctor out of 'er sight! 'E 'ad to fly off to Bruges to get the coffin and to wire half over the world, besides 'aving the two women to tow about, so you mustn't be 'ard on 'im. 'E'll write soon, and explain everything, you may make sure of that, and if 'e don't, why, we shall be after 'im before long! Aldershot, where the Limerick Rangers are quartered, is within a stone's throw of London, and Lord Menzies and

Mr. Nalgett often run over to the Red 'Ouse, and so can Captain Pullen, if he chooses! So, you just make yourself 'appy and it will be all right before long."

"O! I'm all right!" cried Harriet, gaily, "I was only a little startled at the news, so would anyone have been. Come along, Bobby! Let us walk over the dunes to the next town. This cool air will do my head good. Goodbye, Baroness! You needn't expect us till you see us! Bobby and I are going for a good long walk!"

And tucking the lad's arm under her own, she walked off at a tremendous pace, and the pair were soon lost to view.

"I wish that Bobby was a few years older," remarked the Baroness thoughtfully to her husband, as they were left alone, "she wouldn't 'ave made a bad match for him, for she 'as a tidy little fortune, and it's all in Consols. But perhaps it's just as well there's no chance of it! She ain't got much 'eart—I couldn't 'ave believed that she'd receive the news of that poor baby's death, without a tear or so much as a word of regret, when at one time she 'ad it always in 'er arms. She quite forgot all about it, thinking of the man. Drat the men! They're more trouble than they're worth, but 'e's pretty sure to come after 'er as soon as 'e 'ears she's at the Red 'Ouse!"

"But to what good, *mein tear*," demanded the Baron, "when you know he is betrothed to Miss Leyton?"

"Yes! and 'e'll marry Miss Leyton, too. 'E's not the sort of man to let the main chance go! And 'Arriet will console 'erself with a better *beau*. I can read all that without your telling me, Gustave. But Miss Leyton won't get off without a scratch or two, all the same, and that's what I'm aiming at. I'll teach 'er not to call me a female elephant! I've got my knife into that young woman, and I mean to turn it! Confound 'er impudence! What next?"

And having delivered herself of her feelings, the Baroness rose and proceeded to take her evening promenade along the Digue.

CHAPTER 10

The Red House at Holloway was, like its owner, a contradiction and an anomaly. It had lain for many years in Chancery, neglected and uncared-for, and the Baroness had purchased it for a song. She was very fond of driving bargains, and sometimes she was horribly taken in. She had been known to buy a house for two thousand pounds for a mere caprice, and exchange it, six months afterwards, for a dinner service. But as a rule she was too shrewd to be cheated, for her income was not a tenth part of what she represented. When she had concluded her bargain for the Red House, which she did after a single survey of the premises, and entered on possession, she found it would take double the sum she had paid to put it into proper repair. It was a very old house of the Georgian era standing in its own grounds of about a couple of acres, and containing thirty rooms, full of dust, damp, rats, and decay.

The Baroness, however, having sent for a couple of workmen from the firm, to put the tangled wilderness which called itself a garden, into something like order, sent in all her household gods, and settled down there, with William and two rough maid servants, as lady of the Manor. The inside of the Red House presented an incongruous appearance. This extraordinary woman, who could not sound her as-pirates and could hardly write her own name, had a wonderful taste for old china and pictures, and knew a good thing from a bad one. Her drawing-room was heaped with valuables, many of them piled on rickety tables which threatened every minute to overturn them upon the ground. The entrance hall was dingy, bare, and ill-lighted, and the breakfast-room to the side, was furnished with the merest necessities.

Yet the dressing-table in the Baroness's sleeping apartment, was draped in ruby velvet, and trimmed with a flounce of the most costly Brussels lace, which a princess might not have been ashamed to wear. The bed was covered with a duvet of the thickest satin, richly em-broidered by her own hand, whilst the washing stand held a set of the commonest and cheapest crockery. Everything about the house was on the same scale; it looked as though it belonged to people who had fallen, from the utmost affluence to the depths of poverty. Har-riet Brandt was terribly disappointed when she entered it, Bobby's accounts of the magnificence of his home having led her to expect nothing short of a palace.

The Baroness had insisted on her accompanying them to England. She had taken one of her violent fancies to the girl, and nothing would satisfy her but that Harriet should go back with her husband and herself to the Red House, and stay there as long as she chose.

"Now look 'ere," she said in her rough way, "you must make the Red 'Ouse your 'ome. Liberty 'All, as I call it! Get up and go to bed; go out and come in, just when you see fit—do what you like, see what you like, and invite your friends, as if the 'ouse was your own. The Baron and I are often 'alf the day at the boot shop, but that need make no difference to you. I daresay you'll find some way to amuse yourself. You're the daughter of the 'ouse, remember, and free to do as you choose!"

Harriet gladly accepted the offer. She had no friends of her own to go to, and the prospect of living by herself in an unknown city, was rather lonely. She was full of anticipation also that by means of the Red House and the Baroness's influence, she would soon hear of, or see, Captain Pullen again—full of hope that Madame Gobelli would write to the young man and force him to fulfil the promises he had made to her. She did not want to know Prince Adalbert or Prince Loris—at the present moment, it was Ralph and Ralph only, and none other would fill the void she felt at losing him. She was sure there must be some great mistake at the bottom of his strange silence, and that they had but to meet, to see it rectified. She was only too glad then, when the day for their departure from Heyst arrived.

Most of the English party had left the Lion d'Or by that time. The death of Mrs. Pullen's child seemed to have frightened them away. Some became nervous lest little Ethel had inhaled poisonous vapours from the drainage—others thought that the atmosphere was unhealthy, or that it was getting too late in the year for the seaside, and so the visitors dwindled, until the Baroness Gobelli found they were left alone with foreigners, and elected to return to England in consequence.

Harriet had wished to write to Captain Pullen and ask for an explanation of his conduct, but the Baroness conjured her not to do so, even threatened to withdraw her friendship, if the girl went against her advice. The probabilities were, she said, that the young man was staying with his sister-in-law wherever she might be, and that the letter would be forwarded to him from the camp, and fall into the hands of Mrs. Pullen, or Miss Leyton. She assured Harriet that it would be safer to wait until she had ascertained his address, and was sure that any communication would reach him at first hand.

"A man's never the worse for being let alone, 'Arriet," she said. "Don't let 'im think 'e's of too much consequence and 'e'll value you all the more! Our fellows don't care for the bird that walks up to the gun. A little 'olesome indifference will do my gentleman all the good in the world!"

"O! but how *can* I be indifferent, when I am burning to see him again, and to hear why he never wrote to say that he could not come to Brussels," exclaimed Harriet, excitedly. "Do you think it was all falsehoods, Madame Gobelli? Do you think that he does not want to see me anymore?"

Her eyes were flashing like diamonds—her cheeks and hands were burning hot. The Baroness chuckled over her ardour and anxiety.

"He! he! he! you little fool, no, I don't! Anyone could see with 'alf an eye, that he took a fancy for you! You're the sort of stuff to stir up a man and make 'im forget everything but yourself. Now don't you worry. 'E'll be at the Red 'Ouse like a shot, as soon as 'e 'ears we're back in London. Mark my words! it won't be long before we 'ave the 'ole lot of 'em down on us, like bees 'umming round a flower pot."

After this flattering tale, it was disheartening to arrive in town on a chilly September day, under a pouring rain, and to see the desolate appearance presented by the Red House.

It was seven in the evening before they reached Holloway, and drove up the dark carriage drive, clumped by laurels, to the hall door.

After the grand description given by Bobby of his Mamma's barouche lined with olive green satin, Harriet was rather astonished that they should have to charter cabs from the Victoria Station to Holloway, instead of being met by the Baroness's private carriage. But she discovered afterwards that though there was a barouche standing in the coach-house, which had been purchased in a moment of reckless extravagance by Madame Gobelli, there were no horses to draw it, and the only vehicle kept by the Baroness was a very much patched, not to say disreputable looking Victoria, with a spavined cob attached to it, in which William drove the mistress when she visited the boot premises.

The chain having been taken down, the hall door was opened to them, by a slight, timid looking person who Harriet mistook for an upper housemaid.

"Well, Miss Wynward," exclaimed the Baroness, as she stumped into the hall, "'ere we are, you see!"

"Yes! my lady" said the person she addressed, "but I thought, from not hearing again, that you would travel by the night boat! Your rooms are ready," she hastened to add, "only—dinner, you see! I had no orders about it!"

"That doesn't signify," interrupted the Baroness, "send out for a steak and give us some supper instead! 'Ere William, where are you? Take my bag and Miss Brandt's up to our rooms, and, Gustave, you can carry the wraps! Where's that devil Bobby? Come 'ere at once and make yourself useful! What are you standing there, staring at 'Arriet for? Don't you see Miss Wynward? Go and say 'ow d'ye do' to 'er?"

Bobby started, and crossing to where Miss Wynward stood, held out his hand. She shook it warmly.

"How are you, Bobby?" she said. "You don't look much stronger for your trip. I expected to see you come back with a colour!"

"Nonsense!" commenced the Baroness testily, "what rubbish you old maids do talk! What should you know about boys? "Ow many 'ave *you* got? 'Ere, why don't you kiss 'im? You've smacked 'im often enough, *I* know!"

Miss Wynward tried to pass the coarse rejoinder off as a joke, but it was with a very plaintive smile that she replied,

"I think Bobby is growing rather too tall to be kissed, and he thinks so too, don't you, Bobby?"

Bobby was about to make some silly reply, when his Mamma interrupted him,

"O! does he? 'E'll be wanting to kiss the gals soon, so 'e may as well practise on you first! Come! Bobby, do you 'ear what I say? Kiss 'er!"

But Miss Wynward drew up her spare figure with dignity.

"No! my lady!" she said quietly, "I do not wish it!"

"He! he! he!" giggled the Baroness, as she commenced to mount the stairs, "'e ain't old enough for you, that's what's the matter! Come along, 'Arriet, my dear! I'm dog-tired and I daresay you're much the same! Let us 'ave some 'ot water to our rooms. Miss Wynward!"

Harriet Brandt was now ushered by her hostess into a bedroom on the same floor as her own, and left to unpack her bundles and boxes as she best might. It was not a badly furnished room, but there was too much pomp and too little comfort in it. The mantelshelf was ornamented with some rare old Chelsea figures, and a Venetian glass hung above them, but the carpet was threadbare, and the dressing-table was inconveniently small and of painted deal. But as though to atone for these discrepancies, the hangings to the bed were of satin, and the blind that shaded the window was edged with Neapolitan lace. Harriet had not been used to luxuries in the convent, but her rooms in the Lion d'Or had been amply provided with all she could need, and she was a creature of sensual and indolent temperament, who felt any rebuff in the way of her comfort, terribly.

There was an unhomelike feeling in the Red House, and its furniture—and a coldness in their reception, which made the passionate, excited creature feel inclined to sit down and burst into tears. She was on the very brink of doing so, when a tap sounded on the door, and Miss Wynward entered with a zinc can of hot water, which she placed on the washing-stand. Then she stood for a moment regarding the girl as though she guessed what was in her mind, before she said,

"Miss Brandt, I believe! I am so sorry that the Baroness never wrote me with any certainty regarding her arrival, or things would have been more comfortable. I hope you had a good dinner on board!"

"No!" said Harriet, shaking her head, "I felt too ill to eat. But it does not signify, thank you!"

"But you are looking quite upset! Supper cannot be ready for another hour. I will go and make you a cup of tea!"

She hurried from the room again, and presently returned with a small tray on which was set a Sevres cup and saucer and Apostle teaspoon, with an earthenware teapot that may possibly have cost sixpence. But Harriet was too grateful for the tea to cavil whence it came, and drinking it refreshed her more than anything else could have done.

"Thank you, thank you so much," she said to Miss Wynward, "I think the long journey and the boat had been too much for me. I feel much better now!"

"It is such a melancholy house to come to when one is out of sorts," observed her companion, "I have felt that myself! It will not give you a good impression of your first visit to London. Her ladyship wrote me you had just come from the West Indies," she added, timidly.

"Yes! I have not long arrived in Europe," replied Harriet. "But I thought—I fancied—the Baroness gave me the idea that the Red House was particularly gay and cheerful, and that so many people visited her here!"

"That is true! A great many people visit here! But—not such people, perhaps, as a young lady would care for!"

"O! I care for every sort," said Harriet, more gaily, "and you,—don't you care for company, Miss Wynward?"

"I have nothing to do with it, Miss Brandt, beyond seeing that the proper preparations are made for receiving it. I am Bobby's governess, and housekeeper to the Baroness!"

"Bobby is getting rather tall for a governess!" laughed Harriet

"He is, poor boy, but his education is very deficient! He ought to have been sent to school long ago, but her ladyship would not hear of it! But I never teach him now! He is supposed to be finished!"

"Why don't you find another situation then?" demanded Harriet, who was becoming interested in the ex-governess.

She was a fragile, melancholy looking woman of perhaps five and thirty, who had evidently been good-looking in her day and would have been so then but for her attenuation, and shabby dress. But she was evidently a gentlewoman, and far above the menial offices she appeared to fill in the Red House. She gazed at Harriet for a minute in silence after she had put the last question to her, and then answered slowly,

"There are reasons which render it unadvisable! But you, Miss Brandt, have you known the Baroness before?"

"I never saw her till we met at Heyst and she invited me here?" replied the girl,

"O! why did you come? Why did you come?" exclaimed Miss Wynward, as she left the room.

Harriet stood gazing at the door as it closed behind her. *Why had she come?* What an extraordinary question to ask her! For the same reason that other people accepted invitations from their friends—because she expected to enjoy herself, and have the protection of the Baroness on first entering English society! But why should this governess—her dependant, almost her servant—put so strange a question to her? Why had she come? She could not get it out of her mind. She was roused from her train of speculation by hearing the Baroness thumping on the outside panels of her door with her stick.

"Come along," she cried, "never mind dressing! The supper's ready at last and I'm as 'ungry as an 'unter."

Hastily completing her toilet, Harriet joined her hostess, who conducted her down to a large dining-room, wrapt in gloom. The two dozen morocco chairs ranged against the wall, looked sepulchral by the light of a single lamp, placed in the centre of a long mahogany table, which was graced by the fried steak, a huge piece of cheese, bread and butter, and lettuces from the garden. Harriet regarded the preparations for supper with secret dismay. She was greedy by nature, but it was the love of good feeding, rather than a superfluity of food, that induced her to be so. However, when the Baron produced a couple of bottles of the very best champagne to add to the meal, she felt her appetite somewhat revive, and played almost as good a knife and fork as the Baroness. Bobby and Miss Wynward, who as it appeared, took her meals with the family, were the only ones who did not do justice to the supper.

The lad looked worn-out and very pale, but when Miss Wynward suggested that a glass of champagne might do him good, and dispel the exhaustion under which he was evidently labouring, his mother vehemently opposed the idea.

"Champagne for a child like 'im," she cried, "1 never 'eard of such a thing. Do you want to make 'im a drunkard, Miss Wynward?

No! thank you, there 'ave been no 'ard drinkers in *our* family, and 'e shan't begin it! 'Is father was one of the soberest men alive! 'E never took anything stronger than toast and water all the time I knew 'im."

"Of course not, your ladyship," stammered Miss Wynward, who seemed in abject fear of her employer, "I only thought as Bobby seems so very tired, that a little stimulant—"

"Then let 'im go to bed," replied Madame Gobelli. "Bed is the proper place for boys when they're tired! Come, Sir, off to bed with you, at once, and don't let me 'ear anything more of you till tomorrow morning!"

"But mayn't I have some supper?" pleaded Bobby.

"Not a bit of it!" reiterated the Baroness, "if you're so done up that you require champagne, your stomach can't be in a fit state to digest beef and bread! Be off at once, I say, or you'll get a taste of my stick."

"But, my lady—" said Miss Wynward, entreatingly.

"It's not a bit of good, Miss Wynward, I know more about boys' insides than you do. Sleep's the thing for Bobby. Now, no more nonsense, I say—"

But Bobby, after one long look at Harriet Brandt, had already quitted the room. This episode had the effect of destroying Miss Wynward's appetite. She sat gazing at her plate for a few minutes, and then with some murmured excuse of its being late, she rose and disappeared. The Baroness was some time over her meal, and Harriet had an opportunity to examine the apartment they sat in, as well as the dim light allowed her to do. The walls were covered with oil paintings and good ones, as she could see at a glance, whilst at the further end, where narrow shelves were fixed from the floor to the ceiling, was displayed the famous dinner service of Sevres, for which the Baroness was said to have bartered the two thousand lease of her house.

Harriet glanced from the pictures and the china, upon the walls to the steak and bread and cheese upon the table, and marvelled at the incongruity of the whole establishment. Madame Gobelli who, whilst at the Lion d'Or, had appeared to think nothing good enough for her, was now devouring fried steak and onions, as if they had been the daintiest of fare. But the champagne made amends, on that night at least, for the solids which accompanied it, and the girl was quite ready to believe that the poverty of the table was only due to the fact that they had arrived at the Red House unexpectedly. As they reached the upper corridor, her host and hostess parted with her, with much effusion, and passing into their own room, shut the door and locked it noisily. As Harriet gained hers, she saw the door opposite partly unclose to display poor Bobby standing there to see her once again.

He was clothed only in his long nightshirt, and looked like a lanky ghost, but he was too childish in mind to think for one moment that his garb was not a suitable one for a lover to accost his mistress in. She heard him whisper her name as she turned the handle of her own door.

"Why, Bobby," she exclaimed, "not in bed yet?"

"Hush! hush!" he said in a low voice, "or Mamma will hear you! I couldn't sleep till I had seen you again and wished you goodnight!"

"Poor dear boy! Are you not very hungry?"

"No, thanks. Miss Wynward is very kind to me. She has seen after that. But to leave without a word to you. That was the hard part of it!"

"Poor Bobby!" ejaculated Harriet again, drawing nearer to him. "But you must not stay out of bed. You will catch your death of cold!"

"Kiss me then and I will go!"

He advanced his face to the opening of the door, and she put her lips to his, and drew his breath away with her own.

"Goodnight! goodnight!" murmured Bobby with a long sigh. "God bless you! goodnight!" and then he disappeared, and Harriet entered her own room, and her eyes gleamed, as she recognised the fact that Bobby also, was going to make a fool of himself for her sake.

The next morning she was surprised on going downstairs at about nine o'clock, to find a cloth laid over only part of the dining table, and breakfast evidently prepared for one person. She was still gazing at it in astonishment, and wondering what it meant, when Miss Wynward entered the room, to express a hope that Miss Brandt had slept well and had everything that she required.

"O! certainly yes! but where are we going to have breakfast?"

"Here, Miss Brandt, if it pleases you. I was just about to ask what you would like for your breakfast."

"But the Baron and Baroness—"

"O! they started for the manufactory two hours ago. Her ladyship is a very early riser when at home, and they have some four miles to drive."

"The manufactory!" echoed Harriet, "do you mean where they make the boots and shoes?"

"Yes! There is a manufactory in Germany, and another in England, where the boots and shoes are finished off. And then there is the shop in Oxford Street, where they are sold. The Baron's business is a very extensive one!"

"So I have understood, but what good can Madame Gobelli do there? What can a woman know about such things?"

Miss Wynward shrugged her shoulders.

"She looks after the young women who are employed, I believe, and keeps them up to their work. The Baroness is a very clever woman. She knows something about most things—and a good deal that were better left unknown," she added, with a sigh.

"And does she go there every morning?"

"Not always, but as a rule she does. She likes to have a finger in the pie, and fancies that nothing can go on properly without her. And she is right so far that she has a much better head for business than the Baron, who would like to be out of it all if he could!"

"But why can't he give it up then, since they are so very rich?" demanded Harriet.

Miss Wynward regarded her for a moment, as if she wondered who had given her the information, and then said quietly,

"But all this time we are forgetting your breakfast, Miss Brandt! What will you take? An egg, or a piece of bacon?"

"O! I don't care," replied Harriet, yawning, "I never can eat when I am alone! Where is Bobby? Won't he take his breakfast with me?"

"O! he had his long ago with his Mamma, but I daresay he would not mind a second edition, poor boy!"

She walked to the French windows which opened from a rustic porch to the lawn, and called "Bobby! Bobby!"

"Yes, Miss Wynward," replied the lad in a more cheerful tone than Harriet remembered to have ever heard him use before, "what is it?"

"Come in, my dear, and keep Miss Brandt company, whilst she takes her breakfast!"

"Won't I!" cried Bobby, as he came running from the further end of the disorderly garden, with a bunch of flowers.

"They are for you!" he exclaimed, as he put them into Harriet's hand, "I gathered them on purpose!"

"Thank you, Bobby," she replied. "It *was* kind of you!"

She felt cheered by the simple attention. For her hostess to have left her on the very first morning, without a word of explanation, had struck her as looking very much (notwithstanding all the effusive flattery and protestations of attachment with which she had been laden) as if she were not wanted at the Red House.

But when her morning meal was over, and she had been introduced to every part of the establishment under the chaperonage of Bobby—to the tangled overgrown garden, the empty stables, Papa's library, which was filled with French and German books, and Mamma's drawing-room, which was so full of valuable china that one scarcely dared move freely about it—the burning thirst to see, or hear something of Ralph Pullen returned with full force upon Harriet, and she enquired eagerly of Miss Wynward when her hostess might be expected to return.

Miss Wynward looked rather blank as she replied,

"Not till dinner time, I am afraid! I fancy she will find too much to enquire about and to do, after so long an absence from home. I am so sorry, Miss Brandt," she continued, noting the look of disappointment on the girl's face, "that her ladyship did not make this plain to you last night. Her injunctions to me were to see that you had everything you required, and to spare no trouble, or expense on your account! But that is not like having her here, of course! Have you been into the library? There are some nice English works there, and there is a piano in the drawing-room which you might like to use. I am afraid it is not in tune, on account of the rain we have had, and that I have not opened it myself during the Baroness's absence, and indeed it is never used, except to teach Bobby his music lessons on, but it may amuse you despite of anything else."

"O! I daresay I shall find something to amuse myself with," replied Harriet rather sullenly, "I have my own instrument with me, and my books, thank you! But is no one likely to call this afternoon, do you think?"

"This afternoon," echoed Miss Wynward, "are you expecting any of your own friends to see you?"

"O! no! I have no friends in England,—none at least that know I have returned from Heyst. But the Baroness told me—she said the Red House was always full of guests—Prince Adalbert and Prince Loris, and a lot of others—do you think they may come today to see her?"

"O! not in September," replied her companion, "it is not the season now, Miss Brandt, and all the fashionable people are out of town, at the foreign watering-places, or shooting in the country. Her ladyship could never have intended you to understand that the people you have mentioned would come here at any time except between May and July! They *do* come here then—sometimes—but not I expect, as *you* think—not as friends, I mean!

"Not as *friends!* What as, then?" demanded Harriet.

"Well!" returned Miss Wynward, dubiously, "many of them have business with her ladyship, and they come to see her upon it! I generally conduct them to her presence, and leave them alone with her, but that is all I see of them! They have never come here to a party, or dinner, to my knowledge!"

"How very extraordinary!" cried Harriet, "what do they come for then?"

"The Baroness must tell you that!" replied the other, gravely, "I am not in her confidence, and if I were, I should not feel justified in revealing it."

This conversation drove Harriet to her room to indite a letter to Captain Pullen. If she were to be deprived of the society of dukes and princes, she would at least secure the company of one person who could make the time pass pleasantly to her. As she wrote to him, rapidly, unadvisedly, passionately, her head burned and her heart was fluttering. She felt as if she had been deceived—cheated— decoyed to the Red House under false pretences, and she was in as much of a rage as her indolent nature would permit her to be.

The revelations of Miss Wynward had sunk down into her very soul. No parties, no dinners, with princes handing her into the dining-room and whispering soft nothings into her ears all the time! Why had Madame Gobelli so often promised to console her for the loss of Captain Pullen by this very means, and it was a dream, a chimera, they only came to the Red House on business—business, horrid unromantic word—and were shut up with the Baroness. *What* business, she wondered! Could it be about boots and shoes, and if so, why did they not go to the shop, which surely was the proper place from which to procure them! The idea that she had been deceived in this particular, made her write far more warmly and pleadingly perhaps, than she would otherwise have done.

A bird in the hand was worth two in the bush—Harriet was not conversant with the proverb, but she fully endorsed the sentiment. When her letter was written and addressed to the camp at Aldershot, and she had walked out with Bobby to post it in the pillar box, she felt happier and less resentful. At all events she was her own mistress and could leave the Red House when she chose, and take up her abode elsewhere. A hot sun had dried the garden paths and grass, and she spent the rest of the afternoon wandering about the unshaven lawn with Bobby, and lingering on the rotten wooden benches under the trees, with the boy's arm round her waist, and his head drooping on her shoulder.

Bobby was blissfully happy, and she was content. If we cannot get caviar, it is wise to content ourselves with cod's roe. They spent hours together that afternoon, until the dusk had fallen and the hour of dining had drawn nigh. They talked of Heyst and the pleasures they had left behind them, and Harriet was astonished to hear how manly were some of Bobby's ideas and sentiments, when out of sight of his Mamma.

At last, the strident tones of the Baroness's voice were heard echoing through the grounds. Harriet and Bobby leaped to their feet in a moment.

"'Ere, 'Arriet! Bobby! where are you? You're a nice son and daughter to 'ide away from me, when I've been toiling for your benefit all the day."

She came towards them as she spoke, and when Harriet saw how fatigued she looked, she almost forgave her for leaving her in the lurch as she had done.

"I suppose you thought we were both dead, didn't you?" she continued. "Well, we are, almost. Never 'ad such a day's work in my life! Found everything wrong, of course! You can't turn your back for five minutes but these confounded workmen play old 'Arry with your business! I sent off ten fellows before I'd been in the factory ten minutes, and fined as many girls, and 'ave been running all over London since to replace 'em. It's 'ard work, I can tell you!"

She plumped down upon the rotten seat, nearly bringing it to the ground, as she spoke, and burst out laughing.

"You should 'ave seen one man, you would 'ave died of laughing! 'Get out,' I said to 'im, 'not another day's work do you do 'ere!' 'Get out of the factory where I've worked for twenty years?' 'e said, 'Well, then, I shan't, not for you! If the governor 'ad said so, it might be a different thing, but a woman 'as no right to come interfering in business as she knows nothing about!' That's the way the wind lies,' I replied, 'and you want a man to turn you out! We'll soon see if a woman can't do it!' and I took my stick and laid it on his back till he hollered again. He was out of the place before you could say Jack Robinson! 'Ow will that do?' I said to the others, 'who else wants a taste of my stick before 'e'll go!' But they all cleared out before I 'ad done speaking! I laughed till I was ill! But come along, children! It's time for dinner!" As they returned to the house, she accosted Harriet,

"I 'ope you've amused yourself today! You'll 'ave to look after yourself whenever I'm at the factory! But a 'andsome gal like you won't want long for amusement. We'll 'ave plenty of company 'ere, soon! Miss Wynward," she continued, as they entered the dining-room, "Mr. Milliken is coming tomorrow! See that 'is room is ready for 'im!"

"Very good, my lady!" replied Miss Wynward, but Harriet fancied she did not like the idea of Mr. Milliken staying with them.

The dinner proceeded merrily. It was more sumptuous than the day before, consisting of several courses, and the champagne flowed freely. Harriet sitting at her ease and thoroughly enjoying the repast, thought that it atoned for all the previous inconvenience. But a strange incident occurred before the meal was over. The Baron who was carver, asked Bobby twice if he would take some roast beef, and received no answer, which immediately aroused the indignation of the Baroness.

"Do you 'ear what your father is saying to you, Bobby?" she cried, shrilly. "Answer 'im at once or I'll send you out of the room! Will you 'ave some beef?"

But still there was no reply.

"My lady! I think that he is ill," said Miss Wynward in alarm.

"Ill! Rubbish!" exclaimed the Baroness. Being so coarse-fibred and robust a woman herself, she never had any sympathy with delicacy or illness, and generally declared all invalids to be humbugs, shamming in order to attract the more attention. She now jumped up from her seat, and going round to her son's chair, shook him violently by the shoulder.

""'Ere, wake up! what are you about?" she exclaimed, "if you don't sit up at once and answer your father's question, I'll lay my stick about your back!"

She was going to put her argument into effect, when Harriet prevented her.

"Stop! stop! Madame Gobelli!" she exclaimed; "can't you see, he has fainted!"

It was really true! Bobby had fainted dead away in his chair, where he lay white as a sheet, with closed eyes, and limp body. Miss Wynward flew to her pupil's assistance.

"Poor dear boy! I was sure he was not well directly he entered the house," she said.

"Not well!" replied the Baroness, "nonsense! what should ail 'im? 'Is father was one of the strongest men on God's earth! He never 'ad a day's illness in 'is life. 'Ow should the boy, a great 'ulking fellow like 'im, 'ave got ill?"

She spoke roughly, but there was a tremor in her voice as she uttered the words, and she looked at Bobby as though she were afraid of him.

But as he gradually revived under Miss Wynward's treatment, she approached nearer, and said with some tenderness in her tones,

"Well! Bobby, lad, and 'ow do you feel now?"

"Better, Mamma, thank you! only my head keeps going round!"

"Had I not better help him up to his bed, my lady?" asked Miss Wynward.

"O! yes! but I 'ope 'e isn't going to make a fool of 'imself like this again, for I don't 'old with boys fainting like hysterical gals!"

"I couldn't help it, Mamma!" said Bobby faintly.

"O! yes! you could, if you 'ad any pluck! You never saw *me* faint. Nor Gustave either! It's all 'abit! Trundle 'im off to bed, Miss Wynward. The sooner 'e's there, the better!"

"And I may give him a little stimulant," suggested Miss Wynward timidly, recalling the scene of the evening before, "a little champagne or brandy and water—I think he requires it, my lady!"

"O! yes! Coddle 'im to your 'eart's content, only don't let me 'ear of it! I 'ate a fuss! Goodnight, Bobby! Mind you're well by tomorrow morning!"

And she brushed the lad's cheek with her bristly chin.

"Goodnight!" replied Bobby, "goodnight to all!" as he was supported from the room on the arm of Miss Wynward.

The Baroness did not make any further remarks concerning her son, but Harriet noticed that her appetite disappeared with him, and declaring that she had tired herself too much to eat, she sat unoccupied and almost silent for the remainder of the meal.

Chapter 11

Mr. Alexander Milliken arrived punctually upon the morrow.

He was a tall, gaunt, weak-kneed man, with a prominent nose and eyes that required the constant use of glasses. Harriet Brandt could not at first determine his relationship to the Baroness, who received him with one of the rough kisses she was wont to bestow on Bobby and herself.

He established himself in the Red House as if he had been a member of the family, and Harriet frequently surprised him engaged in confidential talk with their hostess, which was immediately stopped on her arrival. She perceived that Miss Wynward had an evident dislike for the newcomer, and never addressed him but in the most formal manner and when it was strictly necessary. The Baroness did not go so often to the manufactory after Mr. Milliken's arrival, but often shut herself up with him in a room with locked doors, after which Mr. Milliken would be much occupied with secretarial work, writing letters with his short-sighted eyes held close to the paper. He was a source of much curiosity to Harriet Brandt, but he need not have been. He was only that very common and unclean animal—the jackal to Madame Gobelli's lion.

He was poor and she was rich, so he did all the dirty work which she was unable, or afraid to do for herself. Mr. Milliken called himself an author and an actor, but he was neither. On account of his accidental likeness to a popular actor, he had once been engaged to play the part of his double at a West-end theatre, but with the waning of the piece, Mr. Milliken's fame evaporated, and he had never obtained an engagement since. His assumed authorship was built on the same scale. He had occasionally penned anonymous articles for newspapers, which had been inserted without pay, but no one in the literary or any other world knew him by name or by fame. Of late he had attached himself to Madame Gobelli, writing her letters for her (of doing which she was almost incapable), and occasionally dabbling in dirtier work, which she was too cunning to do for herself.

Miss Wynward could have told tales of abusive epistles which had been sent through his hand to people, whom the Baroness considered had offended her—of anonymous letters also, which if traced would have landed them both in the County Court. But Mr. Milliken was out at elbows. He found it very convenient to hang about the Red House for weeks together, to the saving of his pocket—receiving *douceurs* sometimes in actual coin of the realm at the hands of his benefactress, and making himself useful to her in any way in return. Lately, notwithstanding her grand promises to Harriet Brandt of introductions to lords and princes, the Baroness had thought it would be a very good thing for her favourite jackal if the young heiress took a fancy for him, and gave him full leave in consequence to go in and conquer if he could. She would praise his appearance and his qualities to the girl, before his very face—calling attention to the fact of what a clever creature he was, and what a fine figure he possessed, and how well he was connected, and advising her in her coarse fashion to cultivate his acquaintance better. She even descended to having visions in the broad daylight, and prophesying the future, for them both.

"'Arriet!" she would suddenly exclaim, "I see a man standing be'ind you!"

"O! gracious!" the girl would reply, jumping in her seat, "I wish you would not say such things, *Madame!*"

"Rubbish! Why shouldn't I say 'em, if they're there? Stop a bit! Let me see 'im plainly! 'E's got dark 'air, slightly sprinkled with grey—a fine nose—deep-set eyes, with bushy eyebrows—no 'air on 'is face—a tall figure, and long 'ands and feet! 'E's living in this world too! Do you know anybody that answers to the description?"

"No!" replied the girl, though she recognised it at once as being meant for Mr. Milliken.

"Well! if you don't know 'im now, you will before long, but it's my belief you've met. And mark my words! you and 'e will be closely connected in life! I shouldn't wonder if 'e turns out to be your future 'usband!"

"O! nonsense!" exclaimed Harriet, trying to speak lightly, "I'm not going to marry anybody, thank you, Madame Gobelli, unless it's one of the princes you promised to introduce me to."

"O! princes are all rubbish!" replied the Baroness, forgetting her former assertions, "they've none of them got any money, and yours wouldn't go far enough for 'em. *They* want a gal with something like five thousand a year at 'er back. I'd rather 'ave an Englishman any day, than a dirty little German prince!"

But Harriet Brandt was not the sort of woman to be forced into an intimacy against her will. Born under an hereditary curse, as she undoubtedly had been, and gifted with the fatal propensity of injuring, rather than benefiting those whom she took a fancy for, she was an epicure in her taste for her fellow creatures, and would not have permitted Mr. Alexander Milliken to take a liberty with her, had he been the last man left upon the earth. She avoided his society as much as it was possible to do, without being rude to her hostess, but as the Baroness was continually calling her to her side, it was difficult to do so. Meanwhile the days went on very differently from what she had anticipated when coming to the Red House. Bobby was languid and indifferent to everything, but hanging about the place where she might have located herself—sitting on the sofa beside her, with his heavy head on her shoulder, and his weak arm wound about her waist.

Miss Wynward feared he must have contracted some species of malaria at the seaside, and Harriet could see for herself that the lad was much altered from the time when they first met—the Baroness alone, either from ignorance or obstinacy, declaring that nothing ailed him but laziness, and she would give him the stick if he didn't exert himself more. Sometimes Harriet took him out with her—for a drive into the country, or to a concert or matinee in London, but what was that compared to the entertainment of Royalty and Aristocracy, which she had been promised. And she had not heard a word from Captain Pullen, though her first letter of appeal had been succeeded by two or three more. Such a rebuff would have driven another girl to despondency or tears, but that was not the effect it had on Harriet Brandt. If you throw a bone to a tigress and then try to take it away, she does not weep—she fights for her prey.

Harriet Brandt, deprived of the flatteries and attentions of Captain Pullen did not weep either, but set her pretty teeth together, and determined in her own mind that if she were to give him up she would know the reason why. She was reckless—she did not care what she did to obtain it, but she would learn the truth of his defalcation if she travelled down to Aldershot for the purpose. She was in this mood one day, when the maid servant who answered the door came to tell her that a lady was in the drawing-room, and desired to see her. The Baroness had gone out that afternoon and taken Mr. Milliken with her, so that Harriet was alone. She eagerly demanded the name of her visitor.

"The lady didn't give me her name," replied the servant, "but she asked if Miss Brandt was at home, plain enough!"

"Go back and say that I will be with her in a minute!" said Harriet.

She had decided in her own mind that the stranger must be Margaret Pullen, bringing her, doubtless, some news of her brother-in-law. She only stayed to smooth her hair, which was rather disordered from Bobby laying his head on her shoulder, before, with a heightened colour, she entered the drawing-room. What was her surprise to encounter, instead of Mrs. Pullen, Miss Leyton—Miss Leyton, who had been so reserved and proud with her at Heyst, and who even though she had sought her out at the Red House, looked as reserved and proud as before. Harriet advanced with an extended hand, but Elinor Leyton did not appear to see the action, as she coldly bowed and sank into her chair again.

Harriet was rather taken aback, but managed to stammer out, "I am very glad to see you, Miss Leyton! I thought you and Mrs. Pullen had forgotten all about me since leaving Heyst."

"We had not forgotten, Miss Brandt," replied Elinor, "but we had a great deal of trouble to encounter in the death of Mrs. Pullen's baby, and that put everything else for a while out of our minds. But—but—lately, we have had reason to remember your existence more forcibly than before!"

She spoke slowly and with an evident effort. She was as agitated as it was in her nature to be the while, but she did not shew it outwardly.

Elinor Leyton had at all times the most perfect command over herself. She was dressed on the present occasion with the utmost neatness and propriety, though she had left her home labouring under a discovery which had pierced her to the very soul. She was a woman who would have died upon the scaffold, without evincing the least fear.

"Reason to remember my existence!" echoed Harriet, "I do not understand you."

"I think you soon will!" said Elinor, as she took three letters from her handbag and laid them on the table, "I do not think you can fail to recognise that handwriting, Miss Brandt!"

Harriet stooped down and read the address upon the envelopes. They were her own letters to Captain Pullen.

"How did you get these?" she demanded angrily, as she seized them in her hand, "is thieving one of your proclivities, Miss Leyton?"

"No, Miss Brandt, thieving, as you elegantly put it, is not one of my proclivities! But Captain Pullen has been staying in the house of my father, Lord Walthamstowe, at Richmond, and left those letters behind him—thrown in the empty grate just as they are, a proof of how much he valued them! One of the housemaids, whilst setting his room in order after his departure, found them and brought them to me. So I determined that I would return them to your hands myself!"

"And have you read them?" demanded Harriet.

"I have read them! I considered it my duty!"

"Your duty!" replied the other, scornfully, "what duty is there in a mean, dishonourable action like that? What right had you to interfere with things that don't belong to you? These letters concern myself and Captain Pullen alone!"

"I deny that, Miss Brandt! They concern me quite as much, if not more—Captain Pullen is my affianced husband! We are to be married

121

in the spring!"

"I don't believe it!" cried Harriet, starting to her feet. "A woman who would read letters not addressed to her, would say anything! You are *not* engaged to be married to Captain Pullen!"

"Indeed! And on what grounds do you refuse to believe my statement?"

"Because he made love to me all the time he was in Heyst! Because he used to kiss me and tell me again and again that I was the only woman who had ever touched his heart! Because he had arranged to follow the Baroness's party to Brussels, only to be near me, and he would have done so, had *you* not prevented him!"

Her great eyes were blazing with indignation and mortified vanity—her slender hands were clenched—she looked as if she were about to spring upon her rival and tear her to pieces—whilst Miss Leyton sat there, calm and collected—and smiled at her ravings.

"You are quite mistaken," she said after a pause, "I have never mentioned your name to Captain Pullen—I had no idea, until those letters fell into my hands, that he had so far forgotten what he owes to me, as to address you in any terms but those of mere acquaintanceship. But now that I *do* know, it must of course be put a stop to at once and for ever! It was to tell you so, that I came here this afternoon."

"Put a stop to! Do you imagine that I am going to give up Captain Pullen at your request? You are vastly mistaken!"

"But you must—you *shall!*" exclaimed Elinor, getting (for her) quite excited. "He is engaged to marry me, and I will not allow him to keep up any communication with you! My decision is final, and you will be good enough to respect it!"

"Your decision is *final!*" cried Harriet in mocking tones. "O! indeed, is it? And what about Ralph's decision! Does that count for nothing? What if Ralph refuses to give me up?"

Elinor rose to her feet, trembling with indignation at the other's boldness.

"You shall not call him 'Ralph'," she exclaimed. "How dare you speak of a man who is nothing to you, in such familiar terms?

"But *is* he nothing to me?" retorted Harriet, "and am I nothing to him? We must have that question answered first. Ralph told me to call him by his name, and he calls me Hally. How can you prevent our doing so? He loves me—he has told me so—and I shall write to him as often as I choose—yes! and I will take him from you, if I choose, and keep him into the bargain! What do you say to that?"

"I say that you are a bold, brazen girl, not fit for me to associate with, and that I refuse to be contaminated by your presence any longer! Let me go!"

She made an effort to gain the door, as she spoke, but Harriet barred her exit.

"No, no, Miss Leyton," she said, "you don't come here to insult me, and then leave before you have heard all I have to say to you! In the first place your assurance today is the first I ever heard of your being engaged to marry Captain Pullen. *He* didn't take the trouble to make it public. He never mentioned you except to say what a cold, reserved, unpleasant nature you had, and how impossible it would be for a man with any human feeling to get on with you! That is what *he* thought! And he said it too, when he had his arm round my waist, and his face close to mine. And now he has come to England, I suppose he is afraid to carry on with me anymore, for fear that you should hear of it! But I don't mean to let him off so easily, I can tell you! He shall answer those letters, which you *say* he threw away in the grate, but which you are just as likely to have pilfered from his desk, before he is many days older!"

"You cannot *make* him answer them," said Elinor, proudly, "whatever you may affirm!"

"Not on paper perhaps, but by word of mouth! I will take them back to him at Aldershot, and see whether he can deny what I have told when he is face to face with me!"

"Surely!—surely!—you would never proceed to so unmaidenly an extremity," exclaimed Elinor, losing sight for a moment of her indignation in her horror at the idea. "You must not think of such a thing! You would create a scandal in the camp! You would be despised for it ever after!"

"I can take care of myself!" replied Harriet, boldly, "you need not fear for me! And if even you *do* get your own way about this matter, you will have the satisfaction all your married life of knowing that your husband was a coward and a traitor to you, even during your engagement, and that you will never be able to trust him further than you can see him, to the end! If you can care for such a husband, take him, for I'm sure I wouldn't. But he shall answer to me for all that!"

"O! Miss Brandt, let me go, pray let me go!" said Elinor in a tone of such unmistakeable pain, that the other involuntarily drew back, and let her push her way past her, to the door.

As Miss Leyton disappeared, Harriet Brandt commenced to pace up and down the length of the drawing-room. It was not the swaying walk of disappointment and despair; it was determined and masterful, born of anger and a longing for revenge. All the Creole in her, came to the surface—like her cruel mother, she would have given over Ralph Pullen to the vivisecting laboratory, if she could. Her dark eyes rolled in her passion; her slight hands were clenched upon each other; and her crimson lips quivered with the inability to express all she felt. Bobby, glancing in upon her from the French windows which opened on the garden, crept to her side and tried to capture her clenched hands, and to keep her restless body still. But she threw him off, almost brutally. At that moment she *was* brutal.

"Leave me alone," she exclaimed impatiently, "don't touch me! Go away!"

"O! Hally," the boy replied, sympathetically, "what is the matter? Has anyone offended you? Let me know? Let me try to comfort you! Or tell me what I shall do to help you."

"Do!" cried the girl, contemptuously, "what could *you* do?—a baby tied to your mother's apron-string! Leave me to myself, I say! I don't want you, or anyone! I want to be alone! Boys are of no use! It requires a *man* to revenge a woman's wrong!"

The lad, after one long look of bitter disappointment, walked quietly away from the spot, and hid his grief in some sequestered part of the garden. Hally despised him—she, who had kissed him and let him lay his head upon her shoulder and tell her all his little troubles—said he was of no use, when she stood in need of help and comfort! When, if she only knew it, he was ready to stand up in her defence against twenty men, if need be, and felt strong enough to defeat them all! But she had called him a baby, tied to his mother's apron-strings. The iron entered into his very soul.

Meanwhile, Elinor Leyton having blindly found her way out of the Red House hailed a passing hansom, and gave the driver directions to take her to a certain number in Harley Street, where Margaret Pullen was staying with her godfather, Doctor Phillips. She knew no one else to whom she could go in this great trouble, which made her feel as if her life had suddenly been cut in two. Yet she made no outward moan. Most young women having kept a bold front, as she had done, towards the enemy, would have broken down, as soon as they found themselves alone. But Elinor Leyton was not in the habit of breaking down. As soon as she had started for her destination, she leaned her head upon the back of the cab, closed her eyes and set her teeth fast together. Her face grew deadly pale, and an observer would have noted the trembling of her lips, and the ball which rose and fell in her throat. But she uttered no sound, not even a sigh—her misery was too deep for words.

Since she had returned to London, Margaret Pullen had stayed with Doctor Phillips, for he had insisted that it should be so. The telegram which had conveyed to Colonel Pullen the news of his little daughter's death, had been answered by one to say that he had applied for immediate leave, and should join his wife as soon as he received it. And Margaret was now expecting his arrival, every day—almost every hour. She looked very sad in her deep mourning dress, as she came forward to greet Elinor, but as soon as she caught sight of her visitor's face, she forgot her own trouble in her womanly sympathy for her friend,

"My dear Elinor!" she exclaimed, "what has brought you to town? You have bad news for me—I can read it in your eyes. Nothing wrong with Ralph, I hope!"

She kissed the girl affectionately, and held her hand, but Elinor did not answer. She turned her white face towards her friend, and bit her lips hard, but the words would not come.

"You are suffering, my poor dear," went on Margaret, tenderly, as she made her sit down, and removed her hat and cloak. "Can't you trust me with your trouble? Haven't I had enough of my own? Ah! cry, that's better, God sends us tears, in order that our hearts may not break! And now, what is it? Is anyone ill at home?"

Elinor shook her head. The tears were rolling slowly one by one, down her marble cheeks, but she jerked them away as they came, as though it were a shame to weep.

After a long pause, she swallowed something in her throat and commenced in a husky voice,

"It concerns Ralph, Margaret! He has been untrue to me! All is over between us!"

"O! surely not!" said Margaret, "have you had a full explanation with him? Who told you he had been untrue? Has Ralph asked for a release from his engagement?"

"No! but he shall have it!"

She then went on to tell the story of the finding of Harriet Brandt's letters in Captain Pullen's grate—and of the interview she had had with the girl that afternoon.

"She did not attempt to deny it," continued Elinor. "On the contrary she declared that he had made love to her all the time he was at Heyst—that he had said she was the only woman who had ever touched his heart, and that no man with human feelings could be happy with such a cold, reserved nature as mine! And if you could see her letters to him, Margaret—I wish I had not given them to her, but she snatched them from my hand—they were too dreadful! I never read such letters from a woman to a man. I did not know they could be written."

"But, Elinor, it strikes me that all this time, you have only heard one side of the question. What does it signify what Miss Brandt may say? The only thing of importance to you is, what Ralph will say."

"But there were her letters—they told their own story! They were full of nothing but 'dearests' and 'darlings', and reminders of how he had embraced her in one place, and what he had said to her in another—such letters as I could not write to a man, if it were to save my life!"

"I can quite understand that! Miss Brandt and you possess two totally different natures. And cannot you understand that a girl like that, half educated, wholly ignorant of the usages of society, with a passionate undeveloped nature and a bold spirit, might write as you have described her doing, against the wishes of the recipient of her letters? You say that Ralph threw her epistles in the grate just as they were. Does that look as if he valued them, or felt himself to be guilty concerning their reception?"

"But, Margaret, you know he *did* make himself conspicuous with the Gobellis and Miss Brandt at Heyst! I think everyone noticed their intimacy!"

"I noticed it also, and I was very sorry for it, but, Elinor, my dear, it was partly your own fault! You were so much opposed to the idea of your engagement to Ralph being made public, that I feared it might lead to some contretemps. And then," she continued gently, "don't be offended if I say that your reserve with him, and your objection to anything like love-making, on his part is in itself calculated to drive a young man to society he cares less for!"

"But—but—still—I love him!" said poor Elinor, with a tremendous effort.

"I know you do," replied Margaret, kissing her again, "and better and more faithfully, perhaps, than half the women who show their love so openly—yet, men are but men, Elinor, and as a rule they do not believe in the affection which is never expressed by caresses and fond words."

"Well! whether I have been right or wrong, it is over now," said Miss Leyton, "and Ralph can go to Miss Brandt or anyone else he chooses for amusement. I shall never stand in his way, but I cannot brook an affront, so I shall write and release him from his promise to me, at once!"

"No, no, Elinor, you must not do anything so rash! I beg—I implore you, to do nothing, until Ralph has had an opportunity of denying the charges brought against him by this girl. They may be utterly untrue! She may be simply persecuting him. Depend upon it, you have only to ask him for an explanation of those letters, and everything will be satisfactorily cleared up."

"You have more belief in him than I have, Margaret! Miss Brandt has great confidence in her cause. She told me that she had not only taken him from me, but she meant to keep him, and expressed her intention of going down to Aldershot and confronting Ralph with the letters she had written him!"

At this intelligence, Margaret grew alarmed for her friend's peace of mind.

"No! no! that must never be," she exclaimed, "that girl must not be permitted to make a scandal in the camp, and get your name perhaps mixed up with it! It must be prevented."

"I fancy you will find that a difficult task," said Elinor, "she seems the most determined young woman I have ever come across. She became so vehement at last, that she frightened me, and I was only too glad to get out of the house."

"Elinor," said Mrs. Pullen suddenly, "will you leave this matter in my hands to settle in my own way?"

"What do you intend to do? See Miss Brandt yourself? I advise you not! She will only insult you, as she did me."

"No! I shall not see her myself, I promise you that, but I will send a proper ambassador to interview Miss Brandt and the Baroness. This sort of thing must not be allowed to go on, and unless Ralph comes forward to second the girl's assertions (which I am sure he will never do), she and her friend Madame Gobelli must be made to understand that if they don't behave themselves, the law will be called into requisition to enforce obedience. I should not be at all surprised if the Baroness were not at the bottom of all this."

"At any rate, it has ruined my life!" said Elinor, mournfully.

"Nonsense! my dear girl, no such thing! It is only an unpleasant episode which will soon be forgotten. But let it make you a little more careful for the future, Elinor. Ralph is a very conceited man. He has been spoilt by the women all his life, *'pour l'amour de ses beaux yeux.'* He has been used to flattery and attention, and when he doesn't get it he misses it, and goes where it is to be found. It is rather a contemptible weakness, but he shares it in common with most of his sex, and you have promised, remember, to take him for better or worse!"

"Not yet, thank goodness!" retorted Elinor, with something of her usual spirit. "He and father got talking together about the marriage, the other day, when he was down at Richmond, and fixed it, I believe, for the spring, but they will have to unfix it again now, if I am not mistaken."

"No such thing," replied Margaret, "and now you have consented—have you not?—to leave the settlement of this other affair in my hands."

"If you wish it, Margaret! But, remember, no compromise! If Ralph has really promised this girl what she says, let him keep his promises, for I will have none of him. And now I must go home or they will wonder what has become of me!"

Margaret was not sorry to see her depart, for she was most anxious to summon Anthony Pennell, her husband's cousin, to her aid, and ask his advice as to what was best to be done in the circumstances.

She had great faith in Anthony Pennell, not only in his genius, which was an accepted thing, but in his good sense, which is not usually found associated with the higher quality. He was a man of about thirty, with a grand intellect—a sound understanding—a liberal mind, and a sympathetic disposition. He had been originally intended for the Bar, but having "taken silk," and made a most promising debut, he had suddenly blossomed into an author, and his first novel had taken London by storm.

He had accomplished the rare feat of being lifted up at once on the waves of public opinion and carried over the heads of all his fellows.

Since his first success, he had continued writing—had given up the law in consequence—and was now making a large and steady income.

But Anthony Pennell's great charm lay in his unassuming manner and modest judgment of his own work. His triumphs were much more astonishing to him than to his friends. In person, he was less handsome than his cousin Ralph Pullen, but much more manly looking, having been a distinguished athlete in his college days, and still finding his best recreation on the cricket field and the golf ground.

Me was very fair, with a white skin, embrowned here and there by sun and outdoor exercise—short, curly hair—a fine figure, standing six toot high, and the bluest of blue eyes. He was smoking in his own chambers late that afternoon, when he received a telegram from Margaret Pullen, "Can you come over this evening?" and as soon as he had changed his lounging coat, he obeyed her summons.

CHAPTER 12

Anthony Pennell was a very fresh, pleasant, and good-looking presentment of a young English gentleman, as he entered the room where Margaret was sitting with Doctor Phillips that evening. It had been arranged between them beforehand, that as little as need be, should be confided to him, of Harriet Brandt's former history. All that was necessary for him to know, was the danger that threatened to blast the future happiness of Ralph Pullen and Elinor Leyton.

"Well! Mrs. Pullen," he said, as he shook hands cordially with Margaret and the doctor, "and what important business is it, that you want to consult me upon? I thought, at the very least, that I should meet my cousin Arthur here!"

"If I had had Arthur, perhaps I should not have needed you," replied Margaret, with a faint smile. "But really Mr. Pennell, I am in want of advice sorely, and the Doctor agreed with me that you would be the best person to whom I could apply!"

"I am at your service, Madam!" said the young man, gaily, as he seated himself.

Then she told him the story of Harriet Brandt—how Ralph had met her at the Lion d'Or, and devoted his time to her—and how she was persecuting him with letters, and had threatened to follow him to the camp and interview him there.

"And it must be put a stop to, you know, Mr. Pennell," she concluded, "not only for Ralph's sake and Elinor's, but for the sake of the Walthamstowes and my husband. I am sure that Arthur would be exceedingly annoyed at any scandal of that sort, and especially as Lord Walthamstowe is so old a friend of his family!"

Anthony Pennell had looked very grave during her recital. After a pause, he said, "Are you sure that Ralph has not given this young lady good cause to run after him?"

"I think not—I hope not! There was very little amusement in Heyst, and this girl, and the people with whom she is now staying— a Baron and Baroness Gobelli, they call themselves—were amongst the visitors to the Lion d'Or. Miss Leyton is rather a stickler for the proprieties, and used to refuse to walk out with Ralph alone in the evenings, and I was too much occupied with my poor darling baby to accompany them," said Margaret, in a faltering voice, "so Ralph took to going to the Baroness's private rooms instead, and became intimate with Miss Brandt!"

"You acknowledge then, that he *was* intimate with her!"

"I think he must have been—because it appears that he had agreed to join their party at Brussels, when—when—my great trouble obliged him to return to England with us instead."

"Did you know this young lady, Mrs. Pullen?"

"I did, and at one time I was rather intimate with her, that is, before the Baroness took her up, when she passed almost all her time with them."

"She is, I suppose, very attractive in person?"

"O! dear no, not at all!" cried Margaret, with a woman's dull appreciation of the charms of one of her own sex, "she has fine eyes, and what men would, I suppose, call a good figure, but no complexion and an enormous mouth. Not at all pretty, but nice-looking at times,—that is all!"

"Clever?" said Pennell, interrogatively.

"I do not think so! She had just come out of a convent school and was utterly unused to society. But she has a very good voice and plays well on the *mandolin!*"

"Ladies are not always the best judges of their own sex," remarked Anthony, turning to Doctor Phillips, "what do *you* say, Doctor? Had you an opportunity of appraising Miss Brandt's beauties and accomplishments for yourself?"

"I would rather say nothing, Mr. Pennell," replied the Doctor. "The fact is, I knew her parents in the West Indies, and could never believe in anything good coming from such a stock. Whatever the girl may be, she inherits terrible proclivities, added to black blood. She is in point of fact a quadroon, and not fit to marry into any decent English family!"

"O! dear!" exclaimed Mr. Pennell laconically,

"And how do you expect me to help you?" he enquired, after a pause.

"I want you to see the Baroness, or Miss Brandt, and tell them that this girl must cease all communication with Captain Pullen," said Margaret, "tell them that he is engaged to marry Miss Leyton—that the marriage is fixed to take place next spring, and that the Waltham-stowe family will be excessively annoyed if any scandal of this sort occurs to break it off."

"Do they not know that such an engagement exists?"

"No! that is the unfortunate part of it! Elinor Leyton is so absurdly scrupulous that she will not have the fact made public, and forbade me to tell Miss Brandt about it! Elinor went to the Red House where Miss Brandt is staying this morning and had a most stormy interview with her. She came here afterwards in a most distressed state of mind. Harriet Brandt had told her that she had secured Ralph Pullen and meant to keep him—that he had told her he loved her—and that Miss Leyton was too cold and prudish a nature for any man to be happy with! Of course Elinor was terribly upset. She seldom shews her feelings, but it was quite impossible for her to disguise them today. I begged her to leave the matter in my hands, and she consented to do so. That is why I telegraphed for you."

"It is rather an awkward predicament!" said Anthony Pennell, thoughtfully, "you will forgive me for saying, Mrs. Pullen, that Ralph is so very likely to have done this sort of thing, that I feel one might be treading on very delicate ground—in fact, putting one's foot in it—by interfering. You know what Ralph is—selfish and indolent and full of vanity. He considers it far too much trouble to make love (as it is called) to a woman, but he will accept any amount of love that is offered him, so long as it gives him no trouble. If this Miss Brandt is all that you and the doctor here, say of her, she may possibly have drawn Ralph on, and taken his languid satisfaction as proof that he agreed to all she said and did. But it will make the denouement just as unpleasant. Besides, how will Ralph himself, take my interference in the matter? He may have some designs on this girl—some ideas in the future connected with her—and will ask what business I had to come between them."

"O! no! Did I not tell you that he had left her letters in his grate?"

"That might be part of his indolent carelessness, or they may have been left there by design, as a means of breaking the ice between himself and Miss Leyton. Is not he, after all, the most proper person to appeal to? Why not wait till your husband returns, and let him speak to his brother?"

"I am so afraid in that case, that Ralph might consider that he had gone too far with Miss Brandt, and honour demanded that he should marry her! And, Mr. Pennell, Doctor Phillips could tell you things, if he chose, to prove to you that Harriet Brandt is not a fit wife for any decent man."

Anthony Pennell thought again for a few minutes—sitting silent with his hand caressing his smooth chin. Then he said:

"If you are very much bent on my doing what I can in this matter, I see only one way to accomplish it. I must enter the Red House under a flag of truce. Did you know this Baroness Gobelli? Can you tell me what sort of woman she is? I never heard the name before!"

"She is quite a character," replied Margaret, "I believe her husband *is* a German Baron, but she was a Mrs. Bates, and is an extraordinary Baroness. A strange mixture also, of vulgarity and refined tastes. She drops all her aspirates, yet talks familiarly of aristocratic and royal titles, she dresses like a cook out on Sundays, and yet has a passion for good paintings and old china."

At the last words, Anthony Pennell pricked up his ears.

"A passion for old china!" he exclaimed, "then there must be some good in her! Cannot you give me an introduction to the Red House on the plea that I am a connoisseur and am desirous of seeing her collection?"

"Of course I can, but how can you approach these people in amity, with a censure of Miss Brandt's conduct in your hand? Madame Gobelli is infatuated with Harriet Brandt! I was telling poor Elinor only this afternoon, that I should not be at all surprised if she were at the bottom of all this unpleasantness."

"She could not be at the bottom of anything unless Ralph had given her cause," replied Mr. Pennell, who had never had a good opinion of his cousin's straightforward dealing, "and however it may turn out, I should think he would have a heavy reckoning to settle with Miss Leyton! This is not the first time, remember! You have not forgotten the trouble Arthur had to get him out of that scrape with the laundress's girl at Aldershot, the year before last!"

"Yes! Arthur told me about it," replied Margaret. "But you are going to help us, this time, Mr. Pennell, are you not?"

"In so far as procuring an introduction to the Baroness, and taking my opportunity to let her know the true state of affairs with Miss Leyton, yes," said Mr. Pennell, "but there, my responsibility must cease. Should Ralph have committed himself in writing, or anything of that sort, you must promise to let them fight it out their own way. I daresay there will be no trouble about the matter. I can see how it has occurred at a glance. Ralph has been merely amusing himself with the girl, and she has taken his philandering in earnest. But I wish he would leave that sort of thing off. It will ruin his married life if he does not!"

"Yes! indeed, and Elinor Leyton really loves him, more, I am sure, than he imagines. She declared this afternoon, that if it were not put a complete stop to, she should break off her engagement. And I think she would be right!"

"So do I," acquiesced Anthony Pennell. "Well! if these people are ordinarily decent, they will, as soon as they hear the truth, prevent their young friend interfering with another woman's rights. Write me the introduction, Mrs. Pullen, and I will pay the Red House a visit as soon as its owner gives me leave. And now let us talk of something pleasanter. How soon do you expect Arthur to arrive?"

"Any day," replied Margaret, "and I am longing so for him to come!"

"Of course you are! Will he remain long in England?"

"Only a few weeks! He has taken three months' leave. Then, I shall return with him to Hoosur.

"And you like the idea of India?"

"O! anything—anything—to find myself with him again," she answered feverishly.

The conversation turned upon more indifferent subjects, and armed with the note of introduction to the Baroness, Anthony Pennell presently took his leave. He did not like the task imposed upon him, and he hardly knew how he should set about it, but on consideration he thought he could do no harm by having a look at the young lady, who had taken the fancy of his fickle-minded cousin Ralph, and leaving his future action to be decided by the interview. He sat down therefore before turning into bed, and wrote a note to the Baroness, enclosing the introduction from Mrs. Pullen, and asking permission to call and inspect her rare collection of china, of which he had heard so much.

His letter reached the Red House on the following morning, at an unfortunate moment, when Madame Gobelli was giving full display to the worst side of her eccentric character.

The Baroness was not a lover of animals, either dogs or horses. She was merciless to the latter and the former she kicked whenever they came in her way. It was considered necessary, however, for the safety of the Red House, that it should be guarded by a watch-dog, and a miserable retriever, which answered to that name, lived in a rotten cask in the stable yard. This unhappy animal, which had neither sufficient food, exercise, nor straw to lie on, was in the habit of keeping up a continuous baying at night, in remonstrance at the cruelty of its treatment, which was a cause of annoyance to the neighbours, who had often written to the Baroness about it in vain.

On the morning in question, a Captain Hill, who lived on one side the Red House, with his parents, sent in his card to Madame Gobelli and asked for an interview. She admitted him at once. She liked men of all sorts, and particularly if they were young and she could kiss them with impunity, under the pretence that she was old enough to be their mother.

She therefore welcomed Captain Hill quite amiably. She came in from the garden to receive him, attired in a Genoa velvet dress that trailed half a yard on the damp ground behind, and a coarse Zulu hat perched on her large bullet head. She was attended by Harriet Brandt, who had been making a tour of the premises with her, and was always eager to see anybody who might call at the Red House. Miss Wynward also, who was dusting the china with a feather brush as the visitor was announced, continued her occupation and without apologising for doing so, or asking leave.

Harriet had not yet been able to determine the exact place which this lady held in the Baroness's household, for she was treated as one of the family, and yet degraded at times to the position of a servant.

The Baroness expected her to cook, or dust rooms, or darn stockings, or do anything required of her, whilst she introduced her to all her friends as if on a perfect equality with themselves. As she entered the drawing-room through one of the French windows, she shook hands familiarly with Captain Hill, and introduced him to both her companions.

"Well!" she went on, "and so you've come to see us at last! I thought you were going to live and die in that tumble-down old place of yours, without so much as a shake of the 'and! I 'ope you're all well at 'ome!

The stranger did not seem to know how to receive these civilities. He had not seated himself, but stood in the centre of the room with his hat in his hand, as though he found a difficulty in stating his errand at the Red House.

"Take a chair," said Madame Gobelli in her rough way, "there's enough and to spare, and my young friend 'ere, won't eat you!"

Still Captain Hill deliberated about accepting her offer.

"Thank you," he commenced, "but I shall not detain you above

134

a few moments. I came to speak to you about your dog, Madame Gobelli. My parents are both very old, and my mother especially delicate—indeed, I fear that she may never rise from her bed again!"

Here his voice faltered a little, but quickly recovering himself he went on,

"She sleeps very little, and that little has now become impossible to her on account of the incessant barking of your yard dog. I am here today by the wish of my mother's medical attendant, Doctor Parker, to tell you that the noise is seriously affecting her health, and to beg that you will adopt some measures to have the annoyance stopped."

As the Baroness understood the reason for which her neighbour had called upon her, her countenance palpably changed. The broad smile faded from her face and was replaced by an ominous frown. If there was one thing which she resented above another, it was being called to task for any disturbance in her household. Without taking any notice apparently of Captain Hill's complaint, she turned to Miss Wynward and said,

"Miss Wynward, come 'ere! Does that dog bark at night?"

"Sometimes, my lady, replied the governess dubiously.

"I don't believe it! You're lying! 'Arriet, does Nelson ever bark so as to disturb anyone?"

"He barks whenever there is a ring at the bell, or a stranger enters the grounds, *Madame*," said Harriet, with politic evasion.

"O! I assure you he does more than that!" interposed the visitor, "the poor animal howls without ceasing. Either he is ill, or the servants do not give him sufficient food!"

But at this censure cast upon her domestics whom she bullied from morning till night, the Baroness's uncontrolled temper burst forth.

"'Ow dare you come 'ere," she exclaimed loudly, "and bring false accusations against my servants? No one in this 'ouse is kept short of food. What do you mean—a rubbishing fellow like you—by coming 'ere, and accusing the Baron of starving 'is animals? There's more money spent upon our animals, I bet, than goes in your poverty-stricken 'ouse-'old in a year!"

Captain Hill was now offended, as he well might be. "I do not know what knowledge you may possess of the exigencies of my parents' household, Madam," he replied, "but what I came here to tell you is this—that from whatever cause it may arise, the howling and whining of your dog is a public nuisance and it must be stopped!"

"Must, must!" exclaimed Madame Gobelli, shaking her stick at him, "and pray 'oo's to make me stop it?"

"I will," said Captain Hill, "the noise is endangering the life of my mother, and I shall insist upon the animal being destroyed, or taken elsewhere. If you cannot take a friendly hint—if you have so callous a nature that the sufferings of an aged and invalid lady cannot excite your sympathy the law shall teach you, that whatever you may fail to feel, you cannot annoy your neighbours with impunity!"

"Fine neighbours indeed!" cried the Baroness, her whole face trembling and contorted with passion. "A beggarly lot of half-pay officers and retired parsons! I'll soon see if you'll be allowed to come riding the 'igh 'orse over me! Confound your impudence! Do you know 'oo I am?"

"A Billingsgate fishwoman, I should imagine, from your language! Certainly not a gentlewoman!" said Captain Hill, his eyes blazing with his wrath.

"'Ang you! I'll soon teach you 'ow to insult a lady that's connected with Royalty!"

At that, the stranger burst into a derisive laugh.

"Down the backstairs!" he muttered to himself, but Madame Gobelli caught the words.

"Get out of my 'ouse," she cried. "'Ere, Miss Wynward, see this fellow out at the front door, and never you let 'im in again, or I'll give you a month's warning! Down the backstairs indeed! Confound you! If you don't clear out this very minute, I'll lay my stick across your back! You'll make me destroy my dog, will you, and just because your trumpery mother don't like 'is barking! Go 'ome and tell 'er to 'old 'er own row! And you accuse my servants of not giving 'im enough to eat. You'd be glad enough to see 'is dinner on your own table once or twice a week. Out with you, I say—out with you at once, and don't let me see your ugly mug and your carroty 'ead in 'ere again, or I'll set the dog you don't like upon you."

Captain Hill had turned white as a sheet with anger.

"You'll hear more of this, Madam, and from my solicitor next time," he said. "Heartless, unfeeling woman! How can you call yourself a mother, when you have no pity for a son's grief at his mother's illness? Pray God you may not have occasion to remember this morning, when you have to part from your own son!"

He rushed from the room as he spoke, and they heard the hall door slam after him. For a minute after he left, there was a dead pause between the three women. His last words seemed to have struck the

Baroness as with a two-edged sword. She stood silent, staring into vacancy, and breathing hard, whilst Harriet Brandt and Miss Wynward regarded each other with furtive dismay. The silence was broken by Madame Gobelli bursting into a harsh laugh.

"I don't fancy 'e will shew 'is face in my 'ouse again, in an 'urry" she exclaimed. "It was as good as a play to watch 'im, trying to brave it out! Confound 'is old mother! Why don't she die and 'ave done with it! I've no patience with old people 'anging on in that way, and worrying the 'ole world with their fads! Well! what is it?" she continued to a maid who brought her a letter.

"By the post, my lady!"

The Baroness broke the seal. There was such a look of scare upon her features, that some people might have thought she was glad to have anything to do that should hide it from her companions. The letter was from Anthony Pennell, whose name was familiar to her, as to all the world.

As she finished its perusal, her manner entirely altered. The broad smile broke out on her countenance—her eyes sparkled—one would have thought she could never be in anything but a beaming good temper.

"'Olloa! 'Arriet!" she exclaimed, "'ere's news for you! 'Oo do you think this letter's from?"

"How can I guess?" replied the girl, though her thoughts had flown at once to Ralph Pullen.

"From Mr. Anthony Pennell, the great author, you know, and own cousin to that rapscallion, Captain Pullen! Now we shall 'ear all about the 'andsome captain! Mr. Pennell says 'e wants to come 'ere and see my china, but I know better! 'E's bringing you a message from 'is cousin, mark my words! I can see it written up be'ind you!"

Harriet's delicate face flushed with pleasure at the news.

"But why shouldn't Captain Pullen have come himself?" she asked, anxiously.

"I can't tell you that! Perhaps 'e is coming, be'ind the other, and this is only a feeler! There's wheels within wheels in these big families, sometimes, you know, and the Pullens are connected with a lot of bigwigs! But we'll 'ave some news, anyway! You just sit down, my dear, and write Mr. Pennell a pretty note in my name—you write a prettier 'and than I do—and say we shall be very pleased to see 'im tomorrow afternoon, if convenient, and I 'ope 'e will stay to dinner afterwards and be introduced to the Baron—will you?"

"O! yes, of course, *Madame*, if you wish it!" replied the girl, smiles dimpling her face at the thought of her triumph over Elinor Leyton.

"Now, Miss Wynward, we must 'ave a first-rate dinner tomorrow for Mr. Pennell, and you and Bobby 'ad better dine at one o'clock, or you'll spoil the table. Let me see! We'll 'ave—"

But turning to enforce her orders, the Baroness discovered that Miss Wynward had quitted the room.

"Why! where 'as the woman gone? Did you see 'er leave the room, 'Arriet?"

"I did not! I was too much occupied listening to you," replied the girl from the table, where she was inditing the answer to Anthony Pennell's note.

"'Ere, Miss Wynward! Miss Wynward!" screamed the Baroness from the open door, but no reply came to her call.

"I must go and see after 'er!" she said, as she stumped from the room, as intent upon procuring a good dinner for one young man, as she had been in insulting the other, and turning him from her doors.

Meanwhile Captain Hill, hot and angry, was striding away in the direction of his own home, when he heard a soft voice calling his name in the rear. He turned to encounter the spare, humiliated form of Miss Wynward.

"Captain Hill," she ejaculated, "I beg your pardon, but may I speak to you for a moment?"

Recognising her as having been in the room, when the Baroness had so grossly insulted him, he waited rather coldly, for her to come up with him.

"Don't think me impertinent or interfering," faltered Miss Wynward, "but I was so shocked—so distressed—I could not let you go without saying how grieved and sorry I am!"

"I do not quite understand you," replied Captain Hill.

"O! yes, surely, did you not see me in the room just now! I felt as if I should die of shame! But if you knew what it is to be dependent—to be unable to speak or to expostulate—you would guess perhaps—"

"Yes! Yes! I think I can understand. But pray don't distress yourself about it! It was my own fault! I should have addressed her first through my solicitor. But I thought she was a gentlewoman!"

"It is her temper that gets the better of her," said Miss Wynward in an apologetic tone, "she is not always so bad as she was this morning!"

"That is fortunate for the world at large," replied Captain Hill, gravely. "I could have forgiven her vulgarity, but not her heartlessness.

I can only think that she is a most terrible woman.

"That is what everybody says," answered his companion, "but she will admit of no remonstrance. She will have her own way, and the Baron is as powerless to refrain her, as you, or I. But that she should so insult a gentleman like yourself, even descending to oaths and personalities—O! I cannot tell you how much I felt it—how ashamed I was, and how anxious that you should not confound me with anything the Baroness said, or did!"

"Indeed," said Captain Hill, holding out his hand, "you need have no fear on that score. I hope I know a gentlewoman when I see her! But tell me, since your eyes are open to all this, how is it that a lady like yourself, can stay under the roof of so terrible a person? There are plenty of other situations to be had! Why do you not leave her, and go elsewhere?"

He was struck by the look of mingled anxiety and fear with which she regarded him.

"O! Captain Hill, there are reasons that are difficult to explain—that I could not tell to anyone on so short an acquaintance. But the Baroness possesses great power—she could ruin me, I believe she could *kill* me if she chose!"

"She threatens you then!"

"Yes!" came from Miss Wynward's lips, but in almost a whisper.

'Well! this is hardly the time and place to discuss such a question," said Captain Hill, "but I should much like to see more of you, Miss Wynward! If you have any time at your disposal, will you come over and see my old mother? She is quite confined to her room, but I know it would please her to have a quiet talk with you!"

A light glistened in Miss Wynward's washed-out eyes, and a smile stole over her countenance.

"Do you really mean it, Captain Hill?"

"I never say anything that I do not mean," he answered, "I am sure both my parents would be glad to give you their advice, and my dear father, who is a clergyman, though past an active ministry, may be able to be of use to you in a more practical way. At any rate, you will come and see us. That is a bargain!" and he held out his hand to her again in farewell.

"O! I will—I will, indeed," exclaimed Miss Wynward, gratefully, "and thank you so very much for the permission. You have put a little hope into my life!"

She seized the hand he proffered her, and kissed it, as an inferior

139

might have done, and then hurried back to the Red House, before he had had time to remonstrate with her on the proceeding.

Chapter 13

When Anthony Pennell received the Baroness's invitation, penned in the delicate foreign handwriting of Harriet Brandt, he accepted it at once. Being out of the season, he had no engagement for that evening, but he would have broken twenty engagements, sooner than miss the chance, so unexpectedly offered him, of meeting in an intimate family circle, the girl who appeared to have led his cousin Ralph's fancy astray. He pictured her to himself as a whitey-brown young woman with thick lips and rolling eyes, and how Ralph, who was so daintily particular where the *beau sexe* was concerned, could have been attracted by such a specimen, puzzled Anthony altogether. The knowledge that she had money struck him unpleasantly, for he could think of no other motive for Captain Pullen having philandered with her, as he evidently had done. At any rate, the idea that there was the least chance of allying herself with their family, must be put out of her head, at once and for ever.

Mr. Pennell amused himself with thinking of the scare he should create at the dinner table, by "springing" the news of Ralph's intended marriage upon them, all at once. Would the young lady have hysterics, he wondered, or faint away, or burst into a passion of tears? He laughed inwardly at the probability! He felt very cruel over it! He had no pity for the poor quadroon, as Doctor Phillips had called her. It was better that she should suffer, than that Elinor Leyton should have to break off her engagement. And, by Margaret Pullen's account, Miss Brandt had been both defiant and insulting to Miss Leyton. She must be a brazen, unfeeling sort of girl—it was meet that she paid the penalty of her foolhardiness.

It was in such a mood that Anthony Pennell arrived at the Red House at five o'clock in the afternoon, that he might have the opportunity to inspect the collection of china that had gained him an entrance there.

The Baroness had promised to be home in time to receive him, but he was punctual and she was not. Harriet Brandt was loitering about the garden, which was still pleasant enough on fine days in the middle of September, when the news that Mr. Pennell was in the drawing-room was brought to her by Miss Wynward. Harriet had been very eager to meet Anthony Pennell—not because she was pining after his cousin, but because her feminine curiosity was strong to discover *why* Ralph had deserted her, and if he had been subjected to undue influence to force him to do so. But now that the time had come, she felt shy and nervous. Suppose he, Mr. Pennell, had seen Miss Leyton meanwhile, and heard all that had taken place between them, when she visited the Red House. And suppose he should take Miss Leyton's part!

Harriet's mind was full of "supposes" as she turned to Miss Wynward and said, "O! I can't go and receive him, Miss Wynward! Mr. Pennell has come to see the Baroness, not me! Cannot you entertain him until she comes home? She will not be long now!"

"Her ladyship's last words to me, Miss Brandt, were, that if she had not returned from the factory by the time Mr. Pennell arrived, you were to receive him and give him afternoon tea in her stead! I hope you will do as her ladyship desired!

"Well! I suppose I must then," replied Harriet, screwing up her mouth, with a gesture of dissatisfaction, "but do send in the tea quickly please!"

"It shall be served, Miss Brandt, as soon as I can get back to make it! Mr. Pennell seems a very pleasant gentleman! I wouldn't mind if I were you!"

Miss Wynward hurried back to the house, as she spoke, and Harriet walked slowly over the lawn towards the drawing-room windows.

Anthony Pennell, who had been bending over some rare specimens of old Chelsea, looked up suddenly as she approached, and was struck dumb with admiration. She had improved wonderfully in looks since she had been in Europe, though the women who lived with her continually, were slow to perceive it. Her delicate complexion had acquired a colour like that of a blush rose, which was heightened by contrast with her dark, glowing eyes, whilst her hair by exposure to the rays of the sun, had caught some of its fire and showed ruddily, here and there, in streaks of auburn.

Her figure, without having lost its lissom grace, was somewhat fuller, and her manner was altogether more intelligent, and less gauche than it had been. But the dark eyes were still looking for their prey, and the restless lips were incessantly twitching and moving one over the other. She was beautifully dressed that evening—she had not been in London for a month, without finding a way to spend her money—and Anthony Pennell, like most artistic natures, was very open to the influence of dress upon a woman. Harriet wore a frock of the palest lemon colour, cut quite plain, but perfect in every line and pleat and fold, and finished off at the throat with some rare lace, caught up here and there with tiny diamond pins.

"By Jove! what a beautiful girl!" was Mr. Pennell's inward ejaculation as he saw her drawing nearer the spot where he stood. It was strange that his first judgment of Harriet Brandt should have been the same as that of his cousin, Ralph Pullen, but it only proves from what a different standpoint men and women judge of beauty. As Harriet walked over the grass, Anthony Pennell noted each line of her swaying figure—each tint of her refined face—with the pretty little hands hanging by her side, and the slumberous depths of her magnificent eyes. He did not, for one moment, associate her with the idea which he had formed of the West Indian heiress who was bent on capturing his cousin Ralph. He concluded she was another young friend who might be partaking of the Baroness's hospitality. He bowed low as she entered through the open French window looking as a Georgian or Cashmerian *houri* might have looked, he thought, if clad in the robes of civilization. Harriet bowed in return, and said timidly,

"I am so sorry that Madame Gobelli is not here to receive you, but she will not keep you waiting more than a few minutes, I am sure. She particularly said that she would not be later than five o'clock."

"She has left a very charming substitute in her place," replied Pennell, with another bow.

"I believe you have come to see the china," continued Harriet, "I do not know much about it myself, but Miss Wynward will be here in a minute, and she knows the name of every piece, and where it came from!"

"That will be eminently satisfactory," rejoined Anthony Pennell, but I happen to be a connoisseur in such things myself. I have one or two charming bits of old Sevres and Majolica in my chambers, which I think the Baroness would like to see if she will honour me with a visit to my little place. A lonely bachelor like myself must take up some hobby, you know, to fill his life, and mine happens to be china. Madame Gobelli appears to have some lovely Chelsea there. I would like to steal one or two of those groups on the cabinet. Will you hold the door open for me, whilst I run away with them?"

At this sally, Harriet laughed, and Mr. Pennell thought she looked even handsomer when she laughed, than when she was pensive.

"Here is the tea!" she cried nervously, as Miss Wynward appeared with the tray. "O! Miss Wynward, surely *Madame* cannot be much longer now! Have you looked down the road to see if she is coming?"

"The carriage has just turned into the stable yard," replied Miss Wynward, and in another minute, the doorway was filled with the ample proportions of the Baroness.

"'Olloa! Mr. Pennell, and so you've stolen a march upon me!" was her first greeting, "'ow are you?" extending her enormous hand, 'ave you been looking at the china? Wait till I've 'ad my tea; I'll shew you one or two bits that'll make your mouth water! It's my 'obby! I used to save my pocket money when I was a little gal to buy china. I remember my grandfather, the Dook of—but there, I 'aven't known you long enough to let you into family secrets. Let's 'ave our tea and talk afterwards! I 'ope 'Arriet "as entertained you well!"

"This young lady—" commenced Anthony Pennell, interrogatively.

"To be sure, Miss 'Arriet Brandt! 'Asn't she introduced 'erself to you? She's like a daughter of the 'ouse to us! We look upon 'er as one of our own, Gustave and me! Miss Brandt from Jamaica! And she knew your cousin, Captain Pullen, too, at Heyst, we all did, and we're dying to 'ear what 'as become of 'im, for 'e's never shewn 'is face at the Red 'Ouse!"

The murder was out now, and Harriet waited tremblingly for the result! What did Mr. Pennell know? What would he say?

But Mr. Pennell said nothing—he was too much startled to speak. *This,* Harriet Brandt—this lovely girl, the quadroon of whom both Doctor Phillips and Mrs. Pullen had spoken so disparagingly?—of whom they had said that she was not fit to be the wife of any decent man? O! they must be fools and blind—or he was dreaming! The Baroness was not slow to see the look upon his face and to interpret it rightly.

"Are you surprised? You needn't look so incredulous! I give you my word that this is 'Arriet Brandt—the same young lady that knew Mrs. Pullen and her brother-in-law and Miss Leyton over at Heyst. What sort of a character 'ave they been giving 'er be'ind 'er back?"

"Indeed, I assure you, *Madame*—" commenced Mr. Pennell, deprecatingly.

"You needn't take the trouble to tell any tarradiddles about it! I can see it in your face! I didn't think much of that cousin of yours from the beginning; 'e's got a shifty sort of look, and as for that cold bit of goods, Miss Leyton, well, all I say is, God 'elp the man that marries 'er, for she's enough to freeze the sun himself! But I liked Mrs. Pullen well enough, and I was sorry to 'ear that she 'ad lost 'er baby, for she was quite wrapt up in it! But I daresay she'll soon 'ave another!''

Without feeling it incumbent on him to enter into an argument as to the probability of the Baroness's last suggestion, Anthony Pennell was glad of the digression, as it gave him an opportunity of slurring over the dangerous subject of Ralph Pullen's character.

"The loss of her child was a very great blow to my poor cousin," he replied, "and she is still suffering from it, bitterly. Else, I have no doubt that you would have seen something of her—and the others," he added in a lower tone. After a slight interval, he ventured to raise his eyes and see how the girl opposite to him, had taken what was said, but it did not appear to have made much impression on her—she was, on the contrary, gazing at him with that magnetic glance of hers as though she wanted to read into his very soul.

"Don't go and say that I want to see 'em," said the Baroness, as having devoured enough cake and bread and butter to feed an ordinary person for a day, she rose and led the way into another room. "I don't want to see anybody at the Red 'Ouse that doesn't want to come, and I 'aven't expected the ladies. But as for Captain Pullen, 'oo made an engagement to follow our party to Brussels, and then never took the trouble to write a line to excuse 'imself for breaking 'is word, why, I say''e's a jerry sneak, and you may tell 'im so if you like! *We* didn't want 'im. 'E proposed to come 'imself, and I engaged 'is room and everything, and then 'e skedaddled without a word, and I call it beastly be'aviour. You mustn't mind my plain speaking, Mr. Pennell. I always say what I think! And I would like to break my stick over Captain Pullen's back and that's the truth."

They were walking along the passage now, on their way to the Baron's library—the Baroness in front with her hand leaning heavily on Pennell's shoulder, and Harriet lingering a little behind. Anthony Pennell pondered a while before he replied. Was this the time to announce Ralph's intended marriage. How would the girl behind them take it?

He turned slightly and looked at her face as the thought passed through his mind. Somehow the eyes that met his reassured him. He began to think it must be a mistake—that she did not care for Ralph as much as Mrs. Pullen had supposed—that she was only offended perhaps (as her hostess evidently was) by the curt and uncivil manner in which he had treated them both. So he replied,

"I have not the slightest excuse to make for my cousin's conduct,

144

Madame Gobelli. It appears to me that he has treated you with very scant civility, and he ought to be ashamed of himself. But as you know, his little niece's death was very sudden and unexpected, and the least he could do, was to escort his sister-in-law and Miss Leyton back to England, and since then—"

"Well! and what since then?" demanded the Baroness, sharply.

"Lord Walthamstowe and he have come to an arrangement," said Pennell, speaking very slowly, "that his marriage with Miss Elinor Leyton shall take place sooner than was at first intended. The Limerick Rangers are under orders for foreign service, and Captain Pullen naturally wishes to take his wife out with him, and though, of course, all this is no excuse for his omitting to write you a letter, the necessary preparations and the consequent excitement *may* have put his duty out of his head. Of course," he continued, "you know that Ralph is engaged to marry Miss Leyton?"

"I 'eard something of it," replied the Baroness reluctantly, "but one never knows what is true and what is not. Anyway, Captain Pullen didn't give out the news"imself! 'E seemed 'appy enough without Miss Leyton, didn't 'e, 'Arriet?"

But turning round to emphasize her words, she found that Harriet had not followed them into the library. Whereupon she became confidential.

"To tell you the truth, Mr. Pennell," she continued, "'e just be'aved like a scoundrel to our little 'Arriet there. 'E ran after the gal all day, and spent all 'is evenings in our private sitting-room, gazing at 'er as if 'e would eat 'er, whilst she sang and played to 'im. 'E never said a word about marrying Miss Leyton. It was all 'Ally, 'Ally, 'Ally' with 'im. And if the gal 'adn't been a deal too clever for 'im, and wise enough to see what a vain zany 'e is, she might 'ave broken 'er 'eart over it. The conceited jackanapes!"

"But she has not fretted," said Anthony Pennell eagerly.

"Not she! I wouldn't let 'er! She's meat for Captain Pullen's master! A gal with fifteen 'undred a year in 'er own 'ands, and with a pair of eyes like that! O! no! 'Arriet can pick up a 'usband worth two of your cousin any day!

"I should think so indeed," replied Mr. Pennell fervently, "I have heard Mrs. Pullen mention Miss Brandt, but she did not prepare me for meeting so beautiful a girl. But I can hardly wonder at my cousin running away from her, Madame Gobelli. Knowing himself to be already engaged, Miss Brandt must have proved a most dangerous companion. Perhaps he found his heart was no longer under his own control, and thought discretion the better part of valour. You must try and look upon his conduct in the best light you can!"

"O! well! it don't signify much any way, for 'e's no miss at the Red 'Ouse, I can tell you, and 'Arriet could marry tomorrow if she chose, and to a man worthy of 'er. But now you must look at my Spode."

She walked up to a tall cabinet at one end of the room, which was piled with china, and took up a fragile piece in her hands.

"Do you see that?" she said, turning up the plate and shewing the mark upon the bottom, "there it is, you see! There's the M. These five pieces are said to be the oldest in existence. And here's a cup of Limoges. And that's Majolica. Do you know the marks of Majolica. They're some of the rarest known! A cross on a shield. The first real bit of china I ever possessed was a Strasbourg. Have you ever seen any Dutch Pottery—marked with an A.P.? I picked that up at an old Jew's shop in the market in Naples. And this Capo di Monte strange to say, in a back alley in Brighton. There's nothing I like better than to grub about back slums and look for something good. Some of my best pieces 'ave come out of pawnbrokers' shops. That plate you're looking at, is old Flemish—more than two 'undred years, I believe! It came out of the rag market at Bruges. There used to be first rate pickings to be 'ad at Bruges and Ghent and in Antwerp some years ago, but the English 'ave pretty well cleared 'em out."

"I never saw a better private collection, Madame Gobelli," said Anthony Pennell, as he gloated over the delicate morsels of Sevres and Limoges and Strasbourg. "The Baron should have had an old curiosity and bric-a-brac establishment, instead of anything so prosaic as boots and shoes."

"O! I couldn't 'ave 'ad it!" exclaimed the Baroness, "it would 'ave gone to my 'eart to sell a good bargain when I 'ad made it! My cups and saucers and plates and teapots are like children to me, and if I thought my Bobby would sell 'em when I was gone, I believe I should rise from my grave and whack 'im."

The woman became almost womanly as her eyes rested lovingly on her art treasures. It seemed incongruous to Pennell, to watch her huge coarse hands, with their thick stumpy fingers and broad chestnut nails, fingering the delicate fabric with apparent carelessness. Cup after cup and vase and plate she almost tossed over each other, as she pushed some away to make room for others, and piled them up on the top of one another, until he trembled lest they should all come toppling down together.

"You are more used to handle these treasures than I am," he remarked presently, "I should be too much afraid of smashing something, to move them so quickly as you do."

"I never broke a bit of china in my life," returned the Baroness energetically. "I've broken a stick over a man's back, more than once, but never 'ad an accident with my plates and dishes. 'Ow do you account for that?"

"You must have a flow of good luck!" said Mr. Pennell, "I am so fearful for mine that I keep all the best under glass!"

"I 'ave more friends to 'elp me than perhaps you know of," said the Baroness, mysteriously, "but it ain't only that! I never let a servant dust it! Miss Wynward does it, but she's too much afraid to do more than touch 'em with the tip of her feather brush. They come to me sometimes and complain that the china is dirty. 'Let it be dirty' I say, *'that* won't break it, but if you clean it, you will!' Ha! ha! ha!"

At that moment Harriet Brandt entered the room, moving sinuously across the carpet as a snake might glide to its lair. Anthony Pennell could not take his eyes off that gliding walk of hers. It seemed to him the very essence of grace. It distracted all his attention from the china.

"The Baron has just come in," observed Harriet to her hostess.

"O! well! come along and leave the rest of the china till after dinner," said Madame Gobelli. "Gustave likes to 'ave 'is dinner as soon as 'e comes 'ome."

She thrust her arm through that of Anthony Pennell, and conducted him to the dining-room, where the Baron (without having observed the ceremony of changing his coat or boots) was already seated just as he had come in, at the table. He gave a curt nod to the visitor as Mr. Pennell's name was mentioned to him, and followed it up immediately by a query whether he would take fish. Mr. Pennell sat out the meal with increasing amazement at every course. He who was accustomed, in consequence of his popularity, to sit at the tables of some of the highest in the land, could liken this one to nothing but a farmhouse dinner.

Course succeeded course, in rapid succession, and there was no particular fault to find with anything, but the utter want of ceremony—the mingling of well-known and aristocratic names with the boot and shoe trade—and the way in which the Baron and Baroness ate and drank, filled him with surprise. The climax was reached when Mr. Milliken, who was late for dinner, entered the room, and his hostess, before introducing him to the stranger, saluted him with a resounding smack on either cheek.

Pennell thought it might be his turn next, and shuddered. But the wine flowed freely, and the Baroness, being in an undoubted good humour, the hospitality was unlimited. After dinner, the Baron having settled to sleep in an armchair, Madame Gobelli proposed that the party should amuse themselves with a game of "Hunt the slippers."

She was robed in an expensive satin dress, but she threw herself down on the ground with a resounding thump, and thrusting two enormous feet into view, offered her slipper as an inducement to commence the game.

Pennell stood aloof, battling to restrain his laughter at the comical sight before him. The Baroness's foot from which she had taken the shoe, was garbed in a black woollen stocking full of holes, which displayed a set of bare toes. But apparently quite unaware of the ludicrous object she presented, she kept on calling out for Harriet Brandt and Miss Wynward to come and complete the circle at which only Mr. Milliken and herself were seated. But Harriet shrunk backwards and refused to play.

"No! indeed, *Madame*, I cannot. I do not know your English games!" she pleaded.

"Come on, we'll teach you!" screamed Madame Gobelli, "'ere's Milliken,"e knows all about it, don't you, Milliken? 'E knows 'ow to look for the slipper under the gal's petticoats. You come 'ere, 'Arriet, and sit next me, and Mr. Pennell shall be the first to 'unt. Come on!"

But Miss Brandt would not "come on". She remained seated, and declared that she was too tired to play and did not care for *les jeux innocens,* and she had a headache, and anything and everything, before she would comply with the outrageous request preferred to her.

Madame Gobelli grumbled at her idleness and called her disobliging, but Anthony admired the girl for her steadfast refusal. He did not like to see her in the familiar society of such a woman as the Baroness—he would have liked still less to see her engaged in such a boisterous and unseemly game as "Hunt the slipper."

He took the opportunity of saying, "Since you are disinclined for such an energetic game, Miss Brandt, perhaps you would oblige me by singing a song! I should so much like to hear the *mandolin.* Mrs. Pullen has spoken to me of your efficiency on it."

"If Madame Gobelli wishes it, I have no objection," replied Harriet.

"O! well! if you are all going to be so disagreeable as not to play a good game," said the Baroness, as Mr. Milliken pulled her on her feet again, "'Arriet may as well sing to us! But a good romp first wouldn't 'ave done us any 'arm!"

She adjourned rather sulkily to a distant sofa with Mr. Milliken, where they entertained each other whilst Harriet tuned her *mandolin* and presently let her rich voice burst forth in the strains of "*Oh! ma Charmante.*" Anthony Pennell was enchanted. He had a passion for music, and it appealed more powerfully to him, than anything else. He sat in rapt attention until Harriet's voice had died away, and then he implored her to sing another song.

"You cannot tell what it is for me, who care more for music than for anything else in this world, to hear a voice like yours. Why! you will create a perfect furore when you go into society. You could make your fortune on the stage, but I know you have no need of that!"

"O! one never knows what one may have need of," said Harriet gaily, as she commenced, "*Dormez ma belle*" and sang it to perfection.

"You must have had a very talented singing master," observed Pennell when the second song was finished.

"Indeed no! My only instructress was a nun in the Ursuline Convent in Jamaica. But I always loved it," said the girl, as she ran over the strings of her *mandolin* in a merry little *tarantelle*, which made everyone in the room feel as if they had been bitten by the spider from which it took its name, and wanted above all other things to dance.

How Pennell revelled in the music and the performer! How he longed to hear from her own lips that Ralph's treatment had left no ill effects behind it.

When she had ceased playing, he drew nearer to her, and under the cover of the Baroness's conversation with Mr. Milliken and the Baron's snores, they managed to exchange a few words.

"How can I ever thank you enough for the treat you have given me!" he began.

"I am very glad that you liked it!"

"I was not prepared to hear such rare talent! My experience of young ladies' playing and singing has not hitherto been happy. But you have great genius. Did you ever sing to Mrs. Pullen whilst in Heyst?"

"Once or twice."

"And to my cousin, Ralph Pullen?"

"Yes!"

"I cannot understand his having treated the Baroness with such scant courtesy. And you also, who had been kind enough to allow him to enjoy your society. You would not have found me so ungrateful. But you have heard doubtless that he is going to be married shortly!"

"Yes! I have heard it!"

"And that has, I suppose, put everything else out of his head! Perhaps it may be as well, especially for his future wife. There are some things which are dangerous for men to remember—such as your lovely voice, for example!"

"Do you think so?" Harriet fixed her dark eyes on him, as she put the question.

"I am sure it will be dangerous for me, unless you will give me leave to come and hear it again. I shall not be able to sleep for thinking of it. Do you think the Baroness will be so good as to enrol me as a visitor to the house?"

"You had better ask her!"

"And if she consents, will you sing to me sometimes?"

"I am always singing or playing! There is nothing else to do here. The Baron and Baroness are almost always out, and I have no company but that of Bobby and Miss Wynward. It is terribly dull, I can tell you. I am longing to get away, but I do not know where to go."

"Have you no friends in England?"

"Not one, except Mr. Tarver, who is my solicitor!"

"That sounds very grim. If you will let me count myself amongst your friends, I shall be so grateful."

"I should like it very much! I am not so ignorant as not to have heard your name and to know that you are a celebrated man. But I am afraid I shall prove a very stupid friend for you."

"I have no such fear, and if I may come and see you sometimes, I shall count myself a very happy man."

"I am generally alone in the afternoons," replied Miss Brandt, sophistically.

In another minute Mr. Pennell was saying goodnight to his hostess and asking her permission to repeat his visit at some future time.

"And if you and Miss Brandt would so far honour me, Madame Gobelli, as to come and have a little lunch at my chambers in Piccadilly, I shall feel myself only too much indebted to you. Perhaps we might arrange a matinee or a concert for the same afternoon, if it would please you? Will you let me know? And pray fix as early a date as possible. And I may really avail myself of your kind permission to come and see you again. You may be sure that I shall not forget to do so. Goodnight! Goodnight, Baron! Goodnight, Miss Brandt!" and with a nod to Mr. Milliken he was gone.

"'Ain't 'e a nice fellow? Worth two of that conceited jackanapes 'is cousin," remarked the Baroness as he disappeared, "what do you think of 'im 'Arriet?"

"O! he is well enough," replied Miss Brandt with a yawn, as she prepared also to take her departure, "he is taller and broader and stronger looking than Captain Pullen—and he must be very clever into the bargain."

"And 'e never said a word about 'is books," exclaimed Madame Gobelli, "only fancy!"

"No! he never said a word about his books," echoed Harriet.

CHAPTER 14

Anthony Pennell had promised to let Margaret Pullen hear the result of his visit to the Red House, and as he entered her presence on the following evening, she saluted him with the queries,

"Well! have you been there? Have you seen her?"

To which he answered soberly,

"Yes! I have been there and I have seen her!"

"And what do you think of her? What did she say? I hope she was not rude to you!"

"My dear Mrs. Pullen," said Pennell, as he seated himself, and prepared for a long talk, "you must let me say in the first place, that I should never have recognised Miss Brandt from your description of her! You led me to expect a gauche schoolgirl, a half-tamed savage, or a juvenile virago. And I am bound to say that she struck me as belonging to none of the species. I sent your note of introduction to Madame Gobelli, and received a very polite invitation in return, in accordance with which I dined at the Red House yesterday."

"You *dined* there!" exclaimed Margaret with renewed interest. "O! do tell me all about it, from the very beginning. What do you think of that dreadful woman, the Baroness, and her little humpty Baron, and did you tell Miss Brandt of Ralph's impending marriage?"

"My dear lady, one question at a time, if you please. In the first place, I arrived there rather sooner than I was expected, and Madame Gobelli had not returned from her afternoon drive, but Miss Harriet Brandt did the honours of the tea-table in a very efficient manner, and

151

with as much composure and dignity as if she had been a duchess. We had a very pleasant time together until the Baroness burst in upon us!"

'Are you chaffing me?" asked Margaret, incredulously. "What do you really think of her?"

"I think she is, without exception, the most perfectly beautiful woman I have ever seen!"

"*What!*" exclaimed his companion. She had thrown herself back in her armchair, and was regarding him as if he were perpetrating some mysterious joke, which she did not understand. "How extraordinary; how very extraordinary!" she exclaimed at length, "that is the very thing that Ralph said of her when they first met."

"But why extraordinary? There are few men who would not endorse the opinion. Miss Brandt possesses the kind of beauty that appeals to the senses of animal creatures like ourselves. She has a far more dangerous quality than that of mere regularity of feature. She attracts without knowing it. She is a mass of magnetism."

"O! do go on, Mr. Pennell! Tell me how she received the news you went to break to her!"

"I never broke it at all. There was no need to do so. Miss Brandt alluded to the magnificent Captain Pullen's marriage with the greatest nonchalance. She evidently estimates him at his true value, and does not consider him worth troubling her head about!"

"You astonish me! But how are we to account then for the attitude she assumed towards Miss Leyton, and the boast she made of Ralph's attentions to her?"

"Bravado, most likely! Miss Leyton goes to the Red House all aflame, like an angry turkey cock, and accuses Miss Brandt of having robbed her of her lover, and what would you have the girl do? Not cry Peccavi, surely and lower her womanhood? She had but one course— to brave it out. Besides, you have heard only one side of the question, remember! I can imagine Miss Leyton being very 'nasty' if she liked!"

"You forget the letters which Miss Brandt wrote to Ralph and which were found in his empty grate at Richmond!"

"I do not! I remember them as only another proof of how unworthy he is of the confidence of any woman."

"Really, Mr. Pennell, you seem to be all on Miss Brandt's side!"

"I am, and for this reason. If your ideas concerning her are correct, she displayed a large amount of fortitude whilst speaking of your brother-in-law yesterday. But my own belief is, that you are mistaken—that Miss Brandt is too clever for Ralph, or any of you— and that she cares no more for him in that way than you do. She considers doubtless that he has behaved in a most ungentlemanly manner towards them all, and so do I. I did not know what excuse to make for Ralph! I was ashamed to own him as a relation."

"Harriet Brandt *did* then confide her supposed wrongs to you!"

"Not at all! When she mentioned Ralph's name, it was like that of any other acquaintance. But when she was out of the room, the Baroness told me that he had behaved like a scoundrel to the girl—that he had never confided the fact of his engagement to her, but run after her on every occasion, and then after having promised to join their party in Brussels, and asked Madame Gobelli to engage his room for him, he left for England without even sending her a line of apology, nor has he taken the least notice of them since!"

"Ah! but you know the reason of his sudden departure!" cried Margaret, her soft eyes welling over with tears.

"My dear Mrs. Pullen," said Anthony Pennell, sympathetically, "even at that sad moment, Ralph might have sent a telegram, or scratched a line of apology. We have to attend to such little courtesies, you know, even if our hearts are breaking! And how can you excuse his not having called on them, or written since? No wonder the Baroness is angry. She did not restrain her tongue in speaking of him yesterday. She said she never wished to see his face again."

"Does she know that Elinor went to the Red House?"

"I think not! There was no mention of her name!"

"Then I suppose we may at all events consider the affair *une chose finie?*"

"I hope so, sincerely! I should not advise Master Ralph to shew his face at the Red House again. The Baroness said she longed to lay her stick across his back, and I believe she is quite capable of doing so!"

"O! indeed she is," replied Margaret, smiling, "we heard a great many stories of her valour in that respect from Madame Lamont, the landlady of the Lion d'Or. Has Miss Brandt taken up her residence altogether with Madame Gobelli?"

"I think not! She told me her life there was very dull, and she should like to change it."

"She is in a most unfortunate position for a young girl," remarked Margaret, "left parentless, with money at her command, and in a strange country! And with the strange stigma attached to her birth—"

"I don't believe in stigmas being attached to one's birth," returned Pennell hastily, "the only stigmas worth thinking about, are those we bring upon ourselves by our misconduct—such a one, for instance, as my cousin Ralph has done with regard to Miss Brandt! I would rather be in her shoes than his. Ralph thinks, perhaps, that being a stranger and friendless she is a fair game—"

"Who is that, taking my name in vain?" interrupted a languid voice at the open door, as Captain Pullen advanced into the room.

Margaret Pullen started and grew very red at being detected in discussing her brother-in-law's actions, but Anthony Pennell, who was always ruffled by his cousin's affected walk and drawl, blurted the truth right out.

"*I* was," he replied, hardly touching the hand which Captain Pullen extended to him, "I was just telling Mrs. Pullen of the high estimation in which your name is held at the Red House!"

It was now Ralph's turn to grow red. His fair face flushed from chin to brow, as he repeated,

"The Red House! what Red House?"

"Did they not mention the name to you? I mean the residence of Madame Gobelli, I was dining there yesterday."

"Dining there, were you? By Jove! I didn't know you were acquainted with the woman. Isn't she a queer old party? Baroness Boots, eh? Fancy, your knowing them! I thought you were a cut above that, Anthony!"

"If the Gobellis were good enough for you to be intimate with in Heyst, I suppose they are good enough for me to dine with in London, Ralph! I did not know until last evening, however, that you had left them to pay for your rooms in Brussels, or I would have taken the money over with me to defray the debt."

Ralph had seated himself by this time, but he looked very uneasy and as if he wished he had not come.

"Did the old girl engage rooms for me?" he stammered. "Well! you know the reason I could not go to Brussels, but of course if I had known that she had gone to any expense for me, I would have repaid her. Did she tell you of it herself?" he added, rather anxiously.

"Yes! and a good many more things beside. As you have happened to come in whilst we are on the question, I had better make a clean breast of it. Perhaps you have heard that Miss Leyton has been to the Red House and had an interview with Miss Brandt!"

"Yes! I've just come from Richmond, where we've had a jolly row over it," grumbled Ralph, pulling his moustaches.

"Your family all felt that that sort of thing could not go on—that it must end one way or the other, and therefore I went to the Red House, ostensibly to view Madame Gobelli's collection of china, but in reality to ascertain what view of the matter she and Miss Brandt took—and to undeceive them as to your being in a position to pursue your intimacy with the young lady any further."

"And what the devil business have you to meddle in my private affairs?" demanded Captain Pullen rousing himself.

"Because, unfortunately, your mother happened to be my father's sister," replied Pennell sternly, "and the scrapes you get in harm me more than they do yourself! One officer more or less, who gets into a scrape with women, goes pretty well unnoticed, but I have attained a position in which I cannot afford to have my relations' names bandied about as having behaved in a manner unbecoming gentlemen."

"Who dares to say that of me?" cried Ralph angrily.

"Everybody who knows of the attention you paid Miss Brandt in Heyst," replied Anthony Pennell, boldly, "and without telling her that you were already engaged to be married. I do not wonder at Miss Leyton being angry about it! I only wonder she consents to have any more to do with you in the circumstances."

"O! we've settled all that!" said Ralph, testily, "we had the whole matter out at Richmond this afternoon, and I've promised to be a good boy for the future, and never speak to a pretty woman again! You need not wonder any more about Elinor! She is only glad enough to get me back at any price!"

"Yes? And what about Miss Brandt?" enquired Pennell.

"Is she worrying about this affair?" asked Captain Pullen, quickly.

"Not a bit! I think she estimates your attentions at their true value. I was alluding to the opinion she and her friends must have formed of your character as an officer and a gentleman."

"O! I'll soon set all that right! I'll run over to the Red House and see the old girl, if you two will promise not to tell Elinor!"

"I should not advise you to do that! I am afraid you might get a warm reception. I think Madame Gobelli is quite capable of having you soused in the horse-pond. You would think the same if you had heard the names she called you yesterday."

"What did she call me?"

"Everything she could think of. She considers you have behaved not only in a most ungentlemanly manner towards her, but in a most dishonourable one to Miss Brandt. She particularly told me to tell you that she never wished to see your face again."

"Damn her!" exclaimed Captain Pullen, wrathfully, "and all her boots and shoes into the bargain. A vulgar, coarse old tradesman's wife! How dare she——"

"Stop a minute Ralph! The Baroness's status in society makes no difference in this matter. You know perfectly well that you did wrong. Let us have no more discussion of the subject."

Captain Pullen leaned back sulkily in his chair. "Well! if I *did* flirt a little bit more than was prudent with an uncommonly distracting little girl," he muttered presently, "I am sure I have had to pay for it! Lord Walthamstowe insists that if I do not marry Elinor before the Rangers start for Malta the engagement shall be broken off, so I suppose I must do it! But it is a doosid nuisance to be tied up at five-and-twenty, before one has half seen life! What the dickens I am to do with her when I've got her, I'm sure I don't know!"

"O! you will find married life very charming when you're used to it!" said Pennell consolingly, "and Miss Leyton is everything a fellow could wish for in a wife! Only you must give up flirting, my boy, or if I mistake not, you'll find you've caught a tartar!"

"I expect to have to give up everything," said the other with a sour mouth.

As soon as he perceived a favourable opportunity, Anthony Pennell rose to take his leave. He did not wish to quarrel with Ralph Pullen about a girl whom he had only seen once, at the same time he feared for his own self-control, if his cousin continued to mention the matter in so nonchalant a manner. Pennell had always despised Captain Pullen for his easy conceit with regard to women, and it seemed to him to have grown more detestably contemptible than before. He was anxious therefore to quit the scene of action. But, to his annoyance, when he bade Margaret good-evening, Ralph also rose and expressed his wish to walk with him in the direction of his chambers.

"I suppose you couldn't put me up for the night, old chappie!" he said with his most languid air.

"Decidedly not!" replied Pennell. "I have only my own bedroom, and I've no intention of your sharing it. Why do you not go back to Richmond, or put up at an hotel?"

"Doosid inhospitable!" remarked Captain Pullen, with a faded smile.

"Sorry you think so, but a man cannot give what he does not possess. You had better stay and keep your sister-in-law company for a little while. I have work to do and am going straight home!"

"All right! I'll walk with you a little way," persisted Ralph, and the two young men left the house together.

As soon as they found themselves in the street, Captain Pullen attacked his cousin, eagerly.

"I say, Pennell, what is the exact direction of the Red House?"

"Why do you want to know?" enquired his companion.

"Because I feel that I owe the Baroness a visit. I acknowledge that I was wrong not to write and make my apologies, but you must know what it is—with a deuce of a lot of women to look after, and the whole gang crying their eyes out, and everything thrown on my shoulders, coffin, funeral, taking them over from Heyst to England, and all—it was enough to drive everything else out of a man's head. You must acknowledge that."

"You owe no excuses to me, Pullen, neither do I quite believe in them. You have had plenty of time since to remedy your negligence, even if you did forget to be courteous at the moment!"

"I know that, and you're quite right about the other thing. I had more reasons than one for letting the matter drop. You are a man and I can tell you with impunity what would set the women tearing my eyes out. I *did* flirt a bit with Harriet Brandt, perhaps more than was quite prudent in the circumstances—"

"You mean the circumstance of your engagement to Miss Leyton?"

"Yes and No! If I had been free, it would have been all the same— perhaps worse, for I should not have had a loophole of escape. For you see Miss Brandt is not the sort of girl that any man could marry."

"Why not?" demanded Pennell with some asperity.

"O! because—well! you should hear old Phillips talk of her and her parents. They were the most awful people, and she has black blood in her, her mother was a half-caste, so you see it would be impossible for any man in my position to think of marrying her! One might get a piebald son and heir! Ha! ha! ha! But putting all that aside, she is one of the demndest fascinating little women I ever came across—you would say so too, if you had seen as much of her as I did—I can't tell you what it is exactly, but she has a drawing way about her, that pulls a fellow into the net before he knows what he is about. And her voice, by Jove!—have you heard her sing?"

"I have, but that has nothing to do that I can see with the subject under discussion. You, an engaged man, who had no more right to philander with a girl, than if you had been married, appear to me to have followed this young lady about and paid her attentions, which were, to say the least of them, compromising, never announcing the fact, meanwhile, that you were bound to Miss Leyton. After which, you left her, without a word of explanation, to think what she chose of your conduct. And now you wish to see her again, in order to apologise. Am I right?"

"Pretty well, only you make such a serious matter out of a little fun!"

"Well, then, I repeat that if you are wise, you will save yourself the trouble, Ralph! Miss Brandt is happily too sensible to have been taken in by your pretence of making love to her. She estimates you at your true value. She knows that you are engaged to Elinor Leyton—that you were engaged all the time she knew you—and, I think, she rather pities Miss Leyton for being engaged to you!"

But this point of view had never presented itself before to the inflated vanity of Ralph Pullen.

"Pities her!" he exclaimed, "the devil!"

"I daresay it seems incomprehensible to you that any woman should not be thankful to accept at your hands the crumbs that may fall from another's table, but with regard to Miss Brandt, I assure you it is true! And even were it otherwise, I am certain Madame Gobelli would not admit you to her house. You know the sort of person she is! She can be very violent if she chooses, and the names she called you yesterday, were not pretty ones. I had much trouble, as your relative, to stand by and listen to them quietly. Yet I could not say that they were undeserved!"

"O well! I daresay!" returned Ralph, impatiently, "let us allow, for the sake of argument, that you are right, and that I behaved like a brute! The matter lies only between Hally Brandt and myself. The old woman has nothing to do with it! She never met the girl till she went to Heyst. What I want to do is to see Hally again and make my peace with her! You know how easily women are won over. A pretty present—a few kisses and excuses,—a few tears—and the thing is done. I shouldn't like to leave England without making my peace with the little girl. Couldn't you get her to come to your chambers, and let me meet her there? Then the Baroness need know nothing about it!"

"I thought you told us just now, that you had had a reconciliation with Miss Leyton on condition that you were to be a good boy for the future. Does that include a surreptitious meeting with Miss Brandt?"

"I suppose not, but we have to make all sorts of promises where women are concerned. A nice kind of life a man would lead, if he consented to be tied to his wife's apron-strings, and never go anywhere, nor see anyone, of whom she did not approve. I swore to everything she and old Walthamstowe asked me, just for peace's sake,—but if they imagine I'm going to be hampered like that, they must be greater fools than I take them for!"

"You must do as you think right, Pullen, but I am not going to help you to break your word!"

"Tell me where the Red House is! Tell me whereabouts Hally takes her daily walks!" urged Captain Pullen.

"I shall tell you nothing—you must find out for yourself!"

"Well! you are damned particular!" exclaimed his cousin, "one would think this little half-caste was a princess of the Blood Royal. What is she, when all's said and done? The daughter of a *mulatto* and a man who made himself so detested that he was murdered by his own servants—the bastard of a—"

"Stop!" cried Pennell, so vehemently that the passers-by turned their heads to look at him, "I don't believe it, and if it is true, I do not wish to hear it! Miss Brandt may be all that you say—I am not in a position to contradict your assertions—but to me she represents only a friendless and unprotected woman, who has a right to our sympathy and respect."

"A friendless woman!" sneered Captain Pullen, "yes! and a doosid good-looking one into the bargain, eh, my dear fellow, and much of your sympathy and respect she would command if she were ugly and humpbacked. O! I know you, Pennell! It's no use your coming the benevolent Samaritan over me! You have an eye for a jimper waist and a trim ankle as well as most men. But I fancy your interest is rather thrown away in this quarter.

"Miss Brandt has a thorny path before her. She is a young lady who will have her own way, and with the glorious example of the Baroness the way is not likely to be too carefully chosen. To tell the truth, old boy, I ran away because I was afraid of falling into the trap. The girl wishes intensely to be married, and she is not a girl whom men will marry, and so—we need go no further. Only, I should not be surprised if, notwithstanding her fortune and her beauty, we should find Miss Harriet Brandt figuring before long, amongst the free lances of London."

"And you would have done your best to send her there!" replied Anthony Pennell indignantly, as he stopped on the doorstep of his

Piccadilly chambers. "But I am glad to say that your folly has been frustrated this time, and Miss Brandt sees you as you are! Goodnight!" and without further discussion, he turned on his heel and walked upstairs.

"By Jove!" thought Ralph, as he too went on his way, "I believe old Anthony is smitten with the girl himself, though he has only seen her once! That was the most remarkable thing about her—the ease with which she seemed to attract, looking so innocent all the while, and the deadly strength with which she resisted one's efforts to get free again. Perhaps it is as well after all that I should not meet her. I don't believe I could trust myself, only speaking of her seems to have revived the old sensation of being drawn against my will—hypnotised, I suppose the scientists would call it—to be near her, to touch her, to embrace her, until all power of resistance is gone. But I do hope old Anthony is not going to be hypnotised. He's too good for that."

Meanwhile Pennell, having reached his rooms, lighted the gas, threw himself into an armchair, and rested his head upon his hands.

"Poor little girl!" he murmured to himself, "Poor little girl!"

Anthony Pennell was a Socialist in the best and truest sense of the word. He loved his fellow creatures, both high and low, better than he loved himself. He wanted all to share alike—to be equally happy, equally comfortable—to help and be helped, to rest and depend upon one another. He knew that the dream was only a dream— that it would never be fulfilled in his time, nor any other; that some men would be rich and some poor as long as the world lasts, and that what one man can do to alleviate the misery and privation and suffering with which we are surrounded, is very little.

What little Pennell could do, however, to prove that his theories were not mere talk, he did. He made a large income by his popular writings and the greater part of it went to relieve the wants of his humbler friends, not through governors and secretaries and the heads of charitable Societies, but from his own hand to theirs. But his Socialism went further and higher than this.

Money was not the only thing which his fellow creatures required—they wanted love, sympathy, kindness, and consideration—and these he gave also, wherever he found that there was need. He set his face pertinaciously against all scandal and back-biting, and waged a perpetual warfare against the tyranny of men over women; the ill-treatment of children; and the barbarities practised upon dumb animals and all living things. He was a liberal minded man, with a heart

160

large enough and tender enough to belong to a woman—with a horror of cruelty and a great compassion for everything that was incapable of defending itself.

He was always writing in defence of the People, calling the attention of those in authority to their misfortunes; their evil chances; their lack of opportunity; and their patience under tribulation. For this purpose and in order to know them thoroughly, he had gone and lived amongst them; shared their filthy dens in Whitechapel, partaken of their unappetising food in Stratford; and watched them at their labour in Homerton. His figures and his kindly face were well-known in some of the worst and most degraded parts of London, and he could pass anywhere, without fear of a hand being lifted up against him, or an oath called after him in salutation. Anthony Pennell was, in fact, a general lover—a lover of Mankind.

And that is why he leant his head upon his hand as he ejaculated with reference to Harriet Brandt, "Poor little girl."

It seemed so terrible in his eyes that just because she was friendless, and an orphan, just because her parents had been, perhaps, unworthy, just because she had a dark stream mingling with her blood, just because she needed the more sympathy and kindness, the more protection and courtesy, she should be considered fit prey for the sensualist—a fit subject to wipe men's feet upon!

What difference did it make to Harriet Brandt herself, that she was marked with an hereditary taint? Did it render her less beautiful, less attractive, less graceful and accomplished? Were the sins of the fathers ever to be visited upon the children?—was no sympathetic fellow-creature to be found to say, "If it is so, let us forget it! It is not your fault nor mine! Our duty is to make each other's lives as happy as possible and trust the rest to God."

He hoped as he sat there, that before long, Harriet Brandt would find a friend for life, who would never remind her of anything outside her own loveliness and lovable qualities.

Presently he rose, with a sigh, and going to his bookcase drew thence an uncut copy of his last work, *God and the People*. It had been a tremendous success, having already reached the tenth edition. It dealt largely, as its title indicated, with his favourite theory, but it was light and amusing also, full of strong nervous language, and bristling every here and there, with wit—not strained epigrams, such as no Society conversationalists ever tossed backward and forward to each other—but honest, mirth-provoking humour, arising from the humorous side of Pennell's own character, which ever had a good-humoured jest for the oddities and comicalities of everyday life.

He regarded the volume for a moment as though he were considering if it were an offering worthy of its destination, and then he took up a pen and transcribed upon the fly leaf the name of Harriet Brandt—only her name, nothing more.

"She seems intelligent," he thought, "and she may like to read it. Who knows, if there is any fear of the sad destiny which Ralph prophesies for her, whether I may not be happy enough to turn her ideas into a worthier and more wholesome direction. With an independent fortune, how much good might she not accomplish, amongst those less happily situated than herself! But the other idea—No, I will not entertain it for a moment! She is too good, too pure, too beautiful, for so horrible a fate! Poor little girl! Poor, poor little girl!"

Chapter 15

The holiday season being now over, and the less fashionable people returned to Town, Harriet Brandt's curiosity was much excited by the number of visitors who called at the Red House, but were never shewn into the drawing-room. As many as a dozen might arrive in the course of an afternoon and were taken by Miss Wynward straight upstairs to the room where Madame Gobelli and Mr. Milliken so often shut themselves up together. These mysterious visitors were not objects of charity either, but well-dressed men and women, some of whom came in their own carriages, and all of whom appeared to be of the higher class of society. The Baroness had left off going to the factory, also, and stayed at home every day, apparently with the sole reason of being at hand to receive her visitors.

Harriet could not understand it at all, and after having watched two fashionably attired ladies accompanied by a gentleman, ascend the staircase, to Madame Gobelli's room, one afternoon, she ventured to sound Miss Wynward on the subject.

"Who were the ladies who went upstairs just now?" she asked.

"Friends of the Baroness, Miss Brandt!" was the curt reply.

"But why do they not come down to the drawing-room then? What does Madame Gobelli do with them in that little room upstairs? I was passing one day just after someone had entered, and I heard the key turned in the lock. What is all the secrecy about?"

"There is no secrecy on my part, Miss Brandt. You know the position I hold here. When I have shewn the visitors upstairs, according to my Lady's directions, my duty is done!"

"But you must know why they come to see her!"

"I know nothing. If you are curious on the subject, you must ask the Baroness."

But Harriet did not like to do that. The Baroness had become less affectionate to her of late—her fancy was already on the wane—she no longer called the attention of strangers to her young friend as the "daughter of the house"—and Harriet felt the change, though she could scarcely have defined where it exactly lay. She had begun to feel less at home in her hostess's presence, and her high spirit chafed at the alteration in her manner. She realised, as many had done before her, that she had outstayed her welcome. But her curiosity respecting the people who visited Madame Gobelli upstairs was none the less. She confided it to Bobby—poor Bobby who grew whiter and more languid every day—but her playful threat to invade the sacred precincts and find out what the Baroness and her friends were engaged upon, was received by the youth with horror. He trembled as he begged her not to think of such a thing.

"Hally you mustn't, indeed you mustn't! You don't know—you have no idea—what might not happen to you, if you offended Mamma by breaking in upon her privacy. O! don't, pray don't! She can be so terrible at times—I do not know what she might not do or say!"

"My dear Bobby, I was only in fun! I have not the least idea of doing anything so rude. Only, if you think that I am frightened of your Mamma or any other woman, you are very much mistaken. It's all nonsense! No one person can harm another in this world!"

"O! yes, they can—if they have *help*," replied the boy, shaking his head.

"Help! what help? The help of Mr. Milliken, I suppose! I would rather fight him than the Baroness any day—but I fear neither of them."

"O! Hally, you are wrong," said the lad, "you must be careful, indeed you must—for my sake!"

"Why! you silly Bobby, you are actually trembling! However, I promise you I will do nothing rash! And I shall not be here much longer now! Your Mamma is getting tired of me, I can see that plainly enough! She has hardly spoken a word to me for the last two days. I am going to ask Mr. Pennell, to advise me where to find another home!"

"No! no!" cried the lad, clinging to her, "you shall not leave us! Mr.

Pennell shall not take you away! I will kill him first!"

He was getting terribly jealous of Anthony Pennell, but Harriet laughed at his complaints and reproaches, as the emanations of a love-sick schoolboy. She was flattered by his feverish longing for her society, and his outspoken admiration of her beauty, but she did not suppose for one moment, that Bobby was capable of a lasting, or dangerous sentiment.

Mr. Pennell had become a familiar figure at the Red House by this time. His first visit had been speedily succeeded by another, at which he had presented Harriet Brandt with the copy of his book—an attention, which had he known it, flattered her vanity more than any praises of her beauty could have done. A plain woman likes to be told that she is good-looking, a handsome one that she is clever. Harriet Brandt was not unintelligent, on the contrary she had inherited a very fair amount of brains from her scientific father—but no one ever seemed to have found it out, until Anthony Pennell came her way. She was a little tired of being told that she had lovely eyes, and the most fascinating smile, she knew all that by heart, and craved for something new.

Mr. Pennell had supplied the novelty by talking to her as if her intellect were on a level with his own—as if she were perfectly able to understand and sympathise with his quixotic plans for the alleviation of the woes of all mankind—with his Arcadian dreams of Liberty, Equality and Fraternity,—and might help them also, if she chose, not with money only, but by raising her own voice in the Cause of the People. Harriet had never been treated so by any one before, and her ardent, impetuous, passionate nature which had a large amount of gratitude in its composition, fixed itself upon her new friend, with a vehemence which neither of them would find it easy to overcome—or to disentangle themselves from.

Her love (eager to repair the void left by the desertion of Captain Pullen) had poured itself, by means of looks and sighs and little timid, tender touches upon Anthony Pennell like a mountain torrent that had burst its bounds, and he had been responsive—he had opened his arms to receive the flood, actuated not only by the admiration which he had conceived for her from the first, but by the intense, yearning pity which her loneliness and friendlessness had evoked in his generous compassionate nature. In fact they were desperately in love with each other, and Harriet was expecting each time he came, to hear Anthony Pennell say that he could no longer live without her. And Bobby looked on from a little distance—and suffered. The next time that Mr. Pennell came to see her, Harriet confided to him the mystery of the upstairs room, and asked his opinion as to what it could possibly mean.

"Perhaps they are people connected with the boot trade," suggested Anthony jestingly, "does *Madame* keep a stock of boots and shoes up there, do you think?"

"O! no! Mr. Pennell, you must not joke about it! This is something serious! Poor Bobby grew as white as a sheet when I proposed to make a raid upon the room someday and discover the mystery, and said that his mother was a terrible woman, and able to do me great harm if I offended her!"

"I quite agree with Bobby in his estimate of his Mamma being a terrible woman," replied Mr. Pennell. "but it is all nonsense about her being able to harm you! I should soon see about that!"

"What would you do?" asked Harriet, with downcast eyes.

"What would I not do to save you from anything disagreeable, let alone anything dangerous. But the Baroness is too fond of you, surely, to do you any harm!"

Harriet pursed up her lips.

"I am not so sure about her being fond of me, Mr. Pennell! She used to profess to be, I know, but lately her manner has very much altered. She will pass half a day without speaking a word to me, and they have cut off wine and champagne and everything nice from the dinner table. I declare the meals here are sometimes not fit to eat. And I believe they grudge me the little I consider worthy my attention."

"But why do you stay here, if you fancy you are not welcome?" asked Pennell, earnestly, "you are not dependent on these people or their hospitality."

"But where am I to go?" said the girl, "I know no one in London, and Miss Wynward says that I am too young to live at an hotel by myself!"

"Miss Wynward is quite right! You are far too young and too beautiful. You don't know what wicked men and women there are in the world, who would delight in fleecing an innocent lamb like you. But I can soon find you a home where you could stay in respectability and comfort, until—until—"

"Until *what,*" asked Harriet, with apparent ingenuousness, for she knew well enough what was coming.

They were seated on one of those little couches made expressly for conversation, where a couple can sit back to back, with their faces turned to one another. Harriet half raised her slumberous black eyes as she put the question, and met the fire in his own. He stretched out his arms and caught her round the waist.

"Hally! Hally! you know—there is no need for me to tell you! Will you come home to me, dearest? Don't ever say that you are friendless again! Here is your friend and your lover and your devoted slave for ever! My darling—my beautiful Hally, say you will be my wife—and make me the very happiest man in all the world!"

She did not shrink from his warm wooing—that was not her nature! Her eyes waked up and flashed fire, responsive to his own; she let her head rest on his shoulder, and turned her lips upwards eagerly to meet his kiss, she cooed her love into his ear, and clasped him tightly round the neck as if she would never let him go.

"I love you—I love you," she kept on murmuring, "I have loved you from the very first!"

"O! Hally, how happy it makes me to hear you say so," he replied, "how few women have the honesty and courage to avow their love as you do. My sweet child of the sun! The women in this cold country have no idea of the joy that a mutual love like ours has the power to bestow. We will love each other for ever and ever, my Hally, and when our bodies are withered by age, our spirits shall still go loving on."

He—the man whose whole thoughts thitherto had been so devoted to the task of ameliorating the condition of his fellow-creatures, that he had had no time to think of dalliance, succumbed as fully to its pleasures now, as the girl whose life had simply been a ripening process for the seed which had burst forth into flower. They were equally passionate—equally loving—equally unreserved—and they were soon absorbed in their own feelings, and noticed nothing that was taking place around them.

But they were not as entirely alone as they imagined. A pale face full of misery was watching them through one of the panes in the French windows, gazing at what seemed like his death doom, too horribly fascinated to tear himself away. Bobby stood there and saw Hally—*his* Hally, as he had often fondly called her, without knowing the meaning of the word—clasped in the arms of this stranger, pressing her lips to his, and being released with tumbled hair and a flushed face, only to seek the source of her delight again. At last Bobby could stand the bitter sight no longer, and with a low moan, he fled to his own apartment and flung himself, face downward on the bed. And Anthony Pennell and Harriet Brandt continued to make love to each other, until the shadows lengthened, and six o'clock was near at hand.

"I must go now, my darling," he said at last, "though it is hard to tear myself away. But I am so happy, Hally, so very, very happy, that I dare not complain."

"Why cannot you stay the evening?" she urged.

"I had better not! I have not been asked in the first instance, and if what you say about the Baroness's altered demeanour towards yourself be true, I am afraid I should find it difficult to keep my temper. But we part for a very short time, my darling! The first thing tomorrow, I shall see about another home for you, where I can visit you as freely as I like! And as soon as it can ever be, Hally, we will be married—is that a promise?"

"A promise, yes! a thousand times over, Anthony! I long for the time when I shall be your wife!"

"God bless you, my sweet! You have made my future life look all sunshine! I will write to you as soon as ever I have news and then you will lose no time in leaving your present home, will you?"

"Not an instant that I can help," replied Harriet, eagerly, "I am longing to get away. I feel that I have lost my footing here!"

And with another long embrace, the lovers parted. As soon as Anthony had left her, Harriet ran up to her room, to cool her feverish face and change her dress for dinner. She was really and truly fond of the man she had just promised to marry, and if anything could have the power to transform her into *a* thinking and responsible woman, it would be marriage with Anthony Pennell. She was immensely proud that so clever and popular a writer should have chosen her from out the world of women to be his wife, and she loved him for the excellent qualities he had displayed towards his fellow men, as well as for the passionate warmth he had shewn for herself.

She was a happier girl than she had ever been in all her life before, as she stood, flushed and triumphant, in front of her mirror and saw the beautiful light in her dark eyes, and the luxuriant growth of her dusky hair, and the carmine of her lips, and loved every charm she possessed for Anthony's sake. She felt less vexed even with the Baroness than she had done, and determined that she would not break the news of her intended departure from the Red House, that evening, but try to leave as pleasant an impression behind her as she could! And she put on the lemon-coloured frock, though Anthony was not there to see it, from a feeling that since he approved of her, she must be careful of her appearance for the future, to do justice to his opinion.

Madame Gobelli appeared to be in a worse temper than usual that evening. She stumped in to the dining-room and took her seat at table without vouchsafing a word to Harriet, although she had not seen her since luncheon time. She found fault with everything that Miss Wynward did, and telling her that she grew stupider and stupider each day, ordered her to attend her upstairs after dinner, as she had some friends coming and needed her assistance. The ex-governess did not answer at first, and the Baroness sharply demanded if she had heard her speak.

"Yes! my lady," she replied, slowly, "but I trust that you will excuse my attendance, as I have made an engagement for this evening!"

Madame Gobelli boiled over with rage.

"Engagement! What do you mean by making an engagement without asking my leave first? You can't keep it! I want you to 'elp me in something and you'll 'ave to come!"

"You must forgive me," repeated Miss Wynward, firmly, "but I cannot do as you wish!"

Harriet opened her eyes in amazement. Miss Wynward refusing a request from Madame Gobelli. What would happen next?

The Baroness grew scarlet in the face. She positively trembled with rage.

"'Old your tongue!" she screamed. "You'll do as I say, or you leave my 'ouse."

"Then I will leave your house!" replied Miss Wynward.

Madame Gobelli was thunderstruck! Where was this insolent menial, who had actually dared to defy her, going? What friends had she? What home to go to? She had received no salary from her for years past, but had accepted board and lodging and cast-off clothes in return for her services. How could she face the world without money?

"You go at your peril," she exclaimed, hoarse with rage, "you know what will 'appen to you if you try to resist me! I 'ave those that will 'elp me to be revenged on my enemies! You know that those I 'ate, *die!* And when I 'ave my knife in a body, I turn it! You 'ad better be careful, and think twice about what you're going to do."

"Your ladyship cannot frighten me any longer," replied Miss Wynward, calmly, "I thank God and my friends that I have got over that! Nor do I believe any more in your boasted powers of revenge! If they are really yours, you should be ashamed to use them."

"Gustave!" shrieked the Baroness, "get up and put this woman from the door. She don't stop in the Red 'Ouse another hour! Let 'er pack up 'er trumpery and go! Do you 'ear me, Gustave? Turn 'er out of the room!"

"*Mein tear! mein tear!* a little patience! Miss Wynward will go quietly! But the law, *mein tear*, the law! We must be careful!"

"Damn the law!" exclaimed the Baroness. "'Ere, where's that devil Bobby? Why ain't 'e at dinner? What's the good of my 'aving a 'usband and a son if neither of 'em will do my bidding!"

Then everyone looked round and discovered that Bobby was not at the table.

"Where's Bobby?" demanded the Baroness of the servant in waiting.

"Don't know, I'm sure," replied the domestic, who like most of Madame Gobelli's dependents, talked as familiarly with her as though they had been on an equality "The last time I saw 'im was at luncheon."

"I will go and look for him," said Miss Wynward quietly, as she rose from table.

"No! you don't!" exclaimed the Baroness insolently, "you don't touch my child nor my 'usband again whilst you remain under this roof. I won't 'ave them polluted by your fingers. 'Ere, Sarah, you go upstairs and see if Bobby's in 'is room. It'll be the worse for 'im if 'e isn't."

Sarah took her way upstairs, in obedience to her employer's behest, and the next minute a couple of shrieks, loud and terrified, proceeded from the upper story. They were in Sarah's voice, and they startled everyone at the dinner table.

"O! what is that?" exclaimed Harriet, as her face grew white with fear.

"Something is wrong!" said Miss Wynward, as she hastily left the room.

The Baroness said nothing, until Miss Wynward's voice was heard calling out over the banisters, "Baron! will you come here, please, at once!"

Then she said,

"Gustave! 'elp me up," and steadying herself by means of her stick, she proceeded to the upper story, accompanied by her husband and Harriet Brandt. They were met on the landing by Miss Wynward, who addressed herself exclusively to the Baron.

"Will you send for a doctor at once," she said eagerly, "Bobby is very ill, very ill, indeed!"

"What is the matter?" enquired the stolid German.

"It's all rubbish!" exclaimed Madame Gobelli, forcing her way past the ex-governess, "'ow can 'e be ill when 'e was running about all the morning? 'Ere, Bobby," she continued, addressing the prostrate figure of her son which was lying face downward on the bed, "get up at once and don't let's 'ave any of your nonsense, or I'll give you such a taste of my stick as you've never 'ad before! Get up, I say, at once now!"

She had laid hold of her son's arm, and was about to drag him down upon the floor, when Miss Wynward interposed with a face of horror.

"Leave him alone!" she cried, indignantly, "Woman! cannot you see what is the matter? Your son has left you! He is *dead!*"

The Baroness was about to retort that it was a lie and she didn't believe it, when a sudden trembling overtook her, which she was powerless to resist. Her whole face shook as if every muscle had lost control, and her cumbersome frame followed suit. She did not cry, nor call out, but stood where the news had reached her, immovable, except for that awful shaking, which made her sway from head to foot. The Baron on hearing the intelligence turned round to go downstairs and dispatch William, who was employed in the stables, in search of a medical man. Miss Wynward took the lifeless body in her arms and tenderly turned it over, kissing the pallid face as she did so—when Harriet Brandt, full of mournful curiosity, advanced to have a look at her dead playmate. Her appearance, till then unnoticed, seemed to wake the paralysed energies of the Baroness into life. She pushed the girl from the bed with a violence that sent her reeling against the mantelshelf, whilst she exclaimed furiously,

"Out of my sight! Don't you dare to touch 'im! This is all *your* doing, you poisonous, wicked creature!"

Harriet stared at her hostess in amazement! Had she suddenly gone mad with grief?

"What do you mean, *Madame?*" she cried.

"What I say! I ought to 'ave known better than to let you enter an 'ouse of mine! I was a fool not to 'ave left you be'ind me at Heyst, to practise your devilish arts on your army captains and foreign grocers, instead of letting you come within touch of my innocent child!"

"You are mad!" cried Harriet, "what have I done? Do you mean to insinuate that Bobby's death has anything to do with me?"

"It is *you* 'oo 'ave killed 'im," screamed the Baroness, shaking her stick, "it's your poisonous breath that 'as sapped 'is! I should 'ave seen it from the beginning. Do you suppose I don't know your 'istory? Do

you think I 'aven't 'eard all about your parents and their vile doings—
that I don't know that you're a common bastard, and that your mother
was a devilish negress, and your father a murderer? Why didn't I listen
to my friends and forbid you the 'ouse?"

"Miss Wynward!" said Harriet, who had turned deadly white at
this unexpected attack, "what can I say? What can I do?"

"Leave the room, my dear, leave the room! Her ladyship is not
herself? She does not know what she is saying!"

"Don't I?" screamed Madame Gobelli, barring the way to the door,
"I am telling 'er nothing but the truth, and she doesn't go till she 'as
'eard it! She has the vampire's blood in 'er and she poisons everybody
with whom she comes in contact. Wasn't Mrs. Pullen and Mademoiselle Brimont both taken ill from being too intimate with 'er, and
didn't the baby die because she carried it about and breathed upon it?
And now she 'as killed my Bobby in the same way—curse 'er!"

Even when reiterating the terrible truth in which she evidently
believed, Madame Gobelli shewed no signs of breaking down, but
stood firm, leaning heavily on her stick and trembling in every limb.

Harriet Brandt's features had assumed a scared expression.

"Miss Wynward!" she stammered piteously, "O! Miss Wynward!
this cannot be true!"

"Of course not! Of course not!" replied the other, soothingly, "her
ladyship will regret that she has spoken so hastily to you tomorrow."

"I shan't regret it!" said the Baroness sturdily, "for it is the truth!
Her father and her mother were murderers who were killed by their
own servants in revenge for their atrocities, and they left their curse
upon this girl—the curse of black blood and of the vampire's blood
which kills everything which it caresses. Look back over your past
life," she continued to Harriet, "and you'll see that it's the case! And
if you don't believe me, go and ask your friend Doctor Phillips, for 'e
knew your infamous parents and the curse that lies upon you!"

"*Madame! Madame!*" cried Miss Wynward, "is this a moment for
such recrimination? If all this were true, it is no fault of Miss Brandt's!
Think of what lies here, and that he loved her, and the thought will
soften your feelings!"

"But it don't!" exclaimed the Baroness, "when I look at my dead
son, I could kill 'er, because she 'as killed 'im."

And in effect, she advanced upon Harriet with so vengeful a look
that the girl with a slight cry, darted from the room, and rushed into
her own.

171

"For shame!" said Miss Wynward, whose previous fear of the Baroness seemed to have entirely evaporated, "how dare you intimidate an innocent woman in the very presence of Death?"

"Don't you try to browbeat me!" replied the Baroness.

"I will tell you what I think," said Miss Wynward boldly, "and that is, that you should blush to give way to your evil temper in the face of God's warning to yourself! You accuse that poor girl of unholy dealings—what can you say of your own? You, who for years past have made money by deceiving your fellow creatures in the grossest manner—who have professed to hold communication with the spiritual world for their satisfaction, when if any spirits have come to you they must have been those of devils akin to your own!

"And because I refused to help you to deceive—to take the place of that miserable cur Milliken and play cheating tricks with cards, and dress up stuffed figures to further your money-getting ends, you threatened me with loss of home and character and friends, until, God forgive me, I consented to further the fraud, from fear of starving. But now, thank Heaven, I have no more fear of you! Yes! you may shake your stick at me, and threaten to take my life, but it is useless! *This,*" pointing to the dead boy upon the bed, "was the only tie I had to the Red House, and as soon as he is dressed for his grave, I shall leave you forever!"

"And where would you go?" enquired the Baroness. The voice did not sound like her own; it was the cracked dry voice of a very old woman.

"That is no concern of yours, my lady," replied Miss Wynward, as she prepared to quit the room. "Be good enough to let me pass! The inexcusable manner in which you have insulted that poor young lady, Miss Brandt, makes me feel that my first duty is to her!"

"I forbid you—" commenced Madame Gobelli in her old tone, but the ex-governess simply looked her in the face and passed on. She made the woman feel that her power was gone.

Miss Wynward found Harriet in her own room, tossing all her possessions into her travelling trunks. There was no doubt of her intention. She was going to leave the Red House.

"Not at this time of night, my dear," said Miss Wynward, kindly, "it is nearly nine o'clock."

"I would go if I had to walk the street all night!" replied Harriet, feverishly.

Her eyes were inflamed with crying, and she shook like an aspen leaf.

"O! Miss Wynward, such awful things to say! What could she mean? What have I done to be so cruelly insulted? And when I am so sorry for poor Bobby too!"

She began to cry afresh as she threw dresses, mantles, stockings, and shoes one on the top of the other, in her endeavours to pack as quickly as possible.

"Let me help you, dear Miss Brandt! It is cruel that you should be driven from the house in this way! But I am going too, as soon as the doctor has been and dear Bobby's body may be prepared for burial. It is a great grief to me, Miss Brandt, I have had the care of him since he was five years old, and I loved him like my own. But I am glad he is dead! I am glad he has escaped from it all, for this is a wicked house, a godless, deceiving and slanderous house, and this trouble has fallen on it as a Nemesis. I will not stay here a moment longer now he has gone! I shall join my friends tomorrow."

"I am glad you have friends," said Harriet, "for I can see you are not happy here! Do they live far off? Have you sufficient money for your journey? Forgive my asking!"

Miss Wynward stooped down and kissed the girl's brow.

"Thank you so much for your kind thought, but it is unnecessary. You will be surprised perhaps," continued Miss Wynward, blushing, "but I am going to be married."

"And so am I," was on Harriet's lips, when she laid her head down on the lid of her trunk and began to cry anew. "O! Miss Wynward, what did she mean? Can there be any truth in it? Is there something poisonous in my nature that harms those with whom I come in contact? How can it be? *How* can it be?"

"No! no! of course not!" replied her friend, "Cannot you see that it was the Baroness's temper that made her speak so cruelly to you? But you are right to go! Only where are you going?"

"I do not know! I am so ignorant of London. Can you advise me?"

"You will communicate with your friends tomorrow?" asked Miss Wynward anxiously.

"O! yes! as soon as I can!"

"Then I should go to the Langham Hotel in Portland Place for tonight at all events! There you will be safe till your friends advise you further. What can I do to help you?"

"Ask Sarah or William to fetch a cab! And to have my boxes placed on it! There is a *douceur* for them," said Harriet placing a handsome sum in Miss Wynward's hand.

"And you will not see the Baroness again?" asked her companion.

"No! no! for God's sake, no. I could not trust myself! I can never look upon her face again!"

In a few minutes the hired vehicle rolled away from the door, bearing Harriet Brandt and her possessions to the Langham Hotel, and Miss Wynward returned to the room where Bobby lay. Madame Gobelli stood exactly where she had left her, gazing at the corpse. There were no tears in her eyes—only the continuous shaking of her huge limbs.

"Come!" said Miss Wynward, not unkindly, "you had better sit down, and let me bring you a glass of wine! This terrible shock has been too much for you."

But the Baroness only pushed her hand away, impatiently.

"Who was that driving away just now?" she enquired.

"Miss Brandt! You have driven her from the house with your cruel and unnecessary accusations. No one liked Bobby better than she did!"

"Has the doctor arrived?"

"I expect so! I hear the Baron's voice in the hall now!"

Almost as she spoke, the Baron and the doctor entered the room. The medical man did what was required of him. He felt the heart and pulse of the corpse—turned back the eyelids—sighed professionally, and asked how long it was since it had happened.

He was told that it was about an hour since they had found him.

"Ah! he has been dead longer than that! Three hours at the least, maybe four! I am afraid there must be an inquest, and it would be advisable in the interests of science to have a post mortem. A great pity, a fine grown lad—nineteen years old, you say—shall probably detect hidden mischief in the heart and lungs. I will make all the necessary arrangements with the Baron. Good evening!"

And the doctor bowed himself out of sight again.

"It is quite true then," articulated the Baroness thickly. "He is gone!"

"O! yes my lady, he is gone, poor dear boy! I felt sure of that!"

"It is quite certain?"

"Quite certain! The body is already stiffening!"

The Baroness did not utter a sound, but Miss Wynward glancing at her, saw her body sway slowly backwards and forwards once or twice, before it fell heavily to the ground, stricken with paralysis.

CHAPTER 16

Doctor Phillips was a great favourite with the *beau sexe*. He was so mild and courteous, so benevolent and sympathetic, that they felt sure he might be trusted with their little secrets. Women, both old and young, invaded his premises daily, and therefore it was no matter of surprise to him, when, whilst he was still occupied with his break-fast on the morning following Harriet Brandt's flight from the Red House, his confidential servant Charles announced that a young lady was waiting to see him in his consulting room.

"No name, Charles?" demanded the doctor.

"No name, Sir!" replied the discreet Charles, without the ghost of a smile.

"Say that I will be with her in a minute!"

Doctor Phillips finished his cutlet and his coffee before he rose from table. He knew what ladies' confidences were like and that he should not have much chance of returning to finish an interrupted meal.

But as he entered his consulting room, his air of indifference changed to one of surprise. Pacing restlessly up and down the carpet, was Harriet Brandt, but so altered that he should hardly have recog-nised her. Her face was puffy and swollen, as though she had wept all night; her eyelids, red and inflamed; her whole demeanour, wild and anxious.

"My dear young lady—is it possible that I see Miss Brandt?" the doctor began.

She turned towards him and coming up close to his side, grasped his arm. "I must speak to you!" she exclaimed, without further pre-liminary, "you are the only person who can set my doubts at rest."

"Well! well! well!" he said, soothingly, for the girl looked and spoke as though her mind were disordered. "You may rely that I will do all I can for you! But let us sit down first!"

"No! no!" cried Harriet, "there is no time, I cannot rest; you must satisfy my mind at once, or I shall go mad! I have not closed my eyes all night—the time was interminable, but how could I sleep? I seemed to be torn in pieces by ten thousand devils!"

"My dear child," said Doctor Phillips, as he laid his hand on hers and looked her steadily in the face, "you are over-excited. You must try to restrain yourself."

He went up to a side table and pouring out some cordial, made her drink it. Harriet gulped it down, and sank back exhausted in a chair. She was weak and worn-out with the excitement she had passed

175

through.

"Come! that is better," said the doctor, as he saw the tears stealing from beneath her closed eyelids, "now, don't hurry yourself! Keep quiet till you feel strong enough to speak, and then tell me what it is that brings you here!"

The allusion appeared to stir up all her misery again. She sat upright and grasped the doctor by the arm as she had done at first.

"You must tell me," she said breathlessly, "you must tell me all I want to know. They say you knew my father and mother in Jamaica! Is that true!"

The old doctor began to feel uncomfortable. It is one thing to warn those in whom you are interested against a certain person, or persons, and another to be confronted with the individual you have spoken of, and forced to repeat your words. Yet Doctor Phillips was innocent of having misjudged, or slandered anyone.

"I *did* know your father and mother—for a short time!" he answered cautiously.

"And were they married to each other?"

"My dear young lady, what is the use of dragging up such questions now? Your parents are both gone to their account—why not let all that concerned them rest also?"

"No! no! you forget that I live—to suffer the effects of their wrong-doing! I *must* know the truth—I will not leave the house until you tell me! Were they married? Am I a—a—bastard?"

"If you insist upon knowing, I believe they were not married—at least it was the general opinion in the Island. But would not Mr. Tarver be the proper person to inform you of anything which you may wish to know?"

Harriet seized his hand and carried it to her forehead—it was burning hot.

"Feel that!" she exclaimed, "and you would have me wait for weeks before I could get any satisfaction from Mr. Tarver, and not then perhaps! Do you think I could live through the agony of suspense? I should kill myself before the answer to my letter came. No! you are the only person that can give me any satisfaction. Madame Gobelli told me to ask you for the truth, if I did not believe her!"

"Madame Gobelli," reiterated the doctor in surprise. "Yes! I was staying with her at the Red House until last night, and then she was so cruel to me that I left. Her son Bobby is dead, and she accused me of having killed him. She said that my father was a murderer and my mother a negress—that they were both so wicked that their own servants killed them, and that I have inherited all their vices. She said that it was *I* who killed Mrs. Pullen's baby and that I had vampire blood in me, and should poison everyone I came in contact with. What does she mean? Tell me the truth, for God's sake, for more depends upon it than you have any idea of."

"Madame Gobelli was extremely wrong to speak in such a manner, and I do not know on what authority she did so. What can she know of your parents or their antecedents?"

"But you—you—" cried Harriet feverishly, "what do *you* say?" Doctor Phillips was silent. He did not know what to say. He was not a man who could tell a lie glibly and appear as if he were speaking the truth. Patients always guessed when he had no hope to give them, however soothing and carefully chosen his words might be. He regarded the distracted girl before him for some moments in compassionate silence, and then he answered:

"I have said already that if a daughter cannot hear any good of her parents, she had better hear nothing at all!"

"Then it is true—my father and mother were people so wicked and so cruel that their names are only fit for execration. If you could have said a good word for them, you would! I can read that in your eyes!"

"The purity and charity of your own life can do much to wipe out the stain upon theirs," said the doctor. "You have youth and money, and the opportunity of doing good. You may be as beloved, as they were—"

"Hated," interposed the girl, "I understand you perfectly! But what about my possessing the fatal power of injuring those I come in contact with! What truth is there in that? Answer me, for God's sake! Have I inherited the vampire's blood? Who bequeathed to me that fatal heritage?"

"My dear Miss Brandt, you must not talk of such a thing! You are alluding only to a superstition!"

"But have I got it, whatever it may be?" persisted Harriet. "Had I anything to do with the baby's death, or with that of Bobby Bates? I loved them both! Was it my love that killed them? Shall I always kill everybody I love? I *must* know—I *will!*"

"Miss Brandt, you have now touched upon a subject that is little thought of or discussed amongst medical men, but that is undoubtedly true. The natures of persons differ very widely. There are some born

177

into this world who nourish those with whom they are associated; they *give out* their magnetic power, and their families, their husbands or wives, children and friends, feel the better for it. There are those, on the other hand, who *draw* from their neighbours, sometimes making large demands upon their vitality—sapping their physical strength, and feeding upon them, as it were, until they are perfectly exhausted and unable to resist disease. This proclivity has been likened to that of the vampire bat who is said to suck the breath of its victims. And it was doubtless to this fable that Madame Gobelli alluded when speaking to you."

"But have I got it? Have I got it?" the girl demanded, eagerly.

The doctor looked at her lustrous glowing eyes, at her parted feverish lips; at the working hands clasped together; the general appearance of excited sensuality, and thought it was his duty to warn her at least a little, against the dangers of indulging such a temperament as she unfortunately possessed. But like all medical men, he temporised.

"I should certainly say that your temperament was more of the *drawing* than the *yielding* order, Miss Brandt, but that is not your fault, you know. It is a natural organism. But I think it is my duty to warn you that you are not likely to make those with whom you intimately associate, stronger either in mind or body. You will always exert a weakening and debilitating effect upon them, so that after a while, having sapped their brains, and lowered the tone of their bodies, you will find their affection, or friendship for you visibly decrease. You will have, in fact, *sucked them dry.* So, if I may venture to advise you I would say, if there is any one person in the world whom you most desire to benefit and retain the affection of, let that be the very person from whom you separate, as often as possible. You must never hope to keep anyone near you for long, without injuring them. Make it your rule through life never to cleave to any one person altogether, or you will see that person's interest in you wax and wane, until it is destroyed!"

"And what if I—marry?" asked Harriet, in a strained voice.

"If you insist upon my answering that question, I should advise you seriously *not* to marry! I do not think yours is a temperament fitted for married life, nor likely to be happy in it! You will not be offended by my plain speaking, I hope. Remember, you have forced it from me!"

"And that is the truth, medically and scientifically—that I must not marry?" she repeated, dully.

"I think it would be unadvisable, but everyone must judge for

178

himself in such matters. But marriage is not, after all, the ultimatum of earthly bliss, Miss Brandt! Many married couples would tell you it is just the reverse. And with a fortune at your command, you have many pleasures and interests quite apart from that very over-rated institution of matrimony. But don't think I am presuming to do more than advise you. There is no real reason—medical or legal—why you should not choose for yourself in the matter!"

"Only—only—that those I cling to most nearly, will suffer from the contact," said Harriet in the same strained tones.

"Just so!" responded the doctor, gaily, "and an old man's advice to you is, to keep out of it as he has done! And now—if there is anything more—" he continued, "that I can do for you—"

"Nothing more, thank you," replied the girl rising, "I understand it all now!"

"Will you not see your old friend, Mrs. Pullen, before you go?" asked the doctor. "She and her husband are staying with me!"

"O! no, no," cried Harriet, shrinking from the idea, "I *could* not see her, I would rather go back at once!"

And she hurried from the consulting room as she spoke.

Doctor Phillips stood for a while musing, after her departure. Had he done right, he thought, in telling her, yet how in the face of persistent questioning, could he have done otherwise? His thoughts were all fixed upon Ralph Pullen and the scenes that had taken place lately with him, respecting this girl. He did not dream she had an interest in Anthony Pennell. He did not know that they had met more than once. He thought she might still be pursuing Ralph; still expecting that he might break his engagement with Miss Leyton in order to marry herself; and he believed he had done the wisest thing in trying to crush any hopes she might have left concerning him.

"A most dangerous temperament," he said to himself, as he prepared to receive another patient, "one that is sufficient to mar a man's life, if not to kill him entirely. I trust that she and Captain Pullen may never meet again. It was evident that my remarks on marriage disappointed the poor child! Ah! well, she will be much better without it!"

And here the discreet Charles softly opened the door and ushered in another lady.

An hour later, Anthony Pennell, who had projected a visit to the Red House that afternoon, received a note by a commissionaire instead, containing a few, hurried lines:

Come to me as soon as you can, I have left Madame Gobelli. I am at the Langham Hotel, and very unhappy!

Needless to say that ten minutes after the reception of this news, her lover was rushing to her presence, as fast as hansom wheels could take him.

He was very desperately and truly in love with Harriet Brandt. Like most men who use their brains in fiction, his work whilst in course of progression, occupied his energies to such an extent that he had no time or thought for anything else. But the burden once lifted; the romance written; the strain and anxiety removed, the pendulum swung in the other direction, and Anthony Pennell devoted all his attention to pleasure and amusement. He had been set down by his colleagues as a reserved and cold-blooded man with regard to the other sex, but he was only self-contained and thoughtful.

He was as warm by nature, as Harriet herself, and once sure of a response, could make love with the best, and as he flew to her assistance now, he resolved that if anything unpleasant had occurred to drive her from the Red House, and launch her friendless on the world, he would persuade her to marry him at once, and elect him her protector and defence.

His fair face flushed with anticipation as he thought of the joy it would be to make her his wife, and take her far away from everything that could annoy or harass her.

Having arrived at the Langham and flung a double fare to the cab driver, he ran up the high staircase with the light step of a boy, and dashed into Harriet's private room. The girl was sitting, much as she had done since returning from her interview with the doctor—silent, sullen, and alone, at war with Heaven and Destiny and all that had conduced to blight the brightest hopes she had ever had.

"Hally, my darling, why is this?" exclaimed Pennell, as he essayed to fold her in his arms. But she pushed him off, not unkindly but with considerable determination.

"Don't touch me, Tony!—don't come near me. You had better not! I might harm you!"

"What is the matter? Are you ill? If so, you know me too well to imagine that I should fear infection."

"No! no! you do not understand!" replied Harriet, as she rose from her seat and edged further away from him, "but I am going to tell you all! It is for that I sent for you!"

Then, waving him from her with her hand, she related the whole story to him—what the Baroness had accused her of, and what Doctor Phillips had said in confirmation of it, only that morning. Pennell had heard something of it before, through Margaret Pullen, but he had paid no attention to it, and now, when Harriet repeated it in detail, with swollen eyes and quivering lips, he laughed the idea to scorn.

"Pooh! Nonsense! I don't believe a word of it," he exclaimed, "it is a parcel of old women's tales. Phillips should be ashamed of himself to place any credence in it, far more to repeat it to you! Hally, my darling! you are surely not going to make yourself unhappy because of such nonsense. If so, you are not the sensible girl I have taken you for!"

"But, Tony," said the girl, still backing from his advances, "listen to me! It is not all nonsense, indeed. I know for myself that it is true! Having been shut up for so many years in the convent dulled my memory for what went before it, but it has all come back to me now! It seems as if what Madame Gobelli and Doctor Phillips have said, had lifted a veil from my eyes, and I can recall things that had quite escaped my memory before, I can remember now hearing old Pete say, that when I was born, I was given to a black wet nurse, and after a little while she was taken so ill, they had to send her away, and get me another, and the next one—*died!* Pete used to laugh and call me the puma's cub, but I didn't know the meaning of it, then.

"And—O! stop a moment, Tony, till I have done—there was a little white child, I can see her so plainly now. They called her little Caroline, I think she must have belonged to the planter who lived next to us, and I was very fond of her. I was quite unhappy when we did not meet, and I used to creep into her nursery door and lie down in the cot beside her. Poor little Caroline! I can see her now! So pale and thin and wan she was! And one night, I remember her mother came in and found me there and called to her husband to send the 'Brandt bastard' back to Helvetia. I had no idea what she meant, but I cried because she sent me home, and I asked Pete what a bastard was, but he would not tell me. And," went on Harriet in a scared tone, "little Caroline *died!* Pete carried me on his shoulder to see the funeral, and I would not believe that Caroline could be in that narrow box, and I struck Pete on the face for saying so!"

"Well! my darling! and if you did, are these childish reminiscences to come between our happiness? Why should they distress you, Hally? Madame Gobelli's insolence must have been very hard to bear—I acknowledge that, and I wish I had been by to prevent it, but you must make excuses for her. I suppose the poor creature was so mad with grief that she did not know what she was saying! But you need never see her again, so you must try to forgive her!"

"But, Anthony, you do not understand me! What the Baroness said was *true*! I see it now! *I killed Bobby!*"

"My dearest, you are raving! *You killed Bobby!* What utter, utter folly! How could you have killed Bobby?"

Harriet passed her hand wearily across her brow, as if she found it too hard to make her meaning plain.

"O! yes, I did! We were always together, in the garden or the house! And he used to sit with his head on my shoulder and his arm round my waist, I should not have allowed it! I should have driven him away! But he loved me, poor Bobby, and it will be the same, Doctor Phillips says, with everybody I love! I shall only do them harm!"

"Hally! I shall begin to think in another moment that you are ill yourself—that you have a fever or something, and that it is affecting your brain!"

"There was a sister at the convent, Sister Theodosia, who was very good to me when I first went there," continued the girl in a dreamy voice, as if she had not heard his words; "and she used to sit with me upon her lap for hours together, because I was sad. But she grew ill and they had to send her away up to the hill, where they had their sanatorium. That made the fourth in Jamaica!"

"Now! I will not have you talk any more of this nonsense," said Pennell, half annoyed by her perseverance, "and to prove to you what a little silly you are to imagine that everyone who falls ill, or dies, who comes within the range of your acquaintance, owes it to your influence, tell me how it is that your father and mother, who must have lived nearer to you than anybody else, did not fall sick and die also.,"

"My parents saw less of me than anybody," replied Harriet, sadly, "they were ashamed of their 'bastard' I suppose! But old Pete loved me, and took me with him everywhere, and he didn't get sick," she concluded, with a faint smile.

"Of course not! See! what rubbish you have been talking—making yourself and me unhappy for nothing at all! So now let me take you in my arms and kiss the remembrance of it away!"

He was about to put his suggestion into execution, but she still shrank from him.

"No! no! indeed you must not! It is all true! I cannot forget Olga Brimont, and Mrs. Pullen, and the baby, and poor Bobby! It is true, indeed it is, and I have been accursed from my birth."

And she burst into a torrent of passionate tears.

Pennell let her expend some for her emotion, before he continued, "Well! and what is to be the upshot of it all!"

"I must part from you," replied the girl, "indeed, indeed I must! I cannot injure you as I have done others! Doctor Phillips said I was not fit for marriage—that I should always weaken and hurt those whom I loved most—and that I should draw from them, physically and mentally until I had sapped all their strength—that I have the blood of the vampire in me, the vampire that sucks its victims' breaths until they die!"

"Doctor Phillips be damned!" exclaimed Pennell, "what right has he to promulgate his absurd and untenable theories, and to poison the happiness of a girl's life, with his folly? He is an old fool, a dotard, a senseless ass, and I shall tell him so! Vampire be hanged! And if it were the truth, I for one could not wish for a sweeter death! Come along, Hally, and try your venom upon me! I am quite ready to run the risk!"

He held out his arms to her again, as he spoke, and she sank on her knees beside him.

"O! Tony! Tony! cannot you read the truth? I love you, dear, I love you! I never loved any creature in this world before I loved you. I did not know that it was given to mortals to love so much! And my love has opened my eyes! Sooner than injure you, whom I would die to save from harm, I will separate myself from you! I will give you up! I will live my lonely life without you, I *could* do that, but I can never, never consent to sap your manhood and your brains, which do not belong to me but to the world, and see you wither, like a poisoned plant, the leaves of which lie discoloured and dead upon the garden path."

Never in the course of their acquaintanceship, had Harriet Brandt seemed so sweet, so pathetic, so unselfish to Anthony Pennell as then. If he had resolved not to resign her from the first, he did so a thousand times more now. He threw his arms around her kneeling figure and lowered his head until it lay upon the crown of her dusky hair.

"My darling! my darling! my own sweet girl!" he murmured, "our destinies are interwoven for ever! No one and nothing shall come between us! You cannot give me up unless you have my consent to doing so. I hold your sacred promise to become my wife, and I shall not release you from it!"

"But if I harmed you?" she said fearfully.

"I do not believe in the possibility of your harming me," he replied, "but if I am to die, which is what I suppose you mean, I claim my right to die in your arms. But whenever it happens, you will have neither hastened, nor retarded it!"

"O! if I could only think so!" she murmured.

"You must! Why cannot you trust my judgment as much as that of Madame Gobelli or old Phillips—a couple of mischief makers. And now, Hally, when shall it be?"

"When shall 'what' be?" she whispered.

"You know what I mean as well as I do! When shall we be married? We have no one to consult but ourselves! I am my own master and you are alone in the world! These things are very easily managed, you know. I have but to go to Doctors' Commons for a special license to enable us to be married at a registrar's office tomorrow. Shall it be tomorrow, love?"

"O! no! no! I could not make up my mind so soon!"

"But why not? Would you live in this dull hotel all by yourself, Hally?"

"I do not know! I am so very unhappy! Leave me, Anthony, for God's sake, leave me, whilst there is time! You do not know the risk you may be running by remaining by my side! How can I consent to let you, whom I love like my very life, run any risk for my sake! O! I love you—I love you!" cried the impassioned girl, as she clung tightly to him. "You are my lord and master and my king, and I will never, *never* be so selfish as to harm you for the sake of my own gratification. You must go away—put the seas between us—never see me, never write or speak to me more—only save yourself, my beloved, save yourself!"

He smiled compassionately, as he would have smiled at the ravings of a child, as he raised her from her lowly position and placed her in a chair.

"Do you know what I am going to do, little woman?" he said cheerfully. "I am going to leave you all alone to think this matter over until tomorrow. By that time you will have been able to compare the opinions of two people who do not care a jot about you, with those of mine who love you so dearly. Think well over what they have said to you, and I have said to you, and you have said to me! Remember, that if you adhere to your present determination, you will make both you and me most unhappy, and do no one any good. As for myself, I venture to say that if I lose you my grief and disappointment will be so great, that, in all probability, I shall never do any good work again. But be a sensible girl—make up your mind to marry me, and give the lie to all this nonsense, and I'll write a book that will astonish the world! Come, Hally, is it to be ruin or success for me?—Ruin to spend my life without the only woman I have ever cared for, or success to win my wife and a companion who will help me in my work and make my happiness complete?"

He kissed her tear-stained face several times, and left her with a bright smile.

"This time tomorrow, remember, and I shall come with the license in my pocket."

CHAPTER 17

Doctor Phillips did not meet Margaret and her husband until luncheon time and then they were full of an encounter which they had had during their morning walk.

"Only fancy, Doctor!" exclaimed Margaret, with more animation than she had displayed of late, "Arthur and I have been shopping in Regent Street, and who do you think we met?"

"I give it up, my dear," replied the doctor, helping himself to cold beef. "I am not good at guessing riddles."

"Ralph and Elinor! They had just come from some exhibition of pictures in New Bond Street, and I never saw them so pleased with each other before. Ralph was looking actually 'spooney' and Elinor was positively radiant."

"*Souvent femme varie,*" quoted Doctor Phillips, shrugging his shoulders.

"O! but, Doctor, it made Arthur and me so glad to see them. Elinor is very fond of Ralph, you know, although she has shewn it so little. And so I have no doubt is he of her, and there would never have been any unpleasantness between them, if it had not been for that horrid girl, Harriet Brandt."

"It is not like you, my dear Margaret, to condemn anyone without a hearing. Perhaps you have not heard the true case of Miss Harriet Brandt. Although I am glad that Ralph has disentangled himself from her, I still believe that he behaved very badly to both the young ladies, and whilst I am glad to hear that Miss Leyton smiles upon him again, I think it is more than he deserves!"

"And I agree with you, Doctor," interposed Colonel Pullen, "I have never seen this Miss Brandt, but I know what a fool my brother is with women, and can quite understand that he may have raised her

185

hopes just to gratify his own vanity. I have no patience with him."

"Well! for Miss Leyton's sake let us hope that this will be his last experience of dallying with forbidden pleasures. But what will you say when I tell you that one of my visitors this morning has been the young lady in question—Miss Brandt!"

"Harriet Brandt!" exclaimed Margaret, "but why—is she ill?"

"O! no! Her trouble is mental—not physical."

"She is not still hankering after Ralph, I hope."

"You are afraid he might not be able to resist the bait! So should I be. But she did not mention Captain Pullen. Her distress was all about herself!"

"O! do tell me about it, Doctor, if it is not a secret! You know I have a kind of interest in Harriet Brandt!"

"When she does not interfere with the prospects of your family," observed the doctor, drily, "exactly so! Well, then, the poor girl is in great trouble, and I had very little consolation to give her! She has left Madame Gobelli's house. It seems that the old woman insulted her terribly and almost turned her out."

"O! that awful Baroness," cried Margaret, "it is only what might have been expected! We heard dreadful stories about her at Heyst. She has an uncontrollable temper and when offended, a most vituperative tongue. Her ill-breeding is apparent at all times, but it must be overwhelming when she is angry. But how did she insult Miss Brandt?"

"You remember what I told you of the girl's antecedents! It appears that the Baroness must have got hold of the same story, for she cast it in her teeth, accusing her moreover of having caused the death of her son."

"Madame Gobelli's son? What! Bobby—O! you do not mean to say that Bobby—is *dead?*"

"Yes! There was but one son, I think! He died yesterday, as I understood Miss Brandt. And the mother in her rage and grief turned upon the poor girl and told her such bitter truths, that she rushed from the house at once. Her visit to me this morning was paid in order to ascertain if such things were true, as the Baroness, very unjustifiably I think, had referred her to me for confirmation."

"And what did you tell her?"

"What could I tell her? At first I declined to give an opinion, but she put such pertinent questions to me, that unless I had lied, I saw no way of getting out of it. I glossed over matters as well as I could, but even so, they were bad enough. But I impressed it upon her that she must not think of marrying. I thought it the best way to put all idea of catching Captain Pullen out of her mind. Let him once get safely married, and she can decide for herself with regard to the next. But at all hazards, we must keep Ralph out of her way, for between you and me and the post, she is a young woman whom most men would find it difficult to resist."

"O! yes! she and Ralph must not meet again," said Margaret, dreamingly. Her thoughts had wandered back to Bobby and Heyst, and all the trouble she had encountered whilst there. What despair had attacked her when she lost her only child, and now Madame Gobelli—the woman she so much disliked—had lost her only child also.

"Poor Madame Gobelli!" she ejaculated, "I cannot help thinking of her! Fancy, Bobby, being—*dead!* And she used to make him so unhappy, and humiliate him before strangers! How she must be suffering for it now! How it must all come back upon her! Poor Bobby! Elinor will be sorry to hear that he is gone! She used to pity him so, and often gave him fruit and cakes. Fancy, his being dead! I cannot believe it."

"It is true, nevertheless! But it is the common lot, Margaret! Perhaps as his mother used to treat him so roughly, the poor lad is better off where he is."

"O! of course, I have no doubt of that! But he was all she had—like me!" said Margaret, with her eyes over-brimming. Her husband put his arms round her, and let her have her cry out on his shoulder.

Then, as he wiped her tears away she whispered,

"Arthur, I should like to go and see her—the Baroness, I mean! I can sympathise so truly with her, I might be able to say a few words of comfort!"

"Do as you like, my darling," replied Colonel Pullen, "that is, if you are sure that the woman won't insult you, as she did Miss Brandt!"

"O! no! no! I am not in the least afraid! Why should she? I shall only tell her how much I feel for her—how much our common loss—"

She could not proceed, and the doctor whispered to the colonel.

"Let her do as she wishes! The best salve for our own wounds is to try and heal those of others!"

Margaret rose and prepared to leave the room. "I shall go at once," she said, "I suppose there is no chance of my meeting Harriet Brandt there!"

"I think not! She told me she had left the Red House for good and all, but she did not say where she was staying! Though, after all, I think she is most in want of comfort of the two."

"O! no!" replied Margaret, faintly, "there is no grief like that of—of—" She did not finish her sentence but left the room hastily in order to assume her walking things.

"Will she ever get over the loss of her child?" demanded Colonel Pullen, gloomily. The doctor regarded him with a half-amused surprise.

"My dear fellow, though it is useless to preach the doctrine to a bereaved mother, the loss of an innocent baby is perhaps the least trying in the category of human ills. To rear the child, as thousands do, to be unloving, or unsympathetic, or ungrateful, is a thousand times worse. But it is too soon for your dear wife to acknowledge it! Let her go to this other mother and let them cry together. It will do her all the good in the world!"

And the doctor, having finished his luncheon, put on his top coat and prepared to make a round of professional calls. Margaret came back ready for her visit.

"I shall not offer to go with you, darling," said the colonel, "because my presence would only be inconvenient. But mind you keep the cab waiting, or you may find some difficulty in getting another in that district. What address shall I give the driver?"

"First to our florist in Regent Street that I may get some white flowers."

In another minute she was off, and in about an hour afterwards, she found herself outside the Red House, which looked gloomier than ever, with all the blinds drawn down. Margaret rang the front door bell, which was answered by Miss Wynward.

"Can I see Madame Gobelli?" commenced Margaret, "I have just heard the sad news, and come to condole with her!"

Miss Wynward let her into the hall and ushered her into a side room.

"You will excuse my asking if you are a friend of her ladyship's," she said.

"I can hardly call myself a friend," replied Margaret, "but I stayed with her in the same hotel at Heyst last summer, and I knew the dear boy who is dead. I was most grieved to hear of his death, and naturally anxious to enquire after the Baroness. But if she is too upset to see me, of course I would not think of forcing my presence upon her!"

"I don't think her ladyship would object to receiving any friend, but I am not sure if she would recognise you!"

"Not recognise me? It is not three months since we parted."

"You do not understand me! Our dear boy's death was so sudden—I have been with him since he was five years old, so you will forgive my mentioning him in such a fashion—that it has had a terrible effect upon his poor mother. In fact she is paralysed! The medical men think the paralysis is confined to the lower limbs, but at present they are unable to decide definitely, as the Baroness has not opened her lips since the event occurred."

"O! poor Madame Gobelli!" cried Margaret, tearfully, "I felt sure she loved him under all her apparent roughness and indifference!"

"Yes! I have been with them so long, that I know her manner amounted at times to cruelty, but she did not mean it to be so! She thought to make him hardy and independent, instead of which it had just the opposite effect! But she is paying bitterly for it now! I really think his death will kill her, though the doctors laugh at my fears!"

"I—I—too have lost my only child, my precious little baby," replied Margaret, encouraged by the sympathetic tenderness in the other woman's eyes, "and I thought also at first that I must die—that I could not live without her—but God is so good, and there is such comfort in the thought that whatever we may suffer, our darlings have missed all the bitterness and sin and disappointments of this world, that at last—that is, sometimes—one feels *almost* thankful that they are safe with Him!"

"Ah! Madame Gobelli has not your hope and trust, Madam!" said Miss Wynward, "if she had, she would be a better and happier woman. But I must tell you that she is in the same room as Bobby! She will not be moved from there, but lies on the couch where we placed her when she fell, stricken with the paralysis, gazing at the corpse!"

"Poor dear woman!" exclaimed Margaret.

"Perhaps you would hardly care to go into that room!"

"O! I should like it! I want to see the dear boy again! I have brought some flowers to put over him!"

"Then, what name shall I tell her ladyship?"

"Mrs. Pullen, say Margaret Pullen whose little baby died at Heyst—then I think she will remember!"

"Will you take a seat, Mrs. Pullen, whilst I go upstairs and see if I can persuade her to receive you!"

Margaret sat down, and Miss Wynward went up to the chamber which had once been Bobby's. On the bed, was stretched the body of the dead boy, whilst opposite to it, lay on a couch, a woman with dry eyes, but palsied limbs, staring, staring without intermission at the silent figure which had once contained the spirit of her son. She did not turn her head as Miss Wynward entered the room.

"My lady," she said, going up to her, "Mrs. Pullen is downstairs and would like to see you! She told me to say that she is Margaret Pullen whose baby died in Heyst last summer, and she knew Bobby and has brought some flowers to strew over his bed. May she come up?"

But she received no answer. Madame Gobelli's features were working, but that was the only sign of life which she gave.

"Mrs. Pullen is so very sorry for your loss," Miss Wynward went on, "she cried when she spoke of it, and as she has suffered the same, I am sure she will sympathise with you. May I say that you will see her?"

Still there was no response, and Miss Wynward went down again to Margaret.

"I think you had better come up without waiting for her consent," she said, "if seeing you roused her, even to anger, it would do her good. Do you mind making the attempt?"

"No," replied Margaret, "but if the Baroness gets very angry, you must let me run away again. I am quite unequal to standing anything like a scene!"

"You will have but to quit the room. Whatever her ladyship may say she cannot move from her couch. She attacked poor Miss Brandt most unwarrantably last evening, but that was in the first frenzy of her grief. She is quite different now!"

"Poor woman!" again ejaculated Margaret, as she followed Miss Wynward, not without some inward qualms, to the presence of Madame Gobelli. But when she caught sight of the immovable figure on the couch, all her fear and resentment left her, overcome by a mighty compassion. She went straight up to the Baroness and bending down tenderly kissed her twitching face.

"Dear *Madame*," she said, "I am—we all are—so truly sorry for your grievous loss. It reminds me of the bitter time, not so long ago, you may remember, when I lost my darling little Ethel, and thought for the while that my life was over! It is so hard, so unnatural, to us poor mothers, to see our children go before ourselves! I can weep with you tear for tear! But do remember—try to remember—that he is safe—that though you remain here with empty arms for a while, death can no more take your boy from you, than a veil over your face can take God's light from you.

"He is there, dear Madame Gobelli— just in the next room with the door closed between you, and though I know full well how bit-

190

ter it is to see the door closed, think of the time when it will open again—when you and I will spring through it and find, not only our dear Bobby and Ethel, but Christ our Lord, ready to give them back into our arms again!"

The Baroness said nothing, but two tears gathered in her eyes and rolled down her flabby cheeks. Margaret turned from her for a minute and walking up to the bed, knelt down beside it in prayer.

"Dear Christ!" she said, "You Who know what our mothers' hearts are called upon to bear, have pity on us and give us Thy Peace! And open our eyes that we may gather strength to realise what our dear children have escaped by being taken home to Thee—the sin, the trouble, the anxiety, the disappointment—and make us thankful to bear them in their stead, and give us grace to look forward to our happy meeting and reunion in the Better Land."

Then she rose and bent over the dead boy.

"Dear Bobby!" she murmured, as she kissed the cold brow, and placed the white blossoms in his hands and round his head. "Goodbye! I know how happy you must be now, in company with the spirits of all those whom we have loved and who have gone home before us— how grateful you must feel to the dear Redeemer Who has called you so early—but don't forget your poor mother upon earth! Pray for her, Bobby,—never cease to ask our dear Lord to send her comfort and peace and joy in believing. For His own dear sake. Amen!"

When she turned again, the Baroness's cheeks were wet with tears and she was stretching forth her arms towards her.

"O!" she gasped, as Margaret reached her side, "I am a godless woman—I am a godless woman!"

"No! no! my dear friend, we are none of us godless," replied Margaret, "we may think we are, but God knows better! We may forsake Him, but He never forsakes us! We should never be saved if we waited till we wanted to be so. It is *He* Who wants *us*—that is our great safeguard! He wanted our two dear children—not to spite us, but to draw us after them. Try to look at it in that light, and then Bobby's death will prove your greatest gain."

"I am a godless woman," repeated the Baroness, "and this is my punishment!" pointing to the bed, "I loved him best of all! My 'eart is broken!"

"So much the better, if it was a hard heart," rejoined Margaret, smiling. "Who was it that said, '*If your heart is broken, give the pieces to Christ and He will mend it again*'? Never think of Bobby, dear Madame

Gobelli, except as with Christ—walking with Him, talking with Him, learning of Him and growing in grace and the love of God daily! Never disassociate the two memories, and in a little while you would hate yourself if you could separate them again. God bless you! I must go back to my husband now!"

"You will come again?" said the Baroness.

"I am afraid I shall have no time! We sail for India on Saturday, but I shall not forget you. Goodbye Bobby," she repeated, with a last look at the corpse, "remember your mother and me in your prayers."

As Miss Wynward let her out of the Red House, she remarked, "I could never have believed that anyone could have had so much influence over her ladyship as you have, Mrs. Pullen. I hope you will come again."

"I shall not be able to do so. But Madame Gobelli will have you to talk to her! You live here altogether, do you not?"

"I have lived here for many years, but I am on the point of leaving. Bobby was my only tie to the Red House, or I should have gone long ago."

"But now that the Baroness is so helpless surely you will delay your departure until she no longer needs you."

"I shall not leave her until she has secured a better woman in my stead. But to tell you the truth, I am going to be married, Mrs. Pullen, and I consider my first duty is towards my future husband and his parents who are very old!"

"O! doubtless! May I ask his name?"

"Captain Hill! He lives in the next house to this—Stevenage! You are surprised, perhaps, that a man who has been in the army should marry a poor governess like myself. That is his goodness. I know that I am worn and faded and no longer young—thirty-three on my last birthday—but he is good enough to care for me all the more for the troubles I have passed through. Mine has been a chequered life, Mrs. Pullen, but I have told Captain Hill everything, and he still wishes to make me his wife! I ought to be a happy woman for the future, ought I not?"

"Indeed yes," said Margaret, heartily, "and I sincerely hope that you may be so! But I can't help thinking of poor Madame Gobelli! Is the Baron good to her?"

"Pretty well!" answered Miss Wynward, "but he is very stolid and unsympathetic! It is strange to think that her heart must have been bound up in that boy, and yet at times she was positively cruel to him!"

"It has all been permitted for some good purpose," said Margaret, as she bade her farewell, "perhaps her remorse and self-accusation are the only things which would have brought her down upon her knees."

She returned home considerably saddened by what she had seen, but in three days she was to accompany her husband to India, and in the bustle of preparation, and the joy of knowing that she was not to be separated from him again, her heart was comforted and at peace. Never once during that time did she give one thought to Harriet Brandt. Miss Wynward had hardly mentioned her name, and no one seemed to know where she had gone. The girl had passed out of their lives altogether.

Margaret only regretted one thing in leaving England—that she had not seen Anthony Pennell again. Colonel Pullen had called twice at his chambers, but had each time found him from home.

Margaret wanted to put in a good word for the Baroness with him. She thought perhaps that he might see her, after a while, and speak a few words of comfort to her. But she was obliged to be content with writing her wishes in a farewell letter. She little knew how hardened Anthony Pennell felt, at that moment, against anyone who had treated the woman he loved in so harsh a manner.

Harriet Brandt spent the time, after her lover had left her to think over and decide upon their mutual fate, in walking up and down the room. She was like a restless animal; she could not stay two moments in the same place. Even when night fell, and the inhabitants of the Langham Hotel had retired to rest, she still kept pacing up and down the room, without thinking of undressing herself or seeking repose, whilst her conscience wrestled in warfare with her inclinations. Her thoughts took her far, far back to the earliest remembrance of which her mind was capable. She thought of her hard, unfeeling, indifferent father—of her gross, flabby sensual mother—and shuddered at the remembrance! What had *she* done?—she said to herself—wherein had *she* sinned, that she should have been cursed with such progenitors?

How had they *dared* to bring her into the world, an innocent yet hapless child of sin—the inheritor of their evil propensities—of their lust, their cruelty, their sensuality, their gluttony—and worst of all, the fatal heritage that made her a terror and a curse to her fellow-creatures? How dared they? *How dared they?* Why had God's vengeance not fallen upon them before they had completed their cruel work, or having accomplished it, why did He not let her perish with them—so that the awful power with which they had imbued her, might have been prevented from harming others?

Harriet thought of little Caroline; of her two nurses; of Sister Theodosia—of Mrs. Pullen's baby; of Bobby Bates; until she felt as though she should go mad. No! no! she would never bring that curse upon her Beloved; he must go far away, he must never see her again, or else she would destroy herself in order that he might escape!

But if she persuaded Anthony to consent to her wishes—if she insisted upon a total separation between them, what would become of her? What should she do? She had no friends in England; Madame Gobelli had turned against her—she was all alone! She would live and die alone. How should she ever get to know people, or to obtain an entrance to Society. She would be a pariah to the end of her life!

And if she did surmount all these obstacles, what would be the result, except a repetition of what had gone before? Strangers would come to know her—to like her—would grow more intimate, and she would respond to their kindness—with the same result. They would droop and fail, die perhaps, like Bobby and the baby—find out that she was the cause and shun her ever after.

"O! God!" cried Harriet in her perplexity and anguish, "I am accursed! My parents have made me not fit to live!"

She passed that night through the agonies of Death—not the death that overtakes the believer in a God and a Future—but the darkness and uncertainty that enwrap the man who knows he is full of sin and yet has no knowledge that His Lord has paid his debt to the uttermost farthing—the doubt and anxiety that beset the unbeliever when he is called upon to enter the dark Valley. The poor child saw her destiny entangling her as in a net—she longed to break through it, but saw no means of escape—and she rebelled against the cruel lot that heredity had marked out for her.

"Why am I to suffer?" she exclaimed aloud; "I have youth and health and good looks, and money—everything, the world would say, calculated to make my life a pleasant one, and yet, I am tortured by this awful thought—that I must keep aloof from everybody, that I am a social leper, full of contagion and death! Doctor Phillips said that the more I loved a person, the more I must keep away from him! It is incredible! unheard-of! Could he have had any motive in saying such a thing?"

The remembrance of her flirtation with Ralph Pullen recurred to her mind, and she seized it, as a drowning man clutches at a straw.

"Was it a plant, after all? Did the old man want to put me off the track of Captain Pullen? Margaret Pullen is staying in the house—he said so—had she asked him to get rid of me if possible? After all, am I torturing myself by believing the story of my fatal power to be true, when it was only a ruse to get rid of me? The Baroness said the same thing, but she was mad about poor Bobby and would have said anything to annoy me—and, after all, what does it amount to? The baby died in teething—heaps of babies do—and Bobby was consumptive from the first—I have heard Miss Wynward say so, and would have died any way, as he grew to be a man and had larger demands made upon his physical strength.

And for the others—what happened to them, happens to all the world. It is fortune *de la guerre*; people drop every day like rotten sheep;—everyone might accuse himself of causing the death of his neighbour. I have been frightening myself with a chimera. Anthony said so, and he must know better than I! And I can't give up Tony—I *can't, I can't, I can't!* It is of no use thinking of it! Besides, he wouldn't let me! He would never leave me alone, until I had consented to marry him, so I may as well do it at the first as at the last."

But the tide of triumphant feeling would be succeeded by a wave of despondency, which threatened to upset all her casuistry.

"But if—*if*—it should be true, and Anthony should—should—O! God! O! God! I dare not think of it! I will kill myself before it shall occur."

When the morning dawned it found her quite undecided—lamenting her unfortunate fate one instant, and declaring that she could never give up her lover the next. She tore off her clothes and took a cold bath, and re-robed herself, but she was looking utterly ill and exhausted when Pennell burst in upon her at eleven o'clock.

"Well, darling," he exclaimed, "and have you made up your mind by this time? Which death am I to die?—suffocated in your dear embrace, or left to perish of cold and hunger outside?"

"O! Tony," she cried, throwing herself into his arms, "I don't know what to say! I have not closed my eyes all night, trying to decide what will be for the best. And I am as far off as ever—only I can never, *never* consent to do anything that shall work you harm!"

"Then I shall decide for you," exclaimed her lover, "and that is that you make me and yourself happy, and forget all the rubbish these people have been telling you! Depend upon it, whatever they may have said was for their own gratification, and not yours, and that they would be quick enough to accept the lot that lies before you, were it in their power!"

"I have been so lonely and friendless all my life," said Harriet, sobbing in his arms, "and I have longed for love and sympathy so much, and now that they have come to me, it is hard, O! *so* hard, to have to give them up."

"So hard, Hally, for *me,* remember, as well as yourself, that we will not make the attempt. Now, I want you to place yourself in my hands, and start for Paris tonight!"

"Tonight?" she cried, lifting such a flushed, startled, happy face from his breast, that he had no alternative but to kiss it again.

"Yes! tonight! What did I tell you yesterday—that I should come with the ring and the license in my pocket! I am as good as my word, and better—for I have given notice to the registrar of marriages in my district, that he is to be ready for us at twelve o'clock today. Am I not a good manager?"

"Tony! Tony! but I have not made up my mind!"

"I have made it up for you, and I will take no refusal! I have calculated it all to a nicety! Married at twelve—back here at one for lunch—a couple of hours to pack up, and off by the four o'clock train for Dover—sleep at the Castle Warden, and cross tomorrow to Paris! How will that do, Mrs. Pennell, eh?"

"O! ought I to do it, ought I to do it?" exclaimed Harriet, with a look of despair.

"If you don't I'll shoot myself. I swear it!"

"No! no! darling, don't say that! It is of you alone that I am thinking! God forgive me if I am doing wrong, but I feel that I cannot refuse you! Take me and do with me as you think best."

After which it came to pass, that Mr. and Mrs. Anthony Pennell started in very high spirits for Dover, by the four o'clock train that afternoon.

CHAPTER 18

A fortnight afterwards, the married couple found themselves at Nice. Much as has been said and sung of the *lune de miel,* none ever surpassed, if it ever reached this one in happiness. Harriet passed the time in a silent ecstasy of delight. Her cup of bliss was filled to overflowing; her satisfaction was too deep for words. To this girl, for whom the world had been seen as yet, only through the barred windows of a convent—who had never enjoyed the society of an intellectual companion before; who had viewed no scenery but that of the island; seen no records of the past; and visited no foreign capital; the first weeks of her married life were a panorama of novelties, her days one long astonishment and delight.

She could not adore Anthony Pennell sufficiently for having afforded her the opportunity of seeing all this, and more especially of feeling it. The presents he lavished upon her were as nothing in her eyes, compared to the lover-like attentions he paid her; the bouquets of flowers he brought her every morning; the glass of lemonade or milk he had ready to supply her need when they were taking their excursions; the warm shawl or mantle he carried on his arm in the evenings, lest the air should become too chilly for her delicate frame after sunset. Money, Harriet had no need of, but love—love she had thirsted for, as the hart thirsts for the water streams, yet had never imagined it could be poured out at her feet, as her husband poured it now.

And Pennell on the other hand, though he had been much sought after and flattered by the fair sex for the sake of the fame he had acquired and the money he made, had never lost his heart to any woman as he had done to his little unknown wife. He had never met anyone like Hally before. She combined the intelligence of the Englishwoman with the *espièglerie* of the French—the devotion of the Creole with the fiery passion of the Spanish or Italian. He could conceive her quite capable of dying silently and uncomplainingly for him, or anyone she loved; or on the other hand stabbing her lover without remorse if roused by jealousy or insult.

He was hourly discovering new traits in her character which delighted him, because they were so utterly unlike any possessed by the women of the world, with whom he had hitherto associated. He felt as though he had captured some beautiful wild creature and was taming it for his own pleasure.

Harriet would sit for hours at a time in profound silence, contemplating his features or watching his actions—crouched on the floor at his feet, until he was fain to lay down his book or writing, and take to fondling her instead. She was an ever constant joy to him; he felt it would be impossible to do anything to displease her so long as he loved her—that like the patient Griselda she would submit to any injustice and meekly call it justice if from *his* hand. And yet he knew all the while that the savage in her was *not* tamed—that at any moment, like the domesticated lion or tiger, her nature might assert itself and become furious, wild and intractable. It was the very uncertainty that pleased him; men love the women of whom they are not quite certain, all the more.

From Nice they wandered to Mentone, but the proximity of the Monte Carlo tables had no charm for Anthony Pennell. He was not a speculating man: his brain was filled with better things, and he only visited such places for the sake of reproduction. Although the autumn was now far advanced, the air of Mentone was too enervating to suit either of them, and Pennell proposed that they should move on to Italy.

"I must shew you Venice and Rome before we return home, Hally," he said, "and when I come to think of it, why should we return to England at all just yet? Why not winter in Rome? Richards is always advising me to take a good, long holiday. He says I overwork my brain and it reacts upon my body—what better opportunity could we find to adopt his advice? Hitherto I have pooh-poohed the idea! Wandering over a foreign country in solitary grandeur held no charms for me, but with you, my darling, to double the pleasure of everything, any place assumes the appearance of Paradise! What do you say, little wife? Shall we set up our tent South until the spring?"

"Don't you feel well, Tony?" asked Harriet, anxiously.

"Never better in my life, dear! I am afraid you will not make an interesting invalid out of me. I am as fit as a fiddle. But I fancy my next novel will deal with Italy, and I should like to make a few notes of the spots I may require to introduce. It is nothing to take me away from you, darling. We will inspect the old places together, and your quick eye and clear brain shall help me in my researches. Is it a settled thing, Hally?"

"O! yes, darling!" she replied, "anywhere with you! The only place I shall ever object to, will be the one where I cannot go with you."

"That place does not exist on this earth, Hally," said Pennell, "but if you are willing, we may as well start tomorrow, for if we leave it too late, we shall find all the best winter quarters pre-engaged."

He left the room, as she thought rather hurriedly, but as he gained the hotel corridor he slightly staggered and leaned against the wall. He had told his wife that he was quite well, but he knew it was not the truth. He had felt weak and enervated ever since coming to Mentone, but he ascribed it to the soft mild atmosphere.

"Confound this dizziness!" he said inwardly, as the corridor swam before his eyes, "I think my liver must be out of order, and yet I have been taking plenty of exercise. It must be this mild moist air. Heat never did agree with me. I shall be glad to get on. We shall find Florence cold by comparison."

He descended to the bureau and announced his intention of giving up his rooms on the morrow, and then ordered a carriage and returned to take Hally out for a drive.

In Florence, they procured rooms in a grand old *palazzo*, furnished with rococo chairs and tables, placed upon marble floors. Harriet was charmed and astonished by the ease with which they got everything *en route*, as though they possessed Aladdin's lamp, she told Pennell, and had but to wish to obtain.

"Ah! Hally!" said her husband, "we have something better than the genie's lamp—we have money! *That* is the true magician in this century. I am very thankful that you have a fortune of your own, my dearest, because I know that whatever happens, my girl will be able to hold her own with the world!"

Harriet grew pale.

"What *could* happen?" she stammered.

"My silly little goose, are we immortal?" he replied, "I make a first-rate income, my dear, but have not laid by enough as yet to leave you more than comfortably off, but with your own money—"

"Don't speak of it, pray don't speak of it!" she exclaimed, with ashen lips, and noting her distress, Pennell changed the subject.

"You are a lucky little woman," he continued, "I wonder what some people would give to possess your income—poor Margaret Pullen for instance."

"Why Mrs. Pullen in particular, Tony? Are they poor?"

"Not whilst Colonel Pullen is on active service, but he has nothing but his pay to depend upon, and whilst he can work, he must. Which means, a residence in India, and perhaps separation from his wife and children—if he should lose his health, a compulsory retirement; and if he keeps it, toiling out there till old age, and then coming home to spin out the remainder of his life on an inadequate pension. A man who accepts service in India should make up his mind to live and die in the country, but so many accidents may prevent it. And at the best, it means banishment from England and all one's friends and relations. Poor Margaret feels that severely I am sure!"

"Has Mrs. Pullen many relations then?"

"She has a mother still living, and several brothers and sisters, besides her husband's family. What a sweet gentle woman she is! She was kind to you, Hally, was she not, whilst you were abroad?"

By mutual agreement they never spoke of Heyst, or the Red House, or anything which was associated with what Pennell called his wife's infatuation regarding herself.

"Yes! she was very kind—at first," replied Harriet, "until—until—it all happened, and they went to England. O! do not let us talk of it!" she broke off suddenly.

"No! we will not! Have you unpacked your *mandolin* yet, Hally? Fetch it, dear, and let me hear your lovely voice again! I shall get you to sing to me when I am in the vein for composing! You would bring me all sorts of beautiful ideas and phantasies!"

"Should I? should I?" exclaimed the girl joyfully. "O! how lovely! I should do a part of your work then, shouldn't I, Tony?—I should inspire you! Why, I would sing day and night for that!"

"No! no! my bird, I would not let you tire yourself! A few notes now and then—they will help me more than enough. I must draw from you for my next heroine, Hally! I could not have a fairer model!"

"O! Tony!"

She rushed to him in the extremity of her delight and hid her face upon his breast.

"I am not good enough, not pretty enough! Your heroines should be perfect!"

"I don't think so! I prefer them to be of flesh and blood, like you!"

He stooped his head and kissed her passionately. "Hally! Hally!" he whispered, "you draw my very life away!"

The girl got up suddenly, almost roughly, and walked into the next room to fetch her *mandolin*.

"No! no!" she cried to herself with a cold fear, "not that, my God, not that!"

But when she returned with the instrument, she did not revert to the subject, but played and sang as usual, to her husband's admiration and delight.

They *did* Florence very thoroughly during the first week of their stay there, and were both completely tired.

"I must really stay at home tomorrow," cried Hally one afternoon on returning to dinner, "Tony, I am regularly fagged out! I feel as if I had a corn upon every toe!"

"So do I," replied her husband, "and I cannot have my darling knocked-up by fatigue! We will be lazy tomorrow, Hally, and lie on two sofas and read our books all day! I have been thinking for the last few days that we have been going a little too fast! Let me see, child!—how long have we been married?"

"Six weeks tomorrow," she answered glibly.

"Bless my soul! we are quite an old married couple, a species of

Darby and Joan! And have you been happy, Hally?"

The tears of excitement rushed into her dark eyes. *"Happy!* That is no word for what I have been, Tony, I have been in Heaven—in Heaven all the while!"

"And so, have I," rejoined her husband.

"I met some nuns whilst I was out this morning," continued Hally, "the sisters of the Annunciation, and they stopped and spoke to me, and were so pleased to hear that I had been brought up in a convent. 'And have you no vocation, my child?' asked one of them. 'Yes! Sister, I replied, 'I have—a big, strong, handsome vocation called my husband.' They looked quite shocked, poor dears, at first, but I gave them a subscription for their orphan schools—one hundred *francs*—and they were so pleased. They said if I was sick whilst in Florence, I must send for one of them, and she would come and nurse me! I gave it as a thanksgiving, Tony—a thanksgiving offering because I am so very happy. I am not a good woman like Margaret Pullen, I know that, but I love you—*I love you!"*

"Who said that you were not a good woman?" asked Pennell, as he drew her fondly to his side, and kissed away the tears that hung on her dark lashes.

"O! I know I am not. Besides, you once said that Margaret Pullen was the best woman you had ever known."

"I think she is very sweet and unselfish," replied Pennell musingly, "she felt the loss of her infant terribly, Doctor Phillips told me, but the way in which she struggled to subdue her grief in order not to distress others, was wonderful! Poor Margaret! how she mourns little Ethel to this day."

"Don't! *don't!"* cried Harriet in a stifled voice, "I cannot bear to think of it!"

"My darling, it had nothing to do with you! I have told you so a thousand times!"

"Yes! yes! I know you have—but I loved the little darling! It is dreadful to me to think that she is mouldering in the grave!"

"Come, child, you will be hysterical if you indulge in any more reminiscences! Suppose we go for a stroll through the Ghetto or some other antiquated part of Florence. Or shall we take a drive into the country? I am at your commands, Madam!"

"A drive, darling, then—a drive!" whispered his wife, as she left him to get ready for the excursion.

It was three hours before they returned to their rooms in the old *palazzo*. Harriet was dull and somewhat silent, and Anthony confessed to a headache.

"I am not quite sure now," he said, as they were dining, "whether a trip to Australia or America would not do us both more good than lingering about these mild, warm places. I think our constitutions both require bracing rather than coddling. Australia is a grand young country! I have often contemplated paying her a visit. What would you say to it, Hally?"

"I should enjoy it as much as yourself, Tony! You so often have a headache now! I think the drainage of these southern towns must be defective!"

"O! shocking! They are famous for typhoid and malarial fevers. They are not drained at all!"

"Don't let us stay here long then! What should I do if you were to fall ill?"

"You are far more liable to fall sick of the two, my darling," returned her husband, "I do not think your beautiful little body has much strength to sustain it. And then what should *I* do?"

'Ah! neither of us could do without the other, Tony!"

"Of course we couldn't, and so we will provide against such a contingency by moving on before our systems get saturated with miasma and mistral. Will you sing to me tonight, Hally?"

"Not unless you very much wish it! I am a little tired. I feel as if I couldn't throw any expression into my songs tonight!"

"Then come here and sit down on the sofa beside me, and let us talk!"

She did as he desired, but Pennell was too sleepy to talk. In five minutes he had fallen fast asleep, and it was with difficulty she could persuade him to abandon the couch and drag his weary limbs up to bed, where he threw himself down in a profound slumber. Harriet was also tired. Her husband was breathing heavily as she slipped into her place beside him. His arm was thrown out over her pillow, as though he feared she might go to sleep without remembering to wish him goodnight! She bent over him and kissed him passionately on the lips.

"Goodnight, my beloved," she whispered, "sleep well, and wake in happiness!"

She kissed the big hand too that lay upon her pillow and composed herself to sleep while it still encircled her.

The dawn is early in Florence, but it had broken for some time before she roused herself again. The sun was streaming brightly into the long, narrow, uncurtained windows, and everything it lighted on was touched with a molten glory. Harriet started up in bed. Her husband's arm was still beneath her body.

"O! my poor darling!" she exclaimed, as though the fault were her own, "how cramped he must be! How soundly we must have slept not to have once moved through the night!"

She raised Tony's arm and commenced to chafe it. How strangely heavy and cold it felt. Why! he was cold all over! She drew up the bedclothes and tucked them in around his chin. Then, for the first time, she looked at his face. His eyes were open.

"Tony, Tony!" she exclaimed, "are you making fun of me? Have you been awake all the time?

She bent over his face laughingly, and pressed a kiss upon his cheek. How stiff it felt! My God! what was the matter? Could he have fainted? She leapt from the bed, and running to her husband's side, pulled down the bedclothes again and placed her hand upon his heart. The body was cold—cold and still all over! His eyes were glazed and dull. His mouth was slightly open. In one awful moment she knew the truth. Tony was—*dead!*

She stood for some moments—some hours—some months—she could not have reckoned the time, silent and motionless, trying to realise what had occurred. Then—as it came upon her, like a resistless flood which she could not stem, nor escape, Harriet gave one fearful shriek which brought the servants hurrying upstairs to know what could be the matter.

"I have killed my husband—I have killed him—it was I myself who did it!" was all that she would say.

Of course they did not believe her. They accepted the unmeaning words as part of their mistress's frenzy at her sudden and unexpected loss. They saw what had happened, and they ran breathlessly for a doctor, who confirmed their worst fears—the *Signor* was dead!

The old *palazzo* became like a disturbed ant-hill. The servants ran hither and thither, unknowing how to act, whilst the mistress sat by the bedside with staring, tearless eyes, holding the hand of her dead husband. But there were a dozen things to be done—half a hundred orders to be issued. Death in Florence is quickly followed by burial. The law does not permit a mourner to lament his Dead for more than four-and-twenty hours.

But the *signora* would give no orders for the funeral nor answer any questions put to her! She had no friends in Florence—for ought they knew, she had no money—what were they to do? At last one of them thought of the neighbouring Convent of the Annunciation and ran to implore one of the good sisters to come to their mistress in her extremity.

Shortly afterwards, Sister Angelica entered the bedroom where Harriet sat murmuring at intervals, "It is *I* who have killed him", and attempted to administer comfort to the young mourner. But her words and prayers had no effect upon Harriet. Her brain could hold but one idea—she had killed Tony! Doctor Phillips was right—it was she who had killed Margaret Pullen's baby and Bobby Bates, and to look further back, little Caroline, and now—now, her Tony! the light of her life, the passion of her being, the essence of all her joy—her hope for this world and the next. She had killed him—*she,* who worshipped him, whose pride was bound up in him, who was to have helped him and comforted him and waited on him all his life—she had killed him!

Her dry lips refused to say the words, distinctly, but they kept revolving in her brain until they dazed and wearied her. The little sister stood by her and held her hand, as the professional assistants entered the death chamber and arranged and straightened the body for the grave, finally placing it in a coffin and carrying it away to a mortuary where it would have to remain until buried on the morrow, but Harriet made no resistance to the ceremony and no sign. She did not even say "Goodbye" as Tony was carried from her sight for ever! Sister Angelica talked to her of the glorious Heaven where they must hope that her dear husband would be translated, of the peace and happiness he would enjoy, of the reunion which awaited them when her term of life was also past.

She pressed her to make the convent her refuge until the first agony of her loss was overcome—reminded her of the peace and rest she would encounter within the cloisters, and how the whole fraternity would unite in praying for the soul of her beloved that he might speedily obtain the remission of his sins and an entrance into the Beatific Presence.

Harriet listened dully and at last in order to get rid of her well-intentioned but rather wearisome consoler, she promised to do all that she wished. Let the sister return to the convent for the present, and on the morrow if she would come for her at the same time, she might take her back with her. She wanted rest and peace—she would be thankful for them, poor Harriet said—only tonight, this one night more, she wished to be alone. So, the good little sister went away rejoicing that she had succeeded in her errand of mercy, and looking forward to bearing the poor young widow to the convent on the morrow, there to learn the true secret of earthly happiness.

When she had gone and the old *palazzo* was quiet and empty, the bewildered girl rose to her feet and tried to steady her shaking limbs sufficiently, to write what seemed to be a letter but was in reality a will. It ran:

> I leave all that I possess to Margaret Pullen, the wife of Colonel Arthur Pullen, the best woman Tony said that he had ever met, and I beg her to accept it in return for the kindness she shewed to me when I went to Heyst, a stranger.
>
> Signed,
>
> Harriet Pennell.

She put the paper into an envelope and as soon as the morning had dawned, she asked her servant Lorenzo to shew her the way to the nearest notary, in whose presence she signed the document and directed him to whom it should be sent in case of her own death.

And after another visit to a *pharmacien*, she returned to the *palazzo* and took up her watch again in the now deserted bedchamber.

Her servants brought her refreshments and pressed her to eat, without effect. All she desired, she told them, was to be left alone, until the sister came for her in the afternoon.

Sister Angelica arrived true to her appointment, and went at once to the bedchamber. To her surprise she found Harriet lying on the bed, just where the corpse of Anthony Pennell had lain, and apparently asleep.

"*Pauvre enfant!*" thought the kind-hearted nun, "grief has exhausted her! I should not have attended to her request, but have watched with her through the night! *Eh donc, ma pauvre,*" she continued, gently touching the girl on the shoulder, "*levez-vous! Je suis ici.*"

But there was no awakening on this earth for Harriet Pennell. She had taken a dose of chloral and joined her husband.

When Margaret Pullen received the will which Harriet had left behind her, she found these words with it, scribbled in a very trembling hand upon a scrap of paper:

> Do not think more unkindly of me than you can help. My parents have made me unfit to live. Let me go to a world where the curse of heredity which they laid upon me may be mercifully wiped out.

The Invisible Tenants of Rushmere

On the banks of the Wye, Monmouthshire.—To be Let, furnished, a commodious Family Mansion, surrounded with park-like grounds. Stabling and every convenience. Only two and a-half miles from station, church, and post-office. Excellent fishing to be procured in the neighbourhood. Rent nominal to a responsible tenant.

Such, with a few trifling additions, was the advertisement that caught my eye in the spring of 18—.

'My dear Jane,' I said, as I handed the paper over to my wife, 'this, I think, is the very thing we want.'

I was a London practitioner, with a numerous family and a large circle of patients; but the two facts, though blessings in themselves, were not without their disadvantages.

The hostages which I had given to fortune had made that strenuous action which attention to my numerous patients supplied incumbent on me; but the consequent anxiety and want of rest had drawn so largely on my mental and physical resources, that there was no need for my professional brethren to warn me of the necessity of change and country air. I felt myself that I was breaking down, and had already made arrangements with a friend to take my practice for a few months, and set me at liberty to attend to my own health. And being passionately fond of fishing, and all country pleasures and pursuits, and looking forward with zest to a period of complete quiet, the residence alluded to (if it fulfilled the promise of its advertisement) appeared to be all that I could desire.

'Park-like grounds!' exclaimed my wife, with animation. 'How the dear children will enjoy themselves.'

'And two and a-half miles from church or station,' I responded eagerly, 'No neighbours, excellent fishing, and at a nominal rent It sounds too good to be true.'

'Oh, Arthur! you must write, and obtain all the particulars this very day. If you put it off, some one will be sure to take the house before we have time to do so.'

'I shall go and see the city agents at once,' I replied, resolutely. 'It is too rare an opportunity to be lost. Only, don't raise your hopes too high, my dear. Advertisements are apt to be deceptive.'

But when I had seen Messrs Quibble & Lye on the subject, it really seemed as though for once they had spoken the truth. Rushmere, the house in question, had been built and furnished for his own use by an old gentleman, who died shortly afterwards, and his heirs, not liking the situation, had placed the property in the agents hands for letting. The owners were wealthy, cared little for money, and had authorised the agents to let the house on any reasonable terms, and it was really a bargain to anyone that wanted it. They frankly admitted that the loneliness of the position of Rushmere was the reason of its cheapness; but when I heard the rent at which they offered to let me take it, if approved of, for three months, I was quite ready to agree with Messrs Quibble & Lye in their idea of a bargain, and that, for those who liked solitude, Rushmere offered extraordinary advantages.

Armed with the necessary authority, I found my way down into Monmouthshire, to inspect the premises on the following day; and when I saw Rushmere, I felt still more disposed to be surprised at the opportunity afforded me, and to congratulate myself on the promptitude with which I had embraced it. I found it to be a good-sized country house, comfortably furnished, and, to all appearance, well built, standing in enclosed grounds, and on a healthy elevation; but, notwithstanding its isolated situation, I was too much a man of the world to believe, under the circumstances, that its greatest disadvantage lay in that fact. Accordingly, I peered eagerly about for damp walls, covered cesspools, unsteady joists, or tottering foundations, but I could find none.

'The chimneys smoke, I suppose?' I remarked, in a would-be careless tone, to the old woman whom I found in charge of the house, and who crept after me wherever I went.

'Chimbleys smoke, sir? Not as I knows of.'

'The roof leaks, perhaps?'

'Deary me, no. You won't find a spot of damp, look where you may.'

'Then there's been a fever, or some infectious disorder in the house?'

'A fever, sir? Why, the place has been empty these six months. The last tenants left at Christmas.'

'Empty for six months!' I exclaimed. 'How long is it, then, since the gentleman who built it died?'

'Old Mr Bennett, sir? He's been dead a matter of fifteen years or more.'

'Indeed! Then why don't the owners of the place sell it, instead of letting it stand vacant?' thought I to myself.

But I did not say so to the old woman, who was looking up in my face, as though anxious to learn what my decision would be.

'No vermin, I hope?' I suggested, as a last resource. 'You are not troubled with rats or mice at night, are you?'

'Oh, I don't sleep here at night, sir, thank heaven!' she answered in a manner which appeared to me unnecessarily energetic. 'I am only employed by day to air the house, and show it to strangers. I go home to my own people at night.'

'And where do your people live?'

'Better than half a mile from here, sir, and ours is the nearest cottage to Rushmere.'

And then—apprehensive, perhaps, that her information might prove a drawback to the letting of the property—she added, quickly,—

'Not but what it's a nice place to live in, is Rushmere, and very convenient, though a bit lonesome.'

I perfectly agreed with her, the 'lonesomeness' of the situation proving no detraction in my eyes.

On my return to London I gave my wife so glowing a description of the house and its surroundings, that she urged me to conclude the bargain at once; and, in the course of a few weeks, I and my family were transplanted from the purlieus of Bayswater to the banks of the Wye. It was the middle of May when we took possession, and the country wore its most attractive garb. The children were wild with delight at being let loose in the flower-bespangled fields, and, as I watched the tributaries of the river, and perceived the excellent sport they promised me, I felt scarcely less excited than the children, Only my wife, I thought, became inoculated with some of the absurd fears of the domestics we had brought with us from town, and seemed to consider the locality more lonely and unprotected than she had expected to find it.

'It's a charming place, Arthur.' she acknowledged, 'and marvellously cheap; but it is certainly a long way from other houses. I find we shall have to send for everything to the town. Not even the country carts, with butter and poultry, seem to call at Rushmere.'

'My dear Jane, I told you distinctly that it was two and a-half miles from church or station, and you read it for yourself in the paper. But I thought we looked out for a retreat where we should run no risk of being intruded on by strangers.'

'Oh yes, of course; only there are not even any farmhouses or cottages near Rushmere, you see; and it would be so very easy for anyone to break in at night, and rob us.'

'Pooh, nonsense! What will you be afraid of next? The locks and bolts are perfectly secure, and both Dawson and I have firearms, and are ready to use them. Your fears are childish, Janie.'

But all my arguments were unavailing, and each day my wife grew more nervous, and less willing to be left alone. So much so, indeed, that I made a practice of seeing that the house fastenings were properly secured each night myself, and of keeping a loaded revolver close to my hand, in case of need. But it damped my pleasure to find that Jane was not enjoying herself; and the country looked less beautiful to me than it had done at first. One night I suddenly awoke, to find that she was sitting up in bed, and in an attitude of expectation.

'My dear, what is the matter with you?'

'Oh, hush ! I am sure that I hear footsteps on the stairs—footsteps creeping up and down.'

I listened with her, but could detect no sound whatever.

'Lie down again, Jane—it is only your imagination. Everyone is fast asleep in bed.'

'I assure you, Arthur, I am not mistaken. Once they came quite near the door.'

'If so, it can only be one of the servants. You don't wish me to get up and encounter Mary or Susan in her nightdress, do you? Consider my morals!'

'Oh no, of course not,' she replied with a faint smile; yet it was some time before she fell to sleep again.

It was not many nights before my wife roused me again with the same complaint.

'Arthur, don't call me silly, but I am *certain* I heard something.'

To appease her fears, I shook off my drowsiness, and, with a lighted candle, made a tour of the house; but all was as I had left it.

Once, indeed, I imagined that I heard at my side the sound of a quick breathing; but that I knew must be sheer fancy, since I was alone.

The only circumstance that startled me was finding Dawson, the man servant, who slept on the ground floor, also awake, and listening at his door.

'What roused you, Dawson?'

'Well, sir, I can hardly say; but I fancied I heard some one going up the stairs a little while ago.'

'You heard me coming down, you mean.'

'No, sir, begging your pardon, it was footsteps going up—lighter than yours, sir. More like those of a woman.'

Yet, though I privately interrogated the female servants on the following day, I could not discover that any of them had been out of their beds; and I forbore to tell my wife what Dawson had said in corroboration of her statement.

Only I was as much annoyed as astonished when, as I finished my catechism of Mary, our head nurse, she informed me that she had made up her mind to leave our service. Mary—my wife's right hand—who had been with us ever since the birth of our first child! The announcement took me completely aback.

'What on earth is your reason for leaving us?' I demanded angrily; for I knew what a blow her decision would be to Jane. 'What have you to find fault with?'

'Nothing with you or the mistress, sir; but I can't remain in this house. I wouldn't stay in it a night longer, if it were possible to get away; and I do hope you and Mrs Delamere will let me go as soon as ever you can, sir, as it will be the death of me.'

'What will be the death of you?'

'The footsteps, sir, and the voices,' she answered, crying. 'I can hear them about the nurseries all night long, and it's more than any mortal can stand—it is, indeed.'

'Are you infected with the same folly?' I exclaimed. 'I see what it is, Dawson has been talking to you. I didn't know I had such a couple of fools in my establishment.'

'Mr Dawson has said nothing to me about nothing, sir,' she answered. 'I hear what I hear with my own ears; and I wouldn't stay a week longer in this 'aunted place, not if you was to strew the floor with golden guineas for me.'

Not possessing either the capability or the inclination to test Mary's fidelity by the means she alluded to, and finding her determination unalterable, I gave her the desired permission to depart; only making it a stipulation that she should not tell her mistress the real reason for her leaving us, but ascribe it to bad news from home, or any other cause.

But though I could not but believe that the woman's idiotic terrors had blinded her judgment, I was extremely surprised to find she should have been so led astray, as I had always considered Mary to possess a remarkably clear head and good moral sense. The wailing and lamentation, from both mother and children, at the announcement of her departure made me still more angry with her obstinacy and folly. But she continued resolute; and we were driven to try and secure someone to fulfil her duties from the neighbouring town.

But here a strange difficulty met us. We saw several fresh, rosy-cheeked maidens, who appeared quite willing to undertake our service, until they heard where we resided; when, by an extraordinary coincidence, one and all discovered that some insurmountable obstacle prevented their coming at all. When the same thing had occurred several times in succession, and Jane appeared worn out with disappointment and fatigue, the landlord of the inn where we had put up for the day appeared at the door, and beckoned me out.

'May I make bold enough to ask if you want a servant to go to Rushmere?' he inquired of me in a whisper.

'Certainly, we do. Our nurse has been obliged to leave us suddenly, and we want some one to supply her place.'

'Then you may give it up as a bad job, sir; for you'll never get one of the country people here about to set a foot in Rushmere—not if you were to live there till the day of your death.'

'And why not?' I demanded, with affected ignorance.

'What! haven't you heard nothing since you've been there, sir?'

'Heard? What should I have heard, except the ordinary noises of the household?'

'Well, you're lucky if you've escaped so far,' returned the landlord, mysteriously; 'but it ain't for long. No one who lives in Rushmere lives there *alone*. I can tell you the whole story if you like?'

'I have no desire to listen to any such folly.' I replied, testily. 'I am not superstitious, and do not believe in supernatural sights or sounds. If the people round about here are foolish enough to do so, I cannot help it; but I will not have the minds of my wife or family imbued with their nonsense.'

'Very good, sir; I hope you may be able to say as much two months hence,' said the man, civilly.

And so we parted.

I returned to Janie, and persuaded her he had told me that all the girls of that town had a strong objection to leave it, which was the reason they refused to take service in the country. I reminded her that Susan was quite competent to take charge of the whole flock until we returned to London; and it would be better after all to put up with a little inconvenience than to introduce a stranger to the nursery. So my wife, who was disappointed with the failure of her enterprise, fell in with my ideas, and we returned to Rushmere, determined to do as best we could with Susan only.

But I could not forget the landlord's earnestness, and, notwithstanding my incredulity, began to wish we were well out of Rushmere.

For a few days after Mary s departure we slept in peace; but then the question of the mysterious footsteps assumed a graver aspect, for my wife and I were roused from deep slumber one night by a loud knock upon the bedroom door, and springing up to answer it, I encountered, on the threshold, Dawson, pale with fright, and trembling in every limb.

'What do you mean by alarming your mistress in this way?' I inquired, angrily.

'I'm very sorry, sir,' he replied, with chattering teeth, 'but I thought it my duty to let you know. There's someone in the house tonight, sir. I can hear them whispering together at this moment; and so can you, if you will but listen.'

I advanced at once to the banisters, and certainly heard what seemed to be the sound of distant voices engaged in altercation; and, light in hand, followed by Dawson, I dashed down the staircase without further ceremony, in hopes of trapping the intruders.

But all in vain. Though we entered every room in turn, not a soul was visible.

I came to the conclusion that the whole alarm was due to Dawson's cowardice.

'You contemptible fool, you are as chicken-hearted as a woman!' I said, contemptuously. 'You hear the frogs croaking in the mere, or the wind blowing through the rushes, and you immediately conclude the house is full of thieves.'

'I didn't say it was thieves,' the man interposed, sullenly; but I took no notice of the muttered remark.

'If you are afraid to sleep downstairs by yourself,' I continued, 'say so; but don't come alarming your mistress again, in the middle of the night, for I won't allow it.'

The man slunk back into his room, with a reiteration that he had not been mistaken; and I returned to bed, full of complaints at having been so unnecessarily roused.

'If this kind of thing goes on,' I remarked to my wife, 'I shall regret ever having set eyes on Rushmere. That a pack of silly maid-servants should see a robber in every bush is only to be expected; but how a sensible man like Dawson, and a woman of education like yourself, can permit your imagination to betray you into such foolish fears, is quite past my comprehension.'

Yet, notwithstanding my dose of philosophy, poor Jane looked so pale upon the following morning, that I was fain to devise and carry into execution a little excursion into the neighbouring country before she regained her usual composure.

Some time passed without any further disturbance, and though upon several occasions I blamed myself for having brought a family, used to a populous city like London, to vegetate in so isolated a spot as Rushmere, I had almost forgotten the circumstances that had so much annoyed me.

We had now spent a month in our temporary home. The fields and hedgerows were bright with summer flowers, and the children passed most of their time tumbling amongst the new-mown hay. Janie had once more regained courage to sit by herself in the dusk, and to rest with tolerable security when she went to bed. I was rejoicing in the idea that all the folly that had marred the pleasure of our arrival at Rushmere had died a natural death, when it was vividly and painfully recalled to my mind by its actual recurrence.

Our second girl, a delicate little creature of about six years old, who, since the departure of her nurse, had slept in a cot in the same room as ourselves, woke me up in the middle of the night by exclaiming, in a frightened, plaintive voice, close to my ear,—

'Papa! papa! do you hear the footsteps? Someone is coming up the stairs!'

The tone was one of terror, and it roused my wife and myself instantly. The child was cold, and shaking all over with alarm, and I placed her by her mother's side before I left the room to ascertain if there was any truth in her assertion.

'Arthur, Arthur! I hear them as plainly as can be,' exclaimed my wife, who was as terrified as the child. 'They are on the second landing. There is no mistake about it this time.'

I listened at the half-opened door, and was compelled to agree with her. From whatever cause they arose, footsteps were to be distinctly heard upon the staircase—sometimes advancing, and then retreating, as though afraid to venture farther; but, still, not to be mistaken for anything but the sound of feet.

With a muttered exclamation, I seized my revolver.

'Don't be alarmed,' I said, hurriedly; 'there is not the slightest occasion for it. And, whatever happens, do not venture on the landing. I shall be quite safe.'

And without further preamble, only desirous to settle the business once for all, and give the intruders on my domains a sharp lesson on the laws of *meum* and *tuum*, I sprang down the staircase. I had not stayed to strike a light; but the moon was shining blandly in at the uncurtained passage window, and the landing was as bright as day. Yet I saw no one there. The thief (if thief it were) must have already taken the alarm, and descended to the lowest regions.

I fancied I could detect the same footsteps, but more distinctly marked, walk by me with a hurried, frightened movement, accompanied by a quick, sobbing breath; and, as I paused to consider what such a mystery could indicate, a pair of heavily-shod feet rushed past me, or seemed to rush, upon the stairs. I heard an angry shout commingle with a faint cry of terror below the landing whereon I stood; then, the discharge of a firearm, followed by a low groan of pain—and all was still.

Dark and mysterious though it appeared to be, I did not dream of ascribing the circumstance to any but a natural cause. But there was evidently no time for hesitation, and in another moment I had flown down the stairs, and stood in the moonlighted hall. It was empty! Chairs, table, hat-stand, stood in their accustomed places; the children's garden hats and my fishing tackle were strewn about; but of animated nature there was not a sign, of the recent scuffle not a trace!

All was quiet, calm, and undisturbed, and, as I gazed around in mute bewilderment, the perspiration stood in thick drops upon my brow and chin.

My first collected thought was for my wife and the best means by which to prevent her sharing the mystification and dread which I have no hesitation in confessing that I now experienced; but as I turned to remount the staircase, I caught sight of some dark mass lying at the further end of the passage, and going up to it, found to my surprise the body of Dawson, cold and insensible.

The explanation of the mystery was before me—so I immediately determined. The man, whom I knew to be replete with superstitious terror, imagining he heard the unaccountable noise of footsteps, had evidently supplied that which had reached my ear, and in his alarm at my approach had discharged his firearm at the supposed marauder. Pleasant for me if he had taken a better aim: So I thought as I dragged his unconscious body into his bedroom, and busied myself by restoring it to sensation.

As soon as he opened his eyes, and was sufficiently recovered to answer me, I asked,—

'What on earth made you discharge your gun, Dawson? I must take it out of your keeping, if your are so careless about using it.'

'I didn't fire, sir.'

'Nonsense! you don't know what you are talking about. I heard the shot distinctly as I came downstairs.'

'I am only telling you the truth, sir. There is the fowling-piece in that corner. I have not drawn the trigger since you last loaded it.'

I went up and examined the weapon. What Dawson had said was correct. It had not been used.

'Then who did fire?' I said, impatiently. 'I could swear to having heard the report.'

'And so could I, sir. It was that that knocked me over.'

'What do you mean?'

'Oh, sir, pray take the mistress and the children away from this place as soon as possible. It's no robbers that go up and down these stairs of nights, sir. It's something much worse than that.'

'Dawson, if you begin to talk such folly to me, I'll discharge you on the spot. I believe the whole lot of you have gone mad.'

'But listen to my story, sir. I had gone to bed last night, as tired as possible, and thinking of nothing but getting a good long sleep. The first thing that roused me was someone trying the handle of my door. I lay and listened to it for some time before I was fully awake, and then I thought maybe you wanted something out of my room, and was trying not to wake me; so I got out of bed and opened the door. But there was nobody there, though I fancied I heard someone breathing hard a few yards off from me. Well, I thought to myself, sir, this is all nonsense; so I came back to bed again, and lay down.

'But I couldn't sleep; for directly the door was closed, I heard the footsteps again, creep, creeping along the passage and the wall, as though some one was crouching and feeling his way as he went Then the handle of the door began to creak and turn again—I saw it turn, sir, with my own eyes, backwards and forwards, a dozen times in the moonlight; and then I heard a heavier step come stumbling down-stairs, and there seemed to be a kind of scuffle. I couldn't stand it no longer, so I opened the door again; and then, as I'm a living Christian, sir, I heard a woman's voice say 'Father!' with a kind of sob, and as the sound was uttered there came a report from the first landing, and the sound of a fall, and a deep groan in the passage below. And it seemed to go right through me, and curdle my blood, and I fell all of a heap where you found me. And it's nothing natural, sir, you may take my word for it; and harm will come of your stopping in this house.'

So saying, poor Dawson, who seemed in real earnest, fell back on his pillow with a heavy sigh.

'Dawson,' I said, critically, 'what did you eat for supper last night?'

'You're never going to put down what I've told you, sir, to supper. I took nothing but a little cold meat, upon my word. And I was as sensible, till that shot knocked me over, as you are this moment.'

'Do you mean to tell me that you seriously believe the report of a firearm could have reached your ears without one having been discharged?'

'But didn't you say you heard it yourself, sir?'

This knocked me over, and I did not know what to answer him. In the attempt to allay what I considered his unreasonable fear, I had forgotten my own experience in the matter. And I knew that I had heard, or imagined I heard, a shot fired, and it would be very difficult for anyone to persuade me I was mistaken. Still, though I held no belief in supernatural agencies, I was an earnest student of the philo-sophical and metaphysical school of Germany, and acquainted with all the revealed wonders of magnetism and animal electricity.

It was impossible to say whether some such effect as I have de-scribed might not have been produced upon my brain by the reflec-tion of the fear or fancy on that of my servant; and that as he had imagined the concussion of firearms, so I might have instantaneously received the impression of his mind. It was a nice question for argu-ment, and not one to be thought over at that moment. All my present business lay in the effort to disabuse Dawson's mind of the reality of the shock it had received.

'I said I fancied I heard something like the report of a firearm; but as none had been fired, of course I must have been mistaken. Come, Dawson, I must go back, or Mrs Delamere will wonder what has be-come of me. I conclude you are not such a coward as to be afraid to be left by yourself?'

'I never feared a man in my life, sir; but the strongest heart can't stand up against spirits.'

'Spirits!' I exclaimed, angrily. 'I wonder what on earth you will talk to me about next? Now, I'll tell you what it is, Dawson—if I hear anything more of this, or am disturbed again at night by your folly, I'll pack you back to London without a character. Do you understand me?'

'I understand you, sir,' the man answered, humbly; and thereupon I left him to himself.

But, as I reascended the staircase, I was not satisfied either with my own half-formed solution of the mystery, or my servant's reception of my rebuke. He evidently would prefer dismissal to passing such another night. I could read the resolution in his face, although he had not expressed it in so many words. When I reached my wife's room, I was still more surprised. Janie and the child lay in a profound slumber. I had expected to find both of them in a state of anxious terror to learn the meaning of the noise that was going on below; but they had evidently heard nothing. This welcome fact, however, only tended to confirm me in the belief I had commenced to entertain, of the whole circumstance being due to some, perhaps yet undiscovered, phase of brain reading, and I fell to sleep, resolved to make a deeper study of the marvels propounded by Mesmer and Kant.

When I awoke, with the bright June sun streaming in at the windows, I had naturally parted with much of the impression of the night before. It is hard to associate any gloomy or unnatural thoughts with the unlimited glory of the summer s sunshine, that streams into every nook and cranny, and leaves no shadows anywhere. On this particular morning it seemed to have cleared the cobwebs off all our brains. The child had forgotten all about the occurrence of the night. I was, as usual, ready to laugh away all ghostly fears and fancies; and even Janie seemed to regard the matter as one of little moment.

'What was the matter last night, Arthur, dear?' she asked, when the subject recurred to her memory. 'I was so sleepy I couldn't keep awake till you came up again.'

'Didn't you hear the fearful battle I held with the goblins in the hall?' I demanded, gaily, though I put the question with a purpose,— 'the shots that were exchanged between us, and the groans of the defeated, as they slunk away into their haunted coal-cellars and cupboards?' 'Arthur, what nonsense! Was there any noise?'

'Well, I frightened Dawson, and Dawson frightened me; and we squabbled over it for the best part of an hour. I thought our talking might have disturbed you.'

'Indeed, it didn't, then. But don't mention it before Cissy, Arthur, even in fun, for she declares she heard someone walking about the room, and I want her to forget it.'

I dropped the subject; but meeting Dawson as I was smoking my pipe in the garden that afternoon, I ventured to rally him on his fright of the night before, and to ask if he hadn't got over it by that time.

'No, sir; and I never shall,' he replied, with a sort of shiver. 'And I only hope you may come to be convinced of the truth of it before it's too late to prevent harm you may never cease to repent of.'

There was so much respectful earnestness in the man's manner, that I could not resent his words nor laugh at them, as I had done before; and I passed by him in thoughtful silence.

What if there were more in all this than I had ever permitted myself to imagine? What if the assertions of my man-servant, the unaffected terror of my wife and child, the fears of my nurse, the evident shrinking of the old woman who had charge of the house, the opposition from the servants of the neighbouring town, combined with what I had heard myself, were not simple chimeras of the brain—fancies engendered by superstition or timidity or ignorance; but indications of a power beyond our control, the beginning and the end of which may alike remain unknown until all things are revealed? I had, with the majority of educated men, manfully resisted all temptation to believe in the possibility of spirits, of whatever grade, making themselves either seen or heard by mortal senses.

I use the word 'manfully,' although I now believe it to be the height of manliness to refuse to discredit that which we cannot disprove, and to have sufficient humility to accept the belief that there are more things in heaven and earth than are dreamt of in our philosophy. But at that juncture I should have considered such a concession both childish and cowardly. Yet, there was sufficient doubt in my mind, notwithstanding the glorious June sun, respecting my adventure of the night before, that I resolved, whatever happened, that I would satisfy myself as to the value of the fears of those about me.

I could not keep my wife and children in a house where they might be liable at any moment to be frightened out of their seven senses, from whatever cause, without ascertaining the reason of it. Some reason there must be, either natural or otherwise; and I determined, if possible, to learn it that very night. I would not tell Dawson or anyone of my intention; but I would keep watch and ward in the old parlour on the ground floor, so as to be ready to rush out at a moment's notice, and seize any intruder who might attempt to disturb us. I still believed—I could not but believe—that the footsteps which so many of us had heard were due to some trickster, who wished to play upon our nerves in that lonely old house. I had heard of such things being done, purposely to keep visitors away; and I determined, whosoever it might be, whether our own servants or strangers, that they must take their chance of being shot down like any other robber.

According to my resolution, I said nothing to Janie, but tried to render the evening as cheerful and merry a one as possible.

I ordered strawberries and cream into the hay-field, and played with my troop of little ones there, until they were so tired they could hardly walk for the short distance that lay between them and their beds. As soon as they were dismissed, and we had returned to the house, I laid aside the newspapers that had arrived by that morning s post, and which I usually reserved for the evening's delectation, and taking my wife upon my knee, as in the dear old courting days, talked to her until she had forgotten everything but the topics on which we conversed, and had no time to brood upon the coming night, and the fears it usually engendered. Then, as a last duty, I carried to Dawson with my own hands a strong decoction of brandy and water, with which I had mixed something that I knew, under ordinary circumstances, must make him sleep till daylight

'Drink this,' I said to him. 'From whatever cause, our nerves were both shaken last night, and a little stimulant will do neither of us harm.'

'Thank you, sir,' he replied, as he finished the tumbler at a draught; 'I don't deny I'm glad to have it. I dread the thoughts of the night before us.'

'Lock your door on the inside,' I added as I left him, 'and don't get up whether the handle moves or not. Then, at all events, you will feel secure till the morrow.'

'Keys won't keep *them* out,' muttered Dawson, as he entered his sleeping apartment.

But I would not notice the allusion, though I understood it.

I went up to bed with my wife as usual; and it was not until I saw she was sound asleep that, habited in my dressing-gown and slippers, I ventured to creep softly out of the room and take my way downstairs again.

It was then about twelve o'clock. The moonlight was as bright as it had been the night before, and made every object distinctly visible. From the loud snoring which proceeded from Dawson's room, I concluded that my opiate had taken due effect, and that I should be permitted to hold my vigil undisturbed. In one hand I grasped a loaded revolver, and in the other a huge knotted stick, so determined was I not to be taken by my tormentors at a disadvantage. I turned into the general sitting-room, which opened on the hall. All was as we had left it; and I ensconced myself on one of the large old-fashioned sofas, trusting to my curiosity to keep me awake.

It was weary waiting. I heard one and then two sound from the big clock in the hall; still there was no other noise to break the silence. I began to relapse into my first belief that the whole business was due to imagination. From this I passed to self-satisfaction; self-satisfaction induced inertion, and inertion brought on heavy sleep. How long I slept I do not know, but I had reason afterwards to think, not more than half-an-hour.

However, that point is immaterial. But what waked me—waked me so completely that in a moment all my faculties were as clear as daylight—was the sound of a hoarse breathing. I sat up on the sofa and rubbed my eyes.

The room was fully lighted by the moon. I could see into each corner. Nothing was visible. The sound I had heard must then have proceeded from outside the door, which was open; and I turned towards it, fully expecting to see Dawson enter in a somnambulistic condition, brought on by his dreams and my soporific.

But he did not appear. I rose and looked into the hall. It was empty, as before. Still the breathing continued, and (as I, with now fully-awakened faculties, discovered) proceeded from a corner of the parlour where stood an old fashioned secretary and a chair. Not daring to believe my senses, I advanced to the spot and listened attentively. The sound continued, and was unmistakably palpable. The breathing was hoarse and laboured, like that of an old man who was suffering from bronchitis or asthma. Every now and then it was interrupted by a short, roupy cough.

What I suffered under this mysterious influence I can hardly tell. Interest and curiosity got the better of my natural horror; but even then I could not but feel that there was something very awful in this strange contact of sound without sight. Presently my eyes were attracted by the chair, which was pushed, without any visible agency, towards the wall. Something rose—I could hear the action of the feet. Something moved—I could hear it approaching the spot where I stood motionless. Something brushed past me, almost roughly—I could feel the contact of a cloth garment against my dressing-gown, and heard the sound of coarsely shod feet leaving the room. My hair was almost standing on end with terror; but I was determined to follow the mystery to its utmost limits, whether my curiosity were satisfied by the attempt or not.

I rushed after the clumping feet into the hall; and I heard them slowly and painfully, and yet most distinctly, commence to toil up the staircase. But before they had reached the first landing, and just as I was about to follow in their wake, my attention was distracted by another sound, which appeared to be close at my elbow—the sound of which Dawson had complained the night before—that of a creeping step, and a stifled sobbing, as though a woman were feeling her way along the passage in the dark.

I could discern the feeble touch as it felt along the wall, and then placed an uncertain hold upon the banisters—could hear the catching breath, which dared not rise into a cry, and detect the fear which caused the feet to advance and retreat, and advance a little way again, and then stop, as though dread of some unknown calamity overpowered every other feeling. Meanwhile, the clumping steps, that had died away in the distance, turned, and appeared to be coming downstairs again. The moon streamed brightly in at the landing window. Had a form been visible, it would have been as distinctly seen as by day. I experienced a sense of coming horror, and drew back in the shadow of the wall. As the heavy footsteps gained the lower landing, I heard a start—a scuffle—a faint cry of 'Father!' and then a curse—the flash of a firearm—a groan—and I remember nothing more.

When I recovered my consciousness, I was lying on the flat of my back in the passage, as I had found poor Dawson the night before, and the morning sun was shining full upon my face. I sat up, rubbed my eyes, and tried to remember how I had come there. Surely the moon had looked in at that window when I saw It last. Then in a moment came back upon my mind all that I had heard whilst holding my vigil during the past night; and I sprang to my feet, to see if I could discover any traces of the tragedy which seemed to have been enacted in my very presence.

But it was in vain I searched the parlour, the passage, and the stairs. Everything remained in its usual place. Even the chair, which I could swear I saw pushed against the wall, was now standing primly before the secretary, and the door of the room was closed, as it usually was when we retired for the night. I slunk up to my dressing-room, anxious that my wife should not discover that I had never retired to rest; and having plunged my head and face into cold water, took my way across the sunlighted fields, to see if the fresh morning air might not be successful in clearing away the confusion with which my brain was oppressed. But I had made up my mind on one point, and that was that we would move out of Rushmere as soon as it was possible to do so. After a stroll of a couple of hours, I re-approached the house. The first person I encountered was the under nurse, Susan, who ran to meet me with a perturbed countenance.

'Oh, sir, I'm so thankful you've come back ! Dawson has been looking for you for the last hour, for poor missus is so ill, and we don't know what on earth to do with her.'

'Ill! In what way?' I demanded quickly.

'That's what we can't make out, sir. Miss Cissy came up crying to the nursery, the first thing this morning, to tell me that her mamma had tumbled out of bed, and wouldn't speak to her; and she couldn't find her papa. So I ran downstairs directly, sir; and there I found my mistress on the ground, quite insensible, and she hasn't moved a limb since.'

'Good heavens!' I inwardly exclaimed, as I ran towards the house, 'is it possible she can have been affected by the same cause?'

I found Janie, as the nurse had said, unconscious; and it was some time before my remedies had any effect on her. When she opened her eyes, and understood the condition she had been in, she was seized with such a fit of nervous terror that she could do nothing but cling to me, and entreat me to take her away from Rushmere.

Remembering my own experience, I readily promised her that she should not sleep another night in the house if she did not desire it. Soothed by my words, she gradually calmed down, and was at last able to relate the circumstance which had so terrified her.

'Did you sleep in my room last night, dear Arthur?' she asked, curiously.

'I did not. But since you awoke, you surely must have been aware of my absence.'

'I know nothing, and remember nothing, except the awful horror that overpowered me. I had gone to sleep very happy last night, and none of my silly fears, as you have called them, ever entered my head. Indeed, I think I was in the midst of some pleasant dream, when I was awakened by the sound of a low sobbing by the bedside. Oh! such a strange, unearthly sobbing' (with a shudder). 'I thought at first it must be poor little Cissy, who had been frightened again, and I put out my hand to her, saying,—"Don't be afraid, dear. I am here." Directly, a hand was placed in mine—a cold, damp hand, with a deathlike, clayey feel about it that made me tremble. I knew at once it was not the child's hand, and I started up in bed, exclaiming,—"Who are you?"

'The room was quite dark, for I had pinned my shawl across the blind to keep the moon out of my eyes before I went to bed, and I could distinguish nothing. Yet still the cold, damp hand clung to mine, and seemed to strike the chill of death into my very bones. When I said, "Who are you?" something replied to me. I cannot say it was a voice. It was more like someone hissing at me through closed teeth, but I could distinguish the name "Emily"

'I was so frightened, Arthur, I did not know what to do. I wrenched my hand away from the dead hand. You were not there, and I called out loudly. I would have leaped out of bed, but that I heard the creeping footsteps, accompanied by the sobbing breath, go round the room, crying, "Father, father!"

'My blood seemed to curdle in my veins. I could not stir until it was gone. I heard it leave the room distinctly, although the door was never opened, and walk upon the landing as though to go downstairs. I was still sitting up in bed listening—listening—only waiting till the dreadful thing had quite gone away, to seek your presence, when I heard a heavy step clumping downstairs, then the report of a gun. I don't know *what* I thought. I remember nothing that followed; but I suppose I jumped out of bed with the intention of finding you, and fainted before I could reach the dressing-room. Oh, Arthur! what was it? What is it that haunts this house, and makes even the sunshine look as gloomy as night? Oh, take us away from it, or I am sure that something terrible will happen!'

'I *will* take you away from it, my dear. We will none of us sleep another night beneath its roof. What curse hangs over it, I cannot tell; but whether the strange sounds we have heard proceed from natural or supernatural causes, they alike render Rushmere no home for us. We will go to the hotel at —— this very day, Janie, and deliver up the keys of Rushmere again to Messrs Quibble & Lye.'

I then related to her my own experience, and that of Dawson; and though she trembled a little whilst listening to me, the idea of leaving the place before nightfall rendered the heavy fear less alarming than it would otherwise have been.

The servants, upon learning the resolution we had arrived at, were only too ready to help us to carry it out. Our personal possessions were packed in an incredibly short time, and we sat down that evening to a comfortable family dinner in the good old-fashioned inn at ——. As soon as the meal was concluded, and the children sent to bed, I said to my wife,—

'Janie, I am going to ring for the landlord, to see if he can throw any light on the cause of our experiences. I never told you that, when we came to this inn to try for a nurse to supply Mary's place, he informed me that nobody from his countryside would live at Rushmere; and asked me, in a manner which assured me he could have said more if he had chosen, if we had not heard anything whilst there. I laughed at the question then, but I do not feel so disposed to laugh at it now; and I am going to beg him to tell me all he may know. If nothing more, his story may form the stratum of a curious psychological study. Would you like to be present at our interview?'

'Oh yes, Arthur; I have quite recovered my nerves since I've lost sight of Rushmere, and I feel even curious to learn all I can upon the subject. That poor, sobbing voice that whispered "Emily"—I shall not forget its sound to my dying day.'

'Ring the bell, dear, and let us ask if the landlord is at leisure. To my mind, your experience of the details of this little tragedy appears the most interesting of all.'

The landlord, a Mr Browser, entered at once; and as soon as he heard my request, made himself completely at home with us.

'After the little rebuff you gave me t'other day, I shouldn't have ventured to say nothing, sir; but when I see your family getting out of the fly this afternoon, I says to Mrs Browser, "If that don't mean that they can't stand Rushmere another night, I'm a pumpkin." And I suppose, now, it did mean it, sir?'

'You are quite right, Mr Browser. The noises and voices about the house have become so intolerable, that it is quite impossible I can keep my family there. Still, I must tell you that, though I have been unable to account for the disturbances, I do not necessarily believe they are attributable to spirits. It is because I do not believe so that I wish to hear all you may be able to tell us, in order, if possible, to find a reason for what appears at present to be unreasonable.'

'Well, sir, you shall hear, as you say, all we have to tell you, and then you can believe what you like. But it ain't I as can relate the story, sir. Mrs Browser knows a deal more than I do; and with your leave, and that of this good lady here, I'll call her to give you the history of Rushmere.'

At this information, we displayed an amount of interest that resulted in a hasty summons for Mrs Browser. She was a fat, fair woman, of middle age, with ruddy cheeks, and a clear blue eye—not at all like a creature haunted by her own weak imagination, or who would be likely to mistake a shadow for a substance. Her appearance inspired me with confidence. I trusted that her relation might furnish me with some clue to the solution of the occurrences that had so confounded us. Safe out of the precincts of Rushmere, and with the lapse of twelve hours since the unaccountable swoon I had been seized with, my practical virtues were once more in the ascendant, and I was inclined to attribute our fright to anything but association with the marvellous.

'Be I to tell the story from the beginning, Browser?' was the first sentence that dropped from Mrs Browser's lips.

Her lord and master nodded an affirmative, whereupon she began:—

'When the gentleman as built Rushmere for his own gratification, sir, died, the house let well enough. But the place proved lonely, and there was more than one attempt at robbery, and people grew tired of taking it. And above all, the girls of the village began to refuse to go to service there. Well, it had been standing empty for some months, when a gentleman and his wife came to look after it. Browser and I—we didn't own this inn at that time, you will understand, sir, but kept a general shop in the village, and were but poorly off altogether, although we had the post-office at our place, and did the best business thereabouts.

'The key of Rushmere used always to be left in our keeping, too, and our boy would go up to show folks over the house. Well, one damp autumn day—I mind the day as if 'twere yesterday, for Browser had been ailing sadly with the rheumatics for weeks past, and not able to lift his hand to his head—this gentleman and lady, who went by the name of Greenslade, came for the keys of Rushmere. I remember thinking Mr Greenslade had a nasty, curious look about his eyes, and that his wife seemed a poor, brow-beaten creature; but that was no business of mine, and I sent Bill up with them to show the house. They took it, and entered on possession at once; and then came the difficulty about the servants.

'Not a soul would enter the place at first. Then a girl or two tried it, and came away when their month was up, saying the house was so lonesome, they couldn't sleep at nights, and the master was so queer-spoken and mannered, they were afraid of him.'

'Don't forget to say what he was used to do at nights,' here put in the landlord.

'La, Browser, I'm a-coming to it. Everything in its time. Well, sir, at last it came to this, that Mrs Greenslade hadn't a creature to help her in anythink, and down she came to ask if I would go to them for a few days. I stared; for there was the shop to be tended, and the post-office looked after, and I hadn't been used to odd jobs like that. But my husband said that he could do all that was wanted in the business; and we were very hard drove just then, and the lady offered such liberal pay, he over-persuaded me to go, if only on trial.

'So I put my pride in my pocket, and went out charring. I hadn't been at Rushmere many days, sir, before I found something was very wrong there. Mr Greenslade hardly ever spoke a word, but shut himself up in a room all day, or went mooning about the fields and common, where he couldn't meet a soul; and as for the poor lady, la! my heart bled for her, she seemed so wretched and broken-down and hopeless. I used often to say to her,—

'"Now, ma'am, do let me cook you a bit of something nice, for you've eaten nothing since yesterday, and you'll bring yourself down to death's door at this rate."

'And she'd answer,—

'"No, thank you, Mrs Browser: I couldn't touch it. I feel sometimes as if I'd never care to eat or drink again."

'And Mr Greenslade, he was just as bad. They didn't eat enough to keep a well-grown child between the two of them.'

'What-aged people were they?' I asked.

'Well, sir, I can hardly say; they weren't young nor yet old. Mr Greenslade, he may have been about fifty, and his lady a year or two younger; but I never took much count of that. But the gentleman looked much the oldest of the two, by reason of a stoop in his shoulders and a constant cough that seemed to tear his chest to pieces. I've known him shut himself up in the parlour the whole night long, coughing away fit to keep the whole house awake. And his breathing, sir—you could hear it half a mile off.'

'He was *assmatical*, poor man! that's where it was,' interposed Mr Browser.

'Well, I don't know what his complaint was called, Browser; but he made noise enough over it to wake the dead. But don't you go interrupting me no more after that fashion, or the gentleman and lady will never understand the half of my story, and I'm just coming to the cream of it.'

'I assure you we are deeply interested in what you are telling us,' I said, politely.

'It's very good of you to compliment me, sir, but I expect it will make matters clearer to you by-and-by. You're not the first tenants of Rushmere I've had to tell this tale to, I can tell you, and you won't be the last, either. One night, when I couldn't sleep for his nasty cough, and lay awake, wishing to goodness he'd go to bed like a Christian, I made sure I heard footsteps in the hall, a-creeping and a-creeping about like, as though someone was feeling their way round the house. "It can't be the mistress," I thought, "and maybe it's robbers, as have little idea the master's shut up in the study." So I opened the door quickly, but I could see nothing.'

'Exactly my own experience,' I exclaimed.

'Ah, sir, maybe; but they weren't the same footsteps, poor dear. I wish they had been, and she had the same power to tread now she had then. The hall was empty; but at the same time I heard the master groaning and cursing most awful in the parlour, and I went into my own room again, that I mightn't listen to his wicked oaths and words. I always hated and distrusted that man from the beginning. The next day I mentioned I had heard footsteps, before 'em both, and the rage Mr Greenslade put himself into was terrible. He said no robbers had better break into his house, or he'd shoot them dead as dogs. Afterwards his wife came to me and asked me what sort of footsteps they seemed; and when I told her, she cried upon my neck, and begged me if ever I heard a woman's step to say nothing of it to her husband.

'"A woman's step, ma'am," I replied; "why, what woman would dare break into a house?"

'But she only cried the more, and held her tongue.

'But that evening I heard their voices loud in the parlour, and there was a regular dispute between them.

'"If ever she should come, Henry," Mrs Greenslade said, "promise me you won't speak to her unless you can say words of pity or of comfort."

'"Pity!" he yelled, "what pity has she had for me? If ever she or any emissary of hers should dare to set foot upon these premises, I shall treat them as house-breakers, and shoot them down like dogs!"

'"Oh no! Henry, no!" screamed the poor woman; "think who she is. Think of her youth, her temptation, and forgive her."

'"I'll never forgive her—I'll never own her!" the wretch answered loudly; "but I'll treat her, or any of the cursed crew she associates with, as I would treat strangers who forced their way in to rob me by night. 'Twill be an evil day for them when they attempt to set foot in my house."

'Well, sir, I must cut this long story short, or you and your good lady will never get to bed tonight.

'The conversation I had overheard made me feel very uncomfortable, and I was certain some great misfortune or disgrace had happened to the parties I was serving; but I didn't let it rest upon my mind, till a few nights after, when I was wakened up by the same sound of creeping footsteps along the passage. As I sat up in bed and listened to them, I heard the master leave the parlour and go upstairs. At the same moment something crouched beside my door, and tried to turn the handle; but it was locked, and wouldn't open.

'I felt very uneasy. I knew my door stood in the shadow, and that whoever crouched there must have been hidden from Mr Greenslade as he walked across the hall. Presently I heard his footsteps coming downstairs again, as though he had forgotten something. He used to wear such thick boots, sir, you might hear his step all over the house. His loaded gun always stood on the first landing; when he reached there he stopped, I suppose it was his bad angel made him stop. Anyway, there was a low cry of "Father, father!"—a rush, the report of the gun, a low groan, and then all was still

'La! sir, I trembled so in my bed, you might have seen it shake under me.'

'I've seen it shake under you many a time,' said Browser.

'Perhaps you would like to tell the lady and gentleman my exact weight, though I don't see what that's got to do with the story,' replied his better half, majestically.

'I don't think I should ever have had the courage to leave my room, sir, unless I had heard my poor mistress fly down the staircase, with a loud scream. Then I got up, and joined her. Oh, it was an awful sight ! There, stretched on the floor-cloth, lay the dead body of a young girl; and my mistress had fainted dead away across her, and was covered with the blood that was pouring from a great hole in her forehead. On the landing stood my master, white as a sheet, and shaking like an aspen leaf.

"'So, this is your doing!" I cried, angrily. "You're a nice man to have charge of a gun. Do you see what you've done? Killed a poor girl in mistake for a robber, and nearly killed your wife into the bargain. Who is this poor murdered young creature? Do you know her?"

"'Know her!" he repeated, with a groan. "Woman, don't torture me with your questions. *She is my own daughter!*"

'He rushed upstairs as he spoke, and I was in a nice quandary, left alone with the two unconscious women. When my poor mistress woke up again, she wanted me to fetch a doctor; but it would have been of no use. She was past all human help.

'We carried the corpse upstairs between us, and laid it gently on the bed. I've often wondered since where the poor mother's strength came from, but it was lent her for the need. Then, sitting close to me for the remainder of the night, she told me her story—how the poor girl had led such an unhappy life with her harsh, ill-tempered father, that she had been tempted into a foolish marriage by the first lover that offered her affection and a peaceful home.

"'I always hoped she would come back to us," said Mrs Greenslade, "for her husband had deserted her, leaving her destitute; and yet, although she knew how to enter the house unobserved, I dreaded her doing so, because of her father's bitter enmity. Only last night, Mrs Browser, I awoke from sleep, and fancied I heard a sobbing in my room. I whispered, 'Who is there?' and a voice replied, 'Emily!' But I thought it was a dream. If I had known—if I had but known!"

'She lay so quiet and uncomplaining on my knee, only moving now and then, that she frightened me; and when the morning broke, I tried to shift her, and said,—

"' Hadn't I better go and see after the master, ma'am?"

'As I mentioned his name, I could see the shudder that ran through her frame; but she motioned me away with her hand.

'I went upstairs to a room Mr Greenslade called his dressing-room, and where I guessed he'd gone; and you'll never believe, sir, the awful sight as met my eyes. I didn't get over it for a month—did I, Browser?'

'You haven't got over it to this day, I'm sometimes thinking, missus.'

'That means I'm off my head; but if it wasn't for my head, I wonder where the business would go to. No, sir—if you'll believe me, when I entered the room, there was the old man dead as mutton, hanging from a beam in the ceiling. I gave one shriek, and down I fell.'

'I don't wonder at it.' cried Janie.

'Well, ma'am, when I came to again, all was confusion and misery.

We had the perlice in, and the crowner's inquest, and there was such a fuss, you never see. Some of Mrs Greenslade's friends came and fetched her away; but I heard she didn't live many months afterwards. As for myself, I was only too glad to get back to the shop and my old man, and the first words I said to him was,—

'"No more charing for me."'

'And now, sir, if I may make so bold, what do you think of the story?' demanded the landlord. 'Can you put this and that together now?'

'It is marvellous!' I replied. 'Your wife has simply repeated the scene which we have heard enacted a dozen times in Rushmere. The footsteps were a nightly occurrence.'

'I heard the voice!' exclaimed Janie, 'and it whispered "*Emily*."'

'The handle of my servant's door was turned. The report of the gun was as distinct as possible.'

'That is what everybody says as goes to Rushmere, sir. No one can abide the place since that awful murder was committed there,' said Mrs Browser.

'And can you account for it in any way, sir?' demanded her husband, slyly. 'Do you think, now that you've heard the story, that the noises are mortal, or that it's the spirits of the dead that causes them?'

'I don't know what to think, Browser. There is a theory that no uttered sound is ever lost, but drifts as an eddying circle into space, until in course of time it must be heard again. Thus our evil words, too often accompanied by evil deeds, live for ever, to testify against us in eternity. It may be that the Universal Father ordains that some of His guilty children shall expurgate their crimes by re-acting them until they become sensible of their enormity; but this can be but a matter for speculation.

'This story leaves us, as such stories usually do, as perplexed as we were before. We cannot tell—we probably never shall tell—what irrefragable laws of the universe these mysterious circumstances fulfil; but we know that spirit and matter alike are in higher hands than ours; and, whilst nature cannot help trembling when brought in contact with the supernatural, we have no need to fear that it will ever be permitted to work us harm.'

This little analysis was evidently too much for Mr and Mrs Browser, who, with a look of complete mystification on their countenances, rose from their seats, and wished us respectfully goodnight; leaving Janie and me to evolve what theories we chose from the true story of the Invisible Tenants of Rushmere.

Still Waters

I often wonder if when, as the Bible tells us, 'the secrets of all hearts shall be revealed,' they will be revealed to our fellow-creatures as well as to the Almighty Judge of men.

I am not usually given to philosophise, but the above remark was drawn from me by the receipt of a letter this morning from my niece, Justina Trevor, announcing the death of her 'dear friend,' Mrs Benson, which recalled the remembrance of an incident that took place a few months since, whilst I was staying at Durham Hall, in Derbyshire, the estate of her late husband, Sir Harry Trevor. I am an old bachelor, though not so old as I look; yet when I confess that I write 'General' before my name, and have served most of my time in hot climates, it will readily be believed that no one would take me for a chicken. It was after an absence of fourteen years that, last November, I arrived in England, and put up at an hotel near Covent Garden, which had been a favourite resort of mine during my last stay in London.

But I soon found that I had made a great mistake, for town was dark, damp, dirty, deserted, detestable; in fact, no adjective, however long and however strong, could convey an adequate idea of the impression made upon me by a review of the great metropolis; and it was with a feeling of intense relief that I perused a letter from my niece Justina, to whom I had duly announced my advent, in which she insisted that her 'dear uncle' must spend his first Christmas in England nowhere but at Durham Hall, with Sir Harry and herself.

Now Justina, if not my only, is certainly my nearest relative, and *I* knew that *she* knew that I was an old fellow on the shady side of sixty-five, with a couple of pounds or so laid by in the Oriental Bank, and with no one to leave them to but herself or her children; but I was not going to let that fact interfere with my prospects of present comfort; and so, ordering my servant to repack my travelling cases, the next day but one saw us *en route* for Derbyshire.

It was evening when I arrived at Durham Hall, but even on a first view I could not help being struck with the munificent manner in which all the arrangements of the household seemed to be conducted, and reflected with shame on the unworthy suspicion I had entertained respecting those two pounds of mine in the Oriental Bank, which I now felt would be but as a drop in the ocean to the display of wealth which surrounded me. The hall was full of guests, assembled to enjoy the hunting and shooting season, and to spend the coming Christmas, and amongst them I heard several persons of title mentioned; but my host and hostess paid as much attention to me as though I had been the noblest there, and I felt gratified by the reception awarded me.

I found my niece but little altered, considering the number of years which had elapsed since I had last seen her; her children were a fine, blooming set of boys and girls, whilst her husband, both in appearance and manners, far exceeded my expectations. For it so happened that I had not seen Sir Harry Trevor before, my niece's marriage having taken place during my absence from England; but Justina had never ceased to correspond with me, and from her letters I knew that the union had been as happy as it was prosperous. But now that I met him I was more than pleased, and voted his wife a most fortunate woman. Of unusual height and muscular build, Sir Harry Trevor possessed one of those fair, frank Saxon faces which look as if their owners had never known trouble. His bright blue eyes shone with careless mirth and his yellow beard curled about a mouth ever ready to smile in unison with the outstretching of his friendly hand.

He was a specimen of a free, manly, and contented Englishman, who had everything he could desire in this world, and was thankful for it. As for Justina, she seemed perfectly to adore him; her eyes followed his figure wherever it moved; she hung upon his words, and refused to stir from home, even to take a drive or walk, unless he were by her side.

'I must congratulate you upon your husband,' I said to her, as we sat together on the second day of my visit. 'I think he is one of the finest fellows I ever came across, and seems as good as he is handsome.'

'Ah, he is, indeed!' she replied, with ready enthusiasm; 'and you have seen the least part of him, uncle. It would be impossible for me to tell you how good he is in all things. We have been married now for more than ten years, and during that time I have never had an unkind word from him, nor do I believe he has ever kept a thought from me.

He is as open as the day, and could not keep a secret if he tried. Dear fellow!' and something very like a tear twinkled in the wife's eyes.

'Ay, ay,' I replied, 'that's right. I don't know much about matrimony, my dear, but if man and wife never have a secret from one another they can't go far wrong. And now perhaps you will enlighten me a little about these guests of yours, for there is such a number of them that I feel quite confused.'

Justina passed her hand across her eyes and laughed.

'Yes, that is dear Harry's whim. He will fill the house at Christmas from top to basement, and I let him have his way, though all my visitors are not of my own choosing. With whom shall I commence, uncle?'

We were sitting on a sofa together during the half-hour before dinner, and one by one the guests, amounting perhaps to fifteen or twenty, came lounging into the drawing-room.

'Who, then, is that very handsome woman with the scarlet flower in her hair?'

'Oh, do you call *her* handsome?' (I could tell at once from the tone of Justina's voice that the owner of the scarlet flower was no favourite of hers.) 'That is Lady Amabel Scott, a cousin of Harry's: indeed, if she were not, she should never come into *my* house. Now, there's a woman, uncle, whom I can't bear—a forward, presuming, flirting creature, with no desire on earth but to attract admiration. Look how she's dressed this evening—absurd, for a home party. I wonder that her husband, Mr Warden Scott (that is he looking over the photograph book), can allow her to go on so! It is quite disgraceful. I consider a flirting married woman one of the most dangerous members of society.'

'But you can have no reason to fear her attacks,' I said, confidently.

The colour mounted to her face. My niece is not a pretty woman—indeed, I had already wondered several times what made Trevor fall in love with her—but this little touch of indignation improved her.

'*Of course not!* But Lady Amabel spares no one, and dear Harry is so good-natured that he refuses to see how conspicuous she makes both him and herself. I have tried to convince him of it several times, but he is too kind to think evil of anyone, and so I must be as patient as I can till she goes. Thank Heaven, she does not spend her Christmas with us! For my part, I can't understand how one can see any beauty in a woman with a turned-up nose.'

'Ho, ho!' I thought to myself; 'this is where the shoe pinches, is it?

And if a lady will secure an uncommonly good-looking and agreeable man all to herself, she must expect to see others attempt to share the prize with her.'

Poor Justina! With as many blessings as one would think heart could desire, she was not above poisoning her life's happiness by a touch of jealousy; and so I pitied her. It is a terrible foe with which to contend.

'But this is but one off the list,' I continued, wishing to divert her mind from the contemplation of Sir Harry's cousin. 'Who are those two dark girls standing together at the side table? and who is that quiet-looking little lady who has just entered with the tall man in spectacles?'

'Oh, those—the girls—are the Misses Rushton; they are pretty, are they not?—were considered quite the *belles* of last season—and the old lady on the opposite side of the fireplace is their mother: their father died some years since.'

'But the gentleman in spectacles? He looks quite a character.'

'Yes, and is considered so, but he is very good and awfully clever. That is Professor Benson: you must know him and his wife too, the "quiet-looking little lady," as you called her just now. They are the greatest friends I have in the world, and it was at their house that I first met Harry. I am sure you would like Mary Benson, uncle; she is shy, but has an immense deal in her, and is the kindest creature I ever knew. You would get on capitally together. I must introduce you to each other after dinner. And the professor and she are so attached—quite a model couple, I can assure you.'

'Indeed! But whom have we here?' as the door was thrown open to admit five gentlemen and two ladies.

'Lord and Lady Mowbray; Colonel Green and his son and daughter; Captain Mackay and Mr Cecil St John,' whispered Lady Trevor, and as she concluded dinner was announced, and our dialogue ended.

As the only persons in whom my niece had expressed much interest were Lady Amabel Scott and Mrs Benson, I took care to observe these two ladies very narrowly during my leisure moments at the dinner-table, and came to the conclusion that, so far as I could judge, her estimate was not far wrong of either of them. Lady Amabel was a decided beauty, notwithstanding the 'turned-up nose' of which her hostess had spoken so contemptuously; it was also pretty evident that she was a decided flirt. During my lengthened career of five-and-sixty years, I had always been credited with having a keen eye for the good points of a woman or a horse; but seldom had I met with such vivid colouring, such flashing eyes, and such bright speaking looks as now shone upon me across the table from the cousin of Sir Harry Trevor. She was a lovely blonde, in the heyday of her youth and beauty, and she used her power unsparingly and without reserve.

My observation quickened by what Justina's flash of jealousy had revealed, I now perceived, or thought I perceived, that our host was by no means insensible to the attractions of his fair guest, for, after conducting her in to dinner and placing her by his side, he devoted every second not demanded by the rights of hospitality to her amusement. Yet, Lady Amabel seemed anything but desirous of engrossing his attention; on the contrary, her arrows of wit flew far and wide, and her bright glances flashed much in the same manner, some of their beams descending even upon me, spite of my grey hairs and lack of acquaintanceship.

One could easily perceive that she was a universal favourite; but as Mr Warden Scott seemed quite satisfied with the state of affairs, and calmly enjoyed his dinner, whilst his wife's admirers, in their fervent admiration, neglected to eat theirs, I could not see that anyone had a right to complain, and came to the conclusion that my niece, like many another of her sex, had permitted jealousy to blind her judgment.

I felt still more convinced of this when I turned to the contemplation of the other lady to whom she had directed my attention—the professor's wife, who was her dearest friend, and through whose means she had first met Sir Harry Trevor. There was certainly nothing to excite the evil passions of either man or woman in Mrs Benson. Small and insignificant in figure, she was not even pleasing in countenance; indeed, I voted her altogether uninteresting, until she suddenly raised two large brown eyes, soft as a spaniel's and shy as a deer's, and regarded me.

She dropped them again instantly, but as she did so I observed that her lashes were long and dark, and looked the longer and darker for resting on perfectly pallid cheeks. *Au reste*, Mrs Benson had not a feature that would repay the trouble of looking at twice, and the plain, dark dress she wore still farther detracted from her appearance. But she looked a good, quiet, harmless little thing, who, if she really possessed the sense Lady Trevor attributed to her, might prove a very valuable and worthy friend. But she was certainly not the style of woman to cause anyone a heartache, or to make a wife rue the day she met her.

And indeed, when, dinner being over, we joined the ladies in the drawing-room, and I saw her surrounded by my grandnephews and nieces, who seemed by one accord to have singled her out for persecution, I thought she looked much more like a governess or some one in a dependent situation than the most welcome guest at Durham Hall. Sir Harry seemed pleased with her notice of his children, for he took a seat by her side and entered into conversation with her, the first time that I had seen him pay his wife's friend so open a compliment. Now I watched eagerly for the 'great deal' that by Justina's account was 'in her;' but I was disappointed, for she seemed disinclined for a tête-à-tête, and after a few futile attempts to draw her out, I was not surprised to see her host quit his position and wander after Lady Amabel Scott into the back drawing-room, whither my niece's eyes followed him in a restless and uneasy manner.

'I promised to introduce you to Mrs Benson, uncle,' she exclaimed, as she perceived that I was watching her, and willy-nilly, I was taken forcible possession of, and soon found myself occupying the chair left vacant by Sir Harry.

'We can so very seldom persuade Mary to stay with us; and when she does come, her visits are so brief that we are obliged to make a great deal of them whilst they last' was part of Justina's introduction speech; and on that hint I commenced to speak of the charms of the country and my wonder that Mrs Benson did not oftener take occasion to enjoy them. But barely an answer, far less an idea, could I extract from my niece's valued friend. Mrs Benson's brown eyes were not once raised to meet mine, and the replies which I forced from her lips came in monosyllables. , I tried another theme, but with no better success; and had just decided that she was as stupid as she looked, when, to my great relief, the professor arrived with a message from Lady Trevor, and bore his wife off into another room.

Several days passed without bringing forth much incident. The gentlemen spent most of their time in. the shooting-covers or hunting-field, and did not meet the ladies until evening re-assembled them in the drawing-room; on which occasions I used to get as far as I could from Lady Trevor and the professor's wife, and in consequence generally found myself in the vicinity of Sir Harry and Lady Amabel. Yet, free and intimate as seemed their intercourse with one another, and narrowly as, in Justina's interest, I watched them, I could perceive nothing in their conduct which was not justified by their relationship, and treated it as a matter of the smallest consequence, until one afternoon about a fortnight after my arrival at Durham Hall.

With the exception of Sir Harry himself, who had business to transact with his bailiff, we had all been out shooting, and as, after a hard day's work, I was toiling up to my bedroom to dress for dinner, I had occasion to pass the study appropriated to the master of the house, and with a sudden desire to give him an account of our sport, incontinently turned the handle of the door. As I did so I heard an exclamation and the rustle of a woman's dress, which were sufficient to make me halt upon the threshold of the half-opened door, and ask if I might enter.

'Come in, by all means,' exclaimed Sir Harry. He was lying back indolently in his armchair beside a table strewn with books and papers,—a little flushed, perhaps, but otherwise himself, and, to my astonishment, quite alone. Yet I was positive that I had heard the unmistakable sound of a woman's dress sweeping the carpet. Involuntarily I glanced around the room; but there was no egress.

Sir Harry caught my look of inquiry, and seemed annoyed. 'What are you staring at, Wilmer?' he demanded, in the curtest tone I had yet heard from him.

'May I not glance round your den?' I replied courteously. 'I have not had the honour of seeing it before.'

Then I entered into a few details with him concerning the day's sport we had enjoyed; but I took care to be brief, for I saw that my presence there displeased him, and I could not get the rustle of that dress out of my mind. As I concluded, and with some remark upon the lateness of the hour, turned to leave the room, a cough sounded from behind a large Indian screen which stood in one corner. It was the faintest, most subdued of coughs, but sufficiently tangible to be sworn to; and as it fell upon my ear I could not help a change of countenance.

'All right!' said my host, with affected nonchalance, as he rose and almost backed me to the door. 'We'll have a talk over all this after dinner, Wilmer; sorry I wasn't with you; but, as you say, it's late. *Au revoir!*' and simultaneously the study door closed upon me.

I was very much startled and very much shocked. I had not a doubt that I was correct in my surmise that Sir Harry had some visitor in his room whom he had thought it necessary to conceal from me; and though Hope suggested that it might have been his wife, Common Sense rose up to refute so absurd an idea. Added to which, I had not traversed twenty yards after leaving him before I met Justina attired in

237

her walking things, and just returning from a stroll round the garden.

'Is it very late, uncle?' she demanded, with a smile, as we encountered one another. 'I have been out with the children. Have you seen Mary or Lady Amabel? I am afraid they will think I have neglected them shamefully this afternoon.'

I answered her questions indifferently, thinking the while that she had no occasion to blame herself for not having paid sufficient attention to Lady Amabel Scott, for that it was she whom I had surprised *tête-à-tête* with Sir Harry Trevor, I had not a shadow of doubt.

Well, I was not the one to judge them, nor to bring them to judgment; but I thought very hard things of Sir Harry's cousin during the dressing hour, and pitied my poor niece, who must some day inevitably learn that it was a true instinct which had made her shrink from her beautiful guest. And during the evening which followed my discovery, I turned with disgust from the lightning glances which darted from Lady Amabel's blue eyes, and the arch smile which helped to make them so seductive.

I could no longer think her beauty harmless: the red curves of her mouth were cruel serpents in my mind; poisoned arrows flew from her lips; there was no innocence left in look, or word, or action; and I found myself turning with a sensation of relief to gaze at the Quaker-like attire, the downcast eyes, and modest appearance of the professor's wife, whilst I inwardly blamed myself for having ever been so foolish as to be gulled into believing that the flaunting beauty of Lady Amabel Scott was superior to Mrs Benson's quiet graces.

I did not have much to say to Sir Harry Trevor during that evening: indignation for his deception towards Justina made me disinclined to speak to him, whilst he, for his part, seemed anxious to avoid me. For a few days more all went on as usual: my host's affability soon returned, and everyone, my niece included, appeared so smiling and contented, that I almost began to think I must have been mistaken, and that there could have been no real motive for concealing Lady Amabel in Sir Harry's room, except perhaps her own girlish love of fun. I tried to think the best I could of both of them; and a day came but too soon when I was thankful that I had so tried.

It was about a week after the little incident related above that Sir Harry Trevor was shooting over his preserves, accompanied by his guests. We had had a capital day's sport and an excellent luncheon—at which latter some of the ladies had condescended to join us—and were beating the last cover preparatory to a return to Durham Hall, when the report of a firearm was quickly followed by the news that Sir Harry Trevor had been wounded.

I was separated from him by a couple of fields when I first heard of the accident, but it did not take me long to reach his side, when I perceived, to my horror, that he was fast bleeding to death, having been shot through the lungs by the discharge of his own gun whilst getting through the hedge. I had seen men die from gunshot wounds received under various circumstances, and I felt sure that Sir Harry's hours were numbered; yet, of course, all that was possible was done at once, and five minutes had not elapsed before messengers were flying in all directions—one for the doctor, another for the carriage, a third for cordials to support the sinking man; whilst I entreated Mr Warden Scott and several others to walk back to the Hall as though nothing particular had happened, and try to prevent the immediate circulation of the full extent of the bad news. Meanwhile, I remained by the wounded man, who evidently suspected, by the sinking within him, that he was dying.

'Wilmer!' he gasped, 'old fellow, have I settled my hash!'

'I trust not. Sir Harry,' I commenced; but I suppose that my eyes contradicted my words.

'Don't say any more,' he replied, with difficulty. 'My head a little higher—thanks. I feel it will soon be over.'

And so he lay for a few moments, supported on my knee, with his fast glazing eyes turned upward to the December sky, and his breath coming in short, quick jerks.

The men who had remained with me seemed as though they could not endure the sight of his sufferings; one or two gazed at him speechless and almost as pale as himself; but the majority had turned away to hide their feelings.

'Wilmer,' he whispered presently, but in a much fainter voice than before, 'it's coming fast now;' and then, to my surprise, just as I thought he was about to draw his last breath, he suddenly broke into speech that was almost a sob—'Oh, if I could only have seen her again! I wouldn't mind it half so much if I could but have seen Pet again! Call her, Wilmer; in God's name, call her!—call Pet to me—only once again—only once! Pet! Pet! Pet!' And with that name upon his lips, each time uttered in a shorter and fainter voice, and with a wild look of entreaty in his eyes, Sir Harry Trevor let his head drop back heavily upon my knees and died.

When the doctor and the carriage arrived, the only thing left for us to do was to convey the corpse of its master back to Durham Hall.

For the first few hours I was too much shocked by the suddenness of the blow which had descended on us to have leisure to think of anything else. In one moment the house of feasting had been turned into the house of mourning; and frightened guests were looking into each other's faces, and wondering what would be the correct thing for them to do. Of my poor niece I saw nothing. The medical man had undertaken to break the news of her bereavement to her, and I confess that I was sufficiently cowardly to shrink from encountering the sorrow which I could do nothing to mitigate.

As I passed along the silent corridors (lately so full of mirth and revelry) that evening, I met servants and travelling-cases at every turn, by which I concluded, and rightly, that the Christmas guests were about at once to take their departure; and on rising in the morning, I found that, with the exception of Lady Amabel and Mr Warden Scott, who, as relatives of the deceased, intended to remain until after the funeral, and the professor and Mrs Benson, on whose delicate frame the shock of Sir Harry's death was said to have had such an effect as to render her unfit for travelling, Durham Hall was clear.

Lady Amabel had wept herself almost dry: her eyes were swollen, her features disfigured, her whole appearance changed from the violence of her grief, and every ten minutes she was ready to burst out afresh.

We had not been together half-an-hour on the following morning before she was sobbing by my side, entreating me to give her every particular of 'poor dear Harry's' death, and to say if there was anything she could do for Justina or the children; and notwithstanding the repugnance with which her conduct had inspired me, I could not repulse her then. However she had sinned, the crime and its occasion were both past—Sir Harry was laid out ready for his burial, and she was grieving for him.

I am an old man, long past such follies myself, and I hope I am a virtuous man; but all my virtue could not prevent my pitying Lady Amabel in her distress, and affording her such comfort as was possible. And so (a little curiosity still mingling with my compassion) I related to her in detail, whilst I narrowly watched her features, the last words which had been spoken by her cousin. But if she guessed for whom that dying entreaty had been urged, she did not betray herself.

'Poor fellow!' was her only remark as she wiped her streaming eyes—'poor dear Harry! Used he to call Justina "Pet"? I never heard

240

him do so.'

Whereupon I decided that Lady Amabel was too politic to be very miserable, and that my pity had been wasted on her.

Of Mrs Benson I saw nothing, but the professor talked about attending the funeral, and therefore I concluded that my niece had invited them, being such intimate friends, to remain for that ceremony.

On the afternoon of the same day I was told that Justina desired to speak to me. I sought the room where she was sitting, with folded hands and darkened windows, with nervous reluctance; but I need not have dreaded a scene, for her grief was too great for outward show, and I found her in a state which appeared to me unnaturally calm.

'Uncle,' she said, after a moment's pause, during which we had silently shaken hands, 'will you take these keys and go down into—into—his study for me, and bring up the desks and papers which you will find in the *escritoire?* I do not like to send a servant.'

I took the keys which she extended to me, and, not able to trust myself to answer, kissed her forehead and left the room again. As I turned the handle of the study door I shuddered, the action so vividly recalled to me the first and last occasion upon which I had done so. The afternoon was now far advanced, and dusk was approaching: the blinds of the study windows also were pulled down, which caused the room to appear almost in darkness. As I groped my way toward the *escritoire* I stumbled over some article lying across my path, something which lay extended on the hearth-rug, and which even by that feeble light I could discern was a prostrated body.

With my mind full of murderous accidents, I rushed to the window and drew up the blind, when to my astonishment I found that the person over whom I had nearly fallen was no other than poor little Mrs Benson, who was lying in a dead faint before the armchair. Fainting women not being half so much in my line as wounded men, I felt quite uncertain in this case how to act, and .without considering how the professor's wife had come to be in the study or for what reason, my first impulse was to ring for assistance. But a second thought, which came I know not how or whence, made me lift the fragile, senseless body in my arms and carry it outside the study door into the passage before I called for help, which then I did lustily, and female servants came and bore the poor 'quiet-looking little lady' away to her own apartments and the care of her husband, leaving me free to execute the errand upon which I had been sent.

Still, as I collected the desk and papers required by my niece, I could not help reflecting on the circumstance I have related as being a strange one, and could only account for it in my own mind by the probable fact that Mrs Benson had required some book from the late Sir Harry's shelves, and, miscalculating her strength, had left her bedroom with the design of fetching it, and failed before she could accomplish her purpose! I heard several comments made on the occurrence, during the melancholy meal which we now called 'dinner,' by her husband and Lady Amabel Scott, and they both agreed with me as to the probable reason of it; and as soon as the cloth was removed the professor left us to spend the evening with his wife, who was considered sufficiently ill to require medical attendance.

We were a rather silent trio in the drawing-room—Lady Amabel, Mr Scott, and I—for ordinary occupations seemed forbidden, and every topic harped back to the miserable accident which had left the hall without a master. The servants with lengthened faces, as though attending a funeral, had dumbly proffered us tea and coffee, and we had drunk them without considering whether we required them, so welcome seemed anything to do; and I was seriously considering whether it would appear discourteous in me to leave the hall and return on the day of the funeral, when a circumstance occurred which proved more than sufficiently exciting for all of us.

I had taken the desk, papers, and keys, and delivered them into my niece's hands, and I had ventured at the same time to ask whether it would not be a comfort to her to see Mrs Benson or some other friend, instead of sitting in utter loneliness and gloom. But Justina had visibly shrunk from the proposal; more than that, she had begged me not to renew it. 'I sent for you, uncle,' she said, 'because I needed help, but don't let anyone make it a precedent for trying to see me. I *couldn't* speak to anyone: it would drive me mad. Leave me alone: my only relief is in solitude and prayer.'

And so I had left her, feeling that doubtless she was right, and communicating her wishes on the subject to Lady Amabel Scott, who had several times expressed a desire to gain admittance to her widowed cousin.

Judge then, of our surprise, equal and unmitigated, when, as we sat in the drawing-room that evening, the door silently Opened and Justina stood before us! If she had been the ghost of Sir Harry himself risen from the dead, she could hardly have given us a greater start.

'Justina!' I exclaimed, but as she advanced toward us with her eyes riveted on Lady Amabel, I saw that something more than usual was the matter, and drew backwards Justina's countenance was deadly pale; her dark hair, unbound from the night before, flowed over the white-dressing gown which she had worn all day; and stern and rigid she walked into the midst of our little circle, holding a packet of letters in her hand.

'Amabel Scott,' she hissed rather than said as she fixed a look of perfect hatred on the beautiful face of her dead husband's cousin, 'I have detected you. You made me miserable whilst he was alive—you know it—with your bold looks and your forward manners and your shameless, open attentions; but it is my turn now, and before your husband I will tell you that—'

'Hush, hush, Justina!' I exclaimed, fearful what revelation might not be corning next. 'You are; forgetting yourself; this is no time for such explanations. Remember what lies upstairs.'

'Let her go on,' interposed Lady Amabel Scott, with wide-open, astonished eyes; 'I am not afraid. I wish to hear of what she accuses me.'

She had risen from her seat as soon as she understood the purport of the widow's speech, and crossed over to her husband's side; and knowing, what I did of her, I was yet glad to see that Warden Scott threw his arm about her for encouragement and support. She may have been thoughtless and faulty, but she was so young, and *he* was gone. Besides, no man can stand by calmly and see one woman pitted against another.

'Of what do you accuse me?' demanded Lady Amabel, with heightened colour.

'Of what do I accuse you?' almost screamed Justina. 'Of perfidy, of treachery, toward him,' pointing to Mr Warden Scott, 'and toward me. I accuse you of attempting to win my dear husband's affections from me—which you never did, thank God!—and of rendering this home as desolate as it was happy. But you failed—you failed!'

'Where are your proofs?' said the other woman, quietly.

'*There!*' exclaimed my niece, as she threw some four or five letters down upon the table—'there! I brought them for your husband to peruse. *He* kept them; generous and good as he was, *he* would have spared you an open exposure, but I have no such feelings in the matter. Are you to go from this house into another to pursue the same course of action, and perhaps with better success? No, not if I can prevent it!'

Her jealousy, rage, and grief seemed to have overpowered her; Justina was almost beside herself. I entreated her to retire, but it was of no avail. 'Not till Warden Scott tells me what he thinks of his wife writing those letters with a view to seducing the affections of a married man,' she persisted.

Mr Scott turned the letters over carelessly,

'They are not from my wife,' he quietly replied.

'Do *you* dare to say so?' exclaimed Justina to Lady Amabel.

'Certainly. I never wrote one of them. I have never written a letter to Harry since he was married. I have never had any occasion to do so.'

The widow turned towards me with an ashen-grey-face, which it was pitiful to behold.

'Whose are they, then?' she whispered, hoarsely.

'I do not know, my dear,' I replied; 'surely it matters little now. You will be ill if you excite yourself in this manner. Let me conduct you back to your room;' but before I could do so she had fallen in a fit at my feet. Of course, all then was hurry and confusion, and when I returned to the drawing-room I found Lady Amabel crying in her husband's arms.

'Oh, Warden dear,' she was saying, 'I shall never forgive myself. This all comes of my wretched flirting. It's no good your shaking your head; you know I flirt, and so does every one else; but I never meant anything by it, darling, and I thought all the world knew how much I loved you.'

'Don't be a goose!' replied her husband, as he put her gently away from him; 'but if you think I'm going to let you remain in this house after what that d—d woman—Oh, here is General Wilmer! Well, General, after the very unpleasant manner in which your niece has been entertaining us, you will not be surprised to hear that I shall take my wife away from Durham Hall tonight. When Lady Trevor comes to her senses you will perhaps kindly explain to her the reason of our departure, for nothing under such an insult should have prevented my paying my last respects to the memory of a man who never behaved otherwise than as a gentleman to either of us.'

I apologised for Justina as best I was able, represented that her mind must really have become unhinged by her late trouble, and that she would probably be very sorry for what she had said by-and-by; but I was not surprised that my arguments had no avail in inducing Mr Scott to permit his wife to remain at Durham Hall, and in a few hours they had left the house. When they were gone I took up the letters, which still lay upon the table, and examined them. They were ad-dressed to Sir Harry, written evidently in a woman's hand, and teemed with expressions of the warmest affection. I was not surprised that the perusal of them had excited poor Justina's wrathful jealousy. Turning to the signatures, I found that they all concluded with the same words, 'Your loving and faithful Pet.' In a moment my mind had flown back to the dying speech of poor Sir Harry, and had absolved Lady Amabel Scott from all my former suspicions. She was not the woman who had penned these letters; she had not been in the last thoughts of her cousin.

Who, then, had been? That was a mystery on which Death had set his seal, perhaps for ever. Before I retired to rest that night I inquired for my poor niece, and heard that she had Mrs Benson with her. I was glad of that: the women were fond of one another, and Justina, I felt, would pour all her griefs into the sympathising ear of the professor's wife, and derive comfort from weeping over them afresh with her. But after I had got into bed I remembered that I had left the letters lying on the drawing-room table, where they would be liable to be inspected by the servants, and blow the breath of the family scandal far and wide. It was much past midnight, for I had sat up late, and all the household, if not asleep, had retired to their own apartments; and so, wrapping a dressing-gown about me, and thrusting my feet into slippers, I lighted my candle, and descended noiselessly to the lower apartments.

But when I reached the drawing-room the letters were gone: neither on the table nor the ottoman nor the floor were they to be seen; and so, vexed at my own carelessness, but concluding that the servants, when extinguishing the lights, had perceived and put the papers away in some place of safety, I prepared to return to my own room.

The bedrooms at Durham Hall were situated on either side of a corridor, and fearful of rousing the family or being caught in *deshabile*, I trod on tiptoe, shading my candle with my hand. It was owing to this circumstance, I suppose, that I had reached the centre of the corridor without causing the least suspicion of my presence; hut as I passed by the apartment where the remains of my unfortunate host lay ready for burial, the door suddenly opened and a light appeared upon the threshold. I halted, expecting to see emerge the figure of my widowed niece, but lifting my eyes, to my astonishment I encountered the shrinking, almost terrified, gaze of the professor's wife.

Robed in her nightdress, pallid as the corpse which lay within, her large frightened eyes apparently the only living things about her, she stood staring at me as though she had been entranced. Her brown hair floated over her shoulders, her feet were bare; one hand held a lighted candle, the other grasped the packet of letters of which I had been in search. So we stood for a moment regarding one another—I taking in these small but important details; she looking as though she implored my mercy and forbearance. And then I drew back with the gesture of respect due to her sex, and, clad in her white dress, she swept past me like a startled spirit and disappeared.

I gained my own room, but it was not to sleep. A thousand incidents, insignificant in themselves, but powerful when welded into one, sprang up in my mind to convince me that Justina and I and everybody had been on a wrong tack, and that in the professor's wife, the 'quiet-looking little lady' with her Quaker-like robes, downcast eyes and modest appearance, in the 'best friend' that my niece had ever possessed, I had discovered the writer of those letters, the concealed visitor in Sir Harry's room, the 'Pet' whose name had been the last sound heard to issue from his dying lips.

For many hours I lay awake pondering over the best course for me to pursue. I could not bear the thought of undeceiving my poor niece, whose heart had already suffered so much; besides, it seemed like sacrilege to drag to light the secrets of the dead. At the same time I felt that Mrs Benson should receive some hint that her presence in Durham Hall, at that juncture, if desired, was no longer desirable. And the next day, finding she was not likely to accord me an interview, I made the reception of the missing letters a pretext for demanding one. She came to her room door holding them in her hand, and the marks of trouble were so distinct in her face that I had to summon all my courage to go through the task which I considered my duty.

'You found these in the drawing-room last night,' I said, as I received them from her.

'I did,' she answered, but her voice trembled and her lips were very white. She seemed to know by instinct what was coming.

'And you went to find them because they are your own?' She made no answer. 'Mrs Benson, I know your secret, but I will respect it on one condition—that you leave the Hall as soon as possible. You must be aware that this is no place for you.'

'I never wished to come,' she answered, weeping.

'I can believe it, but for the sake of your friend, of your husband, of yourself, quit it as soon as possible. Here are your letters—you had better burn them. I only wished to ascertain that they were yours.'

'General Wilmer—' she commenced gaspingly, and then she turned away and could say no more.

'Do you wish to speak to me?' I asked her gently.

'No—nothing; it is useless,' she answered with a tearless, despairing grief which was far more shocking to behold than either Justina's or Lady Amabel's. 'He is gone, and there is nothing left; but thank you for your forbearance—and goodbye.'

So we parted, and to this day, excepting that she is released from all that could annoy or worry her, I have learned nothing more. How long they loved, how much or in what degree of guilt or innocence, I neither know nor have cared to guess at; it is sufficient for me that it was so, and that while Justina was accusing the beautiful Lady Amabel Scott of attempting to win her husband's heart from her, it had been given away long before to the woman whom she termed her dearest friend—to the woman who had apparently no beauty, or wit, or accomplishments with which to steal away a man's love from its rightful owner, but who nevertheless was his 'loving and faithful Pet,' and the last thought upon his dying lips.

Professor and Mrs Benson never returned to Durham Hall. It was not long afterwards that I heard from my niece that his wife's failing health had compelled the professor to go abroad; and today she writes me news from Nice that Mrs Benson is dead. Poor Pet! I wonder if those scared brown eyes have lost their frightened look in heaven?

I believe that Justina has made an ample apology for her rudeness to Lady Amabel and Mr Warden Scott. I know I represented that it was her duty to do so, and that she promised it should be done. As for herself, she is gradually recovering from the effects of her bereavement, and finding comfort in the society of her sons and daughters; and perhaps, amongst the surprises which I have already spoken of as likely to await us in another sphere, they will not be least which prove how very soon we have been forgotten by those we left in the world behind us.

'Sent to His Death!'

I came down to breakfast one morning last autumn, and found a letter on the table from my old friend Bessie Maclean. Bessie and I were girls at school together, and continued our intimacy after we left, until we married and went to different parts of the country. Marriage is a terrible breaker up of old ties; not only by reason of the separation which generally ensues, but because of the new duties it entails. We had both married the men of our hearts, however, and in comfortable circumstances; and so far all was well. But little by little our correspondence, which at first had been so voluminous and detailed, became scanty and irregular.

Bessie had half a dozen children to occupy her time and attention; and I—I had my dear husband to fill up the measure of my life, and felt myself a wicked and ungrateful woman if I even wished for more.

But—there is always a 'but' in the happiest worldly existence, is there not?—Dick and I had no children; and the disappointment had sometimes caused me to shed bitter tears. In secret though; I had never told my husband one-half I felt upon the subject.

Of course he twitted me with it sometimes in a playful manner, which showed that the fact did not sink very deep into his heart, whatever it did in mine. Yet I had thought occasionally that he looked more thoughtful than usual when children were in the room: and the idea made me thoughtful too. Especially I had noticed it when we paid our first visit to Bessie in her new house; for I must tell you that a few months before my story commences, Tom Maclean had bought a large farm in the vicinity of the town where the gaol stands, of which my husband is the governor.

Of course, after so long a separation, Bessie and I were delighted to find we had become near neighbours again; and as soon as ever the Macleans were settled, they invited us both over to Poplar Farm, to stand sponsors to the latest arrival—a little boy whom they called Richard, after my Dick, God bless him! Poplar Farm was ten or twelve miles from Chesterwick, however, so I had not seen my friends more than five or six times since the christening day; and the visits I had paid them had not quite realised the expectations I had formed of meeting Bessie again.

I suppose it was my vile envious nature, or perhaps the quiet life I have led with Dick has made me selfish; but it seemed to me as though all the time my old schoolfellow spent with me was devoted, not to our friendship, or reminiscences of our girlish days, but to talking about her children and telling me of their accomplishments or complaints, or consulting me as to their dresses or amusements. Of course I was pleased at first to be introduced to her fine brood of boys and girls; but I could hardly be expected to feel as much interest in them as their mother did, and I was sorely disappointed to find she had lost so much of hers in me.

She did not seem to care to hear anything about my husband, or how we loved each other in our happy, peaceful home; nor did she even talk much about Tom, with her affection for whom I could have sympathised better than with any other. But he appeared to be almost forgotten or overlooked in her maternal care for the little ones; and she was more anxious that Lily's new hat should become her, or Charley s medicine be swallowed without a fit of obstinacy, than that Mr Maclean should appreciate his dinner, or have his evening hours undisturbed for settling his accounts. I have observed the same thing—oh! scores of times—amongst my married female acquaintances; and the fact has done more to reconcile me to the want of a family than any other.

Not that I believe that the charge of a hundred children could ever make me forget my darling's wants— but there, this is not a love story, so I must try and keep my Dick's name out of it as much as possible.

I had received several letters from Bessie during the last month, which had rather surprised me, as she had grown very lazy at correspondence, as I have said before, and naturally, taking up her residence at Poplar Farm had not made her write oftener, excepting when she required the benefit of my experience with regard to the advantages of her new home. Her two last letters, however, had been written in a very unaccountable strain; and if I had not known she was comfortably and happily situated, I should have imagined it was just the reverse.

'Another letter from Bessie!' I exclaimed, as I broke the seal. 'What on earth can she want now? I suppose she has found out somebody sells whiter flour than Watkins, or better tea than Amyott? I almost believe, Dick, she regrets having left Lincolnshire.'

'I don't know why she should,' replied Dick, as he commenced a raid upon the breakfast-table; 'for, according to Maclean's account, they lived in a perfect swamp there. But why can't the woman look after her own flour and tea? Why is she to worry you about everything in this fashion?'

'Oh! I suppose she thinks, as I have no children, I cannot possibly have anything to do,' I said, laughing; 'for I heard her remark, with regard to Mrs Anderson, who is in the same plight as myself, that it must be quite a charity to give her any employment!'

'Like her impudence,' growled Dick—(I don't think Bessie is a favourite with my husband; perhaps I talked too much about her beforehand),—'I should let her know to the contrary if I were you, Dolly. I believe, with all her fuss and bustle, that you do twice her work in half the time.'

'Ah! I have only *one* baby to look after, you see, though he's a big one,' I said, as I gave his head a squeeze with my disengaged hand; 'but goodness me, Dick, this letter is worse than the last even. Bessie seems really in low spirits now. She says that Mr Maclean's business will take him away from home for a few nights next week, and she wants me to go over and spend them with her in—yes, she actually calls Poplar Farm—"this gloomy ramshackle old place."'

'It's old enough,' said Dick, 'and all the better for it; but it's not "ramshackle." Better walls and roof were never built than those of Poplar Farm. It stands as steady as the gaol'

'But about my going to her, Dick—can you spare me?'

'Can I spare you!' repeated my husband in that tone of voice that, after ten years' marriage, has still the power to make my heart beat faster. 'Of course I can! I could spare you for good and all, if someone would only be obliging enough to take you off my hands; but there's no such luck in store for me. Only mind the days don't stretch themselves into weeks, sweetheart!'

'Into weeks!' I replied, indignantly. 'Have I ever stayed weeks away from you yet, Dick? I'm not even sure that I shall go at all.'

'Yes! you'd better go, Dolly; Bessie Maclean is selfish and egotistical, and somewhat of a fool; but I daresay she's nervous at the idea of remaining in that isolated home by herself, particularly as it is all so strange to her. And you don't know what fear is, old woman!'

'I wish she could overhear the character you give her,' I answered, laughingly. But Dick was right. I am *not* a nervous woman, and if I had been, he would have cured me of it long before. Living in a gaol, and having, of my own free will, constant access to the prisoners, had effectually dispersed any ladylike unreasonable fears I may once have thought womanly and becoming, and made me ashamed of starting at shadows. So, having sent an affirmative answer to my friend's appeal, I set out for Poplar Farm, when the time came, with as much confidence in my powers of protection as though I had been of the sterner sex.

Dick drove me over in the curricle.

It was a bright November morning: one of those days when the air is crisp and exhilarating without being in the least degree cold; a day on which one feels younger, and more hopeful and capable of good— on which one's sorrows seem too paltry for consideration, and one's happiness far more than one deserves. I experienced this sensation in the fullest sense, as I crept as close as I could to my husband's side, and smuggled one hand beneath his arm.

'Holloa!' cried Dick; 'why, what's this? Repenting of your promise already, eh? Oh! you spoony woman, I'm ashamed of you!'

I *was* repenting it, but I did not tell him so. It is good for people who love very much to part sometimes, if only to teach them how great a blessing they possess in each other's affection.

As we drove up the long-neglected drive of Poplar Farm, I could not help thinking that Bessie was right in considering it gloomy. The sun had disappeared again behind an autumn cloud. The trees had shed most of their leaves, which lay in sodden heaps along the paths, and a chilly wind had commenced to blow. I drew my cloak closer against my shoulders, and told Dick what I thought

'Nonsense, Dolly!' he replied. 'The place is well enough; and when Maclean has had time to put it in order, will be one of the prettiest farms in the county. I only wish I had the money to buy such another. But naturally it does not look its best when the trees are bare.'

'Stop!' I cried, suddenly; 'there's the baby. Let me get down and kiss him. That must be the new nurse carrying him, Dick. But what a lugubrious looking young person she is!'

My husband had good-naturedly drawn up by this time, and I had scrambled down to meet my little godson, who was about three months old. But as soon as I had pulled aside the veil that covered his face, I started with surprise.

251

'Oh! how he *has* gone off!' I exclaimed.

The baby, who had been so fat and dimpled and red-faced last time I saw him, was now drawn and white and thin. The change was apparent so that even Dick could see it from the box-seat.

'Whew!' he whistled; 'why, what's the matter with the little chap—is he ill?'

'Oh no! he's not ill. He is perfectly well. You don't think he looks ill, madam?' said the girl who was carrying him, anxiously.

'I don't think I ever saw a child so changed in my life,' I answered, in my blunt fashion. 'Are you the wet-nurse Mrs Maclean told me she had engaged for him?'

'Yes, madam,' she said, in a very low voice.

I raised my eyes, and examined her then for the first time thoroughly; and I could not help observing what a remarkable-looking girl she was. She had the very palest and clearest of complexions—so colourless that it looked like the finest white wax, and her skin was of the texture of satin. Her large, clear, grey eyes, which shone with a limpid light, like agates with water running over them, had a startled look, which might almost have been mistaken for fear, and her delicately cut mouth drooped in the most pathetic manner.

To add to the mournfulness of her appearance, her hair was almost completely hidden beneath her cap, and her dress was the deepest widows mourning. I made a few indifferent remarks about the child, kissed it, and jumped up to my seat again. The nurse was not the person I felt to whom to speak on the subject of the baby's appearance. She made a deep reverence as the carriage moved off, and I saw she was a very superior sort of young woman; but of what account was that, where little Dick's health, and perhaps his life, was concerned?

'Bessie's a greater fool than I took her for,' I exclaimed, indignantly, as we drove on towards the house.

'What's in the wind now?' said Dick.

'Fancy, choosing a wet-nurse for a baby all crape and bombazine and tears. Why, that girl looks as if she cried night and day. I knew Bessie had been weak enough to be persuaded by the doctor to give up nursing baby herself, but she might have exercised a little discretion in the choice of a substitute. The child is half the size he was last month.'

'What a lot we know about babies!' said Dick, in his chaffing way.

'I should hope I know more than half the mothers I meet,' I continued, with some warmth. 'I should be ashamed to be as ignorant as Bessie herself, for instance, though she *has* had six children,' I added, with a little droop in my voice.

'My own Dolly!' said Dick, fondly; and when he says those words in that voice, I don't care for anything else in all the wide, wide world. He wouldn't stay—even to dismount from his box, for we knew Mr Maclean had already left the house, and he thought our chatter would get on better without him, added to which he had duties demanding him at home. So I gave him one long, long kiss, and let him go; and as soon as he was out of sight, turned into the door of Poplar Farm.

Bessie was in the dining-room, where the dinner was already spread, surrounded by her batch of self-willed unruly children. As she came forward to meet me, I saw that she looked tired and worn out, and that her dress was untidy and neglected.

'It is so good of you to come, Dolly,' was her greeting, 'for I am so worried I don't know what I should have done without you.'

'I am very glad to be of use, Bessie; but what worries you—the baby?'

'Dear me! no. It is something quite different. Why should baby worry me? He has his wet-nurse, and she takes him completely off my hands.'

'He is so pulled down,' I said unhesitatingly, for I took an interest in my little godson. 'I met him just now in the drive, and hardly recognised the child. Are you satisfied his nurse does him justice?'

'Oh, perfectly so. She is a most estimable young woman, so quiet and ladylike in her way of speaking. Did you notice her eyes? such a remarkable colour; and her hands are as white as yours or mine.'

'But the baby does not appear to be thriving. He can't inherit her eyes or her hands, you know, and if he could, I don't see that they would be much use to him. What's her name? Where did you find her?'

'She's a Mrs Graham; and she was recommended to me from the Lying-in Hospital at Chesterwick. I'm sorry you don't think baby looks well. Perhaps the change has pulled him down a little, though I really can't see it myself.'

I daresay she did not. Bessie is that sort of woman that never will see anything until it has actually occurred. If her children died, she would make as great a fuss over them—perhaps more—than mothers who have guarded theirs from their infancy upwards; yet she will let them eat improper food, and get damp feet, and remain out in the burning sun without any covering to their heads; and if you remonstrate with her, her invariable excuses, that they have always done so before and got no harm. As if the fact of a wrong being permitted should make it a right; or because we have fallen from the top of a house once without injury, we may cast ourselves thence headlong each day without impunity.

I really never did think, when Bessie and I were girls together, that she would turn out such a ninny.

'What *has* worried you then, since it is not the baby?' I demanded presently.

'Hush! I can't tell you before the children. It's an awful business, and I wouldn't have them hear of it for worlds. Will you lay your bonnet aside, and have dinner with us as you are? or I'm afraid it may get cold. Lily—Charley—Tommy, lay down these toys, and come to the table at once. Put Bessie up on her high chair; and somebody go and call Annie. Ah! Dolly, my dear, how well you have kept your figure! What would I not give to be as slim and neat as you are.'

And although, of course, I would not compare one advantage with the other, yet I must say that the pleasures of having a family would possess a great drawback to me, if I were compelled at the same time to become as rotund and untidy in appearance as poor Bessie is at present And I believe the chief thing Tom Maclean fell in love with was her pretty rounded little figure. Alas! alas!

But I am keeping the early dinner waiting. As soon as it was despatched, with the usual accompaniments of cutting up the children's meat, wiping their mouths, and preventing their throwing the tumblers at each other's heads, Mrs Maclean rose and offered to show me to my bedroom. It was next to her own, and communicated with it by a door.

'This dear old place!' I exclaimed as I entered it; 'you are making it very pretty, Bessie. Aren't you glad that you have come into such a handsome property, instead of having been stuck down in a modern villa, with the plaster on the walls only half-dry?'

But Bessie did not appear to appreciate my congratulations.

'Dolly,' she said, as she sunk down into a chair, 'I would change Poplar Farm for the poorest little villa that was ever built.'

'My dear girl, what do you mean?'

'*Mean!* That the house is haunted, Dolly—'

I confess it; I could not help it: I burst into the loudest and rudest laugh imaginable.

Poplar Farm haunted! What an absurdly unreasonable idea! Why, the last tenants had only just moved out in time to let the Macleans come in, and the house had been freshly papered and painted from basement to attic. There was not a nook nor a corner for a ghost to hide in.

I could not help laughing; and what is worse, I could not stop laughing, until my friend was offended.

'You may laugh as much as you like,' she said at last; 'but I have told you nothing but the truth. Do you mean to say that you consider such a thing impossible?'

'No! I won't go as far as that; but I think it is very uncommon, and very unlikely to occur to—to—to—'

Here I was obliged to halt, for the only words I could think of were, 'to anyone so material as yourself;' and I couldn't quite say that. For though I do not deny the possibility of apparitions, I believe that the person who is capable of perceiving them must be composed of more mind than matter, and there is nothing spiritual nor aesthetic about poor Bessie.

'What is the ghost like, and who has seen it?' I demanded, as soon as I could command my countenance.

'Several of the servants and myself,' replied Bessie; 'and Tom might have seen it, too, if he were not so lazy. But one night when the noises were close to our door, he refused to rouse himself even to listen to them, and told me to go—Well, dear, I really can't repeat what he said; but husbands do not always use the politest language when out of temper, you know!'

'Noises! Then the ghost has been heard as well as seen?'

'Oh yes! and such mournful noises, too. Such weeping and wailing, enough to break one's heart. The first time I saw it, Dolly, I thought I should have died of fright.'

'Tell me all about it.'

'I had been sitting up late one Saturday night mending the children's socks for Sunday, and Tom had been in bed for a good two hours. Everybody was in bed but myself, and I thought, as I carried my single candle up the dark staircase, how silent and ghastly everything appeared. As I turned into the corridor, I heard a gasping sound like a stifled sob. At first I could hardly believe my ears; but when it was repeated, my heart seemed to stand still. I was hesitating whether to go back or forward, and trembling in every limb, when it—this dreadful *thing*—crossed me. It sprung up, I don't know from where, in the darkness, and just looked at me once and rushed away. I nearly sunk to the ground, as you may well imagine I had only just time to get inside my own door, when I tumbled right across the bed, and Tom had to get up and pick up the candlestick, and help undress me; and really, by the way he went on about it, you'd have thought it was all my fault.'

'What was it like? that is the main thing, Bessie.'

'My dear, you don't suppose I looked at it more than I was absolutely obliged. I know *it* was dressed all in white, with snow-white hair hanging over its face, and fearful staring eyes. It's a perfect wonder to me I stand alive here now.'

'And it has been seen since then?'

'Oh, several times, and we hear it every night as regularly as possible about two o'clock in the morning. The cook has seen it—so has the housemaid; and not a servant amongst them would fetch a glass of water from downstairs after ten o'clock, if we were all dying for want of it.'

'A pleasant state of affairs,' I ejaculated; 'and will you take no steps to investigate the mystery, and dissolve the household fears?'

'What steps could I take?''

'Sit up for the apparition, and speak to it; and if it won't answer, take hold of it and see if it is flesh and blood or air.'

'My dear Dolly, I would rather die.'

'Well, I hope you'll wake me up when the sounds begin tonight,' I answered, 'for I am curious to hear them.'

But I didn't tell Bessie that I would be the one to 'bell the cat;' for, though I have little fear, I have no foolhardiness; and if her ghost turned out to be a real one, I had no wish to interfere with it.

In the evening, as much with a view of pointing out the baby's condition to Bessie as for any other reason, I asked her to accompany me to the nursery, and see him put to bed. I found that he slept in a room alone with his wet-nurse, who was engaged in bathing the little creature as we entered. Mrs Graham looked very pretty and delicate as she bent over the bath, attending to the child; but I observed that she never once smiled at nor played with him, as nurses usually do with infants during the process of washing. Little Dick was certainly very attenuated and languid, and even his mother seemed to observe it when pointed out to her. Mrs Graham listened to our conversation with rather an anxious expression on het countenance, and I thought by drawing her out we might gain some clue to the baby's ill health.

'Is your own child strong and vigorous?' I asked her.

'My own child is dead, madam,' she replied.

'It was your first, I presume? You appear very young.'

'It was my first. I was twenty last birthday.'

She seemed unwilling to be more communicative, and I did not like to enter directly on the subject of her husband's death. Poor child! she might have loved him as I did Dick. So, as Bessie had sauntered into the general nursery and left us alone together, I ventured to sound her on another matter, which I thought might be having a secret effect upon her.

'Have you seen anything of this apparition the servants speak of, Mrs Graham?'

'No, madam,' she replied, quietly.

'It is very foolish of people to be frightened of they really don't know what; but no one seems to have been brave enough to try and find out the reason of the mysterious noises heard at night here. You have heard them, perhaps?'

'No, madam,' she said again, without further comment.

'Would it alarm you to see or hear it?' I had forced her now to say something in reply.

'I think not,' she answered, 'I think if spirits can come back from the dead, they must do so only in sympathy with those they have left behind; and, if that is possible, and I thought this one came for me, I should only be too thankful to have a glimpse of its face, or to hear the sound of its voice. I think those people who have so much fear of spirits can never have known what it is to lose any one they would lay down their lives to follow wherever it might lead them.'

She spoke in a low, mournful cadence that touched my heart. Poor girl! she was thinking of her husband and her own desolate condition. I felt for and sympathised with her, and before I left the nursery I took her thin hand and pressed it. She looked surprised, but I had only to say, 'I love my own husband as my life,' to see the tears run into her eyes, and to know she understood me. Still she was by no means a proper person to perform the part of a mother towards little Dick, and I resolved before I left Poplar Farm to try and persuade Bessie to change her.

The rest of the day passed rather monotonously. I worked at one of Dick's shirts, and wondered how I ever could have thought Bessie such a charming companion, whilst she alternatively indulged and scolded her very unpleasant young family. At last they were all despatched to bed, and as soon as decency would permit, I yawned and said I should like to follow their example. So we were all packed away by ten o'clock, my last act having been to pay a visit to Mrs Graham's room, where I had left her fast asleep with my little godson tucked in snugly on her arm. Bessie lay awake for some time talking of the celebrated ghost, but I was too sleepy to be a good listener, and am afraid I dropped off in the midst of her recital. When I waked again, it was by dint of feeling her shake my arm.

'Dolly! Dolly!' she was exclaiming, in a low, hurried voice. 'Listen! there is the sound, and close against the door.'

I had been dreaming of the ghost, and was conscious in a moment, and sitting up in bed. Whatever I had thought of Bessie's tales before, I believed them now, for I could distinctly hear the low, gasping breath which follows an inordinate fit of sobbing, drawn apparently close to us.

'What time is it?' I exclaimed.

'It is just three. I have been listening to it for some time, but did not like to rouse you till I was sure. Is the door locked?'

'Yes; but I will unlock it at once,' I said, springing out of bed.

'No, no! pray do not,' cried Bessie, clinging to me. 'What are you doing? It might come into the room.'

'My dear Bessie, if it is a ghost, no locks can keep it out; and if it is not a ghost, what harm can it do us by entering? Pray be reasonable. We shall never clear up this mystery if we are not a little brave!'

I shook her off, and approached the door, whilst she rushed back to her own bed.

I confess that as I turned the key in the lock I felt very nervous. Do what we will, it is hard to accustom ourselves to think lightly of communication with the dead; neither did I relish the idea of a trick being played us in that lonely house at dead of night. The light was burning brightly in my room, but as I threw the door open, the corridor seemed dark and empty. I stood upon the threshold and looked from right to left. What was that white, tall shadow in the doorway of the spare room?

I called out, 'Who are you? What do you want?' The answer I received was a quick sob and a rustle. Then I saw an indistinct figure move down the passage with a hurried step, and disappear somewhere at the further end.

Shall I confess that for all my boasted strength I had not the courage to follow it? It was one thing to have stood on the threshold of my lighted room and addressed the apparition, and another to venture out into the cold and darkness in pursuit of it. I retreated to Bessie's bedroom instead.

'I have seen it!' I exclaimed. 'I believe that you are right, Bessie, and for the first time in my life I have seen a ghost. I meant to have followed it; but I really felt I couldn't. Tomorrow night I may have more courage. But hark! what is that noise? Isn't it baby crying?'

'Never mind *baby*; Mrs Graham will attend to him,' said Bessie. 'Lock the door again, Dolly dear, do, and get into bed with me, or I sha'n't sleep another wink tonight. I'm shaking from head to foot as it is.'

But the cries from baby's room became more distinct; and my courage had returned to me.

'Let me go and see what is the matter with little Dick first,' I said, taking up the lighted candle.

Bessie yelled at being kept alone in the dark, but I could not have lain down again without ascertaining what ailed the little fellow; so, disregarding her remonstrances, I walked off to Mrs Graham's room. Her door was unlocked, and I entered without knocking.

The child was still crying lustily; and what was my surprise to find his nurse, utterly regardless of the noise, sitting up in bed, with scared wide-open eyes, talking vehemently.

'Go away!' she was exclaiming in a loud voice; 'Go away! and don't come back again. You let the water in each time you open the door: I tell you we don't want you! Go away, I say, and *don't come back again!*'

She halted for a moment at this juncture, and I was about to waken her from what I perceived was a nightmare, when she suddenly clapped her hands before her eyes and screamed.

'Ah, Heavens! a wave—a fearful wave that covers the deck—that covers everything. Where is he? Where is he gone to? I have sent him to his death! Edward! Edward! come back to me! I didn't mean it—I didn't mean it! Ah! Lord have pity on me.'

Her agitation was rising so rapidly, and the baby was crying so violently, that I thought it time to interfere.

'Mrs Graham!' I exclaimed, shaking her by the arm, 'wake up. Don't you hear the baby wants you?'

She turned her big eyes upon me in such a pitiful vacuous way. Then she recognised me, and looked frightened.

'Have I been dreaming? Have I been saying anything? Oh! I am so sorry,' she said apologetically, as she caught up the child and held it to her breast.

'You have only been talking a little in your sleep,' I replied soothingly; 'don't be alarmed; you said nothing out of the common way, and there is no one here but myself.'

She did not answer, but as she held the child I saw how her arms trembled.

'Your agitation is the worst thing possible for the baby, you know; and you must try and calm yourself for his sake,' I continued.

'I should be so sorry to hurt him,' she murmured; 'and I will try and not dream again, if it is possible.'

'Shall I fetch you anything?'

'Oh no, madam, thank you. The best thing I can do is to go to sleep again. There is nothing for me but sleep—and prayer,' she added in a whisper.

I felt deeply interested in this young woman. There was an air of patient mournfulness about her that betokened deep suffering; and as I returned to my room I resolved to do my best to be of use to her. She so completely occupied my thoughts, indeed, that I had forgotten all about the ghost, till Bessie asked me how I could possibly walk through the corridor with so composed a step.

'My dear, I was thinking about baby and his nurse, and quite forgot to be frightened. Yes, they are all right now, and going to sleep again comfortably; and I think the ghost must have followed their example, for certainly there were no signs of its presence as I returned: so I think we had better try to make up for our broken rest by a few hours' sleep.'

Bessie was quite ready to do so; but for my own part I lay awake until the loitering dawn broke through the shuttered windows.

Mr Maclean's absence was really, I found, not to be prolonged beyond the two nights; so I could write Dick word to fetch me home on the following day; but I resolved, before I went, to have some sort of explanatory conversation with Mrs Graham, with respect to her dream of the night before. I told nothing of it to Bessie; for I felt she would spoil everything perhaps by her awkwardness in handling the subject, or wound the poor girl's feelings by too abrupt, a reference to her grief.

But I watched Mrs Graham leave the house at about eleven o'clock to take her little charge out for his morning walk, and as soon as Bessie descended to the kitchen quarters to give her orders for the day, I put on my bonnet and shawl and ran after the nurse. There was a cold wind blowing from the north, and I knew I should find her in the sheltered shrubbery, where she had been told to take the child. It extended for some distance, and when I came up with her we were quite out of sight and hearing of the house.

'A fine cold morning!' I remarked, by way of a beginning.

'Very cold, madam.'

'With the wind in the north. A nasty day for the sea—I pity the ships in the channel.'

To this she made no response.

'Have you ever been on the sea, Mrs Graham?'

'Yes! once!' with a shudder.

'And did you like it?'

'Like it? Oh! for God's sake, madam, don't speak of it, for I cannot bear the thought even.'

'You were unfortunate, perhaps? You had experience of a storm? But the sea is not always rough, Mrs Graham.'

She was silent, and I looked in her face, and saw the tears streaming down it.

'My dear girl,' I said, placing my hand on her shoulder, 'don't think me unkind. I have guessed somewhat of your history, and I feel for you—oh, so deeply. Confide in me; my husband is a man of influence, and I may be of use to you. I see that you are superior to the position you hold, and I have conceived an interest in you. Don't keep your sorrows locked in your own breast, or they will eat out your very heart and life.'

As I spoke she began to sob piteously.

'You are not doing right by this poor little baby, nor his parents,' I continued, by brooding over a silent grief. You will injure his health, when perhaps if you will tell us all, we may be able to comfort you.'

'No one can comfort me, madam! I am beyond all relief.'

'No one dare say that in this world, which God rules according to His will. You cannot tell what solace He may hold in the future for you.'

'I have no future,' she said sadly. 'If you think I am likely to injure this little one,' pressing it tightly to her bosom, 'I am very, very sorry; but to have something to love and care for, seemed to be the only thing to prevent my going mad.'

'Mrs Graham, I don't wish to be impertinently curious, but I want to hear your story. Won't you tell it to me?'

'If you do, you will hate me—as I hate myself.'

'I hardly think that possible. Of what crime can you be guilty, to accuse yourself so bitterly.'

'*I am a murderess!*'

She brought out the words so vehemently that I started. Was it possible she spoke the truth? And yet I had seen in our gaol, such young and superior-looking criminals, that I knew it *might* be possible. My thoughts flew at once to her child.

'Was it the baby?' I cried. 'Oh! my poor child! what drove you to such an awful deed? '

'Do you pity me still?'

'I pity you with all my heart.'

'Ah! madam; you are too good.'

She trembled so violently that I had taken the child from her arms, and as I stood there in the wintry path, she sank down upon her knees before me and kissed the border of my shawl, and hid her face in it and cried.

'Mrs Graham, I cannot believe it!'

'No! you need not believe it. In that sense I did not kill my child. God took it away from me in anger; but I sent its father, my dearly-loved husband, to his death.'

'Sent him to his death!'

'Ah, madam! have pity on me and listen. We had been married but six months, and we loved each other, ah! so dearly. He was a clerk in a city firm, and his employers sent him over to Ireland on business. We could not bear to part—we went together. In order to return to England we embarked in a small sailing vessel, and we had a fearful storm in crossing. The sea ran mountains high, and the women on board were assembled together in a deck cabin. The men to whom they belonged kept looking in every now and then to tell them how we were getting on, and every time the door of the cabin was opened, the sea rushed in and wetted them. They grew impatient, I the most of all; and when my dear husband, in his anxiety lest I should be frightened at our danger, put his head in for the third or fourth time I called out, saying, 'Go away, Edward, and *don't come back again.*' And he went away, and he never did come back. Ah, Heaven! have mercy upon me!'

'My poor girl! how did it happen?'

'He was washed off the deck, madam, by a huge wave that nearly swamped the ship—so they told me afterwards. But I never saw him more! The glimpse I had of his bonnie face as it was thrust in at the half-opened door, beaming with love and anxiety, was the last glimpse I was ever to have in this world—and I sent him to his death. I said, "Go away, and don't come back—and he never came back!"—he never came back!'

Her grief was so violent I almost thought she would have swooned at my feet. I tried to direct her thoughts in another direction.

'Have you no friends to go to, Mrs Graham?'

'None of my own, .madam. I was a soldiers orphan from the Home when Edward married me. And I could not go to his.'

'How did you lose your baby?'

'It died of my grief, I suppose; it only lived a few days. And then they advised me at the hospital to get a situation as wet nurse; and I thought the care of an infant might soothe me a little. But my sorrow is past cure.'

'You have bad dreams at night, I fear.'

'Oh! such awful dreams! He is always calling me—calling me to go to him, and I can find him nowhere; or else I am in the ship again, and see that which I never did see—the cruel wave that washed him from me!'

'Do you feel strong enough to take the child again?'

She had risen by this time, and was, comparatively speaking, calm. She held out her arms mechanically. I put the baby in them, and then stooped and kissed her swollen eyes and burning forehead.

'I will not discuss this subject with you further today,' I said; 'but you have found a friend. Go on with your walk, child, and may God comfort you. I am glad you have told me the story of your grief.'

I hurried back to Bessie, fearful lest she might come in search of me, and insist upon hearing the reason of Mrs Graham's tears. There was no doubt of one thing—another nurse must be found as soon as possible for little Dick, and I must take on myself the responsibility of providing for his present one. But all that required my husband's permission and advice, and I must wait till I had seen and confided in him.

Bessie, who had discovered that, not withstanding my deplorable deficiency in the way of children, I could cut out their garments far better than she could do herself, had provided a delightful entertainment for me in the shape of half-a-dozen frocks to be made ready for the nurse's hands, and the whole afternoon was spent in snipping and piecing and tacking together. But I didn't grumble; my mind was too much occupied with poor Mrs Graham and her pathetic story. I thought of it so much that the temporary fear evoked by the apparition of the night before had totally evaporated. In the presence of a real, substantial human grief, we can hardly spare time for imaginary horrors.

As bedtime recurred, and Bessie and I locked ourselves into our stronghold, I refused the half of the bed she offered me, and preferred to retain my own. I even made up my mind, if possible, not to sleep, but to watch for the mysterious sounds, and be the first to investigate them. So I would not put out my candle, but lay in bed reading long after Bessie's snores had announced her departure to the land of dreams.

I had come to the end of my book, my candle, and my patience, and was just about to give up the vigil as a failure, when I heard footsteps distinctly sounding along the corridor. I was out of bed in a moment, with my hand upon the lock of the door. I waited till the steps had passed my room, and then I turned the key and looked gently out. The same white figure I had seen the night before was standing a little beyond me, its course arrested, as it would appear, by the slight sound of unlocking the door.

'Now or never,' I thought to myself. 'Dick always says I am the bravest woman he ever met, and I will try and prove him true. Why should I be afraid? Even if this *is* a spirit, God is over *it* and us, alike!'

So I stepped out into the passage, just as I should sit down to have a tooth drawn. The figure had recommenced walking, and was some paces farther from me. I followed it, saying softly, 'What are you? Speak to me.' But it did not turn, but went on, clasping its hands, and talking rapidly to itself.

A sudden thought flashed across my mind. In a moment I felt sure that I was right, and had solved the mystery of Poplar Farm. I placed myself full in the path of the apparition, and as the end of the corridor forced it to turn and retrace its steps, I met face to face my poor, pretty Mrs Graham, with the flaxen hair she usually kept concealed beneath her widow's cap, streaming over her shoulders and giving her a most weird and unearthly appearance.

'Edward! Edward!' she was whispering in a feverish, uncertain manner, 'where are you? It is so dark here and so cold. Put out your hand and lead me. I want to come to you, darling; I want to come to you.'

I stretched out my own hand and took hers. She clung to me joyfully.

'Is it you?' she exclaimed, in the undisturbed voice of a sleepwalker. 'Have I found you again? Oh, Edward! I have been trying to find you for so long—so long, and I thought we were parted for ever.'

I drew her gently along to her own room and put her in her bed, whilst she continued to talk to me in the fond, low tones in which she thought she was addressing her dead husband.

★★★★★★

Bessie slept through it all.

Of course I told her all about it next day, and equally, of course, she did not believe half what I said. She did not like the idea of parting with her cherished grievance in the shape of the ghost, nor having the trouble of changing her wet nurse. So I left her, as soon as ever Dick arrived, rather disgusted with the manner in which she had received my efforts for her good, but still determined to do what I could in the way of befriending Mrs Graham. As I told her the last thing, when I ran up to the nursery to say goodbye to little Dick, and received her grateful thanks in reply. 'Only nothing,' she said with a deep sigh, 'could ever do her any good in this world again.'

'But I'm determined to get her out of Poplar Farm,' I said to Dick, as we drove homeward, after I had told him this longwinded story. 'She's killing the baby and herself too. She ought to have a much more cheerful home and active employment. Now, can't you think of something for her to do about the gaol or the hospital, like a dear, darling old boy as you are?'

'Well, I don't quite see how you can take Mrs Maclean's servant away from her against, her will, Dolly. If Mrs Graham leaves, it will be a different thing; but as things are, I'm afraid you ought not to interfere.'

I called him a wretch; but I knew he was right for all that, and determined to take his advice and wait patiently to see how things turned out. And, as it happened, I had not long to wait, for a week afterwards I received this doleful epistle from Bessie:—

'My dear Dolly,—I am perfectly miserable; nothing ever goes right with me. Tom threw Charlie out of the wheelbarrow yesterday, and cut his forehead right across. He will be scarred for life. And nurse has entirely spoiled those frocks you were so kind as to cut out for Lily and Bessie. She is so obstinate, she would have her own way, and the children positively cannot get into them. But the worst news of all is, that Mrs Graham is going to leave me, and I have had to wean baby, and put him on the bottle.'

'Hurrah!' I cried, 'it's all right. I shall get that poor child here after all, and be able to patch up her broken life. No, I sha'n't, though,' I continued, as I went on reading, and then, to my husband's astonishment, I fell on his neck, and burst into tears. 'Oh, Dick, Dick, Dick, I *am* so glad!'

'Halloa! what's up now?' said that vulgar Dick, in his own way of expressing things.

'My darling, she's got him again.'

'Who's got which?'

'Mrs Graham s husband has returned. He wasn't drowned, but let me finish the letter,' and drying my eyes I went on—

'Just imagine how awkward and unpleasant for me. The other evening there was an awful screaming in the kitchen, and when I went down, I found Mrs Graham fainted dead away in the arms of a man. I was very angry at first, naturally; but when she recovered I found it was her husband whom she thought was drowned at sea three months ago. It seems he was picked up insensible by some ship, and taken to Spain, where he had a fever, and was delirious, and all that sort of thing; and when he recovered, he worked his way home before the mast, and had only just found out where his wife lived. But I think it is excessively unreasonable of people to take situations, and say they're widows, and then—'

'Oh, don't read any more of that rubbish, for heaven's sake!' said Dick, irreverently. 'The long and the short of the matter is, that the girl's got her man again.'

'Oh! I *am* so thankful! 'I exclaimed, with the tears still in my eyes; I couldn't help it, they *would* come. 'Poor child! poor, desolate, heartbroken child! What a heaven earth must appear to her today. Dick, will you drive me over to the farm directly after breakfast? I want to see her and congratulate her.'

'You seem to take a vast interest in this Mrs Graham, and her joys and sorrows,' said Dick; 'why is it, Dolly?'

'Because I can sympathise with them so deeply. Because—because—oh, Dick, *you* know—because God has given me—you, and I am the very happiest woman in all the world.'

The Ghost of Charlotte Cray

Mr Sigismund Braggett was sitting in the little room he called his study, wrapped in a profound—not to say a mournful—reverie. Now, there was nothing in the present life nor surroundings of Mr Braggett to account for such a demonstration. He was a publisher and book-seller; a man well to do, with a thriving business in the city, and the prettiest of all pretty villas at Streatham. And he was only just turned forty; had not a grey hair in his head nor a false tooth in his mouth; and had been married but three short months to one of the fairest and most affectionate specimens of English womanhood that ever trans-formed a bachelor's quarters into Paradise.

What more could Mr Sigismund Braggett possibly want? Noth-ing! His trouble lay in the fact that he had got rather more than he wanted. Most of us have our little peccadilloes in this world—awk-ward reminiscences that we would like to bury five fathoms deep, and never hear mentioned again, but that have an uncomfortable habit of cropping up at the most inconvenient moments; and no mortal is more likely to be troubled with them than a middle-aged bachelor who has taken to matrimony.

Mr Sigismund Braggett had no idea what he was going in for when he led the blushing Emily Primrose up to the altar, and swore to be hers, and hers only, until death should them part. He had no con-ception a woman's curiosity could be so keen, her tongue so long, and her inventive faculties so correct. He had spent whole days before the fatal moment of marriage in burning letters, erasing initials, destroying locks of hair, and making offerings of affection look as if he had pur-chased them with his own money. But it had been of little avail. Mrs Braggett had swooped down upon him like a beautiful bird of prey, and wheedled, coaxed, or kissed him out of half his secrets before he knew what he was about. But he had never told her about Charlotte

Cray. And now he almost wished that he had done so, for Charlotte Cray was the cause of his present dejected mood.

Now, there are ladies *and* ladies in this world. Some are very shy, and will only permit themselves to be wooed by stealth. Others, again, are the pursuers rather than the pursued, and chase the wounded or the flying even to the very doors of their stronghold, or lie in wait for them like an octopus, stretching out their tentacles on every side in search of victims.

And to the latter class Miss Charlotte Cray decidedly belonged. Not a person worth mourning over, you will naturally say. But, then. Mr Sigismund Braggett had not behaved well to her. She was one of the 'peccadilloes,' She was an authoress—not an author, mind you, which term smacks more of the profession than the sex—but an 'authoress,' with lots of the 'ladylike' about the plots of her stories and the metre of her rhymes. They had come together in the sweet connection of publisher and writer—had met first in a dingy, dusty little office at the back of his house of business, and laid the foundation of their friendship with the average amount of chaffering and prevarication that usually attend such proceedings.

Mr Braggett ran a risk in publishing Miss Cray's tales or verses, but he found her useful in so many other ways that he used occasionally to hold forth a sop to Cerberus in the shape of publicity for the sake of keeping her in his employ. For Miss Charlotte Cray—who was as old as himself, and had arrived at the period of life when women are said to pray 'Any, good Lord, any!'—was really a clever woman, and could turn her hand to most things required of her, or upon which she had set her mind; and she had most decidedly set her mind upon marrying Mr Braggett, and he—to serve his own purposes—had permitted her to cherish the idea, and this was the Nemesis that was weighing him down in the study at the present moment. He had complimented Miss Cray, and given her presents, and taken her out a-pleasuring, all because she was useful to him, and did odd jobs that no one else would undertake, and for less than any one else would have accepted; and he had known the while that she was in love with him, and that she believed he was in love with her.

He had not thought much of it at the time. He had not then made up his mind to marry Emily Primrose, and considered that what pleased Miss Cray, and harmed no one else, was fair play for all sides. But he had come to see things differently now. He had been married three months, and the first two weeks had been very bitter ones to him. Miss Cray had written him torrents of reproaches during that unhappy period, besides calling day after day at his office to deliver them in person. This and her threats had frightened him out of his life. He had lived in hourly terror lest the clerks should overhear what passed at their interviews, or that his wife should be made acquainted with them.

He had implored Miss Cray, both by word of mouth and letter, to cease her persecution of him; but all the reply he received was that he was a base and perjured man, and that she should continue to call at his office, and write to him through the penny post, until he had introduced her to his wife. For therein lay the height and depth of his offending. He had been afraid to bring Emily and Miss Cray together, and the latter resented the omission as an insult. It was bad enough to find that Sigismund Braggett, whose hair she wore next her heart, and whose photograph stood as in a shrine upon her bedroom mantelpiece, had married another woman, without giving her even the chance of a refusal, but it was worse still to come to the conclusion that he did not intend her to have a glimpse into the garden of Eden he had created for himself.

Miss Cray was a lady of vivid imagination and strong aspirations. All was not lost in her ideas, although Mr Braggett *had* proved false to the hopes he had raised. Wives did not live for ever; and the chances and changes of this life were so numerous, that stranger things had happened than that Mr Braggett might think fit to make better use of the second opportunity afforded him than he had done of the first. But if she were not to continue even his friend, it was too hard. But the perjured publisher had continued resolute, notwithstanding all Miss Cray's persecution, and now he had neither seen nor heard from her for a month; and, manlike, he was beginning to wonder what had become of her, and whether she had found anybody to console her for his untruth. Mr Braggett did not wish to comfort Miss Cray himself; but he did not quite like the notion of her being comforted.

After all—so he soliloquised—he had been very cruel to her; for the poor thing was devoted to him. How her eyes used to sparkle and her cheek to flush when she entered his office, and how eagerly she would undertake any work for him, however disagreeable to perform! He knew well that she had expected to be Mrs Braggett, and it must have been a terrible disappointment to her when he married Emily Primrose.

Why had he not asked her out to Violet Villa since? What harm

269

could she do as a visitor there? particularly if he cautioned her first as to the peculiarity of Mrs Braggett's disposition, and the quickness with which her jealousy was excited. It was close upon Christmas-time, the period when all old friends meet together and patch up, if they cannot entirely forget, everything that has annoyed them in the past, Mr Braggett pictured to himself the poor old maid sitting solitary in, her small rooms at Hammersmith, no longer able to live in the expectation of seeing his manly form at the wicket-gate, about to enter and cheer her solitude. The thought smote him as a two-edged sword, and he sat down at once and penned Miss Charlotte s note, in which he inquired after her health, and hoped that they should soon see her at Violet Villa.

He felt much better after this note was written and despatched. He came out of the little study and entered the cheerful drawing-room, and sat with his pretty wife by the light of the fire, telling her of the lonely lady to whom he had just proposed to introduce her.

'An old friend of mine, Emily. A clever, agreeable woman, though rather eccentric. You will be polite to her, I know, for my sake.'

'An *old* woman, is she?' said Mrs Braggett, elevating her eyebrows. 'And what do you call "old," Siggy, I should like to know?'

'Twice as old as yourself, my dear—five-and-forty at the very least, and not personable-looking, even for that age. Yet I think you will find her a pleasant companion, and I am sure she will be enchanted with you.'

'I don't know that: clever women don't like me, as a rule, though I don't know why.'

'They are jealous of your beauty, my darling; but Miss Cray is above such meanness, and will value you for your own sake.'

'She'd better not let me catch her valuing me for *yours*,' responded Mrs Braggett, with a flash of the eye that made her husband ready to regret the dangerous experiment he was about to make of bringing together two women who had each, in her own way, a claim upon him, and each the will to maintain it.

So he dropped the subject of Miss Charlotte Cray, and took to admiring his wife's complexion instead, so that the evening passed harmoniously, and both parties were satisfied.

For two days Mr Braggett received no answer from Miss Cray, which rather surprised him. He had quite expected that on the reception of his invitation she would rush down to his office and into his arms, behind the shelter of the ground-glass door that enclosed his chair of authority. For Miss Charlotte had been used on occasions to indulge in rapturous demonstrations of the sort, and the remembrance of Mrs Braggett located in Violet Villa would have been no obstacle whatever to her. She believed she had a prior claim to Mr Braggett. However, nothing of the kind happened, and the perjured publisher was becoming strongly imbued with the idea that he must go out to Hammersmith and see if he could not make his peace with her in person, particularly as he had several odd jobs for Christmas-tide, which no one could undertake so well as herself, when a letter with a black-edged border was put into his hand. He opened it mechanically, not knowing the writing; but its contents shocked him beyond measure.

Honoured Sir,—I am sorry to tell you that Miss Cray died at my house a week ago, and was buried yesterday. She spoke of you several times during her last illness, and if you would like to hear any further particulars, and will call on me at the old address, I shall be most happy to furnish you with them.—
Yours respectfully,
Mary Thompson.

When Mr Braggett read this news, you might have knocked him over with a feather. It is not always true that a living dog is better than a dead lion. Some people gain considerably in the estimation of their friends by leaving this world, and Miss Charlotte Cray was one of them. Her persecution had ceased for ever, and her amiable weaknesses were alone held in remembrance. Mr Braggett felt a positive relief in the knowledge that his dead friend and his wife would never now be brought in contact with each other; but at the same time he blamed himself more than was needful, perhaps, for not having seen nor communicated with Miss Cray for so long before her death. He came down to breakfast with a portentously grave face that morning, and imparted the sad intelligence to Mrs Braggett with the air of an undertaker.

Emily wondered, pitied, and sympathised, but the dead lady was no more to her than any other stranger; and she was surprised her husband looked so solemn over it all. Mr Braggett, however, could not dismiss the subject easily from his mind. It haunted him during the business hours of the morning, and as soon as he could conveniently leave his office, he posted away to Hammersmith. The little house in which Miss Cray used to live looked just the same, both inside and outside: how strange it seemed that *she* should have flown away from

271

it forever! And here was her landlady, Mrs Thompson, bobbing and curtseying to him in the same old black net cap with artificial flowers in it, and the same stuff gown she had worn since he first saw her, with her apron in her hand, it is true, ready to go to her eyes as soon as a reasonable opportunity occurred, but otherwise the same Mrs Thompson as before. And yet she would never wait upon *her* again.

'It was all so sudden, sir,' she said, in answer to Mr Braggett's inquiries, 'that there was no time to send for nobody.'

'But Miss Cray had my address.'

'Ah! perhaps so; but she was off her head, poor dear, and couldn't think of nothing. But she remembered you, sir, to the last; for the very morning she died, she sprung up in bed and called out, "Sigismund! Sigismund!" as loud as ever she could, and she never spoke to anybody afterwards, not one word.'

'She left no message for me?'

'None, sir. I asked her the day before she went if I was to say nothing to you for her (knowing you was such friends), and all her answer was, "I wrote to him. He's got my letter." So I thought, perhaps, you had heard, sir.'

'Not for some time past. It seems terribly sudden to me, not having heard even of her illness. Where is she buried?'

'Close by in the churchyard, sir. My little girl will go with you and show you the place, if you'd like to see it.'

Mr Braggett accepted her offer and left.

When he was standing by a heap of clods they called a grave, and had dismissed the child, he drew out Miss Cray's last letter, which he carried in his pocket, and read it over.

You tell me that I am not to call at your office again, except on business, nor to send letters to your private address, lest it should come to the knowledge of your wife, and create unpleasantness between you; but I *shall* call, and I *shall* write, until I have seen Mrs Braggett, and, if you don't take care, I will introduce myself to her and tell her the reason you have been afraid to do so.'

This letter had made Mr Braggett terribly angry at the time of reception. He had puffed and fumed, and cursed Miss Charlotte by all his gods for daring to threaten him. But he read it with different feelings now Miss Charlotte was down there, six feet beneath the ground he stood on, and he could feel only compassion for her frenzy, and resentment against himself for having excited it. As he travelled home from Hammersmith to Streatham, he was a very dejected publisher indeed.

He did not tell Mrs Braggett the reason of his melancholy, but it affected him to that degree that he could not go to office on the following day, but stayed at home instead, to be petted and waited upon by his pretty wife, which treatment resulted in a complete cure. The next morning, therefore, he started for London as briskly as ever, and arrived at office before his usual time. A clerk, deputed to receive all messages for his master, followed him behind the ground-glass doors, with a packet of letters.

'Mr Van Ower was here yesterday, sir. He will let you have the copy before the end of the week, and Messrs Hanleys' foreman called on particular business, and will look in today at eleven. And Mr Ellis came to ask if there was any answer to his letter yet; and Miss Cray called, sir; and that's all'

'*Who* did you say?' cried Braggett.

'Miss Cray, sir. She waited for you above an hour, but I told her I thought you couldn't mean to come into town at all, so she went.'

'Do you know what you're talking about, Hewetson? You said *Miss Cray!*'

'And I meant it, sir—Miss Charlotte Cray. Burns spoke to her as well as I.'

'Good heavens!' exclaimed Mr Braggett, turning as white as a sheet. 'Go at once and send Burns to me.' Burns came.

'Burns, who was the lady that called to see me yesterday?'

'Miss Cray, sir. She had a very thick veil on, and she looked so pale that I asked her if she had been ill, and she said "Yes." She sat in the office for over an hour, hoping you'd come in, but as you didn't, she went away again.'

'Did she lift her veil?'

'Not whilst I spoke to her, sir.'

'How do you know it was Miss Cray, then?'

The clerk stared. 'Well, sir, we all know her pretty well by this time.'

'Did you ask her name?'

'No, sir; there was no need to do it.'

'You're mistaken, that's all, both you and Hewetson. It couldn't have been Miss Cray! I know for certain that she is—is—is—not in London at present. It must have been a stranger.'

'It was not, indeed, sir, begging your pardon. I could tell Miss Cray anywhere, by her figure and her voice, without seeing her face. But

I *did* see her face, and remarked how awfully pale she was—just like death, sir!'

'There! there! that will do! It's of no consequence, and you can go back to your work.'

But anyone who had seen Mr Braggett, when left alone in his office, would not have said he thought the matter of no consequence. The perspiration broke out upon his forehead, although it was December, and he rocked himself backward and forward in his chair with agitation.

At last he rose hurriedly, upset his throne, and dashed through the outer premises in the face of twenty people waiting to speak to him. As soon as he could find his voice, he hailed a hansom, and drove to Hammersmith. Good Mrs Thompson opening the door to him, thought he looked as if he had just come out of a fever.

'Lor' bless me, sir! whatever's the matter?'

'Mrs Thompson, have you told me the truth about Miss Cray? Is she really dead?'

'*Really dead,* sir! Why, I closed her eyes, and put her in the coffin with my own hands! If she ain't dead, I don't know who is! But if you doubt my word, you'd better ask the doctor that gave the certificate for her.'

'What is the doctor's name?'

'Dodson; he lives opposite.'

'You must forgive my strange questions, Mrs Thompson, but I have had a terrible dream about my poor friend, and I think I should like to talk to the doctor about her.'

'Oh, very good, sir,' cried the landlady, much offended. 'I'm not afraid of what the doctor will tell you. She had excellent nursing and everything as she could desire, and there's nothing on my conscience on that score, so I'll wish you good morning.' And with that Mrs Thompson slammed the door in Mr Braggett's face.

He found Dr Dodson at home.

'If I understand you rightly,' said the practitioner, looking rather steadfastly in the scared face of his visitor, 'you wish, as a friend of the late Miss Cray's, to see a copy of the certificate of her death? Very good, sir; here it is. She died, as you will perceive, on the twenty-fifth of November, of peritonitis. She had, I can assure you, every attention and care, but nothing could have saved her.'

'You are quite sure, then, she is dead?' demanded Mr Braggett, in a vague manner.

The doctor looked at him as if he were not quite sure if he were sane.

'If seeing a patient die, and her corpse coffined and buried, is being sure she is dead, *I* am in no doubt whatever about Miss Cray.'

'It is very strange—most strange and unaccountable,' murmured poor Mr Braggett, in reply, as he shuffled out of the doctor's passage, and took his way back to the office.

Here, however, after an interval of rest and a strong brandy and soda, he managed to pull himself together, and to come to the conclusion that the. doctor and Mrs Thompson *could* not be mistaken, and that, consequently, the clerks *must*. He did not mention the subject again to them however; and as the days went on, and nothing more was heard of the mysterious stranger's visit, Mr Braggett put it altogether out of his mind.

At the end of a fortnight, however, when he was thinking of something totally different, young Hewetson remarked to him, carelessly,—

'Miss Cray was here again yesterday, sir. She walked in just as your cab had left the door.'

All the horror of his first suspicions returned with double force upon the unhappy man's mind.

'Don't talk nonsense!' he gasped, angrily, as soon as he could speak. 'Don't attempt to play any of your tricks on me, young man, or it will be the worse for you, I can tell you.'

'Tricks, sir!' stammered the clerk. 'I don't know what you are alluding to. I am only telling you the truth. You have always desired me to be most particular in letting you know the names of the people who call in your absence, and I thought I was only doing my duty in making a point of ascertaining them—'

'Yes, yes! Hewetson, of course,' replied Mr Braggett, passing his handkerchief over his brow, 'and you are quite right in following my directions as closely as possible; only—in this case you are completely mistaken, and it is the second time you have committed the error.'

'Mistaken!'

'Yes!—as mistaken as it is possible for a man to be! Miss Cray *could* not have called at this office yesterday.'

'But she did, sir.'

'Am I labouring under some horrible nightmare?' exclaimed the publisher, 'or are we playing at cross purposes? Can you mean the Miss Cray I mean?'

'I am speaking of Miss Charlotte Cray, sir, the author of *Sweet*

Gwendoline,—the lady who has undertaken so much of our compilation the last two years, and who has a long nose, and wears her hair in curls. I never knew there was another Miss Cray; but if there are two, that is the one I mean.'

'Still I *cannot* believe it, Hewetson, for the Miss Cray who has been associated with our firm died on the twenty-fifth of last month.'

'*Died,* sir! Is Miss Cray dead? Oh, it can't be! It's some humbugging trick that's been played upon you, for I'd swear she was in this room yesterday afternoon, as full of life as she's ever been since I knew her. She didn't talk much, it's true, for she seemed in a hurry to be off again, but she had got on the same dress and bonnet she was in here last, and she made herself as much at home in the office as she ever did. Besides,' continued Hewetson, as though suddenly remembering something, 'she left a note for you, sir.'

'A note! Why did you not say so before?'

'It slipped my memory when you began to doubt my word in that way, sir. But you'll find it in the bronze vase. She told me to tell you she had placed it there.'

Mr Braggett made a dash at the vase, and found the three-cornered note as he had been told. Yes! it was Charlotte's handwriting, or the facsimile of it, there was no doubt of that; and his hands shook so he could hardly open the paper. It contained these words:

'You tell me that I am not to call at your office again, except on business, nor to send letters to your private address, lest it should come to the knowledge of your wife, and create unpleasantness between you; but I *shall* call, and I *shall* write until I have seen Mrs Braggett, and if you don't take care I will introduce myself to her, and tell her the reason you have been afraid to do so.'

Precisely the same words, in the same writing of the letter he still carried in his breast-pocket, and which no mortal eyes but his and hers had ever seen. As the unhappy man sat gazing at the opened note, his whole body shook as if he were attacked by ague.

'It is Miss Cray's handwriting, isn't it, sir?'

'It looks like it, Hewetson, but it cannot be. I tell you it is an impossibility! Miss Cray died last month, and I have seen not only her grave, but the doctor and nurse who attended her in her last illness. It is folly, then, to suppose either that she called here or wrote that letter.'

'Then *who could it have been* sir?' said Hewetson, attacked with a sudden terror in his turn.

'That is impossible for me to say; but should the lady call again, you had better ask her boldly for her name and address.'

'I'd rather you'd depute the office to anybody but me, sir,' replied the clerk, as he hastily backed out of the room.

Mr Braggett, dying with suspense and conjecture, went through his business as best he could, and hurried home to Violet Villa.

There he found that his wife had been spending the day with a friend, and only entered the house a few minutes before himself.

'Siggy, dear!' she commenced, as soon as he joined her in the draw-ing-room after dinner; ' I really think we should have the fastenings and bolts of this house looked to. Such a funny thing happened whilst; I was out this afternoon. Ellen has just been telling me about it.'

'What sort of a thing, dear?'

'Well, I left home as early as twelve, you know, and told the serv-ants I shouldn't be back until dinner-time; so they were all enjoying themselves in the kitchen, I suppose, when cook told Ellen she heard a footstep in the drawing-room. Ellen thought at first it must be cook's fancy, because she was sure the front door was fastened; but when they listened, they all heard the noise together, so she ran upstairs, and what on earth do you think she saw?'

'How can I guess, my dear?'

'Why, a lady, seated in this very room, as if she was waiting for somebody. She was oldish, Ellen says, and had a very white face, with long curls hanging down each side of it; and she wore a blue bonnet with white feathers, and a long black cloak, and—'

'Emily, Emily! Stop! You don't know what you're talking about. That girl is a fool: you must send her away. That is, how could the lady have got in if the door was closed? Good heavens! you'll all drive me mad between you with your folly!' exclaimed Mr Braggett, as he threw himself back in his chair, with an exclamation that sounded very like a groan.

Pretty Mrs Braggett was offended. What had she said or done that her husband should doubt her word? She tossed her head in indigna-tion, and remained silent If Mr Braggett wanted any further informa-tion, he would have to apologise.

'Forgive me, darling,' he said, after a long pause. 'I don't think I'm very well this evening, but your story seemed to upset me.'

'I don't see why it should upset you,' returned Mrs Braggett. 'If strangers are allowed to come prowling about the house in this way, we shall be robbed some day, and then you'll say I should have told you of it.'

'Wouldn't she—this person—give her name?'

'Oh! I'd rather say no more about it. You had better ask Ellen.'

'No, Emily! I'd rather hear it from you.'

'Well, don't interrupt me again, then. When Ellen saw the woman seated here, she asked her her name and business at once, but she gave no answer, and only sat and stared at her. And so Ellen, feeling very uncomfortable, had just turned round to call up cook, when the woman got up, and dashed past her like a flash of lightning, and they saw nothing more of her!'

'Which way did she leave the house?'

'Nobody knows any more than how she came in. The servants declare the hall-door was neither opened nor shut—but, of course, it must have been. She was a tall gaunt woman, Ellen says, about fifty, and she's sure her hair was dyed. She must have come to steal something, and that's why I say we ought to have the house made more secure. Why, Siggy! Siggy! what's the matter? Here, Ellen! Jane! come, quick, some of you! Your master's fainted!'

And, sure enough, the repeated shocks and horrors of the day had had such an effect upon poor Mr Braggett, that for a moment he did lose all consciousness of what surrounded him. He was thankful to take advantage of the Christmas holidays, to run over to Paris with his wife, and try to forget, in the many marvels of that city, the awful fear that fastened upon him at the mention of anything connected with home. He might be enjoying himself to the top of his bent; but directly the remembrance of Charlotte Cray crossed his mind, all sense of enjoyment vanished, and he trembled at the mere thought of returning to his business, as a child does when sent to bed in the dark.

He tried to hide the state of his feelings from Mrs Braggett, but she was too sharp for him. The simple, blushing Emily Primrose had developed, under the influence of the matrimonial forcing-frame, into a good watch-dog, and nothing escaped her notice.

Left to her own conjecture, she attributed his frequent moods of dejection to the existence of some other woman, and became jealous accordingly. If Siggy did not love her, why had he married her? She felt certain there was some other horrid creature who had engaged his affections and would not leave him alone, even now that he was her own lawful property. And to find out who the 'horrid creature' was became Mrs Emily's constant idea. When she had found out, she meant to give her a piece of her mind, never fear! Meanwhile Mr Braggett's evident distaste to returning to business only served to increase his wife's suspicions. A clear conscience, she argued, would know no fear. So they were not a happy couple, as they set their faces once more towards England. Mr Braggett's dread of re-entering his office amounted almost to terror, and Mrs Braggett, putting this and that together, resolved that she would fathom the mystery, if it lay in feminine *finesse* to do so. She did not whisper a word of her intentions to dear Siggy, you may be sure of that! She worked after the manner of her amiable sex, like a cat in the dark, or a worm boring through the earth, and appearing on the surface when least expected.

So poor Mr Braggett brought her home again, heavy at heart indeed, but quite ignorant that any designs were being made against him. I think he would have given a thousand pounds to be spared the duty of attending office the day after his arrival. But it was necessary, and he went, like a publisher and a Briton. But Mrs Emily had noted his trepidation and his fears, and laid her plans accordingly. She had never been asked to enter those mysterious precincts, the house of business. Mr Braggett had not thought it necessary that her blooming loveliness should be made acquainted with its dingy, dusty accessories, but she meant to see them for herself today. So she waited till he had left Violet Villa ten minutes, and then she dressed and followed him by the next train to London.

Mr Sigismund Braggett meanwhile had gone on his way, as people go to a dentist, determined to do what was right, but with an indefinite sort of idea that he might never come out of it alive. He dreaded to hear what might have happened in his absence, and he delayed his arrival at the office for half-an-hour, by walking there instead of taking a cab as usual, in order to put off the evil moment. As he entered the place, however, he saw at a glance that his efforts were vain, and that something had occurred. The customary formality and precision of the office were upset, and the clerks, instead of bending over their ledgers, or attending to the demands of business, were all huddled together at one end whispering and gesticulating to each other. But as soon as the publisher appeared, a dead silence fell upon the group, and they only stared at him with an air of horrid mystery.

'What is the matter now?' he demanded, angrily, for like most men when in a fright which they are ashamed to exhibit, Mr Sigismund Braggett tried to cover his want of courage by bounce.

The young man called Hewetson advanced towards him, with a face the colour of ashes, and pointed towards the ground-glass doors dumbly.

'What do you mean? Can't you speak? What's come to the lot of you, that you are neglecting my business in this fashion to make fools of yourselves?'

'If you please, sir, she's in there.'

Mr Braggett started back as if he'd been shot. But still he tried to have it out.

'*She!* Who's *she?*'

'Miss Cray, sir.'

'Haven't I told you already that's a lie.'

'Will you judge for yourself, Mr Braggett?' said a grey-haired man, stepping forward. 'I was on the stairs myself just now when Miss Cray passed me, and I have no doubt whatever but that you will find her in your private room, however much the reports that have lately reached you may seem against the probability of such a thing.'

Mr Braggett's teeth chattered in his head as he advanced to the ground-glass doors, through the panes of one of which there was a little peephole to ascertain if the room were occupied or not. He stooped and looked in. At the table, with her back towards him, was seated the well-known figure of Charlotte Cray. He recognised at once the long black mantle in which she was wont to drape her gaunt figure—the blue bonnet, with its dejected-looking, uncurled feather—the lank curls which rested on her shoulders— and the black-leather bag, with a steel clasp, which she always carried in her hand. It was the embodiment of Charlotte Cray, he had no doubt of that; but how could he reconcile the fact of her being there with the damp clods he had seen piled upon her grave, with the certificate of death, and the doctor's and landlady's assertion that they had watched her last moments?

At last he prepared, with desperate energy, to turn the handle of the door. At that moment the attention of the more frivolous of the clerks was directed from his actions by the entrance of an uncommonly pretty woman at the other end of the outer office. Such a lovely creature as this seldom brightened the gloom of their dusty abiding-place. Lilies, roses, and carnations vied with each other in her complexion, whilst the sunniest of locks, and the brightest of blue eyes, lent her face a girlish charm not easily described. What could this fashionably-attired Venus want in their house of business?

'Is Mr Braggett here? I am Mrs Braggett. Please show me in to him immediately.'

They glanced at the ground-glass doors of the inner office. They had already closed behind the manly form of their employer.

'This way, madam,' one said, deferentially, as he escorted her to the presence of Mr Braggett.

Meanwhile, Sigismund had opened the portals of the Temple of Mystery, and with trembling knees entered it. The figure in the chair did not stir at his approach. He stood at the door irresolute. What should he do or say?

'Charlotte,' he whispered.

Still she did not move.

At that moment his wife entered.

'Oh, Sigismund!' cried Mrs Emily, reproachfully, 'I knew you were keeping something from me, and now I've caught you in the very act. Who is this lady, and what is her name? I shall refuse to leave the room until I know it'

At the sound of her rival's voice, the woman in the chair rose quickly to her feet and confronted them. Yes! there was Charlotte Cray, precisely similar to what she had appeared in life, only with an uncertainty and vagueness about the lines of the familiar features that made them ghastly.

She stood there, looking Mrs Emily full in the face, but only for a moment, for, even as she gazed, the lineaments grew less and less distinct, with the shape of the figure that supported them, until, with a crash, the apparition seemed to fall in and disappear, and the place that had known her was filled with empty air.

'Where is she gone?' exclaimed Mrs Braggett, in a tone of utter amazement.

'Where is who gone?' repeated Mr Braggett, hardly able to articulate from fear.

'The lady in the chair!'

'There was no one there except in your own imagination. It was my great-coat that you mistook for a figure,' returned her husband hastily, as he threw the article in question over the back of the arm-chair.

'But how could that have been?' said his pretty wife, rubbing her eyes. 'How could I think a coat had eyes, and hair, and features? I am sure I saw a woman seated there, and that she rose and stared at me. Siggy! tell me it was true. It seems so incomprehensible that I should have been mistaken.'

'You must question your own sense. You see that the room is empty now, except for ourselves, and you know that no one has left it. If you like to search under the table, you can.'

'Ah! now, Siggy, you are laughing at me, because you know that would be folly. But there was certainly some one here—only, where can she have disappeared to?'

'Suppose we discuss the matter at a more convenient season,' replied Mr Braggett, as he drew his wife's arm through his arm. 'Hewetson! you will be able to tell Mr Hume that he was mistaken. Say, also, that I shall not be back in the office today. I am not so strong as I thought I was, and feel quite unequal to business. Tell him to come out to Streatham this evening with my letters, and I will talk with him there.'

What passed at that interview was never disclosed; but pretty Mrs Braggett was much rejoiced, a short time afterwards, by her husband telling her that he had resolved to resign his active share of the business, and devote the rest of his life to her and Violet Villa. He would have no more occasion, therefore, to visit the office, and be exposed to the temptation of spending four or five hours out of every twelve away from her side. For, though Mrs Emily had arrived at the conclusion that the momentary glimpse she caught of a lady in Siggy's office must have been a delusion, she was not quite satisfied by his assertions that she would never have found a more tangible cause for her jealousy.

But Sigismund Braggett knew more than he chose to tell Mrs Emily. He knew that what she had witnessed was no delusion, but a reality; and that Charlotte Cray had carried out her dying determination, to call at his office and his private residence, until she had seen his wife!

Lost in the Marshes

In the east coast of the county of Norfolk, there lay a village which shall be distinguished by the name of Corston. It was bounded on the one side by the sea, on the other by the open country, and beside the two or three gentleman farmers whose possessions comprised all the agricultural land within a radius of five miles, it could boast of a church and resident parson—a coastguard with its attendant officer, and above all, close contiguity with Rooklands, the estate of the Earl of Worcester. And those who are acquainted with the moral and social aspect, as it existed forty or fifty years ago, of the more insignificant villages of Norfolk, will acknowledge that Corston was favoured above its fellows.

The sea coast in its vicinity brought many a gay riding party over from Rooklands, either to enjoy the fresh breezes, or to bathe in the sparkling waves from some sequestered nook, whilst the congregation of the church was made up of drafts from some four or five outlying hamlets which had not the advantage of a place of worship of their own. Conceive then what a much larger audience the Corston parson could depend upon, when the women had a prospect of seeing the bonnets from ten miles round (to say nothing of a chance of the Rookland aristocrats taking it into their heads to drive out), in addition to listening to his somewhat uninteresting sermons.

The coastguard, too, was a cause of constant excitement, on account of the Admiralty having been in the habit of bestowing the appointment on old, worn-out, half-pay lieutenants who chose to expire almost as soon as they obtained it, and really, notwithstanding the church and the parson and Rooklands, there was not much in Corston worth living for. But at the time this story opens, the charge of the coast had not long been put in the hands of (comparatively speaking) a young and hale man who bid fair to keep anybody else

283

out of it for a long while to come. His office was no sinecure though, for, notwithstanding the difficulty of landing, the coast was a celebrated one for smugglers, and as soon as the dark months of winter set in there was no lack of work for the preventive officers. For the village of Corston did not, of itself, run down to the sea.

Between it and the ocean there lay the salt marshes, a bleak, desolate tract of land, which no skill or perseverance could reclaim from apparent uselessness. Except to the samphire and cockle-gatherers, the salt marshes of Corston were an arid wilderness which could yield no fruit. Many a farmer had looked longingly across the wide waste which terminated only with the shingled beach, and wondered if it were possible to utilise it. But as it had been from the beginning, so it remained until that day; its stinted vegetation affording shelter for sea-fowl and smugglers' booty only, and its brackish waters that flowed and ebbed with the tides, tainting the best springs on the level ground of Corston. It was the existence of these marshes that rendered the coastguard necessary to the village, which would otherwise have become a perfect nest of smugglers.

As it was, notwithstanding all the vigilance of Mr John Burton and his men, many a keg of spirits and roll of tobacco were landed on the coast of Corston, and many a man in the place was marked by them as guilty, though never discovered. For they who had lived by the salt marshes all their lives were cunning as to their properties, and knew just where they might bury their illegal possessions with impunity when the tide was low, and find them safe when it had flowed and ebbed again. Everyone was not so fortunate. Lives had been lost in the marshes before now—ay, and of Corston men too, and several dark tales were told by the gossips of the village of the quagmires and quicksands that existed in various parts of them, which looked, although they never were, both firm and dry, but had the power to draw man and horse with the temerity to step upon them, into their unfathomable depths.

But if the smugglers kept Mr Burton and his men fully occupied on the sea shore, the poachers did no less for Lord Worcester's band of gamekeepers at Rooklands; and Farmer Murray, who had a drop of Scotch blood running in his veins, and was never so much alive as when his own interests were concerned, had only saved his game for the last three years by having been fortunate enough to take the biggest poacher in Corston, red-handed, and let him off on condition that he became his keeper and preserved his covers from future violence. '*Set a thief to catch a thief* is a time-honoured saying, and Farmer Murray found it answer.

Isaac Barnes, the unscrupulous poacher, became a model game-keeper, and the midnight rest of the inhabitants of Mavis Farm had never been disturbed by a stray shot since; though the eldest son, George Murray, had been heard to affirm that half the fun of his life was gone now that there was no chance of a tussle with the poachers. Such was the state of Corston some forty years ago. The villagers were rough, uneducated, and lawless, and the general condition of the residents, vapid and uninteresting enough to have provoked any amount of wickedness, if only for the sake of change or excitement.

★★★★★★

It was the end of September, and the close of a glorious summer. The harvest had been abundant and the Norfolk soil, which knows so well how to yield her fruits in due season, was like an exhausted mother which had just been delivered of her abundance. The last sheaves of golden corn were standing in the fields ready to be carried to the threshing-barn, the trees in the orchards were weighed down with their wealth of pears and apples, and in every lane clusters of bare-headed children with their hands full of nuts and their faces stained with blackberry juice, proved how nature had showered her bounties on rich and poor alike. Lizzie Locke, who was making her way slowly in the direction of the village, with a huge basket on her arm, stopped more than once to wipe her hot face, and pull the sun bonnet she wore further over her eyes, although in another couple of days the October moon would have risen upon the land.

She was a young girl of not more than eighteen or twenty years, and, as her dress denoted, bred from the labouring classes. Not pretty—unless soft brown hair, a fair skin and delicate features, can make a woman so—but much more refined in appearance than the generality of her kind. The hands that grasped the handle of her heavy basket had evidently never done much hard work, nor were her feet broadened or her back bent with early toiling in the turnip and the harvest fields. The reason of this was apparent as soon as she turned her eyes toward you. Quiet blue eyes shaded by long lashes, that seldom unveiled them—eyes that, under more fortuitous circumstances, might have flashed and sparkled with roguish mirth, but that seemed to bear now a settled melancholy in them, even when her mouth smiled: eyes, in fact, that had been blinded from their birth.

Poor Lizzie Locke! There was a true and great soul burning in her breast, but the windows were darkened and it had no power to look out upon the world. As she stood still for a few moments' rest for the third or fourth time between the salt marshes and Corston, her quick ear caught the sound of approaching horses' feet, and she drew on one side of the open road to let the rider pass. But instead of that, the animal was drawn up suddenly upon its haunches, and a pleasant young voice rang out in greeting to her.

'Why, Lizzie, is that you? What a careless girl you are—I might have ridden over you.'

'Miss Rosa,' exclaimed the blind girl, as she recognised the voice and smiled brightly in return.

'Of course it's Miss Rosa, and Polly is as fresh as a two-year-old this morning. She always is, when she gets upon the marshes. It's lucky I pulled up in time.'

The newcomer, a handsome girl of about the same age as Lizzie, was the only daughter of Farmer Murray, of Mavis Farm. Spoilt, as one girl amongst half-a-dozen boys is sure to be, it is not to be wondered at that Rosa Murray was impetuous, saucy, and self-willed. For, added to her being her father's darling, and not knowing what it was to be denied anything in his power to give her. Miss Rosa was extremely pretty, with grey eyes and dark hair, and a complexion like a crimson rose. A rich brunette beauty that had gained for her the title of the Damask Rose of Corston, and of which no one was better aware than herself.

Many a gentleman visitor at Rooklands had heard of the fame of the farmer's pretty daughter, and ridden over to Corston on purpose to catch a glimpse of her, and it was beginning to be whispered about the village that no one in those parts would be considered good enough for a husband for Miss Rosa, and that Mr Murray was set upon her marrying a gentleman from London, any gentleman from 'London' being considered by the simple rustics to be unavoidably 'the glass of fashion and the mould of form.' Mr Murray was termed a 'gentleman farmer' in that part of the county, because he lived in a substantially-built and well-furnished house, and could afford to keep riding-horses in his stable and sit down to a dinner spread on a table-cloth every day.

But, in reality, his father had commenced life as a ploughman in, that very village of Corston, and it was only necessary to bring Farmer Murray into the presence of Lord Worcester and his fashionable friends to see how much of a 'gentleman' he was. He had made the great mistake, however, of sending his children to be educated at schools above their station in life, the consequence of which was that, whilst their tastes and proclivities remained plebeian as his own, they had acquired a self-sufficiency and idea of their merits that accorded ill with their surroundings and threatened to mar their future happiness. The Damask Rose of Corston was the worst example amongst them of the evil alluded to. She had unfortunately lost her mother many years before, so was almost completely her own mistress, and the admiration her beauty excited was fast turning her from a thoughtless flirt into a heartless *coquette*, the most odious character any woman can assume.

But with her own sex, and when it suited her, Rosa Murray could be agreeable and ingenuous enough, and there was nothing but cordiality in the tone in which she continued her conversation with Lizzie Locke.

'What are you doing out here by yourself, child? You really ought not to go about alone. It can't be safe.'

'Oh, it's safe enough, Miss Rosa. I've been used to find my way about ever since I could walk. I've just come up from the marshes, and I was going to take these cockles to Mavis Farm to see if the master would like them for his breakfast tomorrow.'

'I daresay they will be very glad of them. George and Bob are awfully fond of cockles. What a lot you've gathered, Lizzie. How do you manage to find them, when you can't see?'

'I know all the likeliest places they stick to, Miss Rosa, as well as I do the chimney corner at home. The tide comes up and leaves them on the bits of rocks, and among the boulders, and some spots are regular beds of them. I've been at it half my life, you see, miss, and I just feel for them with my fingers and pick them off, I can tell a piece of samphire, too, by the sound it makes as I tread over it.'

'It's wonderful,' said Rosa; 'I have often been surprised to see you go about just as though you had the use of your eyes. It seems to make no difference to you.'

Poor Lizzie sighed.

'Oh, miss! it makes a vast difference—such a difference as you could never understand. But I try to make the best of it, and not be more of a burden upon aunt and Larry than I need to be.'

'I'm sure they don't think you a burden,' said the other girl, warmly. 'But I wonder I didn't meet you on the marshes just now. I've been galloping all over them.'

'Not past Corston Point, I hope, miss,' exclaimed Lizzie, hurriedly.

'Yes, I have ! Why not?'

'Oh, don't go there again. Miss Rosa. It isn't safe, particularly on horseback. There's no end of quagmires beyond the Point, and you can never tell when you'll come on one and be swallowed up, horse and all.'

Rosa Murray laughed. 'Why aren't *you* swallowed up then, Lizzie?'

'I know my way, miss, and I know the tread of it too. I can tell when the soil yields more than it should at low tide that I'm nearing a quicksand. When the Almighty takes away one sense He sharpens the others to make up for it. But the sands are full of danger; some of them are shifting too, and you can never tell if they're firm today whether they won't be loose tomorrow. Do take heed, Miss Rosa, and never you ride beyond Corston Point without one of the young gentlemen to take care of you.'

'Well, I'll remember your advice, Lizzie, for I don't want to be swallowed up alive. Goodbye.'

She put her horse in motion and cantered on some little way in advance—then suddenly checked him again and turned back. All Rosa Murray's actions, like her disposition, were quick and impulsive.

'By the way, Lizzie, it's our harvest-home supper tonight. You must be sure and make Larry bring you up to the big barn with him.'

The blind girl crimsoned with pleasure.

' Oh, Miss Rosa ! but what should I be doing at your supper? I can't dance, you know. I shall only be in the way.'

'Nonsense ! You can hear the singing and the music; we have made papa get a couple of fiddlers over from Wells; and you can eat some supper. You will enjoy yourself, won't you, Lizzie?'

'Yes, miss, I think so—that is, if Larry and aunt are willing that I should go; but it's very good of you to ask me.'

'You must be sure and come. Tell Larry I insist upon it. We shall all be there, you know, and I shall look out for you, Lizzie, and if I don't see you I shall send someone round to your cottage to fetch you.'

Lizzie Locke smiled and curtsied.

'I'll be sure and tell Larry of your goodness, miss,' she said, 'and he'll be able to thank you better than I can. Here comes a gentleman,' she added, as she withdrew herself modestly from the side of the young lady's horse.

The gentleman, whom Lizzie Locke could have distinguished only as such from the different sound produced by his boots in walking, was Lord Worcester's head gamekeeper, Frederick Darley. He was a young fellow to hold the responsible position he did, being only about thirty years of age, and he had not held it long; but he was the son of the gamekeeper on one of Lord Worcester's estates in the south of England, and his lordship had brought him to Rooklands as soon as ever a vacancy occurred. He was a favourite with his master and his master's guests, being a man of rather superior breeding and education, but on that very account he was much disliked by all the poor people around. Gamekeepers are not usually popular in a poaching district, but it was not Frederick Darley's position alone that made him a subject for criticism.

His crying sin, to use their own term, was that he 'held his head too high.' The velveteen coat he usually wore, with a rose in the button-hole, his curly black hair and waxed moustache, no less than the cigars he smoked and the air with which he affected the society of the gentry, showed the tenants of Rooklands that he considered himself vastly above themselves in position, and they hated him accordingly. The animus had spread to Corston, but Mr Darley was not well enough known there yet to have become a subject for general comment Lizzie Locke had never even encountered him before.

He was walking from the village on the present occasion swinging a light cane in his hand, and as Rosa Murray looked up at the blind girls exclamation, she perceived him close to her horse's head,

'Good morning. Miss Murray,' he said, lifting his hat.

'Good morning,' she replied, without mentioning any name, but Lizzie Locke could detect from the slight tremor in her voice that she was confused at the sudden encounter. 'Were you going down to the beach?'

'I was going nowhere but in search of you.'

'Shall we walk towards home then?' said Rosa, suiting the action to the word. She evidently did not wish the blind girl to be a party to their conversation. She called out 'Goodbye, Lizzie,' once more as she walked her horse away, but before she was out of hearing, the little cockle-gatherer could distinguish her say to the stranger in a fluttered voice,—

'I am so glad you are coming over to our harvest-home tonight.'

'One of the grand gentlemen over from Rooklands come to court Miss Rosa,' she thought in the innocence of her heart, as she turned off the road to take a short cut across the country to Mavis Farm. Meanwhile the couple she alluded to were making their way slowly towards Corston; she, reining in her horse to the pace of a tortoise, whilst he walked by the side with his hand upon the crutch of her saddle.

'Could you doubt for a moment whether I should come?' said Frederick Darley in answer to Rosa's question. 'Wouldn't I go twenty—fifty miles, for the pleasure of a dance with you?'

'You're such an awful flatterer,' she replied, bridling under the compliment; 'but don't make too sure of a dance with me, for papa and my brothers will be there, and they are so horribly particular about me.'

'And not particularly fond of me—I know it, Miss Murray—but I care nothing at all about it so long as—as—'

'As what?'

'*As you are.*'

'Oh, Mr Darley! how can you talk such nonsense?'

'It's not nonsense! it's sober sense—come, Rosa, tell me the truth. Are you playing with me, or not?'

'What do you mean by "playing"?'

'You know. Are you in earnest or in jest? In fact—do you love me better than you love your father and your brothers?'

'Mr Darley! You know I do!'

'Prove it then, by meeting me tonight'

'Meeting you? Are you not coming to the harvest-home?'

'I may look in, but I shall not remain long; I shall only use it as an excuse to come over to Corston. Mr Murray is suspicious of me—I can see that—and your brothers dislike me. I don't care to sit at the table of men who are not my friends, Rosa. But if you will take an opportunity to slip out of the barn and join me in the apple copse, I will wait there for you at ten o'clock.'

'Oh! Frederick—if papa should catch me!'

'I will take care of that ! Only say you'll come.'

'I should like to come—it will be so lovely and romantic. Just like a scene in a novel. But I am afraid it is very wrong.'

'What is there wrong in a moonlight stroll? "The summer nights were made for love," Rosa, and we shall have a glorious moon by nine o'clock tonight. You won't disappoint me, will you?'

'No, indeed I won't; but if anything should be discovered you will promise me—'

'What? I will promise you anything in the world.'

'Only that you will shield me from papa's anger—that you will say it was all your fault. For papa is dreadful when he gets in a temper.'

'If you should be discovered—which is not at all likely—I promise you that, rather than give you back into papa's clutches, I will carry you straight off to Rooklands and marry you with a special licence. Will that satisfy you? Would you consent to be my wife, Rosa?'

'Yes!' she replied, and earnestly, for she had been captivated by the manner and appearance of Frederick Darley for some weeks past, and this was not the first meeting by many that they had held without the knowledge of her father.

'That's my own Damask Rose,' he exclaimed triumphantly; 'give me a kiss, dear, just one to seal the contract; there's no one looking!' He held up his face towards her as he spoke—his handsome *insouciant* face with its bright eyes and smile, and she stooped hers to meet it, and give the embrace he petitioned for.

But someone *was* looking. Almost as Rosa's lips met Darley's a frightened look came into her eyes, and she uttered a note of alarm.

'What is it, darling?'

'It's my brother George! He's coming this way. Oh! go, Mr Darley—pray go across the field and let me canter on to meet him.'

He would have stayed to remonstrate, but the girl pushed him from her, and thinking discretion the better part of valour, he jumped over a neighbouring stile and walked away in the direction she had indicated, whilst she, with a considerable degree of agitation, rode on to make what excuses she best could for the encounter to her brother. George Murray was sauntering along the hedge-row switching the leaves off the hazel bushes as he went, and apparently quite unsuspicious of anything being wrong. But the first question he addressed to his sister went straight to the point.

'Who was that fellow that was talking to you just now, Rosa?'

She knew it would be of no use trying to deceive him, so she spoke the truth.

'It was Mr Darley!'

'What's he doing over here?'

'How should I know? You'd better ask him yourself! Am I accountable for Mr Darley's actions?'

'Don't talk nonsense. You know what I mean perfectly well. Did he come over to Rooklands to see you?'

'To see me—what will you get into your head next?'

'Well, you seemed to be hitting it off pretty well together. What were you whispering to him about just now?'

'I didn't whisper to him.'

'You did ! I saw you stoop your head to his ear. Now look here, Rosa! Don't you try any of your flirtation games on with Darley, or I'll go straight to the governor and tell him.'

'And what business is it of yours, pray?'

'It would be the business of every one of us. You don't suppose we're going to let you marry a gamekeeper, do you?'

'Really, George, you're too absurd. Cannot a girl stop to speak to a man in the road without being accused of wanting to marry him? You will say I want to marry every clodhopper I may dance with at the harvest-home tonight next.'

'That is a very different thing. The ploughboys are altogether beneath you, but this Darley is a kind of half-and-half fellow that might presume to imagine himself good enough to be a match for you.'

'Half-and-half indeed!' exclaimed Rosa, nettled at the reflection on her lover; 'and pray, what are we when all's said and done? Mr Darley's connections are as good as our own, and better, any day.'

'Halloa ! what are you making a row about? I'll tell you what, Rosa. It strikes me very forcibly you want to "carry on" with Lord Worcester's keeper, and you ought to be ashamed of yourself for thinking of it. You—who have been educated and brought up in every respect like a lady—to condescend to flirt with an upstart like that, *a mere servant!* Why, he's no better than Isaac Barnes, or old Whisker, or any of the rest of them, only he's prig enough to oil his hair, and wear a button-hole, in order to catch the eye of such silly noodles like yourself.'

'You've no right to speak to me in this way, George. You know nothing at all about the matter.'

'I know that I found Darley and you in the lane with your heads very close together, and that directly he caught sight of me he made off. That doesn't look as if his intentions were honourable, does it? Now, look you here, Rosa. Is he coming to the barn tonight?'

'I believe so!'

'And who asked him?'

'I don't know,' she replied, evasively; 'papa, perhaps—or very likely Mr Darley thought he required no invitation to join a ploughman's dance and supper.'

'Well, you're not to dance with him if he does come.'

'I don't know what right you have to forbid it.'

'None at all! but if you won't give me the promise I shall go straight to the governor, and let him know what I saw today. *He's* seen something of it himself. I can tell you, and he told me to put you on your guard, so you can take your choice of having his anger or not.'

This statement was not altogether true, for if Farmer Murray *had* heard anything of his daughter's flirtation with the handsome game-keeper, it had been only what his sons had suggested to him, and he did not believe their reports. But the boys, George and Robert, now young men of three or four-and-twenty, had had more than one consultation together on the subject, and quite made up their minds that their sister must not be allowed to marry Frederick Darley. For they were quite alive to the advantages that a good connection for her might afford to themselves, and wanted to see her raise the family instead of lowering it.

Rosa, however, believed her brother's word. Dread of her father's anger actuated in a great measure this belief, and she began to fear lest all communication between Darley and herself might be broken off if she did not give the required promise. And the very existence of the fear opened her eyes to the truth, that her lover was become a neces-sary part of life's enjoyment to her. So, like a true woman and a hunted hare, she temporised and 'doubled.'

'Does papa really think I am too intimate with Mr Darley, George?' she inquired, trembling.

'Of course he does, like all the rest of us.'

'But it's a mistake. I don't care a pin about him.'

'Then it will be no privation for you to give up dancing with him tonight.'

'I never intended to dance with him.'

'Honour bright, Rosa?'

'Well, I can't say more than I have. However, you will. see. I *shall not* dance with him. If he asks me, I shall say I am engaged to you.'

'You can say what you like, so long as you snub the brute. I wonder at his impudence coming up to our "Home" at all. But these snobs are never wanting in "cheek." However, if Bob and I don't give him a pretty broad hint tonight that his room is preferable to his company, I'm a duffer! Are you going in, Rosa?'

For the young people had continued to walk towards their own home, and had now arrived at the farm gates.

'Yes. I've been in the saddle since ten o'clock this morning, and have had enough of it'

'Let me take Polly round to the stables before the governor sees the state you've brought her home in, then,' said George, as his sister dis-mounted and threw him the reins. He could be good-natured enough when he had his own way, and he thought he had got it now with Rosa. But she went up to her chamber bent but on one idea—how best to let Mr Darley know of what had passed between her brother and herself, that he might not be surprised at the caution of her behaviour when they met in the big barn.

★★★★★★

Meanwhile Lizzie Locke having left her basket of cockles at Mavis Farm, had reached her cottage home. Her thoughts had been very pleasant as she journeyed there and pondered on the coming pleasure of the evening. It was not often the poor child took any part in the few enjoyments to be met in Corston. People were apt to leave her out of their invitations, thinking that as she was blind she could not possibly derive any amusement from hearing, and she was of too shrinking and modest a nature to obtrude herself where she was not specially required. She had never been to one of the harvest-home suppers given by Farmer Murray (in whose employ her cousin Laurence worked), though she had heard much of their delights.

But now that Miss Rosa had particularly desired her to come, she thought Larry would be pleased to take her. And she had a print dress nice and clean for the occasion, and her aunt would plait her hair neatly for her, and she should hear the sound of Larry's voice as he talked to his companions, and of his feet whilst he was dancing, and, perhaps, after supper one of his famous old English songs—songs which they had heard so seldom of late, and the music of which her aunt and she had missed so much.

It was past twelve o'clock as she entered the cottage, but she was so full of her grand news that she scarcely remembered that she must have kept both her relations waiting for their dinner of bacon and beans.

'Why, Lizzie, my girl, where on earth have you been to?' exclaimed her aunt, Mrs Barnes, as she appeared on the threshold. Mrs Barnes' late husband had been brother to the very Isaac Barnes, once poacher, now gamekeeper on Farmer Murray's estate, and there were scandal-mongers in Corston ill-natured enough to assert that the taint was in the blood, and that young Laurence Barnes was very much inclined to go the same way as his uncle had done before him. But at present he was a helper in the stables of Mavis Farm.

'I've been along the marshes,' said Lizzie, 'gathering cockles, and they gave me sixpence for them up at the farm; and oh, aunt! I met Miss Rosa on my way back, and she says Larry must take me up to the big barn this evening to their harvest-home supper.'

Laurence Barnes was seated at his mother's table already occupied in the discussion of a huge lump of bread and bacon, but as the name of his master's daughter left Lizzie's lips it would have been very evident to anyone on the look-out for it that he started and seemed uneasy.

'And what will you be doing at a dance and a supper, my poor girl?' said her aunt, but not unkindly. 'Come, Lizzie, sit down and take your dinner; that's of much more account to you than a harvest merrymaking.'

'Not till Larry has promised to take me up with him this evening,' replied the girl gaily, and without the least fear of a rebuff. 'You'll do it, Larry, won't you? for Miss Rosa said they'd all be there, and if she didn't see me she'd send round to the cottage after me. She said, "Tell Larry I *insist* upon it;" she did, indeed!'

'Well, then, I'm not going up myself, and so you can't go,' he answered roughly.

'*Not going yourself!*'

The exclamation left the lips of both women at once. They could not understand it, and it equally surprised them. Larry—the best singer and dancer for twenty miles round, to refuse to go up to his master's harvest-home! Why, what would the supper and the dance be without him? At least, so thought Mrs Barnes and Lizzie.

'Aren't you well, Larry?' demanded the blind girl, timidly.

'I'm well enough; but I don't choose to go. I don't care for such rubbish. Let 'em bide! They'll do well enough without us.'

Lizzie dropped into her seat in silence, and began in a mechanical way to eat her dinner. She was terribly disappointed, but she did not dream of disputing her cousin's decision. He was master in that house; and she would not have cared to go to the barn without Larry. Half the pleasure would be gone with his absence. He did not seem to see that.

'Mother can take you up, Liz, if she has a mind to,' he said, presently.

'*I* take her along of me!' cried Mrs Barnes, 'when I haven't so much as a clean kerchief to pin across my shoulders. You're daft, Larry. I haven't been to such a thing as a dance since I laid your father in the churchyard, and if our Liz can't go without me she must stop at home.'

'I don't want to go, indeed I don't, not without Larry,' replied the blind girl, earnestly.

'And what more did Miss Rosa say to you?' demanded her aunt, inquisitively.

'We talked about the sands, aunt. She'd been galloping all over them this morning, and I told her how dangerous they were beyond Corston Point, and we was getting on so nice together, when someone came and interrupted us.'

'*Someone!* Who's someone?' said Laurence Barnes, quickly.

'I can't tell you; I never met him before.'

''Twas a man, then?'

'Oh yes! 'twas a man—a gentleman! I knew that, because there were no nails in his boots, and he didn't give at the knees as he walked.'

'What more?' demanded Larry, with lowered brows.

'Miss Rosa knew him well, because they never named each other, but only wished "good morning." She said, "What are you doing here?" and he said, "Looking after you." He carried a rose in his hand or his coat, I think, for I smelt it, and a cane, too, for it struck the saddle flap.'

'Well, that's enough,' interrupted Laurence, fiercely.

'I thought you wanted to hear all about it, Larry?'

'Is there any more to tell, then?'

'Only that as they walked away together. Miss Rosa said she was so glad he was coming up to the harvest-home tonight.'

'So *he's* a-going, the cur! ' muttered the young man between his teeth. '*I* know him, with his cane, and his swagger, and his stinking roses; and I'll be even with him yet, or my name's not Larry Barnes.'

It was evident that Mr Frederick Darley was no greater favourite in the cottage than the farm.

'Whoever are you talking of?' said Larry's mother. 'Do you know the gentleman Lizzie met with. Miss Rosa?'

'*Gentleman!* He's no gentleman. He's nothing but a common gamekeeper, same as uncle. But don't let us talk of him any more. It takes the flavour of the bacon clean out of my mouth.'

The rest of the simple meal was performed in silence, and then Mrs Barnes gathered up the crockery and carried it into an outer room to wash.

Larry and Lizzie were left alone. The girl seemed to understand that in some mysterious way she had offended her cousin, and wished to restore peace between them, so she crept up to where he was smoking his midday pipe on the old settle by the fire, and laid her head gently against his knees. They had been brought up from babes together, and were used to observe such innocent little familiarities towards each other.

'Never mind about the outing, Larry. I'm not a bit disappointed, and I'm sorry I said anything about it.'

'That's not true. Liz. You *are* disappointed, and it's my doing; but I couldn't help it. I didn't feel somehow as if I had the heart to go. But I've changed my mind since dinner, and we'll go up to the harvest home together, my girl. Will that content you?'

'Oh, Larry! you *are* good!' she said, raising herself, her cheeks crimsoned with renewed expectation; 'but I'd rather stop at home a thousand times over than you should put yourself out of the way for me.'

A sudden thought seemed to strike the young man as he looked at Lizzie's fair, sightless face. He had lived with her so long, in a sisterly way, that it had never struck him to regard her in any other light. But something in the inflection of her voice as she addressed him, made him wonder if he were capable of making her happier than she had ever been yet. He cherished no other hopes capable of realisation. What if he could make his own troubles lighter by lightening those of poor Liz? Something of this sort, but in much rougher clothing, passed through his half-tutored mind. As it grasped the idea he turned hurriedly towards the girl kneeling at his knee.

'Do you really care about me, lass?' he said. 'Do you care if I'm vexed or not? Whether I come in or go out? If I like my dinner or I don't like it? Does all this nonsense worry you? Answer me, for I want to know.'

'Oh ! Larry, what do you mean? Of course I care. I can't do much for you—more's the pity—without my poor eyes, but I can think of you and love you, Larry, and surely you know that I do both.'

'But would you like to love me more, Liz?'

'How could I love you more?'

'Would you like to have the *right* to care for me—the *right* to creep after me in your quiet way wherever I might happen to go—the *right* to walk alongside of me, with your hand in mine, up to the harvesting home tonight; eh, Liz?'

The girl half understood her cousin's meaning, but she was too modest not to fear she might be mistaken. Larry could never wish to take *her*, blind and helpless, for his *wife*.

'Larry, speak to me more plainly; I don't catch your meaning quite.'

'Will you marry me then, Liz, and live along of mother and me to the end of your life?'

'*Marry you!*—Be your *wife! Me! Oh,* Larry, you can't mean it! never.'

'I do mean it,' replied her cousin with an oath; 'and I'll take you as soon as ever you'll take me if you will but say the word.'

'But I am *blind,* Larry.'

'Do you suppose I don't know that? Perhaps I likes you blind best.'

'But I am so useless. I get about so slowly. If anything was to happen to aunt, how could I keep the house clean and cook the dinners, Larry? You must think a bit more before you decide for good.'

But the poor child's face was burning with excitement the while, and her sightless eyes were thrown upwards to her cousin's face as though she would strain through the darkness to see it.

'If anything happened to mother, do you suppose I'd turn you out of doors, Liz? And in any case, then, I must have a wife or a servant to do the work—it will make no difference that way. The only question is, do you want me for a husband?'

'Oh ! I have loved you ever so!' replied the girl, throwing herself into his arms. 'I couldn't love another man, Larry. I know your face as well as if I had seen it, and your step, and your voice. I can tell them long before another body knows there's sound a-coming.'

'Then you'll have me?'

'If you'll have *me.*' she murmured in a tone of delight as she nestled against his rough clothes.

'That's settled, then, and the sooner the banns are up the better! Here, mother! Come along and hear the news. Lizzie has promised to marry me, and I shall take her to church as soon as we've been cried.'

'Well! I *am* pleased,' said Mrs Barnes. 'You couldn't have got a neater wife, Larry, though her eyesight's terribly against her, poor thing! But I'm sure of one thing, Liz, if you can't do all for him that another woman might, you'll love my lad with the best among them, and that thought will make me lie quiet in my grave.'

The poor cannot afford the time to be as sentimental over such things as the rich. Larry kissed his cousin two or three times on the forehead in signification of the compact they had just entered into, and then he got up and shook himself, and prepared to go back to his afternoon work.

'That's a good job settled,' he thought as he did so; 'it will make Lizzie happy, and drive a deal of nonsense may be out of my head. But if ever I can pay out that scoundrel Darley I'll do it, if it costs me the last drop of my blood.'

The blind girl regarded what had passed between her cousin and herself with very different feelings. Condemned, by reason of her in-firmity, to pass much of her young life in solitude, the privation had repaid itself by giving her the time and opportunity for an amount of self-culture which, if subjected to the rough toil and rougher pleasures of her class, she never could have attained. Her ideas regarding the sanctity of love and marriage were very different from those of other Corston girls. She could never have 'kept company,' as they termed it, with one man this month and another the next.

Her pure mind, which dwelt so much within itself, shrank from the levity and coarseness with which she had heard such subjects treated, and believing, as she had done, that she should never be married, she had pleased herself by building up an ideal of what a husband should be, and how his wife would love and reverence him. And this ideal had always had for its framework a fancied portrait of her cousin Laurence. In reality, this young fellow was an average specimen of a fresh-faced country youth, with plenty of colour and flesh and muscle.

But to the blind girl's fancy he was perfection. Her little hands from babyhood had traced each feature of his face until she knew every line by heart, and though she had never acknowledged it even to herself, she had been in love with him ever since she was capable of understanding the meaning of the term. So that although his proposal to marry her had come as a great surprise, it had also come as a great glory, and set her heart throbbing with the pleasant consciousness of returned affection.

She was in a flutter of triumph and delight all the afternoon, whilst Larry was attending to his horses, and hardly knew how to believe in her own happiness. Her aunt brushed and plaited her long hair for her till it was as glossy and neat as possible, and tied her new cherry-coloured ribbon round the girl's throat that she might not disgrace her son's choice at the merry-making. And then Lizzie sat down to wait for her affianced lover's return, the proudest maid in Corston. Larry came in punctually for his tea, and the first thing he did was to notice the improvement in his little cousin's appearance; and indeed joy had so beautified her countenance that she was a different creature from what she had been on the sands that morning.

The apathy and indifference to life had disappeared, and a bright colour bloomed in her soft cheeks. As she tucked her hand through her cousin's arm, and they set off to walk together to Farmer Murray's harvest-home, Mrs Barnes looked after them with pride, and declared that if poor Liz had only got her sight they would have made the handsomest couple in the parish. Larry was rather silent as they went up to the barn together, but Liz was not *exigeante*, and trotted by his side with an air of perfect content. When they arrived they found the place already full, but the 'quality' had not yet arrived, and until they did so, no one ventured to do more than converse quietly with his neighbour, although the fiddlers from Wells were all ready and only waiting a signal to strike up.

But in those days the working men did not consider their festival complete without the presence of the master, and it would have been a sore affront if the members and guests of the household had not also joined them in order to open the ball and set the liquor flowing. In these days of Radicalism perhaps they find they can get on just as well without them. Larry still kept Lizzie's arm snugly tucked within his own as he described to her how beautiful the walls of the barn looked hung with flags and decorated with flowers and evergreens, and what a number of lamps there were, and what a lot of liquor and eatables were stowed away at the further end. He was still talking to her rapidly, and, as she imagined, somewhat uneasily, when a cheer rose up from a group of rustics outside, and Larry gave a start that almost disengaged her from his clasp.

'What's the matter?' she demanded, 'Is it the gentry coming, Larry?'

'Yes! 'tis they, sure enough. Keep close to me, Liz—I don't want to part from you, not for one moment.'

'Oh, Larry! that do make me feel so happy,' she whispered. As she spoke, the party from Mavis Farm entered the barn and were received with a shout of welcome. Mr Murray, a fine, hale old gentleman, and his sons came first; then Miss Rosa, looking rather conscious, tripping after her brothers in a white muslin dress. The farmer advanced to the beer barrel, and having filled his glass, drank success to all present, and asked them to give three cheers for a bountiful harvest When that ceremony was completed the fiddlers struck up a merry country dance, and every one was at liberty to drink and caper about The young people from Mavis Farm all took part in the first dance, and Rosa Murray came up and asked Larry if he would be her partner on the occasion. She ought in fairness to have opened the ball with her father's bailiff or one of the upper servants, but she preferred the young groom, with whom she held daily intercourse, and she was accustomed to go her own way without reference to anybody's feelings. As she approached the cousins she gave Lizzie a kindly welcome.

'I am so glad you have come up, Lizzie; and now your cousin must get you a nice seat until this dance is ended, for I intend him to open the ball with me.'

This was considered a great honour on the part of the villagers, and the blind girl coloured with pleasure to think that her *fiancé* had been selected for the ceremony.

'Oh, Miss Rosa, you *are* good! Larry, why don't you thank the young lady, and say how proud you shall be to dance alongside of her?'

But Larry said nothing. He reddened, it is true, but more from confusion than pleasure, and he was so long a time settling Lizzie to his satisfaction, that Rosa was disposed to be angry at his dilatoriness, and called out to him sharply that if he were not ready she should open the ball with someone else. Then he ran and took his place by her side, and went through the evolutions of 'down the middle' and 'setting at the corners' with a burning face and a fast-beating heart.

Poor Laurence Barnes! His young mistress's constant presence in the stables and familiarity with himself had been too much for his susceptible nature. She was to him, in the pride of her youthful loveliness and the passport it afforded her for smiling upon all classes of men, as an angel, rather than a woman, something set too high above for him ever to reach, but yet with the power to thrill his veins and make his hot blood run faster. The touch of her ungloved hand in the figures of the dance made him tremble, and the glance of her eyes sickened him, so that as soon as the terrible ordeal was concluded he made her an awkward salute, and rushed from her side to that of the beer barrel, to drown his excitement in drink. And it was just there that he had left Lizzie Locke.

'That was beautiful, Larry,' she exclaimed, with glowing cheeks. 'I could hear the sound of your feet and Miss Rosa's above all the others, even when you went to the further end of the barn. It must be lovely to be able to dance like that. But it has made you thirsty, Larry. That's the third glass, isn't it?'

'Yes, lass, it's made me thirsty. But don't you keep counting my glasses all the evening, or I shall move your chair a bit further off.'

She laughed quietly, and he flung himself upon the ground and rested his arm upon her knee. He seemed to feel safer and more at peace when by Lizzie's side, and she was quite happy in the knowledge that he was there. The Mavis Farm party did not dance again after the ball had been opened, at least Miss Rosa did not. But she moved about the barn restlessly. Sometimes she was in, and sometimes she was out. She did not seem to know her own mind for two minutes together.

'Why is that fellow Darley skulking about here, Larry?' demanded Isaac Barnes of his nephew. 'I've seen his ugly face peeping into the barn a dozen times. Why don't he come in or stay out? I hate such half-and-half sneaking ways.'

Larry muttered an oath, and was about to make some reply, when George Murray came up to them.

'Is that Mr Darley I see hanging about the barn door, Isaac?' he inquired of their own keeper.

'That it be, Master George; and as I was just saying to Larry here, why not in or out? What need of dodging? He don't want to catch no one here, I suppose?'

'He'd better try. I'd soon teach him who the barn belongs to.'

'And I'd back you, Master George,' cried Larry resolutely. The strong-brewed Norfolk ale was giving him a dash of Dutch courage.

'Would you, Larry? That's right! Well, I can't be in all parts of the barn at once, and father wants me to take the bottom of the supper-table, so you keep your eye on Mr Darley for me, will you? and if he looks up to anything, let me know.'

'I'm your man, Master George,' replied Larry heartily.

Rosa was near enough to them to overhear what had passed. Her brother had intended she should do so. But when he set his wit against that of a woman he reckoned without his host. Rosa had been on the look-out for Frederick Darley from the beginning of the evening, and during the first greeting, had managed to slip a little note into his hand, warning him of her brother s animosity, and begging him to keep as much as possible out of their sight until an opportunity occurred for her joining him in the apple copse. Now, she felt afraid of what might happen if there were an encounter between the two young men, and decided at once that her best plan would be, as soon as she saw George safely disposed of at the supper-table, to tamper with his spy.

And unfortunately Rosa Murray knew but too well how to accomplish this. Young Barnes' infatuation had not been unnoticed by her. She would have been aware of it if a cat had admired her. She knew his hand trembled when he took her foot to place her in the saddle, and that he became so nervous and agitated when she entered the stable as often to have to be recalled to a sense of his duty by a sharp rebuke from the head groom. She had known it all for months past, and it had pleased her. She was so vain and heartless that she thought nothing of what pain the poor fellow might be undergoing.

She laughed at his presumption, and only considered it another feather in her cap. But now she saw her way to make use of it. The dancing had recommenced, and was proceeding with vigour, and the huge rounds of beef and legs of mutton on the supper-table were beginning to be served out. George was in full action, leading the onslaught with his carving-knife, when Rosa Murray approached Laurence Barnes.

'Won't you dance again, nor go and have your supper, Larry dear?' Lizzie was asking, with a soft caress of her hand upon the head laid on her knee.

'I don't want to dance no more,' said Larry, 'and I sha'n't sup till the table's clearer and you can sup with me, Liz.'

'That's very good of you, Barnes,' said Rosa, who had caught the words; 'but if you'll take Lizzie to the table now, I'm sure George will find room for you both.'

'No thank you, miss,' he answered; 'I promised Master George to bide here till he came back, and I mustn't break my word.'

'Then I shall sit here with you, and we'll all have supper together by-and-by,' replied Rosa. 'Have you been gathering cockles again this afternoon, Lizzie.'

'Oh no, miss!' said Lizzie, blushing at the recollection of how her afternoon had been employed; 'it's high tide at four o'clock now, and I haven't been out of the house again today.'

'Did your cousin tell you how she scolded me for riding in the salt marshes, Barnes?'

'Well! it *is* dangerous, miss, for such as don't know the place. I mind me when Whisker's grandfather strayed out there by himself—'

'Oh, Larry!' cried Lizzie, 'don't go to tell that terrible tale. It always turns me sick!'

'Is that what they call the Marsh Ghost, Barnes? Oh ! I must know all about it. I love ghost stories, and I have never been able to hear the whole of this one. Where does it appear, and when?'

'Lizzie here can tell you better than me, miss—she knows the story right through.'

'It's a horrible tale, Miss Rosa. You'll never forget it, once heard.'

'That's just why I want to hear it; so, Lizzie, you must tell it me directly. Don't move, Barnes, you don't inconvenience me. I can sit up in this corner quite well.'

'Well, miss, if you *must* hear it,' began the blind girl, 'it happened now nigh upon twenty years ago. Whisker's grandfather, that used to keep the lodge at Rooklands, had grown so old and feeble the late lord pensioned him off and sent him home to his own people. He hadn't no son in Corston then, miss, because they was both working in the south, but his daughter-in-law, his first son's widdy, that had married Skewton the baker, she offered to take the old man in and do for him. Lord Worcester allowed him fifty pounds a-year for life, and Mrs Skewton wanted to take it all for his keep, but the old man was too sharp for that, and he only gave her ten shillings aweek and put by the rest, no one knew where nor for what.

'Well, miss, this went on for three or four years may be, and then poor Whisker had grown very feeble and was a deal of trouble, and his sons didn't seem to be coming back, and the Skewtons had grown tired of him, so they neglected him shamefully. I shouldn't like to tell you, miss, all that's said of their beating the poor old man and starving him, and never giving him no comforts. At last he got quite silly and took to wandering about alone, and he used to go out on the marshes, high or low tide, without any sense of the danger, and everybody said he'd come to harm some day.

'And so he did, for one day they carried his body in from Corston Point quite dead, and all bruised with the rocks and stones. The Skewtons pretended as they knew nothing about how he'd come to his death, but they set up a cart just afterwards, and nothing has ever been heard of the old man's store of money, though his sons came back and inquired and searched far and near for it. But about six months after— Larry! 'tisn't a fit tale for Miss Rosa to listen to!'

'Nonsense, Lizzie ! I wouldn't have the ghost left out for anything. It's just that I want to hear of.'

'Well, miss, as I said, six months after old Whisker's death he began to walk again, and he's walked ever since.'

'Where does he walk?'

'Round and round Corston Point every full moon, wringing his hands and asking for his money. They say it's terrible to see him.'

'Have you ever seen him, Barnes?'

Larry coloured deeply and shook his head. The peasantry all over England are very susceptible to superstition, and the Corston folk were not behindhand in their fear of ghosts, hobgoblins, and apparitions of all sorts. This young fellow would have stood up in a fight with the best man there, but the idea of seeing a ghost made his blood curdle.

'Dear me, miss, no,' said Lizzie, answering for him, 'and I hope he never may. Why, it would kill him.'

'Nonsense, Lizzie. Barnes is not such a coward, I hope.'
Something in Miss Murray's tone made the blood leap to her retainer's face.

'I'm not a coward, miss,' he answered quickly.

'Of course not; I said so. But any man would be so who refused to go to Corston Point by night for fear of seeing old Whisker's ghost He walks at full moon, you say! Why, he must be at it tonight, then! There never was a lovelier moon.'

'Don't, miss,' urged Lizzie, shivering.

'You silly goose! I don't want you to go. But, I must say, I should like to try the mettle of our friend here.'

'I beg your pardon, miss; did you mean that for me?' said Larry quickly.

'Yes, I did, Barnes. What harm? I should like to see someone who had really seen this ghost, and I'll give my gold watch chain to the man who will go to Corston Point tonight and bring me a bunch of the samphire that grows upon the top of it.'

Larry's mind was in a tumult. Some wild idea of rendering himself admirable in Rosa Murray's eyes may have influenced his decision—or the delight of possessing her watch chain may have urged him on to it Anyway, he rose up from the floor, and with chattering teeth, but a resolute heart, exclaimed,—

'I'll take you at your word, miss. I'll go to Corston Point and bring you the samphire, and prove to you that Larry Barnes is not a coward.'

'Larry, Larry, you'll never do it!' cried Lizzie.

'Let me alone, my girl. I've made up my mind, and you won't turn it.'

'You *are* a brave fellow, Barnes,' said Rosa. 'I believe you're the only man in Corston that would have taken my wager. And, mind, it's a bargain. My gold watch chain for your bunch of samphire and news of old Whisker's ghost.' She was delighted at the idea of getting him out of the way.

'But, Larry! Miss Rosa! Think of the danger,' implored poor Lizzie. 'Oh, he'll never come back; I know he'll never come back.'

'What are you afraid of, Lizzie? Doesn't Barnes know the sands as well as you do? And the moonlight is as bright as day. It's silly to try and stop him.'

'But he's going to be my husband, miss,' whispered Lizzie, weeping, into Miss Murray's ear.

'Oh! if that's the case, perhaps he'd better follow your wishes,' rejoined Rosa coldly. 'Mine are of no consequence, of course, though I'd have liked Barnes to wear my chain—we've been such good company together, haven't we, Larry?'

Her smile, and the way in which she spoke his name, determined him. He had heard the whispered conversation between her and Lizzie, and he felt vexed—he didn't know why—that it should have occurred.

'Be quiet, Liz,' he said, authoritatively. 'What's to be has nothing to do with this. I'm only too glad to oblige Miss Rosa, even with a bit of samphire. Goodbye, my girl, and goodbye, miss; it's close upon the stroke of ten, so you mayn't see me again till tomorrow morning; but when you do, it'll be *with the bunch of samphire in my hand!*'

He darted away from them as he spoke, and left the barn; whilst Lizzie Locke, disappointed at his departure, and frightened for his safety, wept bitterly. But the noise around them was so great, and everyone was so much occupied with his or her own pleasure, that little notice was taken of the girl's emotion.

'Come, Lizzie, don't be foolish,' urged Miss Murray, in a whisper, afraid lest the errand on which she had sent Larry should become public property. 'Your lover will be back in an hour, at the latest'

'He'll never come back, miss! You've sent him to his death; I feel sure of it,' replied Lizzie, sobbing.

'This is too ridiculous,' said Rosa. 'If you intend to make such a fool of yourself as this, Lizzie, I think you had much better go home to your aunt. Shall I send Jane Williams back with you? You know her; she's a kind girl, and she'll lead you as safely as Larry would.'

'No; thank you, miss; Larry said he would return to the barn with your samphire, and I must wait here till he comes—if ever he comes,' she added mournfully.

'Well, you've quite upset me with all this nonsense, and I must have a breath of fresh air. If Master George, or papa, should ask for me, Lizzie, say I've got a headache, and gone home for a little while. I'll be round again before Larry's back; but if anything should keep me, tell him he shall have the chain tomorrow morning. For he's a brave fellow, Lizzie, and whether he sees the ghost or not, he shall keep my watch chain as a wedding present.'

She patted the blind girl's hand before she tripped away; but no amount of encouragement could have driven the conviction from Lizzie Locke's breast that her lover was a doomed man; and added to this, she had an uncomfortable feeling in her heart (though too undefined to be called jealousy), that his alacrity in complying with his young mistress's request arose from something more than a desire to maintain his character for courage in her eyes. So the poor child sat by the beer barrel, sad and silent, with her face buried in her hands; and so she remained till midnight had sounded from the church clock, and the lights were put out, and the festivities concluded, and some kind neighbour led her back to her aunt's house. But neither Miss Rosa nor Larry had returned.

******

Miss Rosa's 'breath of fresh air' meant, of course, her appointment with Frederick Darley in the apple copse. She had got Larry nicely out of the way (notwithstanding the fears of his betrothed), and there was no obstacle in her path as she left the barn and approached the place of meeting. She had taken the precaution to wrap a large dark shawl round her white dress, and, thus concealed, crept softly down the lane and through the lower meadow unobservant or unheeding that her father's terrier, Trim, had followed her footsteps.

Mr Darley was in waiting for her, and a lover-like colloquy ensued. He did not again mention the subject of marriage, at which Rosa was somewhat disappointed; for she believed that, notwithstanding her brother's assertions to the contrary, Mr Murray might not refuse his consent to her becoming Frederick Darley's wife; and he certainly was the handsomest man round about. Lord Worcester himself not excepted. But in the midst of their tender conversation, as Darley was telling Rosa he loved her better than ever man had loved woman in this world before, Trim commenced wagging his tail and snuffing the grass.

'What is the matter?' cried Rosa in alarm. 'Down, Trim, down—be quiet, sir! Oh, Frederick ! surely no one can be coming this way.'

'Don't be afraid,' said her companion; 'throw your shawl over your head and trust to me. I will answer for it that no one shall molest you whilst under my protection.'

But he had not calculated upon having to make his words good in the presence of her father and brother.

Trim would not lie down, nor be quiet, but kept on with his little signals of warning, until two dark figures could be discerned making their way towards them over the grass, when he bounded away to meet them. Rosa guessed who the newcomers must be, and her heart died within her for fear. She would have screamed, but Darley placed his hand before her mouth. There was no escape for the lovers, even if an attempt to escape would not have increased suspicion, for the apple copse was a three-cornered field that had but the one entrance through which they had come. In another moment the four had met, and Rosa recognised her father and her brother George.

How they had guessed they would find her there she did not stay to ask or even think. All her thought was how to shield herself from the farmer's anger. The fact was that George had wished to seat his sister at the supper-table, when, finding that she and Darley and Larry had all three mysteriously disappeared, he had communicated his suspicions and the events of the morning to his father, and they had sallied forth together in search of the missing daughter, and were on their way to the farm, where they had been told she had gone, when Trim's unwarrantable interference led them to the very spot.

Mr Murray's rage was unbounded. He did not wait for any explanations, but walked up straight to Rosa and demanded,—

'Is this my daughter?'

The girl was too frightened to speak as she clung to her lover's arm, but Darley, perceiving that an amicable settlement was out of the question, replied in the same tone,—

'What right have you to ask, sir?'

'The right of a father, Mr Darley, who has no intention to let disgrace be brought into his family by such as you.'

He pulled Rosa by the arm roughly as he spoke, and dragged the shawl from her face.

'So it is you, you jade; and you would try and deceive your father, who has never refused you a thing in his life. That's the gratitude of women. However, you'll pay for it. You've had your first clandestine meeting and your last. No more gamekeeper's courtships for you if I know it.'

'By what right, Mr Murray, do you insult me, or this young lady, in my presence? If I have persuaded her to do a foolish thing, I am sorry for it, but you cannot give a harsher name to a lover's moonlight walk.'

'I do give it a harsher name, sir, and you know it deserves it. A lover's moonlight walk indeed! You mean a scoundrel's endeavour to get an innocent girl into his clutches.'

'Papa! papa! you are quite mistaken. Mr Darley has asked me to marry him. He will marry me tomorrow by special licence if you will only give your consent.'

'Marry you tomorrow! you poor fool! You've been swallowing every lie he chose to tell you. He can't marry you tomorrow nor any

308

day, and for a good reason. *He's a married man already.'*

Rosa screamed, George uttered an oath, and Darley darted forward.

'Who told you so, Mr Murray?'

'Never mind who told me; you know it is true. Can you deny that you left a wife down south when you came to Rooklands? Lord Worcester does not know it, perhaps, but there are those who do.'

'Who is your informant?' repeated Darley.

'I shall not tell you; but if you don't clear out of my meadow and Corston within half-an-hour, and promise never to show your face here again, I'll lay the whole story before his lordship.'

'Are you going, or shall I kick you out?' inquired George.

Frederick Darley thought upon the whole he'd better go. He turned on his heel with an oath, and slunk out of the apple copse like a beaten cur.

'Come, my girl,' said Farmer Murray, not unkindly, as he commenced to walk homeward, with his hand still on Rosa's arm; 'you've been a fool, but I hope you've been nothing worse. Never see nor speak to the man again, and I'll forgive you.'

'Oh, papa! is it really true?' she answered, sobbing.

'It's as true as Heaven, Rosa! It was Larry Barnes told it me a week ago, and he had it from one of the Whiskers, who worked near Lord Worcester's estate in Devon, and knew Mrs Frederick Darley by sight. You've had a narrow escape, my girl, and you may thank Larry for it'

'Poor Larry!' sighed Rosa; and if she could have known what was happening to poor Larry at that moment, she would have sighed still deeper. He had accepted her wager, and rushed off at her bidding to get the bunch of samphire that grew at the top of Corston Point. His brain was rather staggered at the idea of what he had undertaken, but he had been plentifully plied with Farmer Murray's "Old October," and it was a bright, moonlight night, so that he did not find the expedition after all so terrible as he had imagined.

The salt marshes were very lonely, it is true, and more than once Larry turned his head fearfully over his shoulder, to find that nothing worse followed him than his own shadow; but he reached the Point in safety, and secured the samphire, without having encountered old Whisker's ghost. Then his spirits rose again, and he whistled as he commenced to retrace his steps to the village. He knew he had been longer over the transaction than he had expected, and that he should be unable to see Miss Rosa that night; but he intended to be up at the farm the very first thing in the morning, and give the bunch of samphire into her own hands.

He did not expect to receive the watch chain; he had not seen the ghost, and had not earned it; but Larry's heart was all the lighter for that. He would not have exchanged a view of the dreaded spectre even for the coveted gold chain that had hung so long round the fair neck of his divinity. But as he turned Corston Point again, he started back to see a figure before him. The first moment he thought it must be old Whisker's ghost, but the next convinced him of his error. It was only Mr Darley—Lord Worcester's gamekeeper! He had been so absorbed in angry and remorseful thought since he left the apple copse that he had unwittingly taken the wrong turning, and now found himself upon the wide, desolate waste of the salt marshes, and rather uncertain on which side to find the beaten track again which led to the road to Rooklands. The two men were equally surprised and disgusted at encountering one another.

'What are you doing here?' demanded Darley, insolently.

'What business is that of yours?' replied the other. 'The salt marshes belong to me, I suppose, as much as they do to you.'

'You're not likely to have business here at this time of night. You've been dogging my footsteps,' said Darley, without the least consideration for probability.

'Follow *you!*' exclaimed Larry, with a big oath; 'it would be a long time before I'd take the trouble to care what happened to you. And since you ask my business here, pray what may yours be? You didn't think to find Farmer Murray's daughter in the marshes at twelve o'clock at night, did you?'

'You insolent hound! how dare you take that young lady's name upon your lips in my presence?'

'I've as good a right to name her as you have—perhaps better. It was at her bidding I came here tonight. Did she send you here, too?'

'I shall not condescend to answer your question nor to link our names together. Do you know what you are?'

'I know what *you* are, Mr Darley, and that's a villain!'

Poor Larry had said he would have it out with him, and he thought his time had come. A sudden thought flashed through Darley's brain that here was the informer who had stopped his little game with the farmer's pretty daughter.

'Are you the man,' he demanded fiercely, 'who has thought fit to inform Mr Murray of my antecendents?'

'Antecedents' was a long word for Larry's comprehension, but he grasped the meaning somehow.

'If you'd say, am I the man who told the master that you have got a wife and children down in Devonshire, I answer "Yes;" and I hope he's told you of it, and kicked you out of the barn tonight for a scoundrel, as you are, to try and make love to his daughter.'

'You brute!' cried Darley, throwing off his coat; 'I'll be revenged on you for this if there's any strength left in my arm.'

'All right,' replied the young countryman; 'I've longed to punch your head many and many a day. I'm glad it's come at last. There's plenty of room for us to have it out here, and the devil take the hindmost.'

He flew at his adversary as he spoke, and fastened his hands on to his coat-collar. Larry was the younger and the stronger built man of the two; but Frederick Darley had had the advantage of a politer education, in which the use of his fists was included, so that after a very little while it would have been evident to any bystander that Barnes was getting the worst of it. He had energy and muscle and right on his side, but his antagonist, unfortunately, possessed the skill, and after he had stood on the defensive four or five times, he seized his opportunity, and with a dexterous twist threw Larry heavily from him on the ground.

The young man fell backward, crashing his skull against a projecting fragment of rock, and then lay there, bleeding and unconscious. Darley glanced around him—not a creature was in sight. The broad harvest moon looked down placidly upon the deed of blood he had just committed, but human eyes to see it there were none. Finding that Barnes neither stirred nor groaned, he stooped down after a while, and laid his hand upon his heart. It had stopped beating. The body was getting cold. The man was dead!

Darley had not intended this, and it alarmed him terribly. His first idea was what he should do to secure his own safety. If he left the body there, would it be discovered, and the guilt traced home to him, or would the incoming tide carry it out to sea, and wash it up again, weeks hence perhaps, as a drowned corpse upon the shore? He thought it might. He hoped it would. He remembered Larry's words, that Miss Rosa had sent him there that night. It was known, then, that he had gone to the marshes, and the fact was favourable.

He dragged the corpse a little way upon the sands that it might the sooner be covered by the water; but finding it left deep traces of its progress, he lifted it with some difficulty upon his shoulders, and after carrying it perhaps a couple of dozen yards towards the sea, flung it with all his force before him. What was his amazement at seeing the body immediately sink in what appeared to be the solid ground, and disappear from view? Was it magic, or did his senses deceive him? Darley rubbed his eyes once or twice, but the miracle remained the same.

The sand, with its smooth, shining surface, was before him, but the corpse of Larry Barnes had vanished. With a feeling of the keenest re-lief—such relief as the cowardly murderer who has cheated the gallows must experience—the gamekeeper settled his clothes, glanced once or twice fearfully around him, and then, retracing his steps, ran until he had gained the high road to Rooklands. But retribution dogged his murderous feet, and he was destined never to reach his master's home. When the morning dawned upon Corston, a fearful tale was going the round of its cottages. The dead body of Lord Worcester's game-keeper had been found on the borders of the estate, shot through the heart, as it was supposed, in an encounter with poachers, as traces of a fierce struggle were plainly visible around him.

And Laurence Barnes was missing!

The two circumstances put together seemed to provide a solution of the mystery. Everyone in Corston knew that poor Larry had not been entirely free from the suspicion of poaching, and most people had heard him abuse Frederick Darley, and vow to have vengeance upon him. What more likely, then, that Larry, having been taken at his old tricks, had discharged his rusty gun at the gamekeeper, and sent him out of the world to answer for all his errors. This was the light by which Corston folk read the undiscovered tragedy. All, that is to say. but two, and those two were the dead man's mother and his betrothed, who knew of his visit to the Point, and fully believed that old Whisker had carried him off.

The murder of Frederick Darley made quite a sensation in Cor-ston. Lord Worcester gave his late gamekeeper a handsome funeral, and monument in the churchyard; and Rosa Murray lost her spir-its and her looks, and wore a black ribbon on her bonnet for three months, although she dared not let her father know the reason why. But Darley had been so generally disliked that, when the first horror at his death had subsided, people began to think he was a very good riddance, and though Rosa still looked grave if anyone mentioned his name, there was a certain young farmer who rode over from Wells to see her every Sunday, on whom the gossips said she seemed to look with considerable favour. And so, in due course of time, the name of Darley appeared likely to become altogether forgotten.

But not so Larry Barnes. Larry was a native of Corston, and, had been a general favourite there, and his mother still lived amongst them to keep his memory green. No one in the village thought Larry was dead, except Lizzie and Mrs Barnes. The rustics believed that, finding he had shot Darley, he had become alarmed and ran away—left the country, perhaps, in one of the numerous fishing smacks that infest the coast, and gone to make his fortune in the 'Amerikys.' Larry would come back some day—they were assured of that—when the present lord was dead and gone, perhaps, and the whole affair was forgotten; but they were certain he was alive, simply because they were. But Lizzie Locke knew otherwise—Lizzie Locke, to whom a glimpse of heaven had been opened the day of his death, and to whom the outer life must be as dark as the inner henceforward.

She mourned for Larry far more than his mother did. Mrs Barnes had lived the best part of her life, and her joys and her sorrows were well-nigh over, but the poor blind girl had only waked up to a consciousness of what life might hold for her on the awful day on which hope seemed blotted out for ever. From the moment her cousin left the barn at Rosa's bidding, Lizzie drooped like a faded flower. That he never returned from that fatal quest was no surprise to her. She had known that he would never return. She had waited where he had left her till all the merry-making was over, and then she had gone home to her aunt, meek, unrepining, but certain of her doom. She had never been much of a talker, but she seldom opened her mouth, except it was absolutely necessary, after that day.

But she would take her basket whenever the tide was low, and walk down to Corston Point and sit there—sometimes gathering cockles, but oftener talking to the dead, and telling him how much she had loved him. The few who had occasionally overheard her soliloquies said they were uncanny, and that Lizzie Locke was losing her wits as well as her eyes. But the blind girl never altered her course. Corston Point became her home, and whenever it was uncovered by the tide, she might be seen sitting there beside her cockle basket, waiting for— she knew not what, talking to—she knew not whom.

★★★★★★

The autumn had passed, and the winter tides had set in. Rosa Murray never rode upon the Corston marshes now—she was more pleasantly engaged traversing the leafless lanes with the young farmer from Wells. Most people would have thought the fireside a better place to mourn one's dead by than out on the bleak marsh; yet Lizzie Locke, despite her cotton clothing and bare head, still took her way there every morning, her patient, sightless eyes refusing to reveal the depths of sorrow that lay beneath them. One day, however, Mrs Barnes felt disposed to be impatient with the girl. She had left the house at eight o'clock in the morning and had not returned home since, and now it was dark, and the neighbours began to say it was not safe that Lizzie should remain out alone on such a bitter night, and that her aunt should enforce her authority to prevent such lengthy rambles.

Two or three of the men went out with lanterns to try and find her, but returned unsuccessful, and they supposed she must have taken shelter at some friend's house for the night. Lizzie Locke knew the marshes well, they said (no one in Corston better), and would never be so foolish as to tempt Providence by traversing them in the dark, for the currents were at their worst now, and the quicksands were shifting daily. The logs and spars of a ruined wreck of a year before had all come to the surface again within a few days, and with them a keg of pork, preserved by the saline properties of the ground in which it had been treasured, so that its contents were as fresh as though they had been found yesterday.

Inquiries were made for the blind girl throughout the village, but no one had seen anything of her, and all that her friends could do was to search for her the first thing in the morning, when a large party set out for Corston Point, Mrs Barnes amongst them. Their faces were sad, for they had little hope that the cruel tide had not crawled over the watching girl before she was aware of it, and carried her out to sea. But as they neared the Point they discovered something still crouched upon the sand.

'It can't be Lizzie,' said the men, drawing closer to each other, though a bright, cold sun was shining over the February morning, 'It can't be nothing mortal, sitting there in the frost, with the icy waves lapping over its feet.'

But Mrs Barnes, who had rushed forward, waved her arms wildly, and called to them,—

'*It's him!* It's my Larry, washed up again by the sands; and poor Lizzie has found him out by the touch of her finger.'

The men ran up to the spot, and looked upon the sight before them. The corpse of Larry Barnes, with not so much as a feature changed by the hand of Time—with all his clothes intact and whole, and a bunch of samphire in his breast—lay out upon the shining sands, stiff as marble, but without any trace of decomposition upon his fresh young features and stalwart limbs. (This is a fact, the corpse of a fisherman having been preserved in like manner for some nine months when buried in the salt marshes of Norfolk). And beside him, with her cheek bowed down upon his own, knelt Lizzie Locke. Lizzie, who had braved the winter's frost, and withstood the cold of a February night, in order to watch beside the recovered body of her lover.

'Lizzie!' exclaimed Mrs Barnes. 'Look up now; I've come to comfort thee ! Let us thank Heaven that he's found again, and the evil words they spoke of him must be took back.'

But the blind girl neither spoke nor stirred.

'Can't thee answer, my lass?' said Isaac the poacher, as he shook her by the arm.

The answer that she made was by falling backwards and disclosing her fair, gentle face—white and rigid as her lover's.

'Merciful God ! she is dead!' they cried.

Yes, they were right. She was dead—she was at rest. What she had waited for she had found. What she had striven for she had gained. How many of us can say the same? Larry had been restored to her. The shifting quicksand had thrown him upon earth again, and had she not been there, his body might have been washed out to sea, and no further knowledge gained of his fate. But she had saved his dust for consecrated ground—more, she had saved his character for the healing of his mother's heart.

For in his breast there still reposed the bunch of samphire he had periled his life to gather for the farmer's daughter, and, grasped tight in his hand, they found the neck-cloth of Lord Worcester's gamekeeper—a crimson, silk neck-cloth, recognised by all three—and which Larry had seized and held in the last deadly struggle. And the men of Corston looked on it and knew the truth—that their comrade was no murderer, but had fallen where he was found in a quarrel (probably pre-arranged) with Frederick Darley; and they cursed the gamekeeper in their hearts.

But Lizzie was at rest—happy Lizzie Locke! sleeping in the quiet churchyard at Corston, with her cheek pillowed on her Larry's breast.

A Midsummer's Nightmare; Or, The Amateur Detective

I am an author. I am something worse than that—I am a Press writer. I am worse than that still—I am a Press writer with a large wife and a small family. And I am an Amateur Detective! I don't mean, of course, that I reckon the last item as part of my profession, but my friends always come to me if they are in any difficulty, and set me to do all kinds of queer jobs, from restoring and reconciling a truant husband to his wife, to making the round of the 'Homes for Lost Dogs' in order to find Lady Softsawder's pet poodle.

Even Jones couldn't complete his great work, *The Cyclopaedia of the Brain*, without asking my assistance (for a consideration, of course) with his fifth section, 'The Origin of Dreams.' Jones is full of fire and imagination, but he does not care for plodding, and he knew me of old for a good steady compiler. I agreed with alacrity. 'The Origin of Dreams' would fill those hungry little mouths of mine for three months at the very least. But how to do it whilst they gaped around me!—how to cover the one table in my solitary sitting-room with valuable works of reference at the risk of their being touched by greasy fingers!—how to wade through volume after volume, placing a mental mark there and a material one here, whilst my offspring either surreptitiously removed the one or irretrievably obliterated remembrance of the other, by attracting my attention to the manner in which they attempted to scalp each other's heads or gouge out each other's eyes! I tried it for a week in vain.

My Press work I had been accustomed to do at office, but this, which was to be based upon the contents of certain ponderous black-lettered tomes which Jones had been collecting for ages past, must be carried on at home, and the noisy, wearisome day gave me no time for reflection, and left me without energy to labour at night I was about to resign the task in despair—to tell Jones to give it to some more capable or more fortunate labourer in the wide field of speculation—when Fate came to my rescue in the person of the Hon. Captain Rivers, Lord Seaborne's son.

'My dad's in an awful way about his ward, young Cockleboat,' he remarked to me, in his friendly manner, 'and he wants your assistance, Trueman, if you'll give it him.'

'Why, what's the matter. Captain Rivers? '

'Haven't you heard? Cockleboat's made a fool of himself. He fell in love with a nursemaid, or a barmaid, or some such sort of person—he, with his twenty thousand a-year in prospect; and when the governor remonstrated with him—told him 'twas nonsense and couldn't be, and all that sort of thing, he actually ran away!'

'Left Lord Seaborne's house?'

'Of course, and without a word of explanation. Now, dad doesn't want to make the affair public, you know, unless it becomes necessary, so he hasn't said a word to the police; but he wants you to find out where Cockleboat is—you're so clever at that sort of thing—and just bring him home again.'

'An easy task, certainly. And you don't even know which way the lad has gone?'

'Well, we think we've traced him to Norwich, and dad thought if you wouldn't mind going up there for a bit, and keeping your eyes open; of course we should make it worth your while, you know, you might hear something of the young scamp for us.'

'What on earth can be his motive for leaving home?'

'Well, perhaps the lady lives up that way, or Julian may have got it into his head that he'll work to support her. He is but twenty last birthday, and will not be of age, by his father's will, for the next five years—very lucky for him, as it's turned out, that he will not be.'

'True. I think I remember seeing the lad at Lady Godiva's last season. Didn't he act there in some private theatricals or charades?'

'I believe he did. Now, Trueman, what's your decision? Will you go to Norwich for us or not?'

'I will start tomorrow if your father wishes it.'

The offer had come most opportunely; even as Captain Rivers was speaking it had flashed through my mind that here was the very opportunity that I desired to carry out my project of writing the fifth section of Jones' *Cyclopaedia*;—a remote lodging in one of the back streets of the quiet old city of Norwich, whence I could carry on my inquiries all day, and where I might sit up and write out my notes all night. And Lord Seaborne's generosity in such cases was too well known to permit of any doubt on the subject whether I should not (by accepting his proposal) be killing two birds with one stone. So I did accept it, with gratitude, and having obtained all the information possible respecting the mysterious disappearance of Master Julian Cockleboat, I packed up the black-lettered tomes, and; embracing my smiling wife and children, who appeared rather pleased than otherwise at the prospect of getting rid of me for a few weeks, started for Norwich.

I have a great respect for old county towns: there is a dignified sobriety and sense of unimpeachable respectability about them that impresses me. I like their old-world institutions and buildings—their butter crosses and market steps; their dingy bye streets with kerbstones for pavements; their portentous churches and beadles; their old-fashioned shops and goods and shopmen. I like the quiet that reigns in their streets, the paucity of gas they light them up with, the strange conveyances their citizens ply for hire—in fact, I like everything with which the world in general finds fault. So it was with a sense of pleasure I found myself wandering about the streets of Norwich, on the look-out for some place in which to lay my head. I had rather have been there than at the seaside, although it was bright July weather, and I knew the waves were frothing and creaming over the golden sands beneath a canopy of cloudless blue sky. I preferred the shaded, cloister-like streets of the county town, with its cool flags under my feet, and its unbroken sense of calm.

I did not turn into the principal thoroughfares, with their gay shops and gayer passengers, but down the less-frequented bye-ways, where children playing in the road stopped open-mouthed to watch me pass, and women's heads appeared above the window-blinds, as my footfall sounded on the narrow pavement, as though a stranger were something to be stared at. Many windows held the announcement of 'Rooms to Let,' but they were too small—too modern, shall I say—too fresh-looking to take my fancy.

I connected space and gloom with solitude and reflection, and felt as if I could not have sat down before a muslin-draped window, filled with scarlet geraniums and yellow canadensis, to ponder upon *The Origin of Dreams*, to save my life. At last I came upon what I wanted. Down a narrow street, into which the sun seemed never to have penetrated, I found some tall, irregular, dingy-looking buildings—most of which appeared to be occupied as insurance, wine, or law offices,—and in the lower window of one there hung a card with the inscription, 'Apartments for a Single Gentleman.'

It was just the place from which to watch and wait—in which to ponder, and compare, and compose,—and I ascended its broken steps, convinced that the birthplace of 'The Origin of Dreams' was found. A middle-aged woman, with an intelligent, pleasing face answered my summons to the door. The weekly rent she asked for the occupation of the vacant apartments sounded to me absurdly low, but perhaps that was due to my experience of the exorbitant demands of London landladies. But when I explained to her the reason for which I desired her rooms, namely, that I might sit up at night and write undisturbed, her countenance visibly fell.

'I'm afraid they won't suit you, then, sir.'

'Why not?' Have you any objection to my studying by night?'

'Oh, no, sir. You could do as you pleased about that!'

'What then? Will your other lodgers disturb me?'

Her face twitched as she answered, 'I have no other lodgers, sir.'

'Do you live in this big house, then, by yourself?'

'My husband and I have been in charge of it for years, and are permitted to occupy the lower floor in consideration of keeping the upper rooms (which are only used as offices in the daytime) clean and in order. But the clerks are all gone by five o'clock, so they wouldn't interfere with your nightwork.'

'What will, then?'

'I'm afraid there are a good many rats about the place, sir. They *will* breed in these old houses, and keep up a racket at night'

'Oh, I don't mind the rats,' I answered, cheerfully. 'I'll catch as many as I can for you, and frighten away the others. If that is your only objection, the rooms are mine. May I see them?'

'Certainly, sir,' she said, as she closed the door behind me and led the way into two lofty and spacious chambers, connected by folding-doors, which had once formed the dining-saloon of a splendid mansion.

'The owners of the house permit us to occupy this floor and the basement, and as it's more than we require, we let these rooms to lodgers. They're not very grandly furnished, sir, but it's all neat and clean.'

She threw open the shutters of the further apartment as she spoke, and the July sun streamed into the empty room. As its rays fell upon the unmade bed, my eye followed them and caught sight of a deep indentation in the mattress. The landlady saw it also, and looked amazed.

'Someone has been taking a *siesta* here without your permission,' I said, jestingly; but she did not seem to take my remark as a jest.

'It must be my good man,' she answered, hurriedly, as she shook the mattress; 'perhaps he came in here to lie down for a bit. This hot weather makes the best feel weak, sir.'

'Very true. And now, if you will accept me as a lodger, I will pay you my first week's rent, and whilst I go back to the railway-station to fetch my valise, you must get me ready a chop or a steak, or anything that is most handy, for my dinner.'

All appeared to be satisfactory. My landlady assented to everything I suggested, and in another hour I was comfortably ensconced under her roof, had eaten my steak, and posted a letter to my wife, and felt very much in charity with all mankind. So I sat at the open window thinking how beautifully still and sweet all my surroundings were, and how much good work I should get through without fear of interruption or distraction. The office clerks had long gone home the upper rooms were locked for the night, only an occasional patter along the wide uncarpeted staircase reminded me that I was not quite alone. Then I remembered the rats, and 'The Origin of Dreams;' and thinking it probable that my honest old couple retired to bed early, rang the bell to tell my landlady to be sure and leave me a good supply of candles.

'You're not going to sit up and write tonight, sir, are you?' she inquired. 'I am sure your rest would do you more good; you must be real tired.'

'Not at all, my good Mrs Bizzey' (Did I say her name was Bizzey?), 'I am as fresh as a daisy, and could not close my eyes. Besides, as your friends, the rats, seem to make so free in the house, I should burn a light any way to warn them they had better not come too near me.'

'Oh, I trust nothing will disturb you sir,' she said, earnestly, as she withdrew to fetch the candles.

I unpacked my book-box and piled the big volumes on a side table. How imposing they looked! But I had no intention of poring over them that night. 'The Origin of Dreams' required thought—deep and speculative thought; and how could I be better circumstanced to indulge in it than stationed at that open window, with a pipe in my mouth, looking up at the dark blue sky bespangled with stars, and listening (if I may be allowed to speak so paradoxically) to the silence—

for there is a silence that can be heard?

When Mrs Bizzey brought me the candles, she asked me if I required anything else, as she and Mr Bizzey were about to retire to the marital couch, which I afterwards ascertained was erected in the scullery. I answered in the negative, and wished her goodnight, hearing her afterwards distinctly close the door at the head of the kitchen stairs and descend step by step to the arms of her lord and master. But Mrs Bizzey's intrusion had murdered my reverie. I could not take up the chain of thought where she had severed the links. The night air, too, seemed to have grown suddenly damp and chilly, and I pulled down the window sash with a jerk, and taking out my note-book and writing-case drew a chair up to the table and commenced to think, playing idly with my pen the while.

Soon the divine afflatus (the symptoms of which every successful writer knows so well) came down upon me. I ceased to think—or rather to be aware that I was thinking. My pen ran over the paper as though some other hand guided it than my own, and I wrote rapidly, filling page after page with a stream of ideas that seemed to pour out of my brain involuntarily. Time is of no account under such circumstances, and I may have been scribbling for one hour or for three, for aught I knew to the contrary, before I was roused to a sense of my position by hearing a footfall sound through the silent, deserted house.

Now, although I have described my condition to be such as to render me impervious to outer impressions, I am certain of one thing—that no noise, however slight, had hitherto broken in upon it. It was the complete absence of sound that had permitted my spirit to have full play irrespective of my body; and directly the silence was outraged, my physical life re-asserted its claims, and my senses became all alive to ascertain the cause of it. In another moment the sound was repeated, and I discovered that it was over my head—not under my feet. It could not, then, proceed from either of the old couple, whom I had heard lock themselves up together down below. Who could it be?

My first idea, emanating from my landlady's information that the noise might proceed from rats, I had already dismissed with contempt. It was the reverberation of a footstep. There could be no doubt about that; and my next thought naturally flew to burglars, who were making an attempt on the safes in the offices above. What could I do? I was utterly unarmed, and to go in pursuit of midnight robbers in so defenceless a condition would be simply delivering myself into their power. I certainly might have shied a couple of Jones' black-lettered books at their heads, for they were ponderous enough to knock any man down, but I might not take a steady aim, and it is better not to attempt at all than to attempt and fail.

Meanwhile, the sounds overhead had increased in number and become continuous, as though someone had commenced to walk up and down the room. Surely no midnight thief would dare to create so much disturbance as that! Detection of his crime would be inevitable. Or did he trust to the sound sleep of the porter and his wife in the kitchen below, not knowing that I, existent and wakeful, intervened between himself and them?

In another minute I believe that I should have cast all consequences to the winds, and rushed, not *in*, but *up* to the rescue, forgetting I was a husband and a father, and armed with Jones' patent self-acting leveller, alone have ascended to the upper story to investigate the cause of the midnight disturbance I heard. Only—*I didn't!* For before I had had time to shoulder my weapons and screw my courage up to the sticking-point, another sound reached my ears that made the patent levellers drop on the table again with a thump,—the sound, not of a step, but a groan—a deep, hollow, unmistakable groan, that chilled the marrow in my bones to such a degree that it would have been a disgrace to any cook to send them up to table.

I knew then that I must have been mistaken in my first theory, and that the sounds I overheard, whether they proceeded from mortals or not, had no connection with the nefarious occupation of housebreakers. But they had become a thousand times more interesting, and I listened attentively.

The groan was followed by some muttered words that sounded like a curse, succeeded by louder tones of reproach or anger. Then the footsteps traversed the floor again, and seemed to be chasing someone or something round and round the room. At last I heard another groan, followed by a heavy fall.

I started to my feet. Surely Mr and Mrs Bizzey must have been roused by such an unusual commotion, and would come upstairs to learn the reason! But no!—they did not stir. All was silent as the grave below, and above also. The noises had suddenly ceased. I appeared to be alone in the empty house. It was all so strange that I put my hands up to my head and asked myself if I were properly awake. I was hardly satisfied on this point before the sounds recommenced overhead, and precisely in the same order as before. Again I listened to the pacing feet—the groan—the curse—the chase—the fall! Each phase of the ghostly tragedy—for such I now felt sure it must be—was repeated in rotation, not once, but a couple of dozen or more times; and then at last the disturbance ceased as suddenly and as unexpectedly as it had commenced.

I looked at my watch. It was three o'clock, and already the early birds on the look-out for the worm had begun to herald the dawn with a few faint twitters in the trees in the cloister. I threw off my clothes impatiently, and lying down in my bed, gave myself up, not to sleep, but reflection on what was best to be done. I had not the slightest doubt left as to the cause of the noises I had heard. My landlady might ascribe them to rats, but were she closely questioned she would probably acknowledge the truth—that she knew the sounds to proceed from spirits, popularly called ghosts; which accounted for all her hesitation and change of countenance when speaking to me about the apartments, also for the low price she asked for her rooms, and her evident wish to dissuade me from sitting up at night.

Naturally the poor woman was afraid she should never secure a lodger if the truth were known; but as far as I was concerned, she was altogether mistaken—I was not afraid of her ghosts. On the contrary, as I lay in bed and thought on what had just occurred, I congratulated myself that, by a third strange coincidence, my visit to Norwich promised to turn out all that I could desire.

I must 'lay' these ghosts, of course—*i.e.*, if they interfered with my graver work; but to have the opportunity of doing so was the very thing my heart was set upon. Is my reader surprised to hear this? Then I must take him further into my confidence.

When I confessed I was an author, Press writer, amateur detective, and father of six children, I did not add the crowning iniquity, and write myself down a believer in ghosts and spiritualism. Every man acknowledges himself a spirit, and to have been created by the power of a spirit. Most men believe that spirits have the capability of free volition and locomotion, and many that they have exercised these powers by re-appearing to their fellow spirits in the flesh. But to assert publicly that you believe in all this because you have proved it to be the truth, is to throw yourself open to the charge of being a dupe, or a madman, or a liar. Therefore I had preferred until then to keep my faith a secret My children's bread depended in a great measure on the reputation I kept up as a man of sense, and I had not dared to risk it by attempting to put my theories into practice. Not that I was entirely ignorant of the rules pertaining to the science of spiritualism. Under cover of the darkness that hides all delinquencies, I had attended several circles gathered for the sole purpose of investigating the mysteries of other worlds; but it had always been accomplished with the utmost secrecy, as my wife was hysterically disposed, and the mere mention of a spirit would have upset the house for days together.

I had never, therefore, had the opportunity of pursuing spiritualism on my own account; and until the day broke I lay awake, congratulating myself on the good luck that had thrown me, cheek by jowl, with a party of ready-made ghosts, whom a very little encouragement would, I trusted, induce to pay me a visit in my own apartments.

All the next day I wandered through the streets of Norwich and in the country surrounding them, speculating—not on the whereabouts of Julian Cockleboat, nor 'The Origin of Dreams'—but how I should persuade my landlady to help me unravel the mysterious occurrence of the night before. At last I bethought me that 'honesty is the best policy' after all, and decided that I would make a clean breast of my suspicions and desires. If Mrs Bizzey were a sensible woman, she would prove only too ready to aid me in ridding her apartments of visitors that must injure their reputation; and, at all events, I could but try her. So I opened the subject on the very first opportunity. The woman was clearing away my tea-things the same evening, when she remarked that I had not eaten well.

'I am afraid you sit up too much at night, sir, to make a good appetite.'

'Other people seem to sit up in this house at night as well as myself, Mrs Bizzey,' I replied, significantly.

'I don't understand you,' she said, colouring,

'Why, do you mean to say you never hear noises;—that you were not disturbed last night, for instance, by the sound of groans and voices, and of someone falling about in the upper rooms?'

'Oh, sir, you don't mean to tell me as you've heard them already!' exclaimed Mrs Bizzey, clasping her hands and letting a teacup fall in her agitation. 'If you go too, you'll be the third gentleman that has left within a fortnight on that account; and if a stop ain't put to it, the house will get such a name that nobody will put a foot inside the door for love or money.'

'But I don't mean to go, Mrs Bizzey; on the contrary, I should be very sorry to go; and if you and your husband will consent to help me, I will do my best to stop the noises altogether,' for the idea of forming a little circle with these worthy people had suddenly flashed into my mind.

'How can me and my good man help you, sir?'

'Is Mr Bizzey at home? If so, go downstairs and fetch him up here, and I will explain what I mean to you both at the same time.'

She left the room at once, and in a few minutes returned with a dapper-looking little old fellow, in knee-breeches and a red plush waistcoat, who pulled his forelock to me on entering.

'This is Mr Bizzey, sir, and I've been telling him all you say as we came up the stairs.'

I leant back in my chair, folded my hands, and looked important.

'I suppose you must have heard the science of spiritualism mentioned?' I commenced, grandly.

'The science of *what*, sir?' inquired Mr Bizzey, with a puzzled air.

'Of spiritualism—*i.e.*, the power of converse or communication with disembodied spirits.'

'Lor'! you never mean "*ghosts*," sir?' said the old woman.

'I do, indeed, Mrs Bizzey. I suppose you believe that spirits (or ghosts, as you call them) may re-appear after death?'

'Oh, yes,' interposed the husband; 'for I mind the night that my poor mother lay dying, there was an apparition of a turkey-cock that sat upon the palings opposite our cottage, and when it fluttered off 'em with a screech, just for all the world like a real turkey, you know, sir, she turned on her side suddenly, and give up the ghost. I've always believed in apparitions since then.'

'And when my sister Jane lay in of her last,' chimed in Mrs Bizzey, 'there was a little clock stood on the mantel-shelf that had always been wound up regular and gone regular ever since she was married; and we was moving a lot of things to one side, and we moved that clock and found it had stopped; and the nurse, she said to me, "Mark my words if that's not a warning of death;" and, sure enough, Jane died before the morning, which makes me so careful of moving a clock since then that I'd rather go three miles round than touch one if a body lay sick in the house.'

'I see that you both take a most sensible view of the business, and are fully alive to the importance attached to it,' I answered; 'I hope, therefore, to secure your assistance to find out what these unusual and mysterious noises in your house portend, and what the authors require us to do for them.'

Then—whilst the old man scratched his head with bewilderment, and the old woman looked scared out of her seven senses—I explained to them, as well as I was able, the nature of a *séance*, and asked them if they would come and sit at the table with me that evening and hold one.

'But, lawk a mussy, sir, you never want to speak to them!' cried Mrs Bizzey.

'How else are we to ascertain for what reason these spirits disturb your lodgers and render your rooms uninhabitable by their pranks?'

'I should die of fright before we had been at it five minutes,' was her comment; but her husband was pluckier, and took a more practical view of the matter.

'You'll just do as I bid you, missus, and hold your chatter. There's no doubt these noises are a great nuisance—not to say a loss—and if this gentleman will be good enough to try and stop them, and can't do without us, I'll help him for one, and you will for another.'

Mrs Bizzey protested, and wept, and was even refractory, but it was all of no avail, and before we separated it had been agreed we should meet again at ten o'clock, and hold a *séance*. There was some whispering between the old couple after that that I did not quite understand, but as it ended by Mrs Bizzey ejaculating, 'Nonsense; I tell you the house will be quiet enough by ten o'clock,' I concluded he was referring to some expected visitor, and dismissed the subject from my mind. As soon as they had disappeared I delivered myself up to self-gratulation. I was really going to hold a *séance*, under my own direction and the most favourable circumstances, with a large haunted house at my command, and no one to be any the wiser for my dabbling in the necromantic art. I took out an old number of the *Spiritualist*, and referred to the directions for forming circles at home. I prepared the paper, pencils, and speaking tubes, and symmetrically arranged the table and chairs.

Nothing was wanted when Mr and Mrs Bizzey entered my room at the appointed hour—he looking expectant, and she very much alarmed. I was prepared for this, however, and insisted upon their both joining me in a glass of whisky and hot water before commencing the sitting, alleging as a reason the fact that the presence of spirits invariably chills the atmosphere, whether in summer or winter. So I mixed three bumping tumblers of toddy, strong enough to give us the courage we required for the occasion; and after we had (according to the directions) engaged for some little time in light and friendly conversation, I induced my friends to approach the table.

It was now, I was glad to see by my watch, about half-past eleven—

just about the time when the mysterious sounds had commenced the night before; and having lowered the lamp, much to Mrs Bizzey's horror, until it was represented by a mere glimmer of light, I instructed her husband and herself how to place their hands upon the table, linked with mine, and the *séance* began.

I had enjoined perfect silence on my companions, and after we had been sitting still for about fifteen minutes, during which I had watched in vain for some symptoms of movement on the part of the table, we all heard distinctly the sound of a foot creeping cautiously about the upper rooms, upon which Mrs Bizzey, too frightened to shriek, began to weep, and her husband, in order to stop her, pinched her violently in the dark.

'Hush!' I exclaimed, almost as agitated as the woman. 'Do not disturb them for your life, and whatever you may see, don't scream.'

'La, sir, you never mean to say that they'll come downstairs?'

'I cannot say what they may do. I think I hear a step descending now. But remember, Mrs Bizzey, they will not hurt you, and try and be brave for all our sakes.'

We were in a state of high nervous excitement for the next five minutes, during which the same noises I had heard the night before were repeated overhead, only that the curses were louder and delivered with more determination, and the falls appeared to succeed each other like hail.

'Oh, sir, what are they a–doing?' exclaimed Mrs Bizzey, paralysed with terror. 'They must be killing each other all round.'

'Hush!' I replied. 'Listen, now. Someone is pleading for love or for mercy. How soft and clear the voice is!'

'It sounds for all the world like my poor sister Jane when she was asking her husband to forgive her for everything she had done amiss,' said the old woman.

'Perhaps it is your sister Jane, or some of your relations,' I replied. 'She may want you to do something for her. Would you be afraid if she were suddenly to open the door and come into the room?'

'Oh, I don't know, I'm sure, sir; but I hope she mayn't. It makes me curdle all over only to think of it.'

'They're quieter now. Let us ask if there is anyone present who wishes to peak to us,' I said; and addressing the t:able to that effect, I commenced to spell out the alphabet rather loudly— 'A, B, C,' *etc.*

Whether from my nervousness, or the united strain we laid upon it, I know not, but the table certainly began to rock at that juncture, though I could make neither head nor tail of its intentions. Treating it in the orthodox manner by which Britons invariably attempt to communicate with a foreigner who does not understand one word of the language spoken, I began to bawl at the table, and my A, B, C must have reverberated through the empty house.

Again the old woman whispered mysteriously to the old man, but he dismissed her question with an impatient answer; and my attention was too much attracted in another direction at that moment to give much heed of what they were doing. My ear had caught the sound of a descending footstep, and I felt sure the spirits were at last about to visit us *in propriae personae.*

But dreading the effect it might have on Mrs Bizzey's nerves, I purposely held my tongue, and applied myself afresh to a vigorous repetition of the alphabet, striving to cover the approaching footstep by the noise of my own voice, although I was trembling with excitement and delight at the successful issue of my undertaking. At last I plainly heard the footstep pause outside the door, as though deliberating before it opened it. The old man was apparently too deaf or too absorbed to notice it, and his wife was in a state of helpless fright. I alone sufficiently retained my senses to see the door slowly open, and a white-robed figure—a real, materialised spirit—stand upon the threshold. The gesture of delight, which I could not repress, roused my companions from their reverie; and as soon as Mrs Bizzey turned and saw the figure, she recognised it.

'It's Jane!' she screamed. 'It's my own poor sister Jane come back from the grave to visit me again, with her red hair and blue eyes; I can see 'em as plain as plain. I'll die of the shock, I know I shall!'

'Nonsense!' I exclaimed, sternly, fearful, lest by her folly she should scare the newly-born spirit back to the spheres. 'If it is your sister, speak to her as you used to do. Tell her you are glad to see her, and ask if she wants anything done.'

'Oh, Jane!' said the old woman, half falling upon her knees, 'don't come anigher me, for mercy's sake! I never kept nothing of yourn back from the children except the old blue dress, which it wouldn't have been no use for them to wear, and the ring, which I had asked you to give me a dozen times in your life, and you had always refused. I'd give 'em both back now if I could, Jane, but the gownd have been on the dust-heap these twenty years past, and the ring I sold the minute my man was laid up with rheumatis. Forgive me, Jane, forgive me!'

'*Why, what on earth are you making such a row about?*' replied the spirit.

I leapt to my feet in a moment.

'This is some shameful hoax!' I exclaimed. 'Who are you, and what do you do here?'

'I should think I might put the same question to you, since I find you sitting in the dark, at dead of night, with my landlord and landlady.'

'Lor', Mr Montmorency, it's never you, sir!' ejaculated old Bizzey, with a feeble giggle.

The voice seemed familiar to me. Who on earth was this Mr Montmorency, who had intruded upon our *séance* at the most important juncture? I turned up the lamp and threw its light full upon his features. 'Good heavens!' I exclaimed, 'it's Julian Cockleboat'

The young man was equally astonished with myself.

'Did Lord Seaborne send you after me?' he said, guessing the truth at once. 'And how did you find out I was lodging here?'

'Aha, my boy!' I replied, unwilling to deny the *kûdos* with which he credited me, 'that's my secret. Do you suppose I have gained the name of the amateur detective among my friends for nothing? No, no! I am in Norwich expressly for the purpose of restoring you to your guardian, and as I knew that to show my hand more openly would be to scare you off to another hiding place, I devised this little plan for making you reveal yourself in your true character.'

'Did Robson tell you, then, that I had taken an engagement at the theatre here?'

'Never you mind, Mr Cockleboat; it is quite sufficient that I knew it. This is a proper sort of house to play hide-and-seek in, isn't it?'

I was dispersing the table and chairs again with angry jerks as I spoke, fearful lest my attempted investigation of the occult mysteries should be discovered before I had removed its traces.

'Still I can't understand how you discovered that Mr Montmorency was myself, although naturally my night rehearsals must have disturbed you. But you told me you had no other lodgers,' continued Julian Cockleboat reproachfully, to the Bizzeys.

'And you said the same thing to me,' I added, in similar tones.

'Well, sir—well, Mr Montmorency, I'm very sorry it should have happened so,' replied the landlord, turning from one to the other, 'but it's all my old woman's fault, for I said to her—'

'You did nothing of the sort,' interrupted his better half; 'for when I come to you and told you as a second gentleman wanted rooms here, it was you as said, "Let him have the little room upstairs, and no one will be ever the wiser if he takes his meals out of a day."'

'But we never thought—begging your pardon, Mr Montmorency—as you'd take such a liberty with the upper offices as to make noises in them as should disturb the whole house.'

'Well, what was I to do?' replied the young man, appealing to me. 'They've given me three leading parts to get up at a fortnight's notice, and if I don't study them at night I have no chance of being ready in time.'

'In fact,' I said, oracularly, 'you've been cheating each other all round. Mr Bizzey has cheated his employers by letting apartments to which he has no right; you have cheated the Bizzeys by using one which you never hired of them; and I have—'cheated myself,' I might have added, but I stopped short and looked wise instead.

'And it was never no ghosts after all!' said Mrs Bizzey, in accents of disappointment, as her husband marched her downstairs.

★★★★★★

There is nothing more to tell. I reconciled Mr Julian Cockleboat to his guardian and his destiny; and I wrote 'The Origin of Dreams,' the best part, by the way (as all the critics affirmed), of *The Cyclopaedia of the Brain*. I made more money by my little trip than six months of ordinary labour would have brought me; and Lord Seaborne speaks of me to this day, amongst his acquaintances, as the 'very cleverest amateur detective he has ever known.'

And so I am.

'Mother'

It was close upon Easter. The long, dark days of Lent, with their melancholy ceremonials, were nearly over, and, as if in recognition of the event, the sun was shining brightly in the heavens. The hawthorn bushes had broken into bloom, and the wild birds were bursting their little throats in gratitude. The boys were almost as wild and joyous as the birds, as they rushed about the playground, knocking each other over in the exuberance of their glee, and forgetting to be angry in the remembrance that the next day would be Holy Thursday, when they should all go home to their fathers and mothers to spend the Easter holidays. I alone of the merry throng sat apart under the quick-set hedge, joining in neither game nor gaiety, as I wondered, with the dull, unreasoning perception of childhood, why I had been the one selected, out of all that crowd of boys, to have no part in their anticipation or their joy.

Even poor, lame Jemmy, who had no remembrance of his father or his mother, and who had been, in a way, adopted by our schoolmaster, and lived all the year round, from January to December, in the same dull house and rooms, looked more cheerful than I did. He was incapacitated by his infirmity from taking part in any of the noisy games that were going on around us, yet he smiled pleasantly as he came limping up towards me on his crutches, and told me that Mrs Murray (who bestowed on him all the mother's care he would ever know) had promised, if he were good, to give him a donkey ride during Easter week, and some seeds to plant in his strip of garden.

'What's the matter with you, Charlie?' he asked presently; 'aren't you glad to be going home?'

'Oh! I don't care,' I answered, listlessly.

'Don't *care* about seeing your father and mother again!'

'I haven't got a mother,' I rejoined, quickly.

'Is your mother dead, like mine? Oh, I *am* sorry! But your father loves you for them both, perhaps.'

'No, he doesn't! He doesn't care a bit about me. He never asks to see me when I do go home; and he frightens me. I wish I might stay all the holidays with Mrs Murray, like you do.'

'That *is* bad,' quoth the lame child. 'Well, maybe they'll forget to send for you, Charlie, and then we'll have fine times together, you and I.'

I had not the same hope, however. I knew that if by any oversight my father forgot to send the servant for me, that my schoolmaster would take the initiative and despatch me home himself.

How I dreaded it. The gloomy, half-closed house, the garden paths, green with damp and thick with weeds, the servants acting entirely upon their own authority, and the master querulous, impatient, and unjust, either shut up in his own room brooding over the past and present, or freely distributing oaths, complaints, and sometimes even blows, amongst the unfortunate inmates of his household. As for myself, I seldom came within the range of his arm without being terrified away, and it had been a great relief to me when I returned home for the previous Christmas holidays to find that he was absent, and the term of my penance passed peacefully, if nothing else. But now he was at home again, so my master informed me, my father had never dreamt of writing to me, and I looked forward to the coming visit with dread. A strange, unnatural state of things for a child of eight years old, who had never known a mother's love nor care, had never even heard her name mentioned by any one with whom he was connected,

'What was your mother like?' continued Jemmy, after a few minutes' pause, during which we two unfortunates had been ruminating upon our lot. 'Had she light-coloured hair, like Mrs Murray, or dark, like the cook?'

'I don't know,' I answered, sadly. 'I never saw her, that I remember.'

'Haven't you got a likeness of her at home?' he demanded with surprise. 'Wait till I show you mine.'

He fumbled about in his waistcoat, and produced a much faded daguerreotype of an ordinary-looking young woman in old-fashioned habiliments.

'Isn't she beautiful?' he exclaimed, with weak enthusiasm as he pressed the miniature to his lips.

'Oh, how I wish she hadn't died! I know I should have loved her so much!'

I made no reply. Poor Jemmy's imagination did not run so fast as mine. If my mother had lived to side with my father, where should I have been between them? I turned my face away, and sighed.

It was strange that I had no idea of what my mother had been like. I had never even formed one, neither had I any relation to whose memory I might have appealed on the subject. My father lived a solitary, aimless life in the old neglected house I have alluded to, seldom leaving his own apartments, except at meal times, and certainly never asking any friend to enter them to bear him company. The servants had their parents, or lovers, or brothers, to visit them by stealth in the kitchen, but the master sat by himself, gloomy and preoccupied, and irritable almost to frenzy when provoked. No wonder I wished that I could have spent the Easter holidays with Mrs Murray. But a great surprise was in store for me. The boys had hastily concluded the game of football they had been carrying on during my colloquy with Jemmy, when Mrs Murray came smiling down the playground in search of me.

'I've a piece of news for you, Master Vere,' she exclaimed. 'Someone is waiting to see you in the parlour.'

'Not papa!' I said, quickly.

'No; not your papa,' replied Mrs Murray, laying her hand compassionately on my shoulder, ' but a new friend—a lady whom you will like very much indeed.'

'A *lady!*' I repeated, in utter bewilderment, whilst my schoolmates crowded round Mrs Murray, with the question, 'Is she come to take Vere home?'

'Perhaps! most probably,' was her answer, whilst exclamations of 'Oh, I say, that's a jolly shame. It isn't fair. School doesn't break up till tomorrow. *We* sha'n't get off today, try as hard as we may,' greeted her supposition from every sideband I, trembling like a culprit, affirmed that I would much rather not be introduced to the pleasures of home one hour earlier than was needful.

'Come into the parlour, dear, and see the lady,' Mrs Murray replied, 'and we will decide what to do afterwards.'

So my face and hair were hurriedly washed and arranged, and I sheepishly followed my master's wife to the formal little apartment dedicated to the reception of visitors, where we found the lady she had alluded to.

Shall I ever forget her face as she rose to greet me, and drew me into her arms! Such a fair, sweet, fresh face as it was, but with an amount of sorrowful thought pictured in the serious eyes.

'And so this is Charlie Vere,' she said, as she gazed into my features. 'I should have known you anywhere, my darling, from your likeness to your father! And now do you guess who I am?'

'No!' I answered, shyly; for Mrs Murray had slipped away and left me all alone with the stranger.

'I am your mother, dear; your new mother who means to love you very dearly, and I have come to take you home!'

Mother and Home! How sweet the dear familiar words sounded in my ears; familiar alas! to everyone but me. The hawthorn blossoms in the playground seemed to smell sweeter than they had done before, as she pronounced them, and the birds' chorus rang out harmoniously. 'Will papa be there?' I asked, nervously.

'Papa! of course! What would home be without your father?'

I had found it much pleasanter without him than with him hitherto, but some instinct made me hold my tongue.

'Don't you love papa, dear?' the lady went on softly. 'Don't you think that he loves you?'

'I don't know,' I said, picking my fingers.

'Poor child! Perhaps you have thought not, but that will all be altered now. But you have not yet told me if you will like to have me for a mother!'

'I think I shall like you very much!'

'That's right, so we will go home together and try to make each other happy. You want a mother to look after you, dear child, and I want a little boy to love me. We will not part again, Charlie, now I have found you, not for the present, at all events. You have been too long away from home as it is. That is why I came today. I could not wait till tomorrow, even: I was so impatient to see you and to take you home.'

How she dwelt and lingered on the word and repeated it, as though it gave her as much happiness to listen to as it did me.

'Will *you* be there?' I asked, presently.

'Of course, I shall—always! What would be the use of a mother, Charlie, if she didn't live in the house close to you, always ready to heal your troubles and supply your wants to the utmost of her power?'

'Oh! let us go at once!' I exclaimed, slipping my hand into hers. All dread of my father seemed to have deserted me. The new mother was a guardian angel, under whose protection I felt no fear. She was delighted with my readiness.

'So we will, Charlie! We need not even wait for your box to be packed. Mrs Murray can send on everything tomorrow. And papa will be anxious until he sees us home again!'

My father anxious about me! That was a new thing to be wondered at. I was too much of a baby still to perceive that his anxiety would be for *her*—not for me! I had not yet been able to grasp the idea that she was his wife. I only regarded her as my new mother.

As we passed out of the house, I asked leave to say goodbye to my friend Jemmy.

'His mother is dead, like mine,' I said, in explanation. 'He will be so pleased to hear that I have got a new one.'

'Poor boy!' she sighed; 'we will ask him to spend the summer holidays with you Charlie. A great happiness like ours should make us anxious to make others happier.'

And when Jemmy came forward on his crutches, and smiled his congratulations on the wonderful piece of news I had to give him, she stooped down and kissed his forehead. Then we passed out of the playground together, I clinging to her hand, and proud already to hear the flattering comments passed upon her appearance by the other boys, and to remember that from that time forward she was to be called *my mother.*

★★★★★★

Lilyfields, as my fathers house was designated, was not more than ten or twelve miles from the school; but we had to make a little railway journey to reach it, and I thought I had never travelled so pleasantly before. My new mother laughed so often and chatted so continuously to me, that I caught the infection of her mirthful loquacity, and, long before we got home, had revealed so much of my past life and feelings, that more than once I brought a shadow over her sunny face, and closed her smiling lips with a sigh. But as we left the train and commenced to walk tot wards Lilyfields, my old fears showed symptoms of returning, and my sudden silence, with the tightening clasp of my hand, did not pass unobserved by my companion.

'What is the matter, Charlie? Of what are you afraid?'

'Won't papa be angry with me for coming back before the holidays begin?' I whispered.

Her clear laugh rang over the peaceful meadows we were traversing.

'If he is angry with anyone, he must be so with me, as I fetched you home Charlie.'

'And you are not afraid of him?'

'*Afraid!*' The sweet serious eyes she turned upon me as she ejaculated the word were just about to deprecate so monstrous an idea, when they caught sight of an approaching figure, and danced with a thousand little joys instead.

'There he is!' she exclaimed excitedly.

She ran up to him, dragging me with her.

He took her in his arms (there was not another living soul within sight of us) and embraced her fervently, whilst I stood by, open-mouthed with astonishment.

'My angel,' he murmured, as she lay there, with her face pressed close to his; 'life has been insupportable without you.'

'Ah, Harold! it does me good to hear you say so; and I am so glad to get back to you again. See! here is Charlie waiting for his father to welcome him home.'

She lifted me up in her arms—big boy as I was—and held me towards him for a kiss. How strange it was to feel my father kiss me; but he did so, though I think his eyes never left her face the while. Then he took her hand, and held it close against his heart, and they walked through the silent, balmy-breathed fields together. As I entered the house I could hardly help exclaiming aloud at the marvellous changes that had taken place there. Not an article of furniture had been changed, not a picture moved from its place, yet everything looked bright as the glorious spring.

The rooms had been thoroughly cleaned, and lace curtains, snowy tablecloths, and vases of flowers, with here and there a bright bit of colour in the shape of a rug, or a piece of china, had transformed the house—not into a paradise—but into *a home*. Even my father was changed like his surroundings. He looked ten years younger, as with nicely kept hair, and a becoming velveteen lounging coat, he sunk down into an easy-chair, and deprecated, whilst he viewed with delight, the alacrity with which my new mother insisted upon removing his boots and fetching his slippers.

It was such a novelty to both of us to be attended to in any way, that I was as much surprised as he to find that the next thing she did was to take me upstairs, and tidy me for tea herself, showering kisses and love words upon me all the while. Oh! the happy meal that followed. How unlike any we had taken in that house before! I, sitting up at table, with my plate well provided; my father in his arm-chair, looking up with loving eyes at each fresh proof of her solicitude for

him, and my new mother seated at the tea-tray, full of smiles and innocent jests, watching us both with the utmost affection; but apparently
too excited to eat much herself. Once my father noticed her want of
appetite and reproached her with it.

'I am too happy to eat, Harold!' was her reply.

'Too happy,' he repeated in a low voice, '*really* too happy! No regrets, my Mary, no fears! Your future does not terrify you. You would
not undo the past if it were in your power!'

'Not one moment of it, Harold! If I ever think of it, with even a
semblance of regret, it is that it did not begin ten years sooner.'

'God bless you' was all he answered. If I had not been such a child
I should have echoed the words; for before many days were over my
head, the whole of my joyous young life was an unuttered blessing
upon her. The darkness of fear and despondency—the most unnatural
feelings a young child can entertain—had all passed away. I no longer
dreaded my father's presence; on the contrary, it was my greatest treat
to bear him company as he worked in the garden, or whistled over his
carpentering, or accompanied my mother in strolls about the country.

He never shut himself up in his room now, unless she was shut in
too; and although his new-born love was for *her*, and not for me, the
glory of it was reflected in his treatment of me.

So I was very happy, and so was he, and so most people would
have thought my mother to be. But though she never appeared before
my father without a bright face, she was not always so careful in my
presence, thinking me, perhaps, too young to observe the changes in
her countenance; and sometimes when she and I were alone together,
I marked the same look steal over her which I had observed on the
occasion of our first meeting—an undercurrent of thoughtful sad-
ness—the look of one who had suffered, who still suffered, from a pain
which she kept to herself.

Once I surprised her in tears—a violent storm of tears, which she
was powerless for some time to control; and I eagerly inquired the
reason of them.

'Mamma, mamma, what is it, mamma? Have you hurt your foot?
Did Prince bite you? Have you got a pain anywhere?'

My childish mind could not comprehend that her tears should
flow for any other than a physical reason. Did not papa and I love her
dearly? and she was afraid of no one, and she never went to school.
What possible cause could she have for tears?

My mother composed herself as soon as she was able, and laid her burning face against my cheek.

'Will my little boy love me always?' she asked—'always—always—whatever happens.'

'Always, dear mamma. Papa and I would die if we hadn't you. Oh, you don't know what it was like before you came here!'

'Then mamma will never again be so silly as to cry,' said my mother, as she busied herself over some occupation to divert her thoughts.

But although this was the only time she betrayed herself so openly before me, I often detected the trace of weeping on her face, which she would try to disguise by excessive mirth.

So the years went on, until one bright summer's day a little sister was born in our house. I hailed the advent of this infant with the greatest possible delight. It was such a new wonderful experience to have a playmate so dependent on me, and yet so entirely my own. I positively worshipped my little sister, although her birth was the signal for my being sent back to school, but this time only as a weekly boarder.

Hitherto my mother had taught me herself, and very sorry I was to give up those delightful lessons, which were rendered so easy by the trouble she took to explain them to me; but her time was too much taken up with her baby to allow her to devote sufficient to me. Besides, I was now eleven years old, growing a great lad, and able to take every advantage of the education afforded me at Mr Murray's school.

My old friend, lame Jemmy, who had spent many a pleasant week at Lilyfields meanwhile, was still there to welcome me back and make me feel less of a stranger; and my father took away the last sting of the new arrangement by buying me a sturdy pony on which to ride backwards and forwards every week to see my mother and him.

But the greatest pang which I experienced was parting, even for a few days, with baby Violet. I cried over her so much, indeed, that I made my mother cry too, as she asked God to bless the boy who had been a true son to her. I was very glad to think she loved me so much, for I loved her dearly in return; but as I galloped back to Lilyfields every Saturday afternoon, my thoughts were all for the dimpled baby sister whom I would carry about in my arms, or roll with amongst the newly-mown grass, rather than with those who had proved themselves to be real parents to me,—she from the commencement of her knowledge of me, and he from the date of his knowing her. It was my mother alone I had to bless for it all. But I had grown accustomed to happiness by this time, and took it as my due.

My parents were very proud of their little daughter, who grew into a lovely child, but she did not seem to afford them as much pleasure as pride. Sometimes I detected my mother looking at her as we romped together, with more pain in the expression of her face than anything else. Once she caught her suddenly to her bosom, and kissed her golden curls with passion, exclaiming,—

'Oh, my heart, if I were to go, what would become of you?—what *would* become of you?'

I was still too young to grasp the full meaning of her words, but I knew my mother meant that if she died, no one would take such good care of Violet as she had done. So I marched up to her confidently, with the assurance that *I* would take that responsibility upon my own shoulders.

'Don't be afraid, mamma! As soon as I am a man, I mean to get a house all to myself, and the best rooms in it shall be for Violet'

She looked at me with her sweet, earnest, searching gaze for a moment, and then folded me in one embrace with her own child.

'Father's boy!' she murmured, caressingly over me—'father's brave, loving boy! No, Charlie, I will not be afraid! If it be God's will that I should go, I will trust Violet to father and to you.'

★★★★★★

Meanwhile my father was a very contented man. He had undergone much the. same change as myself, and forgotten, in. the sunshine that now surrounded him, all the miserable years he had spent in that once desolate mansion.

I do not suppose a happier nor more peaceful family existed than we were, No jars nor bickering ever disturbed the quiet of the household; everything seemed to go as smoothly as though it had been oiled. We were like the crew of some ship, safely moored within a sunny harbour, never giving a thought to what tempests might be raging outside the bar.

Every Saturday when I rode home on my pony, I found my father either working out of doors if it were summer, or indoors if it were winter, but always with the same satisfied easy smile upon his countenance, as though he had no trouble in the world, as indeed he had not; for my mother warded off the most trifling annoyance from him as though he were a sick child, that must not be upset; whilst she threaded her quiet way through the kitchen and bedrooms, with little Violet clinging to her gown, regulating the household machinery by her own supervision, that no accident might occur to ruffle her husband's temper.

I believed her in those days—I believe her still to be the noblest woman ever planned. One thing alone puzzled me—or rather, I should say, seemed strange to me, for I did not allow it to go the length of puzzlement—and that was why we had so few visitors at Lilyfields. True, my father had made himself so unsociable in the old days that strangers might well have been shy of intruding themselves upon him now; but my mother was so sweet and gentle, I felt it must be their loss rather than hers, that so few people knew her. When, as a lad of fifteen, I mentioned this circumstance to her, she put it aside as a matter of course.

'When I made up my mind, Charlie, to try as far as in me lay, to render the remainder of your father's life happy, I was perfectly aware that I should have to depend for companionship upon him alone. We have each other, and we have you and Violet. We want no other society but yours.'

Still, I thought the clergyman and his wife might sometimes have come to see us, as they did the rest of their parishioners, and I should have liked an occasional game of play with the sons of Squire Roberts up at the Hall. But, with the exception of the doctor, who sometimes came in for a chat with my father, no one but ourselves ever took a meal at Lilyfields.

As I grew still older, and others remarked on the circumstance in my hearing, I came to the conclusion that my father must have offended his own friends by marrying my mother, whose connections might be inferior to his own. This idea was confirmed in my mind by observing that she occasionally received letters she was anxious to conceal, which, knowing the frankness of her disposition, and her great love for him, appeared very strange to me. One day, indeed, my suspicions became almost certainties. It so happened that my mother had appeared very fidgety and unlike herself at the breakfast-table, and more than once had spoken to Violet and me in a voice hardly to be recognised as her own.

We felt instinctively that something was the matter, and were silent, but my father, who was not well, seemed irritated by the unusual annoyance. He wished to remain quietly at home that morning, but my mother found a dozen reasons why he should ride to the neighbouring town and take me with him. He combated her wish for some time, till, finding that her arguments were revolving themselves into entreaty, his affection conquered his irresolution, and we set off together.

It was not a genial day for a ride, and the trifling commissions my mother had given us to execute were not of sufficient consequence to turn the duty into a pleasure. I was rather pleased than otherwise, therefore, when we had left Lilyfields some miles behind us, to find that my pony had cast a shoe, and to be able, according to my father's direction, to turn back and walk it gently home again, whilst he went forward to do my mother's bidding.

When I reached Lilyfields I left the animal in the stables, and, walking up to the house, gained the hall before anyone was sensible of my approach. What was my surprise to hear a loud altercation going on within the parlour. My first impulse was to open the door; but as my mother turned and saw me standing on the threshold, she came forward and pushed me back into the hall.

'Go away!' she whispered hurriedly; 'go upstairs; hide yourself somewhere, and do not come down until I call you!'

Her eyes were bright as though with fever, and a scarlet spot burned on either cheek. I saw she was labouring under the influence of some strong excitement, and I became intensely curious to learn the reason.

'Whom have you in there?' I demanded, for I had caught sight of another figure in the drawing-room.

'Oh! you wish to know who I am, young man, do you?' exclaimed a coarse, uncertain voice from the other side the half-opened door. 'Well, I'm not ashamed of myself, as *some* people ought to be, and you're quite welcome to a sight of me if it'll give you any pleasure.'

The door was simultaneously pulled open, and a woman stood before me.

How shall I describe her.

She may have been beautiful, perhaps, in the days long past, but all trace of beauty was lost in the red, blotchy, inflamed countenance she presented to my gaze. Her eyes were bloodshot; her hair dishevelled; her dress tawdry and untidy, and if she had even been a gentlewoman, which I doubted, she had parted with every sign of her breeding. As she pushed her way up behind my mother—looking so sad and sweet and ladylike beside her—she inspired me with nothing but abhorrence.

'Who is this person?' I repeated, with an intimation of disgust that apparently offended the stranger, for in a shrill voice she commenced some explanation which my mother was evidently most anxious I should not hear.

'Oh, Charlie! do you love me?' she whispered.

'Mother! yes!'

'Then go up to your room, now, *at once*, and wait there till I come to you! I will speak to you afterwards—I will tell you *all*—only go now!'

She spoke so earnestly that I could not refuse her request, but did as she desired me at once, the woman I had seen, screaming some unintelligible sentence after me as I ascended the stairs. But when I found myself alone, the scene I had witnessed recurred rather unpleasantly to my memory. It was an extraordinary circumstance to see a stranger at all within our walls; still more so a woman, and one who dared to address my mother in loud and reproachful tones. And I was now sixteen, able and willing to defend her against insult, why, therefore, had she not claimed my services to turn this woman from the house, instead of sending me upstairs, as she might have done little Violet, until she had settled the matter for herself?

But then I remembered the trouble my mother had taken to get my father and me away from Lilyfields that morning, and could not believe but that she had foreseen this visitation and prepared against it. It was then as I had often supposed. She had relations of whom she was ashamed, with whom she did not wish my father to come in contact Poor mother! If this was one of them, I pitied her! I believed the story I had created myself so much, that I accepted it without further proof, and when my mother entered the room, and laying her head against my shoulder, sobbed as if her heart would break, I soothed her as well as I was able, without another inquiry as to the identity of the person with whom I had found her.

'Don't tell your father, Charlie!' she said, in parting. 'Don't mention a word to anyone of what you have seen today. Promise me, darling! I shall not be happy till I have your word for it!'

And I gave her my word, and thought none the less of her for the secrecy, although I regretted it need be.

Not long after this my father articled me, at my own request, to an architect in London, and my visits to the happy home at Lilyfields became few and far between. But I had the consolation of knowing that all went well there, and that I was taking my place in the world as a man should do.

I had worked steadily at my profession for two years, and was just considering whether I had not earned the right to take a real good long holiday at Lilyfields (where Violet, now a fine girl of seven years old, was still my favourite plaything), when I received a letter from the doctor of the village—desiring me to come home at once as my father was ill, beyond hope of recovery. I knew what that meant—that he was already gone; and when I arrived at Lilyfields I found it to be true; he had died of an attack of the heart after a couple of hours' illness. The shock to me was very great I had never loved my father as I did my mother; the old childish recollections had been too strong for that, but the last few years he had permitted me to be very happy, and I knew that to *her* his loss must be irreparable. Not that she exhibited any violent demonstration of grief.

When I first saw her, I was surprised at her calmness. She sat beside my father's body, day and night, without shedding a tear; and she spoke of his departure as quietly as though he had only gone on a journey from which she fully expected him to return. But though her eyes were dry, they never closed in sleep, and every morsel of colour seemed to have been blanched out of her face and hands. So the first day passed, and when the second dawned, I, having attained the dignity of eighteen years, thought it behoved me to speak of my late father's affairs and my mother's future.

'Where is father's will, mother?'

'He never made one, dear!'

'Never made a will! That was awfully careless.'

'Hush, Charlie!'

She would not brook the slightest censure cast on her dead love.

'But there *must* be a will, mother.'

'Darling, there is none! It was the one thought that disturbed his last moments. But I am content to let things be settled as they may.'

'Lilyfields will be yours of course, and everything in it,' I answered decidedly.

'No one has a better right to them than you have. And you and Violet will live here to your lives' end, won't you?'

'Don't ask me, dear Charlie, don't think of it—not just yet at least! Let us wait until—until—it is all over, and then decide what is best to be done!'

Before it was all over; matters were decided for us.

It was the day before the funeral. I had just gone through the mournful ceremony of seeing my father's coffin soldered down, and, sad and dispirited, had retired to my own room for a little rest, when I heard the sound of carriage wheels up on the gravel drive. I peered over the window blind curiously, for I had never heard of my father's

343

relations, and had been unable in consequence to communicate with any of them. A lumbering hired fly, laden with luggage, stopped before the door, and from it descended, to my astonishment, the same woman with the fiery red face whom I had discovered in my mother's company two years before. I decided at once that, whatever the claims of this stranger might be, she could not be suffered to disturb the widow in the first agony of her crushing grief, and, quick, as thought, I ran down into the hall and confronted her before she had entered the house.

'I beg your pardon, madam,' I commenced, 'but Mrs Vere is unable to see anyone at present. There has been a great calamity in the family, and—'

'I know all about your calamity,' she interrupted me rudely 'if it were not for that I shouldn't be here.'

'But you cannot see Mrs Vere!' I repeated.

'And pray who *is* Mrs Vere?' said the woman.

'My mother,' I replied proudly, 'and I will not allow her to be annoyed or disturbed.'

'Oh! indeed, young man. It strikes me you take a great deal of authority upon yourself; but as I mean to be mistress in my own house, the sooner you stop that sort of thing the better! Here! some of you women!' she continued, addressing the servants who had come up from the kitchen to learn the cause of the unusual disturbance. 'Just help the flyman up with my boxes, will you—and look sharp about it.'

I was thunderstruck at her audacity.

For a moment I did not know what to answer. But when this atrocious woman walked past me into the parlour, and threw herself into my dead father's chair, I followed her, and felt compelled to speak.

'I do not understand what you mean by talking in this way,' I said. 'Mrs Vere is the only mistress in this house, and—'

'Well, young man, and suppose *I* am Mrs Vere!'

'I can suppose no such thing. You cannot know what you are talking about. My mother—'

'*Your mother!* And pray, what may your name be and your age?'

'Charles Vere; and I was eighteen last birthday,' I said, feeling compelled, I knew not by what secret agency, to reply.

'Just so! I thought as much! Well, I am Mrs Vere, and I am your mother!'

'*My mother!* You must be mad, or drunk! How dare you insult the dead man in his coffin upstairs. My mother! Why, she died years ago, before I can remember.'

'Did she? That's the fine tale. Madam, who's been taking my place here all this time, has told you, I suppose. But I'll be even with her yet. I'm your father's widow, and all he's left behind him belongs to me, and she'll be out of this house before another hour's over her head, or my name's not Jane Vere!'

'You lie!' 'I exclaimed passionately. This tipsy, dissipated, coarse-looking creature, the woman who bore me, and whom I had believed to be lying in her grave for sixteen years and more. Was it wonderful that at the first blush my mind utterly refused to credit it? The angry accusation I have recorded had barely left my lips, when I looked up and saw *my mother*—the woman who had come as an angel of light into my father's darkened home, and watched over me with the tenderest affection since—standing on the threshold, pale and peaceful in her mourning garb, as the Spirit of Death itself

'Mother! say it is not true,' I cried as I turned towards her.

'Oh, Charlie, my darling boy! my brave, good son! Be quiet! bear it like a man; but it is true!'

'This—this woman was my father's *wife!*'

'She was!'

'And *you*, mother!' I exclaimed in agony.

'I was only the woman that he loved, Charlie,' she answered, with downcast eyes. 'You must think no higher of me than that!'

'I think the very highest of you that I can. You were my fathers loving companion and friend for years: you saved his life and his reason! You were *his* true, true wife, and *my* mother. I shall never think of you in any lower light.'

My emotion had found vent in tears by that time. It was all so new and so horrible to believe, and my mothers hand rested fondly on my bowed head.

Then that other woman, whose existence I can never recall without a shuddery seized her hateful opportunity, and levelled the most. virulent abuse at my poor martyr mother's head. Words, such as I had never heard from a female before, rained thickly from her lips, until I lost sight of my own grief in my indignation at the shower of innuendoes which were being hurled at the person dearest to me of all the world.

'Be silent,' I said in a loud authoritative voice. 'Were you twenty times my mother I would not permit you to speak as you are speaking now. If it is true that you were my father's wife, why were you not in your proper place, instead of leaving your lawful duties to another?'

'Oh! madam here can answer that question better than myself. She knows well enough there was no room left for me where she was.'

'Untrue!' murmured my mother, but without any anger. 'I would have shielded your character from your boy's censure, as I have done for so long, but justice to the dead compels me to speak. You left this borne desolate for many miserable years before I entered it. You deserted your child in his infancy, but your husband had so good and forgiving a heart that, when you cried to him for pardon, he took you back again and condoned your great offence, and therefore, when you left him a second time, the law contained no remedy for his wrong. He was compelled to live on—alone—dishonoured and comfortless, whilst you—you can best tell your son what your life has been since.'

'Anyway I am Mrs Vere,' retorted the other, 'and my husband has died intestate, and his property belongs to me, so I'll thank you to take your brat, and clear out of my house before the sun goes down.'

'Oh! mother, this is infamous! It can never be!'

'It *must* be, Charlie! It is the law. I knew all this when I consented to come here as your father's wife. He never deceived me for a single moment; and if I have any regret that he put off providing against this contingency until it was too late, it is only for fear lest he should be regretting it also.'

'But, my dear, *dear* love!' she added in a lower tone, 'I acquit you of this as of all things. I know your great love for me never failed, and I am content!'

'I will not believe it without further proof!' I exclaimed. 'I will send Ellen at once for the solicitor. I cannot leave you alone with this horrid woman!'

'Hush, Charlie! she is your mother.'

'I will not acknowledge it. *You* are the only mother I have ever had—the only mother I ever will have to my life's end.'

Mr Chorberry, the solicitor, came without delay, but he could give me no comfort. My poor father, by that strange indifference which has been the curse of so many, had put off making his will until it was too late, by reason of which he had left the one to whom he owed most in the world, the woman who had sacrificed friends and reputation to spend her life in a dull country home, administering to his pleasures, entirely dependent on her own resources for support— whilst the faithless, drunken creature he had the misfortune to be still chained to, walked in as the lawful wife, and claimed her share of the property. There was only one drop of balm in his decision. I, as my father's son, shared what he had left behind him, but my angel mother and dear baby-sister were cast upon the world to shift for themselves. And this was the law.

Oh, father! did your spirit look down from whichever sphere it had been translated to, and witness this?

'But, surely,' I said to Chorberry, 'there can be no necessity for my mother leaving Lilyfields before the funeral?'

'Of course there is no necessity; but do you think it advisable, under the circumstances, that she should remain? Mrs Vere has the legal power to enforce her departure, and I am afraid will not be slow to use it.'

My mother evidently was of one mind with him, for in an incredibly short space of time she had packed her belongings. Mrs Vere, standing over her meanwhile to see she did not purloin anything from the house, and was waiting in the hall with little Violet, ready to go to the house of the clergyman's wife, who, to her honour, having heard how matters stood at Lilyfields, had promptly sent my mother an invitation to the vicarage for the night.

'Are you ready, dear mother?' I said sadly, as I joined her in the hall, and drew her arm within my own.

'Well, Mr Charles, I suppose I shall see you back again here before long?' screamed the shrill voice of Mrs Vere down the staircase.

I started.

See me back! Was it possible that this woman believed I intended to make friends with her?

'We've been parted long enough, it strikes me,' she continued; 'and now your father's gone, and left no one behind him but yourself, I suppose you'll be looking out for my share of the property at my death, so we may as well let bygones be bygones—eh?'

'I wish for none of your property, madam,' I answered haughtily, 'since the law gives it to you you are welcome to keep it.'

'Charlie, dear, think what you may be resigning,' urged my mother in my ear.

'I think of nothing but *you*, mother!'

'Hoity, toity! here's manners,' cried the other woman. 'You seem to forget. Master Charlie, that *I'm your mother!*'

Still holding my mother's hand, I turned and confronted her.

'I forget nothing, madam! I wish I could; but I remember that *here* stands the woman who laboured where you refused to work; who loved, where you had insulted and betrayed; who was faithful where you were faithless and undeserving; and, I say, that here stands my dead father's true wife; and here stands, in God's sight, *my mother!* The blessing of man may not have sanctified her union, but the blessing of heaven shall be upon it and upon her—upon the creatures she rescued from a living death and upon the gracious hand with which she did it, until time itself shall be no more.'

So saying, I passed with my mother beyond the gates of Lilyfields, to make a new life for her in some quiet spot where she might outlive her grief, and to repay, if possible, by the protection and support of my manhood, the love she had given me as a little child

ALSO FROM LEONAUR
AVAILABLE IN SOFTCOVER OR HARDCOVER WITH DUST JACKET

MR MUKERJI'S GHOSTS *by S. Mukerji*—Supernatural tales from the British Raj period by India's Ghost story collector.

KIPLINGS GHOSTS *by Rudyard Kipling*—Twelve stories of Ghosts, Hauntings, Curses, Werewolves & Magic.

THE COLLECTED SUPERNATURAL AND WEIRD FICTION OF WASHINGTON IRVING: VOLUME 1 *by Washington Irving*—Including one novel 'A History of New York', and nine short stories of the Strange and Unusual.

THE COLLECTED SUPERNATURAL AND WEIRD FICTION OF WASHINGTON IRVING: VOLUME 2 *by Washington Irving*—Including three novelettes 'The Legend of the Sleepy Hollow', 'Dolph Heyliger', 'The Adventure of the Black Fisherman' and thirty-two short stories of the Strange and Unusual.

THE COLLECTED SUPERNATURAL AND WEIRD FICTION OF JOHN KENDRICK BANGS: VOLUME 1 *by John Kendrick Bangs*—Including one novel 'Toppleton's Client or A Spirit in Exile', and ten short stories of the Strange and Unusual.

THE COLLECTED SUPERNATURAL AND WEIRD FICTION OF JOHN KENDRICK BANGS: VOLUME 2 *by John Kendrick Bangs*—Including four novellas 'A House-Boat on the Styx', 'The Pursuit of the House-Boat', 'The Enchanted Typewriter' and 'Mr. Munchausen' of the Strange and Unusual.

THE COLLECTED SUPERNATURAL AND WEIRD FICTION OF JOHN KENDRICK BANGS: VOLUME 3 *by John Kendrick Bangs*—Including twor novellas 'Olympian Nights', 'Roger Camerden: A Strange Story', and ten short stories of the Strange and Unusual.

THE COLLECTED SUPERNATURAL AND WEIRD FICTION OF MARY SHELLEY: VOLUME 1 *by Mary Shelley*—Including one novel 'Frankenstein or the Modern Prometheus', and fourteen short stories of the Strange and Unusual.

THE COLLECTED SUPERNATURAL AND WEIRD FICTION OF MARY SHELLEY: VOLUME 2 *by Mary Shelley*—Including one novel 'The Last Man', and three short stories of the Strange and Unusual.

THE COLLECTED SUPERNATURAL AND WEIRD FICTION OF AMELIA B. EDWARDS *by Amelia B. Edwards*—Contains two novelettes 'Monsieur Maurice', and 'The Discovery of the Treasure Isles', one ballad 'A Legend of Boisguilbert' and seventeen short stories to cill the blood.

LEONAUR

ALSO FROM LEONAUR

AVAILABLE IN SOFTCOVER OR HARDCOVER WITH DUST JACKET

THE COMPLETE FOUR JUST MEN: VOLUME 2 *by Edgar Wallace*—*The Law of the Four Just Men & The Three Just Men*—disillusioned with a world where the wicked and the abusers of power perpetually go unpunished, the Just Men set about to rectify matters according to their own standards, and retribution is dispensed on swift and deadly wings.

THE COMPLETE RAFFLES: 1 *by E. W. Hornung*—*The Amateur Cracksman & The Black Mask*—By turns urbane gentleman about town and accomplished cricketer, life is just too ordinary for Raffles and that sets him on a series of adventures that have long been treasured as a real antidote to the 'white knights' who are the usual heroes of the crime fiction of this period.

THE COMPLETE RAFFLES: 2 *by E. W. Hornung*—*A Thief in the Night & Mr Justice Raffles*—By turns urbane gentleman about town and accomplished cricketer, life is just too ordinary for Raffles and that sets him on a series of adventures that have long been treasured as a real antidote to the 'white knights' who are the usual heroes of the crime fiction of this period.

THE COLLECTED SUPERNATURAL AND WEIRD FICTION OF WILKIE COLLINS: VOLUME 1 *by Wilkie Collins*—Contains one novel 'The Haunted Hotel', one novella 'Mad Monkton', three novelettes 'Mr Percy and the Prophet', 'The Biter Bit' and 'The Dead Alive' and eight short stories to chill the blood.

THE COLLECTED SUPERNATURAL AND WEIRD FICTION OF WILKIE COLLINS: VOLUME 2 *by Wilkie Collins*—Contains one novel 'The Two Destinies', three novellas 'The Frozen deep', 'Sister Rose' and 'The Yellow Mask' and two short stories to chill the blood.

THE COLLECTED SUPERNATURAL AND WEIRD FICTION OF WILKIE COLLINS: VOLUME 3 *by Wilkie Collins*—Contains one novel 'Dead Secret,' two novelettes 'Mrs Zant and the Ghost' and 'The Nun's Story of Gabriel's Marriage' and five short stories to chill the blood.

FUNNY BONES *selected by Dorothy Scarborough*—An Anthology of Humorous Ghost Stories.

MONTEZUMA'S CASTLE AND OTHER WEIRD TALES *by Charles B. Cory*—Cory has written a superb collection of eighteen ghostly and weird stories to chill and thrill the avid enthusiast of supernatural fiction.

SUPERNATURAL BUCHAN *by John Buchan*—Stories of Ancient Spirits, Uncanny Places & Strange Creatures.